Musings and Meditations

Robert Silverberg

reflections on science fiction, science, and other matters

nonstop press • *new york*

MUSINGS AND MEDITATIONS
Reflections on Science-Fiction, Science, and Other Matters

By Robert Silverberg

For Sheila Williams and Gardner Dozois, who published most of these.
And for Barry Malzberg, with whom I have been discussing such subjects
as these for more than forty years.

First Edition:
2011

Book design by Luis Ortiz
Production by Nonstop Ink

ISBN 978-1933065-20-5

PRINTED IN THE UNITED STATES OF AMERICA

www.nonstop-press.com

 Nonstop Press

Contents

THREE
Being A Writer

FOUR
Colleagues

FIVE
The Worlds We Live In

SIX
Something Of Myself

Foreword:

Reflections Of An Opinion-Monger

I'VE BEEN A PROFESSIONAL SCIENCE FICTION WRITER for something more than fifty-five years now, and I've been writing *about* science fiction for even longer than that, starting back around 1950 when I was a mere teenage fan, much given to making dogmatic statements about sf stories and writers in the amateur magazines ("fanzines") of the day. Back then, any sf aficionado who happened to own a typewriter felt empowered to cut loose with uninhibited blasts of opinion on all matters having to do with their favorite kind of reading matter, just as vast hordes of bloggers do today. A few of those fanzines, particularly in their earliest days, were elegantly printed from hand-set type; but most were crudely produced items reproduced by such methods, largely obsolete today, as mimeography, hektography, and dittography. I know. I published one of them myself, an effusion called *Spaceship*, between 1949 and 1955, abandoning it only when I moved over from the pontificating side of things to the productive side and became a professional science fiction writer.

But I didn't stop expressing opinions about my chosen field. I started getting paid for them, is all.

A bibliography of my published work shows that I was doing book reviews for three of the science fiction magazines (*Infinity*, *Science Fiction Adventures*, and *Science Fiction Stories*) as far back as 1958. I continued doing reviews, on and off, for this magazine and that, for a decade or so, but by then so many of my colleagues were also my close friends that I began to feel diffident about criticizing their work in public, and I stopped doing reviews. I did, however, write more formal essays on the genre, some of them as introductions to the many anthologies I was editing in the 1960s and 1970s, or as prefaces to collections of my own stories, and others as essays on specific themes, such as 1969's "Characterization in Science Fiction" or 1971's "Science Fiction in an Age of Revolution." These were sporadic efforts, a piece every year or so; but in 1978 I began to write a regular column of opinion for one of the magazines, and, with scarcely an intermission, I have continued to do so for more than thirty years so far.

This is the second collection of the essays I've done in those thirty-plus years. The first, *Reflections and Refractions*, was published in 1997 by Underwood Books, and its 425 pages included most — not all — of my magazine pieces written between 1973 and 1996. This new volume picks up the thread from there and collects much of my 1996-2010 work (and one from 1995).

Many of the essays collected in this book, and in its predecessor, are personal ones. I don't just mean that they represent my own opinions — that should go without saying — but that a good many of them deal with my own books and stories, with my own life, with my own experience of being a science fiction writer. That should cause no surprise, and I offer no apologies. I was a teenager when I set out to become a professional science fiction writer, and I am well along in my seventies as I write this now, which means that pretty much the entirety of what by now has been quite a long life has seen me deeply enmeshed in the art and craft of science fiction. It has been my life's work in the way that the art of medicine is a doctor's life work or the art of architecture is an architect's life work. Willie Mays would not talk about baseball, I suspect, without mentioning some of the important games he took part in during his playing career. It's equally impossible for me to talk about science fiction without illustrating some of my arguments by referring to my own experience as a writer. Hence you will find that this book of opinionated comment is very Silverberg-oriented. If you see that as a monument to mad egotism, well, put the book back on the shelf and go no further. If you see it as a quasi-autobiographical series of statements about science fiction by someone who has loved it and tried to serve it well for the past six decades — so far — then I think you will find much to interest you here.

The magazine that put me in the business of regular public opinion-mongering was called *Galileo*, which was pretty much a shoestring operation, published out of Boston by a bunch of people whose main excuse for publishing it was that they were passionate about science fiction, and edited by the ambitious and determined Charles C. Ryan.

I suppose you would have to call *Galileo* a semi-pro operation, considering its irregular publishing schedule, its not-quite-ready-for-prime-time format, and its basically subscriptions-only distribution scheme. But so far as its editorial content went it was as professional as any sf magazine of its era. Looking through my file of *Galileo*, I see its contents page studded with such names as Connie Willis, Joan D. Vinge, John Kessel, Alan Dean Foster, and Lewis Shiner, each them writers in the early years of careers that soon would shine with high accomplishment. Veterans like Brian Aldiss, Harlan Ellison, Marion Zimmer Bradley, and Jack Williamson had stories in it too; and there were non-fiction pieces by the likes of Carl Sagan, Arthur C. Clarke, Hal Clement, and Frederik Pohl. All in all, it seemed to me a fine place for me to set up shop in as a pontificator.

I very much wanted to do some pontificating, too. After a quarter of a century as a professional science fiction writer, I had wandered into a time of personal and creative crisis that had led me, late in 1974, to retire from writing fiction "forever." A great deal of my motivation for walking away from my career had to do with the changing nature of science fiction publishing in the United States in the mid-1970s. The exciting revolution of concepts and literary technique that had acquired the label of "the New Wave" had failed in a big way; the ambitious work of the writers who were considered to be part of the New Wave was swiftly going out of print, and what was coming in was the first surge of Star Trek novelizations, Tolkien imitations, juvenile space adventure books, and other highly commercial stuff that I had no interest in writing or reading. I felt crowded out by all the junk; and, having also hit a period of mental burnout after years of high-level productivity, I was too tired to fight back against the overwhelming trend toward more juvenile sf. So I simply picked up my marbles and walked away, intending my disappearance from the field to be permanent.

When Charlie Ryan approached me about doing a regular column three and a half years later, I was still deep in my irrevocable and permanent retirement, but I had begun to feel as though I were living a weirdly posthumous existence. It was apparent to my friends, if not yet to me, that I was growing increasingly troubled and confused by my extended period of self-imposed silence. Although I had had plenty of offers to write my kind of science fiction on quite generous terms, I wasn't yet ready to get back into the business of writing fiction again; but I wanted to write *something*, if only to re-establish my connection with the field of fiction that had been the center of my imaginative experience since my boyhood. The truth was that I missed science fiction and my role in shaping it. I could no longer bear to be invisible, after so many years at the center of things. So I accepted *Galileo*'s invitation to do a regular commentary piece gladly and eagerly, and with some relief.

And what sort of things was I writing about, thirty years ago in those old *Galileo* columns?

In the first one of all I noted that science fiction writers, long a notably underpaid crew, were suddenly getting huge advances from book publishers and many were now able, for the first time, to make their livings as full-time writers, something that only a handful of us had been able to manage when I broke in in the 1950s. "I am not, repeat *not*, in any way objecting to the sudden prosperity that has engulfed nearly all science fiction writers," I said. "But I do feel some qualms about the ease with which young writers can make themselves self-supporting these days. I know that beyond doubt that I was injured as a writer by having things too easy in my twenties....Maybe the best science fiction really *is* written by part-time writers."

Well, time has taken care of that problem. Most new sf writers now get very modest sums indeed for their work, and very few are able to set up shop as full-time pros. Even a lot of veterans are returning to their day jobs. We no longer have to worry, most of us, about the agony of excessive prosperity.

I had more to say on the same subject in the second column. In the third, I talked about the packaging and marketing of sf books as it applied to my own long novel *Lord Valentine's Castle*, which was soon about to appear. (My four-year retirement from writing fiction had ended and I was definitely back in harness with the bit between my teeth.) "Of course we're not going to market the book as science fiction," my editor had told me. "We'll handle it as a straight mainstream novel." It was a noble attempt to break me out of the science fiction ghetto, which had been so constricting for us all. But I did point out to him that the novel takes place on a planet umpteen light-years from here and some fifteen thousand years in the future, which made mainstream handling a bit questionable, and in the end they marketed it as science fiction and did reasonably well that way. Today sf remains what they call "category fiction" — that is, ghetto stuff — and the advent of computerized bookselling makes it most improbable that that will ever change.

In the fourth column I noted the death of the New Wave, that school of highly experimental, even avant-garde sf, that had its little era between 1966 and 1972 or thereabouts. I expressed no regrets for the excesses of the New Wave, but suggested that it had at least succeeded in boosting the general literary level of sf beyond the old pulp standards, and the effects of that would probably be permanent. By and large, I think I was right.

Column four went on to examine the New Wave's rejection of old-fashioned notions of plot in favor of stylistic experimentation: "We stand at the threshold of the 1980s; we have survived a time of revolution; we have, I hope, integrated our divergent excesses into something more harmonious; now let us produce a science fiction that avoids both elitism and subliteracy, fiction that holds readers so that they stand spellbound as we tell our tales, and cannot choose but hear." Did we? I surely hope so.

And in the fifth *Galileo* column I grumbled about the spelling errors in some recently published books and cited the legal phrase, *Falsus in uno, falsus in omnibus* — "False in one thing, false in everything." If a writer doesn't know how to spell, can we trust him to know anything else? And if a publisher doesn't bother to correct the writer's spelling errors, how much attention is the publisher paying to other aspects of his book, like inconsistencies of plot? I still feel that it's a writer's job to get everything right, from the spelling of words to the name of the capital of Albania. But here we are, decades later, and — well, I don't want to get started on the current state of knowledge of such things as spelling and grammar, let alone geography.

Galileo closed up shop with its sixteenth issue, dated January, 1980, which contained the sixth of my columns, dealing with science fiction conventions and the interactions there between readers and writers. Scarcely had it been laid to rest but I had an offer from Elinor Mavor, then the editor of the venerable *Amazing Stories*, to move my column to her magazine. Which indeed I did, beginning with the May, 1981 *Amazing*; and there it remained for thirteen years, through a change of publisher, three changes of editor, one change in the column's name (from "Opinion" to "Reflections"), and a total transformation of the magazine's format. Issue after issue, Silverberg spouting off on this topic or that for something like a hundred columns.

Then *Amazing* too went under, and, caught without a podium for my orations and accustomed after sixteen years to holding forth, I quickly accepted Gardner Dozois' invitation in the spring of 1994 to transfer the site of my column to *Asimov's Science Fiction*, and there I have remained, even after Gardner retired as editor and his place was taken by Sheila Williams. It is my hope that both the magazine and I enjoy enough longevity to allow me to equal Isaac's record for long-term column production. I have had a column in each issue since the one dated July, 1994, except for one at a time when I was struggling to finish a novel that was running greatly overdue, and my wife Karen stepped in and wrote that month's essay on my behalf. (Not as a ghost-writer, mind you. She got her own byline.) The bulk of this second collection of my essays is made up of those *Asimov's* columns, interspersed with some occasional pieces written as introductions for various books.

In the foreword to *Reflections and Refractions* I had this to say about the essays in that book, and much of it is equally relevant to this volume:

"They cover a span of thirty years or so of my life. The tone of my essay-writing has changed, somewhat, during my five-decade evolution from wiseacre brat to somber and weary *eminence grise*.

But certain positions remain consistent.

"From start to finish, for example, these essays are grounded in my belief that the world we inhabit and the universe that contains it are intensely interesting places full of wonders and miracles, and that one way we can bring ourselves closer to an appreciation, if not an understanding, of those wonders and miracles is through reading science fiction. There is also — consistently — the recognition that not all science fiction is equally valuable for that purpose, that in fact a lot of it is woeful junk; and I can be seen, again and again, expressing the same kind of displeasure with mediocre, cynical, or debased science fiction that I was voicing when I sounded off at [*Amazing Stories* editor] Howard Browne in 1952.

"Which is not to say that I haven't written plenty of stories myself over those forty years that fail to live up to my own lofty standards of execution, some because my skills have not been equal to my vision, and some because circumstances (like the need to pay the rent) led me to knock out some quick piece of formula prose instead of taking the time to turn out another award-winning classic. I am as human as the next guy, after all.

"But my own literary sins, and they are numerous, haven't kept me from crying out in the public square against those who, for the sake of a dollar or two, would transform science fiction into something less than it can be. I know how the finest sf can pry open the walls of the universe for an intelligent and inquisitive reader, for it has done that for me since I was ten or eleven years old, and it angers me to see writers and editors and publishers refusing even to make the attempt. In my own best fiction I have tried to achieve for other readers what H.G. Wells and Jules Verne and Robert A. Heinlein and Isaac Asimov and Jack Vance and A.E. van Vogt and Theodore Sturgeon and fifty other wonderful writers achieved for me ever since the time I first stumbled, wide-eyed and awe-struck, into the world of science fiction. And in many of the essays in this book I try, perhaps with the same naive idealism that I aimed at poor Howard Browne in 1952, to advocate the creation of more science fiction of that high kind and to urge the spurning of the drab simple-minded stuff that leads us away from the real exaltation that an intense encounter with the fabric of space and time can provide.

"There are also some essays here examining the foibles and oddities of the present-day world. I have to confess that even the best of science fiction writers have no more access to the secret recesses of space and time than you do; the sources of their fiction lie in part in their own souls, in part in the reading and studying that they do, and in part in their observation of the world around them. I do plenty of observing, and plenty of rueful shaking of my head; and because I am a man of profound common sense (or, as some might say, a man of increasingly crotchety prejudices) I deplore a lot of what I see. Since I have a thousand words a month at my disposal in which to express my thoughts, I often tell my readers about those deplorable things, perhaps with some hope of winning allies in my lifelong crusade against idiocy and irrationality, or — perhaps — just to get some things off my chest.

"My basic attitude in these essays, I suppose, can be called libertarian/ conservative, though a lot of people nowadays who call themselves libertarians or conservatives often say things that appall me. (I am not such a doctrinaire libertarian that I favor the abolition of government inspection of food products or an end to government regulation of the manufacturers of medicines; I am not such a doctrinaire conservative that I look kindly on governmental attempts to legislate personal morality, or favor mandatory religious instruction in state schools. And so forth.)

"Very likely you will find me advocating a number of positions with which you disagree. It would surprise me if you didn't. If we all held the same set of beliefs on everything, the world would be a dreary thing indeed, and so would this book. Grant me, as a minimum, that in all my thinking I am trying to grope my way toward sane answers to crazy problems, and if I come to conclusions that you don't share, it's not because I'm a black-hearted villain or an eager oppressor of the unfortunate but because — having spent a lot of my life imagining myself living a million light-years from Earth or a million chronological years from the present day — I've come to feel that a lot of what goes on all around me in the actual world I inhabit doesn't make a lot of sense, and, because I have the privilege of saying so in print, I do say so, with the small and faint hope that I am thereby nudging the world a little closer to rationality.

"And, finally, there are some pieces in here that deal with my long career as a science fiction writer: editors I have dealt with, writers I have known, events in my writing life, commentary on my own books and stories. Whatever else the life of a professional writer can sometimes be — exhausting, frustrating, bewildering, even frightening — it is rarely dull; and it has been my great good luck to spend nearly half of this rapidly expiring twentieth century right in the midst of that strange and wonderful literary microcosm called science fiction publishing. I've known almost everyone involved in it, and experienced just about everything that an sf writer can experience, and I have a lot of tales to tell about those experiences, some of which — just a few — I tell here. It's as close to a formal autobiography as I'll ever write, I suspect.

"I offer these reminiscences and self-referential essays without apology, not only because I enjoyed writing them but also because I think you'll them of interest. (Modesty is not a trait widely found among writers. The successful ones are those who are convinced, at least while they're actually at work, that what they're writing, whatever it may be, is inherently interesting to other people and will find an immediate, eager, happy audience. Without that conviction, I imagine it would be very hard for writers to push themselves all the way from the first page of a story to the last.)

"So, then. Herewith a bunch of essays on science fiction, science, and various other matters, written by someone who has very gradually grown old and gray dreaming about far galaxies and other dimensions and somehow still keeps at it, writing stories about people and places who never existed. Being a professional science fiction writer is, I have to admit, a very peculiar way to have spent your whole adult life. But so be it; that is the choice I made, unhesitatingly, a long time ago; and here are some of the thoughts that have occurred to me along the way."

For this second volume of collected essays I am grateful to Luis Ortiz of Nonstop Press, who made it possible to exist; to Gardner Dozois and Sheila Williams, who gave me the space in their magazine to sound off, month after month; to Barry Malzberg, over many decades a valuable correspondent with whom I can test my opinions, and to Tony Adams, for dedicated bibliographical research that made it ever so much easier for me to compile a mass of unrelated short pieces into a coherent book; and, above all, to my wife Karen, who not only listened to the early versions of many of these columns as I talked them out around the house, but who suggested the themes for a number of them.

— **Robert Silverberg**
Oakland, California
March, 2010

ONE
Science Fiction In General

The Great Tradition

THE DISTINGUISHED MODERN RUSSIAN POET JOSEPH BRODSKY once remarked that he wrote to please his predecessors, not his contemporaries. It's an illuminating comment — Brodsky was not only a great poet but also a brilliant thinker, two things that don't automatically go together — and it set me wondering about my own attitudes and practices as a writer.

He wrote to please his predecessors. I wonder which poets he meant by that. Brodsky was born in Russia in 1940. He was a man of outspoken views, which brought him a prison term (1964-65) for "social parasitism." He remained troublesome to the Soviet government, though, and was forced into exile in 1972, settling in the United States. There he attained worldwide fame as a poet and a critic, writing his essays in English and his poems in Russian, which he then translated into English. His work brought him the Nobel Prize for Poetry in 1987 and many a lesser award. In 1991 President Bush named him poet laureate of the United States. He was only 55 when he died in 1996.

I have no doubt that Alexander Pushkin was one of the poets to whom Joseph Brodsky inwardly offered his work for approval: all Russian poets work in the shadow of Pushkin. Among the modern Russians whom he would have regarded as watching and judging his poetry would certainly have been Anna Akhmatova and Osip Mandelstam, and, I would guess, Boris Pasternak. But the multicultural Brodsky would surely not have limited his list of revered predecessors to Russian poets alone: he declared Frost, Hardy, and Auden to be among his favorites, and I suspect that when he wrote he looked also toward the whole of the great poetic tradition from Homer and Virgil and Horace onward: Dante, Shakespeare, Milton, Pope, Keats, Byron,

Yeats, Eliot, and on and on. And humbly saw himself as a successor in that glorious line.

What, you may ask, does all this have to do with science fiction, and the science fiction of R. Silverberg in particular?

I've been writing the stuff for more than forty-five years, now. That's by no means the longest career in modern science fiction; among writers currently active, I can point to such folk as Poul Anderson, Frederik Pohl, Frank M. Robinson, Gordon R. Dickson, Jack Vance, and five or six others who began publishing five or ten years before I did — a list topped by Jack Williamson, whose first stories appeared seven years before I was born. Still, a forty- five-year career makes me a distinctly senior figure in a field in which most of the current top writers are less than fifty years old. It's a long enough time to make me ask the big question of myself. Have I, with all of my vast output of stories and novels, been adding anything significant to the great tradition of modern science fiction, or have I simply been taking up a lot of space in print?

(The quick answer, lest you think I'm pleading for your approval here, is, yes, I think my work in its totality has been worth the trees that died for it.) But I arrive at that bit of self-approval in a Brodskyesque fashion, by looking backward at the writers who shaped my imagination and assessing, as well as I can, my place among them.

Science fiction has changed a great deal since I broke in as a new writer in 1954. Back then it was a magazine-based field. Paperback publishing in the United States was just getting under way, and scarcely any hardcover publishers would touch anything so odd and esoteric as sf. For those who loved to read or write it, everything was centered in three important monthly magazines: *Astounding Science Fiction* (now *Analog*), *Galaxy*, and *Fantasy & Science Fiction*. It was in those magazines where things happened first, although the work of a privileged few writers (Heinlein, Asimov, Bradbury) did eventually find its way into book form a year or two after its magazine appearance.

The editors of those magazines — John W. Campbell, Horace L. Gold, and Anthony Boucher, respectively — were powerful personalities who had significant and distinct ideas about what constituted a good science fiction story. The leading writers of the day — Theodore Sturgeon, Henry Kuttner, Isaac Asimov, James Blish, Alfred Bester, Clifford Simak, Frederik Pohl, Cyril Kornbluth, Arthur C. Clarke, Poul Anderson, Philip K. Dick, Robert Sheckley, Philip José Farmer, etc. — wrote short stories, novelets, and occasional novels for Campbell, Gold, and Boucher, and what they couldn't place with them went to the secondary (and lower-paying) magazines, edited by such people as Robert Lowndes, Larry Shaw, Howard Browne, Samuel Mines, and Sam Merwin, Jr. Those men also had firm ideas about the nature of what they wanted to publish, and the combination of strong editorial personalities and a dazzling constellation of first-rate writers working in the field all at once had a mighty impact on me as a teenage would-be science fiction writer. My tastes as a reader and my whole approach as a writer were formed by the great science fiction magazines of that bygone period.

Today just a few science fiction magazines still survive, and, however excellent their product may be, their impact on the overall publishing scene is not great. The heart of the sf action is in book publishing, primarily paperbacks, although a good many hardcover science fiction books appear every year. As a result we have a changed paradigm of excellence in science fiction. In the old days, the standard of excellence was set by Messrs. Campbell, Gold, and Boucher and to a certain degree by some of the lesser editors. The stories that they bought and published month after month represented, ipso facto, the ideal form of science fiction, the sort of thing that any young writer should aspire to create.

Today, though, where everything is dominated by sales figures, editors tend to be self-effacing figures and the size of a writer's sales determines the value of his work. The writer who proves to have potent popular appeal becomes a defining case: book publishers will seek the work of such a writer with avidity, and will urge other writers to write "in the tradition of" X or Y or Z, even if the work of X and Y and Z is crude subliterate junk. Thus the writer who manages somehow to sell fifty or sixty thousand copies of his last novel in hardcover format, or half a million paperbacks, becomes an 800-pound gorilla who reshapes the field in his own image. Style, character, plot, ingenuity of concept — these are all secondary to the dollar return.

I was raised in a different tradition. I was fighting for a place on the contents pages of magazines full of stories by the likes of Sturgeon, Blish, Bradbury, Clarke, Anderson, and Bester. I couldn't hope to match their level of attainment — not at nineteen, I couldn't! — but I knew that I had damned well better *try*. Which meant mastering the techniques by which stories are constructed, and then applying those techniques to the special kind of ideation that is science fiction.

One of my masters was James Blish, the precise, waspish, and formidable author of a multitude of brilliant stories now largely forgotten today. "We know," Blish wrote in a 1952 essay that had enormous effect on me, "that there is a huge body of available technique in fiction writing, and that the competence of a writer — entirely aside from the degree of his talent — is determined by how much of this body he can use. (Talent is measured in some part by how much he adds to it.)" Elsewhere in the same piece he observed, "Technical competence in story-telling is of course not the sole factor which turns a piece of fiction into a work of art. Freshness of idea, acuity of observation, depth of emotional penetration are all crucial; and there are other such factors. But technical competence is the one completely indispensable ingredient; the use of an old idea, for instance, is seldom fatal in itself, but clumsy craftsmanship invariably is."

This sounds a little quaint, in the era of gigantic, clumsily written novels linked into infinitely long series, each volume of which sells more copies than all of Jim Blish's books together. Modern-day commodified publishing has put an entirely new spin on things for the science fiction writer: acuity of observation, depth of emotional penetration, freshness of idea, and all those other things dear to the best sf writers of Blish's generation are often seen now as impediments to a book's success, and the writer who is most avidly courted by the publishers is the one who has found the most efficacious way of reaching great hordes of readers who are looking, evidently, for the prose equivalent of television.

Which doesn't mean that good writing is extinct in science fiction — as the work of Kim Stanley Robinson, Joe Haldeman, Walter Jon Williams, Ursula K. Le Guin, Nancy Kress, and James Patrick Kelly, to name just the first half dozen that come into my mind out of a long list of outstanding modern writers, amply demonstrates. But then there are all those awful books with the glitzy covers that get the big sales, and sell and sell and sell, and jostle the more classical kind of science fiction out of print. Those are the books the editors really crave; they merely tolerate the other kind.

I don't begrudge the writers of those books, many of whom are good friends of mine, their whopping sales figures. They have the great skill of knowing how to give the public what the public wants, and they are rewarded accordingly, and so be it. I applaud their immense commercial success. I just don't have to read their books myself.

No, I'm back there in the era of Campbell, Gold, and Boucher most of the time. Those are the editors I'm still trying to please, and I still want the admiration of my colleagues of that period, too. When I set out to write a book or a story, I do, of course, want it to reach a wide and enthusiastic audience, and I'm only too well aware that most of the people who wrote for and read *Galaxy* and *Astounding* and *F&SF* in 1953 aren't around any more. My work depends on the approbation of today's readership.

But in my own mind, the plaudits I want are those of the writers who fed my imagination when I was in my teens. Like Brodsky looking over his shoulder at Pushkin and Frost and Yeats, I write even now for Blish and Bester and Pohl, for Ted Sturgeon and Henry Kuttner, even for H. G. Wells. I like to regard myself as one of the last survivors of that group, upholding the great tradition they created. And so I'm engaged in a constant dialog with the past — forever seeking to prove to myself that I'm worthy of moving in the company of my idols of half a century ago.

Asimov's Science Fiction, **December, 1999**

The Final Voyage of Odysseus

"THE ETERNAL SILENCE OF THESE INFINITE SPACES TERRIFIES ME," Blaise Pascal noted in his *Pensées,* that extraordinary jumble of philosophical jottings that the seventeenth-century French philosopher set down toward the close of his life. The startling phrase leaps up suddenly at the reader just a few lines below the equally famous passage in which Pascal declares, "A human being is only a reed, the weakest in nature, but he is a thinking reed. To crush him, the whole universe does not have to arm itself. A mist, a drop of water, is enough to kill him. But if the universe were to crush the reed, the man would be nobler than his killer, since he knows that he is dying, and that the universe has the advantage over him. The universe knows nothing about him." And then, a sudden, jarring leap to the next level of response, as powerful as it is unexpected, that stunning line:

The eternal silence of these infinite spaces terrifies me.

I've been thinking about those infinite spaces, and their terrifying eternal silences, quite a bit since the death last year of Poul Anderson. Poul was the poet of the spaceways. More than anyone else in modern science fiction, he made us feel the immensity of space, the darkness of it, the silence, and, yes, the terror of which Pascal spoke three and a half centuries ago. From such early works as *The Snows of Ganymede* and *No World of Their Own* on through *Tau Zero* and "Call Me Joe" to the most recent of his innumerable novels and stories, he showed us the strangeness and awesomeness of the universe in a way that was at once exhilarating and sobering.

The danger is, in science fiction, that we get too chummy with the universe. We reduce it in our stories to something that is quickly comprehensible and readily traversible, and allow our spacefarers to pop back and forth through its billions of light-years and its myriad of galaxies with the same sort of ease with which I might travel from San Francisco to Chicago tomorrow in the course of a single afternoon. It's a convenient way of story-telling, yes. But its big fault is that it allows everything to get *much* too easy. I remember myself as a boy of fifteen, who had already read more science fiction than was good for him, aiming a flashlight into the blackness of a summer night in Massachusetts and thinking that the beam of my little light must inevitably travel on and on forever, reaching outward into the galaxy at a rate of 186,000 miles per second until it came to Betelgeuse or Rigel or Aldebaran. Well, no: the atmosphere of Earth was in the way, and that flashlight beam probably managed no more than the first few hundred yards of the journey to the stars. But at that moment I saw no reason why I could not send messages to the peoples of the far galaxies with it. I knew what a light-year was; I knew how far away those galaxies are. Yet I had come away from my extensive reading of science fiction, somehow, with a sense not of the hugeness of the universe but of its ready accessibility. And so I innocently tried to send semaphore signals to the natives of Procyon XIX with my two-dollar tin flashlight.

Even our best writers are guilty of making the cosmos seem an excessively cozy place. Consider Isaac Asimov's famous Foundation series, in which the inhabitants of the *twenty-five million inhabited worlds* of the Galactic Empire zip merrily about from planet to planet, going from Trantor to Siwenna to Terminus ever so much more easily than a citizen of Rome could have gone from Naples to Alexandria. The Foundation novels are charming and delightful books, and science fiction readers will cherish them to the end of time, but their great flaw is that they reduce interstellar travel to the level of a trip on the New York subway system. (Isaac didn't like to fly, and rarely went very far from New York City.) Frank Herbert's Dune books, though set in a very different sort of stellar empire, nevertheless have the same inescapable flaw. All galactic-empire stories do. They are inherently reductive in nature. They turn whole clusters of stars into downscaled metaphors that make them seem to be nothing more than aggregations of counties and towns, and they make the gigantic dark emptinesses between the galaxies seem like the grassy patches of scruffy wasteland that separate the suburbs of one medium-sized city from the suburbs of the next.

That is, I suppose, the only way such books can be written. Without easy faster-than-light travel that carries with it no great relativistic consequences there can be no galactic-empire novels; but once you let those nifty warp-speed spacedrives into the story, the true wonder and terror that comes from contemplating the hugeness of the cosmos must inevitably leak away. Poul Anderson, of course, wrote as many faster-than-light tales as anybody. But he did, more often than not, see space travel as something qualitatively different from a commuter jaunt, and there are passages in his best books in which his characters, confronting the universe in all its grandeur, are humbled by that grandeur and communicate that humility to us.

One great character of literature who never let humility stand in his way, and yet who surely stared outward into the unfathomable universe with the same mixture of awe and hungry fascination that Poul Anderson showed us so often, was Odysseus, King of Ithaca. He was the prototypical explorer, burning with the need to look upon the mysteries that lie beyond the horizon.

Homer's immortal epic poem traces Odysseus's ten–year–long journey homeward from the Trojan War, taking him from island to island around the Mediterranean in a way that demonstrates that the insatiably curious Odysseus was not in as much of a hurry to get home as many of us, under the same circumstances, would have been. He wanted to see and experience everything that lay in his path, and did. (SF writers have been rewriting *The Odyssey* ever since. Fletcher Pratt did it fifty years ago in a fine novella called "The Wanderer's Return"; Philip José Farmer's *The Green Odyssey* appeared a few years later; and more recently we have had, among many others, the *Star Trek: Voyager* series.)

Odysseus made one last voyage after his return from Troy. Homer doesn't tell us about it, but Dante does, in the twenty–sixth canto of *The Inferno,* and it's a wonderful story, which I'm sure Poul Anderson must have known. It shows Odysseus ("Ulysses," Dante calls him, using the Latin form) as a perfect Andersonian voyager, awed but in no way cowed by the unattainability of the unconquered worlds that lie before him.

It is a story that Dante apparently invented, since there seems to be no Greek or Roman antecedent for it. Dante, recounting his journey through Hell, is deep in the Eighth Circle now, among the "Fraudulent Counselors," those who had injured others through trickery. Cunning Odysseus has been sent to Hell for devising the Trojan horse, by which Troy finally was conquered. To Dante the shade of Odysseus tells a tale, not the familiar one of his journey home to Ithaca, but of what happened afterward, when, driven by "the restless itch to rove," he felt impelled to leave his beloved wife and his aged father and his son and set forth once more, "on the deep and open sea, with a single ship and that little band of comrades who even then had not deserted me."

Off they go on a final Odyssey, westward into the Mediterranean, with Africa on their left and the coast of Spain on their right, until they find themselves staring at the open sea, the uncharted Atlantic. "Brothers," Odysseus says, "you who have passed through a hundred thousand perils to reach this place, do not deny yourself this last exploit. Here lies a chance to learn for yourself what lies in this unknown world on the far side of the sun, where no people dwell." He tells his men that they had not been born to live in brutish ignorance, but for the pursuit of knowledge and excellence: and so they put their shoulders to their oars and eagerly go forward into the unplumbed ocean that stands before them.

The path Odysseus takes goes toward the southwest. On and on they go, presumably toward the place we now know as Brazil. Soon they pass the Equator; the familiar northern stars slip below the horizon, and they sail beneath the unfamiliar constellations of the other hemisphere. At last a mountain looms before them in the sea, "dark in the distance," says Odysseus, "and so lofty and so steep, I had never seen its like before." It is, Dante will explain to us much later in his great poem, the mountain of Purgatory; but Odysseus has no knowledge of that. He and his crew rejoice at the sight of land, and head vigorously toward it. But then a fierce storm comes toward them out of the newly discovered shore, and the voyagers' ship is caught by whirlwinds and spun three times around. The fourth spin is the fatal one: the stern rises, the prow sinks, and the sea closes over Odysseus and his men, for Odysseus must not reach Purgatory, but is destined to burn forever among his fellow tricksters in Hell's Eighth Circle.

The failure of Odysseus's final voyage is not important. What matters is that he made it: that he stood by the Pillars of Hercules, looking westward into the great ocean that no one before him had dared to enter, and, putting aside all terror and awe, urged his companions forward for the sake of the pursuit of knowledge and excellence.

A great dark ocean lies all about our world. Blaise Pascal looked up into it and shivered with primordial terror. I looked up into it once and aimed my flashlight at the inhabitants of the stars. Again and again Poul Anderson reminded us that venturing into that black void would be something quite different from taking the 9:15 train from Penn Station to Connecticut, something frightening and humbling, but that some of us — some — would attempt that voyage even so.

Asimov's Science Fiction, **February, 2002**

Beaming it Down

THE IDEA OF BEAMING ELECTRICITY DOWN TO EARTH from satellites in space is back in the news, now that worldwide concern over global warming is bringing about some rethinking of our current ways of generating power. Power plants that burn coal, oil, or natural gas create combustion-product problems. Nuclear power plants have spooked certain segments of the population since the Three Mile Island and Chernobyl events of a generation ago, though the fact that they are actually quite safe these days and have none of the emission problems of fossil-fuel plants has begun to attract support for them even from environmentalists who long opposed them. Hydroelectric power and wind power are also carbon-free, but generating them involves building giant dams or covering great swathes of land with windmills, which engenders ecological problems of its own. The use of solar-power panels also is land-intensive, and in any case is suitable only where long hours of sunlight can be consistently counted upon. And so, since the relentless rate of growth in annual demand for electrical power is unlikely to slow down in the years ahead, the concept of shipping power down from space is getting major attention these days, nearly eighty years after it first turned up in science fiction.

One big backer this time around is the Pentagon, which issued a report in October 2007 asserting that beaming energy down from space satellites would provide "affordable, clean, safe, reliable, sustainable, and expandable energy for mankind." Those powerful political buzzwords are to be found in a seventy-five-page study conducted for the Defense Department's National Security Space Office, which has been examining potential energy sources for worldwide U.S. military operations. The Pentagon people do note, however, that although the technology for building such space-based power plants already exists, the cost of lifting thousand of tons of apparatus for collecting and transmitting the energy into space would be formidable.

While the Defense Department ponders the budgetary aspects of such a project, the tiny Pacific nation of Palau — twenty thousand inhabitants scattered over a cluster of islands — is ready to go ahead. Palau got involved after the American entrepreneur Kevin Reed, speaking at the Fifty-Eighth International Astronautical Congress in India in September 2007, suggested that Palau's Helen Island would be a fine site for a demonstration project in which a satellite in orbit three hundred miles up would ship down microwave beams carrying one megawatt of power, enough to run a thousand homes. A 260-foot rectifying antenna, or "rectenna," would act as the receiver. Since Helen Island is uninhabited, there would be no immediate economic benefit, but the pilot rig, Reed said, would at least demonstrate the safety of power transmissions from space.

The government of Palau quickly showed interest in the scheme, suggesting that it might well be extended to the populated islands of the archipelago. "We are keen on alternative energy," said Palau's president, Tommy Remengasau. "And if this is something that can benefit Palau, I'm sure we'd like to look at it." Reed has organized an American-Swiss-German consortium and is looking for corporate financing for the estimated eight hundred million dollar cost of the system, which he thinks can be in operation as early as 2012.

NASA has for many years been studying much more grandiose ideas for beaming power down from space. One NASA plan involves satellites in geostationary orbits, 22,300 miles up, that would be equipped with arrays of solar panels eighteen square miles in size and transmit power continuously to rectennas of similar vast area on Earth. Each of these orbiters would yield twice as much power as Hoover Dam, and, according to studies independently carried out in Japan, the beams from them would be no more dangerous than microwave ovens, though no-go zones would have to be established to keep aircraft out of their path. Another proposal — and I am indebted to sf writer Allen Steele for details of this one — is the SunTower, an array of photovoltaic cells ten miles long in orbit six hundred miles high, that would collect solar energy (available twenty-four hours a day up there, remember), convert it into electricity, and send it via low-power microwave beams to rectennas on Earth. The cost of hoisting all this hardware into space and assembling it there would be enormous, of course, but once the initial investment had been made, limitless supplies of carbon-free electricity would head our way.

The progenitor of the modern proposals for beaming power down from space seems to be Peter Glaser of the Arthur D. Little Corporation, who first set it forth in an article in *Science* in 1968. Gerard K. O'Neill, an advocate for the development of permanent space stations who had been working on space-colonization plans for NASA, expanded on Glaser's ideas in a 1976 book, *The High Frontier*, that led to a flood of further books and studies. Of course, power-generating stations in space began to turn up in science fiction, also. The Canadian writer Donald Kingsbury, who attended a 1977 meeting of the American Astronautical Society in San Francisco where much attention was paid to the theme of the industrialization of space, embodied the idea in a 1979 novella, "The Moon Goddess and the Son," and then a 1986 novel of the same name. In 1981, rocketry expert G. Harry Stine published under his "Lee Correy" pseudonym the novel *Space Doctor*, about the problems of constructing a power satellite in geosynchronous orbit. Allen Steele's 1989 novel *Orbital Decay* shows a gang of rough-hewn construction guys working aboard a space satellite called Olympus Station — nicknamed "Skycan" — to build a power-transmission plant. And plenty of other writers have dealt with the subject since.

But the history of the power-satellite theme in science fiction goes back much farther than that — to 1931, astonishingly, and Murray Leinster's novelette "Power Planet," which, like so many Leinster stories, introduced a startling new idea to our field.

Leinster is not much spoken of in the sf world nowadays, but he was a major figure fifty years ago, commonly thought of as "the Dean of Science Fiction." He was a courtly, soft-spoken Virginian, born in 1896, whose real name was Will F. Jenkins. Though he had hoped to become a scientist, circumstances did not allow him to go beyond an eighth-grade education. Nevertheless, he pursued a lifelong interest in technology, maintaining a home laboratory from which flowed scores of patentable inventions, while at the same time carrying on a major career as a fiction writer under the "Leinster" pseudonym, with science fiction as one of his specialties. It was Murray Leinster who gave us the concept of parallel worlds in "Sidewise in Time" (1934), did one of the first generation-ship interstellar stories in that year's "Proxima Centauri," and wrote a definitive tale of the problem of communication with aliens in his classic novelette "First Contact" in 1945. His other major contributions to science fiction over the course of a fifty-year career would make a long list.

"Power Planet" appeared in the January 1931 issue of the pioneering sf magazine *Amazing Stories*. The magazine science fiction of that era was mostly pretty creaky work, but "Power Planet," despite some crude pulp touches, remains surprisingly readable today. It presents us with fiction's first power-generating space station: "The Power Planet, of course," Leinster writes, "is that vast man-made disk of metal set spinning about the sun to supply the Earth with power. Everybody learns in his grammar-school textbooks of its construction just beyond the Moon and of its maneuvering to its present orbit by a vast expenditure of rocket fuel. Only forty million miles from the sun's surface, its sunward side is raised nearly to red heat by the blazing radiation. And the shadow side, naturally, is down to the utter cold of space. There is a temperature drop of nearly seven hundred degrees between the two sides, and Williamson cells turn that heat-difference into electric current, with an efficiency of 99 percent. Then the big Dugald tubes — they are twenty feet long on the Power Planet — transform it into the beam which is focused always on the Earth and delivers something over a billion horsepower to the various receivers that have been erected." The space station itself is ten miles across, "and it rotates at a carefully calculated speed so that the centrifugal force at its outer edge is very nearly equal to the normal gravity of Earth. So that the nearer its center one goes, of course, the less is that force, and also the less impression of weight one has."

This is astonishing stuff for 1931. Where did Leinster/Jenkins get the idea?

The earliest known reference to an orbiting space station is in Edward Everett Hale's story "The Brick Moon" (1869), in which a satellite built of brick is launched into orbit by huge flyweels. Kurt Lasswitz' 1897 novel, *Auf Zwei Planeten* (*Of Two Planets*), describes Martian space stations shaped like spoked wheels in orbit above the Earth. Neither of these says anything about power generation, of course: the first story comes from the pre-electrical age, the second from the dawning era of commercial power generation on Earth. For the idea of a power-generating satellite we have to look to the German rocketry experimenter and space-exploration propagandist Hermann Oberth, whose 1929 book *By Rocket Into Interplanetary Space* (an expansion of his 1922 doctoral thesis, rejected by his university as "too utopian") speaks of an orbiting station 625 miles above sea level that would use immense mirrors to transmit light beams to Earth for lighting and heating large areas.

Perhaps Leinster had read something about Oberth's orbiter in Hugo Gernsback's magazine *Wonder Stories*, since Gernsback kept up with European speculative thought and frequently ran articles about it. Leinster may also have known of the work of Nikola Tesla, the brilliant Croatia-born inventor and physicist who was a fountain of dazzling and revolutionary scientific ideas but died impoverished in 1943 at the age of eighty-six. As far back as the 1890s, Tesla was trying to create a system of wireless transmission of electrical energy across great distances using a high-power ultraviolet beam. Sf writer Geoffrey Landis tells me that Hugo Gernsback was a great advocate of Tesla's work and often featured him in his magazine *Electrical Experimenter*, which Leinster/Jenkins very probably read.

Short of rummaging through dozens of fragile old magazines, I have no way of knowing whether Hugo Gernsback planted the seed that led to "Power Planet." But it is just as likely that Leinster, the inveterate gadgeteer and demonstratably ingenious author of dozens of strikingly original science fiction stories, came up with the idea of power satellites on his own. In any case, the credit for introducing the idea to science fiction, and doing it in so presciently plausible a way, must go to him.

Will such power planets be built? I think they will. Not immediately, maybe, but diminishing fossil-fuel supplies on Earth and ever-expanding electricity demand make it inevitable, perhaps not in my lifetime but quite possibly in yours, and certainly in your children's. And remember: Murray Leinster said it first.

Asimov's Science Fiction, October/November, 2008

Glimpses Of The Future

I SPOKE LAST TIME OF MY INSATIABLE BOYHOOD CURIOSITY, and how my discovery of science fiction when I was ten or eleven years old helped to feed that frustrating hunger to visit other times and places that I could not in any other way gratify. And that set me thinking about those first science fiction stories that I read, back there in the mid-1940s, which had such a vast and permanent impact on my developing mind. In particular, the ones that showed me the far future that I knew I would never live to see: what I thought of then, and still in part do regard, as the most valuable function of science fiction.

What were they like, those visions of the future that kept me awake and in a fever of speculative fantasy during so many nights of my boyhood? How do they look, fifty years later? Quaint and creaky, are they? Or do they still have the power to excite my imagination, even now and stir my mind with a sense that I am somehow being granted an authentic look at the eons to come?

The earliest sources of science fiction that I was able to draw upon were books — books that I found in the public library, or that I wangled as gifts from relatives, or was actually able to buy for myself (for a dollar or two, which was what many hardcover books cost back then) with my saved-up pittance of an allowance. From the library came the novels of H.G. Wells — *The War of the Worlds*, *The Island of Dr. Moreau*, and three or four others, paramount among them *The Time Machine*, with that wondrous vision of a dying sun and Earth's last living thing hopping fitfully about in the blood-red waters of an icy sea — a vision that has never lost its power for me. I also found Don Wollheim's pioneering paperback anthology *The Pocket Book of Science Fiction* there. From Macy's Book Department came three spectacular anthologies, Groff Conklin's *Best of Science Fiction* and *A Treasury of Science Fiction*, and *Adventures in Time and Space*, edited by Raymond Healy and J. Francis McComas. And then, a little while later — it was 1948, now — I began reading John Campbell's *Astounding Science Fiction* and Raymond A. Palmer's garish magazine *Amazing Stories*, and quickly went on to add the other pulp sf magazines of the day to my list, *Startling Stories* and *Planet Stories* and *Thrilling Wonder Stories* and *Super-Science Stories*.

I have before me now a lot of the books and magazines that sent my head spinning in the days when Harry Truman was President. Is the magic still there? Let me paw the yellowing pages, and see what time has done to yesterday's visions of tomorrow.

Here's a passage from A.E. van Vogt's "The Weapons Shop," first published in 1942:

> "The sign of the weapon shop was, he saw, a normal-illusion affair. No matter what his angle of view, he was always looking straight at it. When he paused finally in front of the great display window, the words had pressed back against the store front, and were staring unwinkingly down on him....
>
> "There was another sign in the window, which read:
> "THE FINEST ENERGY WEAPONS IN THE KNOWN UNIVERSE.
>
> "A spark of interest struck fire inside Fara. He gazed at that brilliant display of guns, fascinated in spite of himself. The weapons were of every size, ranging from tiny little finger pistols to express rifles. They were made of every one of the light, hard, ornamental substances: glittering glassein, the colorful but opaque Ordine plastic, viridescent magnesitic beryllium. And others."

Yes. Simple stuff, but it does it for me, still. I need only encounter a few passages of that story's limpid prose and I am back in 1949, trembling with anticipation as I peer through a window into the millennia ahead. And when I read about that sign that you're always looking right at, I picture in my mind those little plastic guns of viridescent magnesitic beryllium, and something goes click in my mind and I am in the town of Glay, seven thousand years in the future.

Then there's this — the opening of Poul Anderson's "Tomorrow's Children," of 1947:

> "Ten miles up, it hardly showed. Earth was a cloudy green and brown blur, the vast vault of the stratosphere reaching changelessly out to spatial infinities, and beyond the pulsing engine there was silence and serenity no man could ever touch. Looking down, Hugh Drummond could see the Mississippi gleaming like a drawn sword, and its slow curve matched the contours shown on his map. The

hills, the sea, the sun and wind and rain, they didn't change. Not in less than a million slow-striding years, and human efforts flickered too briefly in the unending night for that.

"Farther down, though, and especially where cities had been —"

Oh, my, the power of that line: "*especially where cities had been*"! The whole radioactive post-civilized world that we all expected and dreaded then uncoiled before my twelve-year-old eyes; and though we seem to have been spared the nightmare world of Anderson's story, I see that wrecked and sizzling world once again, now, as I re-read.

Or the truly unattainable remote future, limned for me by John W. Campbell, Jr., writing as "Don A. Stuart," in 1937's "Forgetfulness":

"The city flamed before him. Across ten — or was it twenty — thousand millenniums, the thought of the builders reached to this man of another race. A builder who thought and dreamed of a mighty future, marching on, on forever in the aisles of time. He must have looked from some high, wind-swept balcony of the city to a star-sprinkled sky — and seen the argosies of space: mighty treasure ships that swept back to this remembered home, coming in from the legion worlds of space, from far stars and unknown, clustered suns; Titan ships, burdened with strange cargoes of unguessed things.

"And the city peopled itself before him; the skies stirred in a moment's flash. It was the day of Rhth's glory then! Mile-long ships hovered in the blue, settling, slow, slow, home from worlds they'd circled. Familiar sights, familiar sounds, greeting their men again. Flashing darts of silver that twisted through mazes of the upper air, the soft, vast music of the mighty city."

Stirs the old nostalgia, yes, indeed: that yearning for futures past that comes over me whenever I think of those old magazines and the unabashedly romantic prose. How grateful I am, to these great writers, for having created these visions for me as I came stumbling wide-eyed into the world of science fiction!

There's so much more that I remember fondly from that era: Heinlein's rolling roads, and Lewis Padgett's Twonky and his Time Locker, and the Build-a-Man Set of William Tenn's "Child's Play," and the robot bartender of Anthony Boucher's "Q.U.R." Those images and dozens just as vivid set my mind aflame, as images out of other, later stories must have done for yours a generation later. (I hope some of them were mine!) Looking at these old stories now, I'm immensely gladdened to see that they still hold their magic for me, and not simply because they evoke nostalgia in me, but because of the intensity with which their authors strived to invent the future.

Let me leave you with the other pre-eminent passage of my boyhood reading, the one that hit me every bit as hard as the scene in Wells' *Time Machine* of that dismal snow-flecked beach at the end of time. This is from H.P. Lovecraft's novella "The Shadow Out of Time," of 1936: one of Lovecraft's few excursions into pure science fiction, in which a twentieth-century college professor has a strange adventure that takes him both backward and forward in time:

> "I learned...that the entities around me were of the world's greatest race, which had conquered time and sent exploring minds into every age....I seemed to talk, in some odd language of claw clicking, with exiled intellects from every corner of the solar system. There was a mind from the planet we know as Venus, which would live incalculable epochs to come, and one from an outer moon of Jupiter six million years in the past. Of earthly minds there were some from the winged, star-headed, half-vegetable race of paleogean Antarctica; one from the reptile people of fabled Valusia; three from the furry prehuman Hyperborean worshippers of Tsathoggua; one from the wholly abominable Tcho-Tchos; two from the Arachnid denizens of earth's last age, five from the hardly Coleopterous species immediately following mankind, to which the Great Race was some day to transfer its keenest minds *en masse* in the face of horrible peril....
>
> "I talked with the mind of Yiang-Li, a philosopher from the cruel Empire of Tsan-Chan, which is to come in 5,000 AD; with that of a general of the great-headed brown people who held South Africa in 50,000 BC; with that of a twelfth-century Florentine monk named Bartolomeo Corsi; with that of a king of Lomar who ruled that terrible polar land one hundred thousand years before the squat, yellow Inutos came from the west to engulf it...."
>
> "I talked with the mind of Nug-Soth, a magician of the dark conquerors of 16,000 AD;...with that of Khepnes, an Egyptian of the 14th Dynasty, who told me the hideous secret of Nyarlathotep; with that of a priest of Atlantis' middle kingdom; with that of Crom-Ya, a Cimmerian chieftain of 15,000 BC; and with so many others that my brain can not hold the shocking secrets and dizzying marvels I learned from them...."

Infinite reach; infinite possibilities. That passage left me stunned and gasping. It still does. It gave me what I knew I could never have in reality, a sweeping look down the corridors of time; and I have sought ever since, both as a reader and a writer, to replicate that experience and those others of my early reading years that I've quoted here — to gain once again that sense of doors opening onto enormous vistas of other realities.

Asimov's Science Fiction, March 1997

Cause and Effect

ONE OF THE MOST INSIGHTFUL ATTEMPTS TO DE-FINE SCIENCE FICTION ever made was an essay called "Social Science Fiction" by — who else? — Isaac Asimov, written in 1953 for Reginald Bretnor's superb book, *Modern Science Fiction*. Isaac had this to say, back then:

> Let us suppose it is 1880 and we have a series of three writers who are each interested in writing a story of the future about an imaginary vehicle that can move without horses by some internal source of power; a horseless carriage, in other words. We might even make up a word and call it an automobile.
>
> Writer X spends most of his time describing how the machine would run, explaining the workings of an internal-combustion engine, painting a word-picture of the struggles of the inventor, who after numerous failures, comes up with a successful model. The climax of the yarn is the drama of the machine, chugging its way along at the gigantic speed of twenty miles an hour between a double crowd of cheering admirers, possibly beating a horse and carriage which have been challenged to a race. This is gadget science fiction.
>
> Writer Y invents the automobile in a hurry, but now there is a gang of ruthless crooks intent on stealing this valuable invention. First they steal the inventor's beautiful daughter, whom they threaten with every dire eventuality but rape (in these adventure stories, girls exist to be rescued and have no other uses). The inventor's young assistant goes to the rescue. He can accomplish his purpose only by the use of the newly invented automobile. He dashes into the desert at an unheard of speed of twenty miles an hour to pick

up the girl who otherwise would have died of thirst if he had relied on a horse, however rapid and sustained the horse's gallop. This is adventure science fiction.

Writer Z has the automobile already perfected. A society exists in which it is already a problem. Because of the automobile, a gigantic oil industry has grown up, highways have been paved across the nation, America has become a land of travelers, cities have spread out into suburbs, and — what do we do about automobile accidents? Men, women, and children are being killed by automobiles faster than by artillery shells or airplane bombs. What can be done? What is the solution? This is social science fiction.

I leave it to the reader to decide which is the most mature and which (this is 1880, remember) is the most socially significant. Keep in mind the fact that social science fiction is not easy to write. It is easy to predict an automobile in 1880; it is very hard to predict a traffic problem. The former is really only an extrapolation of the railroad. The latter is something completely novel and unexpected.

I have just been reading an astonishing sf novel by a writer whose work is probably unfamiliar to most of you: José Saramago, who is Portuguese. The novel is called *Blindness* and it is a stunning exemplar of Asimovian social science fiction: an examination of the consequences for society of a single astounding deviation from our established reality.

Perhaps the book is really fantasy rather than science fiction, since Saramago's premise is not an easy one to accept at face value, and he makes no attempt to provide a scientific rationale for it. He simply states it, turns it loose to generate his plot, and lets it run its course, without ever attempting to offer any sort of explanation of how such a thing might have happened. No matter. Even if the primary situation is basically fantastic, his handling of it is purely science fictional, the steady and meticulous examination of the consequences — *all* of them — of a single remarkable departure from the reality we know. As the author himself said in an interview a couple of years ago, "There is not much imagination in *Blindness,* just the systematic application of the relation of cause and effect."

He states his speculative situation on the first page: in the midst of heavy urban traffic (the city is never mentioned; perhaps it is Lisbon) the car at the head of the middle lane stops for a traffic light and remains halted when the light turns green. Horns begin to honk. Drivers get out of their cars to investigate. A breakdown of some sort? No. The driver inside the stopped car shouts, "I am blind, I am blind." Between one moment and the next he has lost his vision. The only thing he can see is a white glow.

"These things happen," a woman says. "It will pass. Sometimes it's nerves." A good Samaritan offers to drive the hapless man home, and does, taking him to his nearby apartment and leaving him there. (And stealing his car when he departs.) The man stumbles around the apartment in bewilderment. His wife comes home: he explains his predicament. Hastily she leafs through the telephone book, finds an eye doctor, hails a taxi when she discovers the car is missing, and brings him to the doctor's office.

Six or seven patients are waiting there already — an old man with cataracts, a boy with a squint, a young woman with conjunctivitis, and several more. But so strange is the case of the driver who went blind at the wheel of his car that the doctor orders him shown immediately into the consulting room while the others wait. He examines the man's eyes and can find nothing organically wrong. "Your blindness at this moment defies explanation," he tells the man. In the evening, at home, he discusses the case with his wife and searches through his reference books without success.

By morning, several other cases of the same sort of blindness — the white glow, not the usual blackness that loss of vision brings — have been reported throughout the city. It begins to become apparent that a baffling epidemic of blindness has begun.

At this point let's look at those Asimovian categories again. The writer of gadget science fiction (the Hugo Gernsback school of SF) would halt the story after the situation has been stated so that he can deliver a long lecture on the mechanics of vision. The rest of the tale would show the steady spreading of this inexplicable plague of blindness and would depict a brilliant young medical researcher's ultimately triumphant struggle to find a cure.

As for the writer of adventure sf (the pulp-magazine school of the 1940s), he would let us know fairly quickly that the blindness is the result of a beam being flashed down from space by an invading army of aliens. With all of Earth demoralized by the onset of such instant blindness, it will be an easy matter for the monsters from space to achieve its conquest — but for the heroic efforts of a band of brave men who just happened to be in a subterranean cave at the time of the attack, and who now emerge, aided by hastily improvised blindness shields, to wage a valiant war of defense that ends in the total rout of the invaders.

Whereas the writer of social science fiction would examine in meticulous detail the cascading consequences of the one strange event that set his story in motion, looking at them with regard to the effects that such an event might have on human society.

And that is exactly what José Saramago does. For it turns out that the earliest victims of the blindness can all be linked directly to the first man, the rush-hour driver. The Samaritan who steals his car goes blind. Likewise the taxi driver who takes the first blind man and his wife to the eye doctor, and the first blind man's wife. So do the patients in the eye doctor's waiting room, the squinting boy and the man with the eye patch and the rest. *The eye doctor himself loses his vision.* Of all those who come in contact with the first blind man or the earliest group of victims, only the doctor's wife, for some miraculous reason, retains her sight.

The local officials instantly conclude that the blindness is contagious, transmitted by direct contact. Since no one understands what causes it, that's as reasonable a theory as any; and so, on grounds of "public safety," the early victims are rounded up and confined, under guard, in an abandoned mental hospital that happens to be available. This is Saramago's jumping-off point for an examination of the convergence of paranoia and totalitarianism in modern civilization. Step by step he shows us the return to a state of primitive nature within and without the camp — fear of the blindness drives these otherwise civilized people into a state approaching savagery in the name of self-defense, and only a few inspired leaders retain enough sanity to hold some shreds of civilization together. And as the blindness continues to spread until society has collapsed altogether, we realize that Saramago has been writing not only a classic end-of-the-world novel but also an allegory of the failures of human communication in daily life.

It is a remorseless, harrowing novel. You are drawn along from one grim situation to another, each of them utterly plausible *within the context of the defined situation,* and depicted in merciless and wholly believable detail. And when the ending comes — it is more of a release than a real ending — you are left stunned by the power of the book you have just read.

If the novel is as good as all that, though, why was it not a Hugo or Nebula nominee in the year of its publication? Why are you hearing about it now, probably, for the first time?

Because José Saramago is not a science fiction writer, simply a writer who deviated into a sort of science fiction for this one magnificent novel. But, though he has no Hugos or Nebulas to his credit, it is not as though his great literary accomplishments have gone completely unnoticed in the world beyond the confines of the sf readership. In October, 1998 — a couple of years after the publication of *Blindness* — José Saramago was awarded the Nobel Prize for Literature.

Asimov's Science Fiction, July, 2001

Dancing Through The Apocalypse

HUMANKIND SEEMS TO TAKE A CERTAIN GRISLY DELIGHT in stories about the end of the world, since the market in apocalyptic prophecy has been a bullish one for thousands or, more likely, millions of years. Even the most primitive of protohuman creatures, back there in the Africa of Ardipithecus and her descendants, must have come eventually to the realization that each of us must die; and from there to the concept that the world itself must perish in the fullness of time was probably not an enormous intellectual leap for those hairy bipedal creatures of long ago. Around their prehistoric campfires our remote hominid ancestors surely would have told each other tales of how the great fire in the sky would become even greater one day and consume the universe, or, once our less distant forebears had moved along out of the African plains to chillier Europe, how the glaciers of the north would someday move implacably down to crush them all. Even an eclipse of the sun was likely to stir brief apocalyptic excitement.

I suppose there is a kind of strange comfort in such thoughts: "If I must die, how good that all of you must die also!" But the chief value of apocalyptic visions, I think, lies elsewhere than in that sort of we-will-all-go-together-when-we-go spitefulness, for as we examine the great apocalyptic myths we see that not only death but resurrection is usually involved in the story — a bit of eschatological comfort, of philosophical reassurance that existence, though finite and relatively brief for each individual, is not totally pointless. Yes, the tale would run, we have done evil things and the gods are angry and the world is going to perish, in a moment, in the twinkling of an eye, but then will come a reprieve, a second creation, a rebirth of life, a better world than the one that has just been purged.

What sort of end-of-the-world stories our primordial preliterate ancestors told is something we will never know, but the oldest such tale that has come down to us, which is found in the 5000 year old Sumerian epic of Gilgamesh, King of Uruk, is an account of a great deluge that drowns the whole Earth, save only one man, Ziusudra by name, who manages to save his family and set things going again. Very probably the deluge story had its origins in memories of some great flood that devastated Sumer and its Mesopotamian neighbors in prehistoric times, but that is only speculation. What is certain is that the theme can be found again in many later versions: the Babylonian version gives the intrepid survivor the name of Utnapishtim, the Hebrews called him Noah, to the ancient Greeks he was Deucalion, and in the Vedic texts of India he is Manu. The details differ, but the essence is always the same: the gods, displeased with the world, resolve to destroy it, but then bring mankind forth for a second try.

Floods are not the only apocalypses that religious texts offer us. The Norse myths give us a terrible frost, the Fimbulwinter, in which all living things die except a man and a woman who survive by hiding in a tree; they follow the usual redemptionist course and repeople the world, but then comes an even greater cataclysm, Ragnarok, the doom of the gods themselves, in which the stars fall, the earth sinks into the sea, and fire consumes everything — only to be followed by yet another rebirth and an era of peace and plenty. And the Christian tradition provides the spectacular final book of the Bible, the Revelation of St. John the Divine, in which the wrath of God is visited upon the Earth in a host of ways (fire, plague, hail, drought, earthquakes, flood, and much more), leading to the final judgment and the redemption of the righteous. The Aztecs, too, had myths of the destruction of the world by fire — several times over, in fact — and so did the Mayas. Even as I write this, much popular excitement is being stirred by an alleged Mayan prediction that the next apocalypse is due in 2012, which has engendered at least three books and a movie, so far.

Since apocalyptic visions are nearly universal in the religious literature of the world, and apparently always have been, it is not surprising that they should figure largely in the fantasies of imaginative storytellers. Even before the term "science fiction" had been coined, stories of universal or near-universal extinction brought about not by the anger of the deities but by the innate hazards of existence were being written and achieving wide popularity. Nineteenth-century writers were particularly fond of them. Thus we find such books as Jean-Baptiste de Grainville's *The Last Man, or Omegarus and Syderia* (1806) and Mary Shelley's *The Last Man* (1826), which was written under the shadow of a worldwide epidemic of cholera that raged from 1818 to 1822. Edgar Allan Poe sent a comet into the Earth in "The Conversation of Eros and Charmion" (1839). The French astronomer Camille Flammarion's astonishing novel of 1893, *La Fin du Monde*, or *Omega* in its English translation, brought the world to the edge of doom — but only to the edge — as another giant comet crosses our path. H.G. Wells told a similar story of near-destruction, almost surely inspired by Flammarion's, in "The Star" (1897). In his classic novel *The Time Machine* (1895) Wells had already taken his time traveler to the end of life on Earth and beyond ("All the sounds of man, the bleating of sheep, the cries of birds, the hum of insects, the stir that makes the background of our lives — all that was over.")

Another who must certainly have read Flammarion is his compatriot Jules Verne, who very likely drew on the latter sections of *Omega* for his novella, "The Eternal Adam" (1905). Here Verne espouses a cyclical view of the world: Earth is destroyed by a calamitous earthquake and flood, but the continent of Atlantis wondrously emerges from the depths to provide a new home for the human race, which after thousands of years of toil rebuilds civilization; and we are given a glimpse, finally, of a venerable scholar of the far future looking back through the archives of humanity, "bloodied by the innumerable hardships suffered by those who had gone before him," and coming, "slowly, reluctantly, to an intimate conviction of the eternal return of all things."

The eternal return! It is the theme of so much of this apocalyptic literature. That phrase of Verne's links his story to the core of Flammarion's own belief that our own little epoch is "an imperceptible wave on the immense ocean of the ages" and that mankind's destiny is, as we see in his closing pages, to be born again and again into universe after universe, each to pass on in its turn and be replaced, for time goes on forever and there can be neither end nor beginning.

Rebirth after catastrophe is to be found, also, in M.P. Shiel's magnificent novel *The Purple Cloud* (1901), in which we are overwhelmed by a mass of poisonous gas, leaving only one man — Adam is his name, of course — as the ostensible survivor, until he finds his Eve and life begins anew. No such renewal is offered in Frank Lillie Pollock's terminally apocalyptic short story "Finis" (1906), though, which postulates a gigantic central star in the galaxy whose light has been heading toward us for an immense span of time and now finally arrives, so that "there, in crimson and orange, flamed the last dawn that human eyes would ever see."

There is ever so much more. Few readers turn to apocalyptic tales these days for reassurance that once the sins of mankind have been properly punished, a glorious new age will open; but, even so, the little *frisson* that a good end-of-the-world story supplies is irresistible to writers, and the bibliography of apocalyptic fantasy is an immense one. Garrett P. Serviss's *The Second Deluge* (1912) drowns us within a watery nebula. G. Peyton Wertenbaker's "The Coming of the Ice" (1926) brings the glaciers back with a thoroughness that makes the Norse Fimbulwinter seem like a light snowstorm. (I had a go at the same theme myself in my 1964 novel, *Time of the Great Freeze*, but, unlike Wertenbaker, I opted for a thaw at the end.) Philip Wylie and Edwin Balmer's *When Worlds Collide* (1933) tells us of an awkward astrophysical event with very unpleasant consequences for our planet. Edmond Hamilton's "In the World's Dusk" (1936) affords a moody vision of the end of days, millions of years hence, when one lone man survives and "a white salt desert now covered the whole of Earth. A cruel glaring plain that stretched eye-achingly to the horizons...." Robert A. Heinlein's story "The Year of the Jackpot" (1952) puts the end much closer — 1962, in fact — when bad things begin to happen in droves all around the world, floods and typhoons and earthquakes and volcanic eruptions worthy of the Book of Revelation, culminating in a lethal solar catastrophe. J.T. McIntosh's *One in Three Hundred* (1954) also has the sun going nova, at novel length. And, of course, the arrival of atomic weapons in 1945 set loose such a proliferation of nuclear-holocaust stories that it would take many pages to list them all.

The possible variations on the theme are endless. As Robert Frost wrote nearly a century ago,

> Some say the world will end in fire,
> Some say in ice.
> From what I've tasted of desire
> I hold with those who favor fire.
> But if it had to perish twice,
> I think I know enough of hate
> To know that for destruction ice
> Is also great
> And would suffice.

Fire or ice, one or the other — who knows? The final word on finality is yet to be written. But what is certain is that we will go on speculating about it ... right until the end.

Introduction to *It's The End of the World*, 2010

Hic Rhodus, Hic Salta

CAREFUL READERS OF THIS COLUMN WILL KNOW THAT THE SCIENCE FICTION of "Murray Leinster," which was the pseudonym of Will F. Jenkins, has been on my mind for the past couple of issues. Another of his works has crossed my path now: the best-known of his stories, "First Contact" (1945), which deals — brilliantly — with the problems that humans will face on their initial encounter with an alien starship in interstellar space.

The first problem, of course, is figuring out how to speak with the aliens. Leinster solves this in his usual efficient way: " 'We've hooked up some machinery,' said Tommy, 'that amounts to a mechanical translator.' " After some plausible-sounding engineering talk about frequency modulation and short-wave beams, Tommy goes on to tell his captain, "We agreed on arbitrary symbols for objects, sir, and worked out relationships and verbs and so on with diagrams and pictures. We've a couple of thousand words that have mutual meanings. We set up an analyzer to sort out their short-wave groups, which we feed into a decoding machine. And then the coding end of the machine picks out recordings to make the wave groups we want to send back. When you're ready to talk to the skipper of the other ship, sir, I think we're ready."

All very neat and clever. Communication is opened between the two ships, and Leinster can proceed to the real focus of the story — the ticklish issue of interstellar diplomacy. If this is not the first use in science fiction of that handy gadget, the electronic translating machine, it is certainly one of the earliest and best. From then on, spacefarers voyaging into alien territory in the pages of magazines like *Astounding* and *Galaxy* routinely uncorked their translating machines as needed, thus allowing them to get on to their interstellar tasks and the authors to get on to their story's plot requirements.

All very convenient for us writers. Your protagonist comes across an alien, pulls out a device no bigger than an iPod (and how that great gadgeteer Murray Leinster would have loved iPods!) and interspecies communication becomes as easy as Pi. But it's all a little on the glib side, too. How well, one wonders, would these marvelous translating machines work in reality? In a 2003 column that discussed the vagaries of the here-and-now translating programs (terrestrial languages only) that are available all over the Internet I had this to say:

> Science fiction writers, as you know, are in the habit of equipping their spacefaring heroes with translating devices that swiftly and accurately render unfamiliar alien languages into lucid English. We have always suspected that creating such a device would be, of course, easier said than done. In Kim Stanley Robinson's 1990 story "The Translator," which pokes lethal fun at the concept of a translating machine, a hapless Earthman meeting with two alien species at once has one group tell him things like "*Warlike viciously now descendant fat food flame death*" while the other comes through the translating gizmo with sounds that can be translated, the machine says, as "*1. Fish market. 2. Fish harvest. 3. Sunspots visible from a depth of 10 meters below the surface of the ocean on a calm day. 4. Traditional festival. 5. Astrological configuration in galactic core.*"

What causes me now to reflect once again on the unlikelihood of our getting to understand the speech of alien beings is my stumbling across a choice example of mistranslation of a language we know very well — Latin — done not by a computer but by actual human beings, highly intelligent ones, a translation that has been bungled and rebungled for hundreds of years until we no longer can be sure of the original meaning.

In a 1953 essay by the Swiss scholar Herbert Luthy on the writings of the philosopher Montaigne I came upon a Latin phrase that was new to me and left unexplained in Luthy's text: *Hic Rhodus, hic salta.* I still remember some of the Latin that I studied more than fifty years ago, and my first attempt at a translation produced "*Here is Rhodes, dance here.*" Which made little sense to me; but then I recalled that in Italian, a language of which I have some knowledge, the verb *saltare* means "to jump." Perhaps the phrase quoted by Luthy was late Latin, I thought; late Latin was practically Italian: "*Here is Rhodes, jump here.*" But that seemed just as nonsensical. Off I went to my Latin dictionary. I found the verb *salire*, meaning "to jump," which gave rise to a later verb, *saltare,* which in Latin meant "to jump repeatedly," i.e. "to dance," from which the Italian verb for jumping came, though Italian has a different word meaning "to dance." ("Salire," in Italian, has lost its old Latin meaning and now means "to climb," by the way.) I also found the noun *saltus,* meaning "a leap" or "a jump." Well, whether jump or dance, the phrase still was baffling. So my next stop was Google.

The Google link for *Hic Rhodus, hic salta* traced the phrase back to one of Aesop's fables. Aesop, if he existed at all, was a Greek who lived in the sixth century BC, but the earliest texts of his fables that have come down to us are Latin versions of the first or second century AD, and in those the phrase is given as *Hic Rhodus, hic saltus*, which means, essentially, "Here [is] Rhodes, here [make your] jump." The fable concerns a fellow who has returned after having been away from home for a while and begins bragging about the feats of athletic valor that he had performed while traveling. In Rhodes, he claims, he took part in a long-jump contest and made such a jump that not even an Olympic athlete could equal it. Whereupon a skeptical bystander calls his bluff, saying, and I translate freely, "All right: let's pretend that this is Rhodes. Now jump!"

That explained the phrase, but not why Herbert Luthy had used the imperative verb *salta*, with its connotation of dancing, in place of the Latin noun *saltus*, "a jump," that we find in our texts of Aesop. The answer, I learned, is that Karl Marx is to blame, or maybe Friedrich Hegel.

Hegel, it seems, had used the phrase — first in Greek, and then in Latin with *saltus* — in the preface to his *Philosophy of Right* (1821). He doesn't explain it, and in fact doesn't seem to understand its Aesopian meaning, because he appears to think it connotes jumping over the entire *island* of Rhodes. He goes on to give it a German translation — *Hier ist die Rose, hier tanze*, meaning "Here is the rose, dance here." Apparently the switch from "Rhodes" to "rose" involves a pun in Greek, substituting *rodon* ("rose") for *Rodos* ("Rhodes"). The rose Hegel is talking about seems to be the symbol of the mystic order of the Rosicrucians, my source tells me, an explanation I did not find helpful.

Marx comes into the story because he is responsible for the garbled *salta* translation, perhaps working backward to Latin from Hegel's pun. In a book published in 1852 he gave the phrase as *Hic Rhodus, hic salta*, which, since it refers to dancing rather than jumping, has no Aesopian meaning, and then in Hegel's punning mistranslation, "Here is the rose, dance here." Hegel, at least, seemed to know he was punning. But Marx appears to think that he is translating, although *Rhodus* in this context can only be the Latin name of the island off the coast of Asia Minor, not the Latin word for "rose," which is, you will be relieved to know, *rosa*. Nevertheless, Marx's essentially meaningless mistranslation of the Aesopian punchline, minus the rest of the fable, seems to have passed into philosophical discourse as a tag with the original Aesopian meaning, that is, something like "put up or shut up."

An interesting twist now enters the tale: the possibility that phrase in its original form may not have included a reference to the island of Rhodes at all. As I noted above, the original Greek texts of Aesop's fables have been lost for more than a thousand years. Aesop himself first is mentioned in Greek literature in the fifth century BC, more than a hundred years after he supposedly lived, but, like Homer, he is a legendary figure about whom we know nothing that can be regarded as trustworthy. Probably someone of that name did compose some fables, but other fables that we regard as the work of Aesop may well have been the work of others, and the biographical information we have about him is best thought of as fiction.

A biography of the scholar Demetrius of Phalerius dating from the fourth century BC credits Demetrius with having compiled a collection of "Aesopic fables," but his book has not survived to our time. For our knowledge of the fables ascribed to Aesop we must turn to several Latin translations dating from the early days of the Roman Empire, one by a certain Babrius, another by a certain Phaedrus. And in the case of the fable of the boastful jumper, one student of the fables suggests, these early translators may have given us an inaccurate version of the Greek original.

I've already mentioned that the Greek name for the island of Rhodes is *Rodos*. But *rodos*, without the capital letter (and the early Greeks were very haphazard about capitalizing), is the Greek word for the long rod that pole-vaulters use to propel themselves over the bar. So the original tale may have finished with the skeptical onlooker saying, "All right: here's a rod. Now let's see you jump!" By using the wrong meaning for *rodos*, the Latin translator was forced to insert Rhodes as the site of the braggart's exploit, and, later, Karl Marx (with some help from Hegel) added another layer of confusion by using *rodon*, "rose," instead of *rodos*, "Rhodes" or "rod."

If you have been having difficulty following this tangled tale, let me assure you that you are not the only one. I have taken you through it simply to show you that translating from one language to another is no easy matter. Classical Greek was still a living language in the time of Tiberius Caesar when Phaedrus was making his Latin translation of Aesop, and yet it is possible that Phaedrus misunderstood the Greek text's use of *rodos* and thus brought the isle of Rhodes into the tale. Hegel, who, like all educated men in the nineteenth century, was quite at home in Latin and Greek, had not fully understood the Latin text of the proverb where it mentions Rhodes, and then had — deliberately, it seems — given it a further twist to make it read "Here is the rose, dance here," which Marx — who surely knew the classical languages also — picked up and passed along, making it available now in transmogrified form for Herbert Luthy to baffle me with a century later. If these brilliant men couldn't get one of Aesop's fables straight, what luck do you think a translating machine is going to have with the poetry of Betelgeuse XIX?

Asimov's Science Fiction, **January, 2009**

Science Fiction In The Fifties:
The Real Golden Age

HISTORIANS OF SCIENCE FICTION OFTEN SPEAK OF THE YEARS 1939-42 as "the golden age." But it was more like a false dawn. The real golden age arrived a decade later, and — what is not always true of golden ages — we knew what it was while it was happening.

That earlier golden age was centered entirely in a single magazine, John W. Campbell's *Astounding Science Fiction*, and the war aborted it in midstride. Campbell steered a middle course between the heavy-handed science-oriented stories preferred by the pioneering sf magazine editors Hugo Gernsback and T. O'Conor Sloane and the cheerfully lowbrow adventure fiction favored by pulp editors Ray Palmer and Mort Weisinger. He wanted smoothly written fiction that seriously explored the future of science and technology for an audience of intelligent adult readers — and in the four years of that first golden age he found an extraordinary array of brilliant new writers (and re-energized some older ones) to give him what he wanted: Robert A. Heinlein, Isaac Asimov, Theodore Sturgeon, A.E. van Vogt, Jack Williamson, Clifford D. Simak, L. Sprague de Camp, and many more.

The decade of the Fifties is often thought nowadays to have been a timid, conventional, strait-laced time, a boring and sluggish era that was swept away, thank heaven, by the free-wheeling, permissive, joyous Sixties. In some ways, that's true. For science fiction, no. The decade of the Fifties, staid as it may have been in matters of clothing, politics, and sexuality, was also a period that saw the first artificial space satellites placed in orbit around the Earth; the beginning of the end of legal racial segregation in the United States; and, in the small world of science fiction, a grand rush of creativity, a torrent of new magazines and new writers bringing new themes and fresh techniques that laid the foundation for the work of the four decades that followed. An exciting time for us, yes: truly a golden age.

The disruptions of the Second World War scattered Campbell's talented crew far and wide. Some, like Asimov, van Vogt, and Simak, managed to provide Campbell with an occasional story during the war years, as did some lesser figures of the first Campbell pantheon who now were reaching literary maturity — Henry Kuttner, Fritz Leiber, Eric Frank Russell. Others — Heinlein, Williamson, de Camp — vanished from science fiction "for the duration," as the phrase went then. They all came back after the war, and with their aid Campbell attempted, with moderate success, to restore *Astounding* Somehow, though, the magazine never quite became the dazzling locus of excitement that it had been a decade earlier.

And then, suddenly, the Fifties arrived — and with the new decade came a host of new science fiction magazines and a legion of gifted new writers. The result was a spectacular outpouring of stories and novels that swiftly surpassed both in quantity and quality the considerable achievement of the Campbellian golden age.

Many of Campbell's original stars were still in their prime, indeed had much of their best work still ahead. But now there was the new generation of writers, most born between 1915 and 1928. They had been too young to have been major contributors to the pre-war *Astounding*; but now they came blossoming into literary maturity all at once. I mean such writers as Jack Vance, James Blish, Poul Anderson, Damon Knight, "William Tenn", Frederik Pohl, Arthur C. Clarke, C.M. Kornbluth, Ray Bradbury, Alfred Bester, and, a little later, Algis Budrys, Marion Zimmer Bradley, Philip K. Dick, Robert Sheckley, Philip José Farmer, Walter M. Miller, Jr., James E. Gunn, and others.

Most of these newcomers had learned what they knew about science fiction by reading Campbell's magazine. Nearly all (Bradbury was the major exception) subscribed to Campbell's insistence that even the most speculative of science fiction stories ought to be founded on a clear understanding of real-world science and human psychology and his belief in the importance of employing a lucid, straightforward narrative style.

But most of these new writers did their best work for editors other than Campbell. That was a significant change. In the Forties, Campbell was the only market for serious science fiction; those who could not or would not write the relatively sophisticated sort of fiction that Campbell wanted to publish wrote simple, low-pay action-adventure stories for his gaudy-looking pulp-paper competitors, such magazines as *Planet Stories*, *Super Science Stories*, and *Startling Stories*.

As the Fifties dawned, two of the pulps, *Startling* and *Thrilling Wonder Stories*, were beginning to welcome science fiction of the more complex Campbellian kind under the editorship of Sam Merwin, Jr. But the basic task of most of them still was to supply simple adventure fiction to an audience primarily made up of boys and half-educated young men.

The first harbinger of the new era was *The Magazine of Fantasy*, a dignified-looking magazine in the small "digest-sized" format that *Astounding* had adopted during the war. The first issue, on sale in the autumn of 1949, sold for the premier price of 35 cents a copy, ten cents more than *Astounding*, and contained a mixture of new short stories, more fantasy than science fiction, by such people as Theodore Sturgeon and Cleve Cartmill (the latter a minor Campbell writer), and classic reprints by British writers like Oliver Onions, Perceval Landon, and Fitz-James O'Brien, that gave the magazine a genteel, almost Victorian tone. But right at the back of the magazine was an astonishing, explosive science fiction story by the poet Winona McClintock: science fiction, yes, but nothing that John Campbell would ever have published, for it was profoundly anti-scientific in theme, and exceedingly literary in tone. It was closest in manner to the sort of fiction that Ray Bradbury had begun to publish in just about every American magazine from *Weird Tales* to *Harper's*, but never in *Astounding*.

The Magazine of Fantasy, by all appearances, was the sort of quiet little literary quarterly that would find a quiet little audience and expire after two or three issues. But its second issue, though still in the same elegant format, showed a notable transformation. The name of the magazine now was *The Magazine of Fantasy and Science Fiction*, and — though there still were a couple of nineteenth-century reprints — most of the issue was science fiction. Not Campbellian science fiction, to be sure: nothing that explored and even extolled the coming high-tech future. Ray Bradbury himself was on hand, with a tale of hallucinatory spaceflight ("The Exiles"), and two of Campbell's regulars, L. Sprague de Camp and Fletcher Pratt, with a funny little fantasy. Damon Knight and Margaret St. Clair, writers just beginning their careers, contributed stories which, though they fit almost anyone's definition of science fiction, Campbell would surely have rejected for their frivolity and their scientific irrelevance. The whole tone of the magazine was light, playful, experimental.

And yet one of Campbell's own regulars was in charge: Anthony Boucher, the author of a baker's dozen of stories for *Astounding* and its short-lived fantasy companion, *Unknown Worlds*, between 1942 and 1946. He and his co-editor, J. Francis McComas, were familiar with Campbell's objectives and were quite willing to concede the high-tech audience to him, staking out a position for themselves among readers whose orientation lay more in the direction of general literature, fantasy, even detective fiction, but who had a liking for the vivid concepts of science fiction as well.

F&SF, as the magazine came to be known, prospered and grew in the Fifties, quickly going from quarterly to bi-monthly publication and then to monthly. Its pages were a home for scores of writers new and old who chafed at John Campbell's messianic sense of the function of science and his growing literary dogmatism. Bradbury was a frequent contributor. So was Sturgeon. Alfred Bester, a peripheral figure in the Campbell *Astounding*, produced a group of remarkable short stories in a unique pyrotechnic style.

Poul Anderson, a Campbell discovery in 1947 and a regular in his magazine ever since, gave Boucher and McComas dozens of stories that went beyond Campbell's ever-narrowing editorial limits. So did James Blish and C.M. Kornbluth, who had served their apprenticeships in the pre-war pulp magazines but whose talents were coming now into their real flowering. And for a multitude of new writers launching what would prove to be spectacular careers — Philip K. Dick, Robert Sheckley, Avram Davidson, Richard Matheson, J.T. McIntosh, and on and on and on — the amiable, sympathetic Boucher-McComas style of editing proved to be so congenial that they rarely if ever offered stories to Campbell at all.

While *F&SF* was hitting its stride in the first months of the new decade, another Campbell protege was busily readying the first issue of his new science fiction magazine — one intended not to be a genteel literary adjunct to Campbell's *Astounding*, but as its direct and ferociously aggressive competitor. He was Horace L. Gold; his magazine was *Galaxy Science Fiction*, which became the dominant and shaping force of this decade of science fiction as *Astounding* had been for the last one.

Gold, a fiercely opinionated and furiously intelligent man, had begun writing science fiction professionally since his teens, publishing stories even before Campbell's ascent to the editorial chair in 1937, and had worked as an associate editor for a pulp-magazine chain just before the war. He had written some outstanding stories for Campbell in those years too; but then he went off to service, and when he returned it was with serious war-related psychological disabilities from which he was years in recovering.

By 1950, though, Gold was vigorous enough to want to make a head-on attack on Campbell's editorial supremacy: to edit a magazine that would emulate the older editor's visionary futuristic range while at the same time allowing its writers a deeper level of psychological insight than Campbell seemed comfortable with. His intention was to liberate Campbell's best writers from what was now widely felt to be a set of constrictive editorial policies, and to bring in the best of the new writers as well; and to this end he offered his writers a notably higher rate of pay than *Astounding* had been giving them.

The first issue of *Galaxy*, resplendent in a gleaming cover printed on heavy coated stock, was dated October, 1950. Its contents page featured five of Campbell's star authors — Clifford D. Simak, Isaac Asimov, Fritz Leiber, Theodore Sturgeon, Fredric Brown — along with the already celebrated newcomers Richard Matheson and Katherine MacLean. The second issue added Damon Knight and Anthony Boucher to the roster; the third, another recent Campbell star, James H. Schmitz. A new Asimov novel was serialized in the fourth issue; the fifth had a long story by Ray Bradbury, "The Fireman," which would be the nucleus of his novel *Fahrenheit 451*. And so it went all year, and for some years thereafter. The level of performance was astonishingly high. Every few months *Galaxy* brought its readers stories and novels destined for classic status: Alfred Bester's *The Demolished Man*, Pohl and Kornbluth's *The Space Merchants* (called "Gravy Planet" in the magazine), Heinlein's *The Puppet Masters*, James Blish's "Surface Tension," Wyman Guin's "Beyond Bedlam," and dozens more. Though the obstreperous Gold was a difficult, well-nigh impossibly demanding editor to work with, he and his magazine generated so much excitement in the first half of the Fifties that any writer who thought at all of writing science fiction wanted to write for *Galaxy*.

Nor were *Galaxy* and *F&SF* the only new markets for the myriad of capable new writers. Suddenly it was science fiction time in American magazine publishing. Title after title came into being, until by 1953 there were nearly forty of them, whereas in the past there had never been more than eight or nine at once. The new magazines, some of which survived only two or three issues, included *Other Worlds, Imagination, Fantastic Universe, Vortex, Cosmos, If, Science Fiction Adventures*, and *Space Science Fiction*. Long-established pulp magazines like *Startling Stories, Planet Stories*, and *Thrilling Wonder Stories* upgraded their literary standards and drew outstanding contributions from the likes of Arthur C. Clarke, Jack Vance, Henry Kuttner, Ray Bradbury, and Theodore Sturgeon. A trio of ephemeral pulps that had perished in the wartime paper shortage — *Future Fiction, Science Fiction Stories*, and *Science Fiction Quarterly* — were revived after an eight-year lapse.

It was a heady time, all right. The most active writers of the period, people like Sturgeon, Dick, Sheckley, Anderson, Farmer, Blish, Pohl — were in their twenties and thirties, an age that is usually a writer's most productive period, and with all those magazines eager for copy, there was little risk of rejection. In the earlier days when one editor had ruled the empire and a story he turned down might very well not find a home anywhere else, science fiction was too risky a proposition for a professional writer; but now, with twenty or thirty magazines going at a time, the established writers knew they could sell everything they produced, and most of them worked in a kind of white heat, happily turning out fiction with gloriously profligate productivity and, surprisingly, at a startlingly high level of quality as well.

You will note that so far I have spoken of science fiction entirely as a magazine-centered medium. Until the decade of the Fifties, there was essentially no market for science fiction books at all. The paperback revolution had not yet happened; the big hardcover houses seemed not to know that science fiction existed; and, though some of the great magazine serials of the earlier Campbell era, novels by Heinlein and Asimov and Leiber and De Camp, were finding their way occasionally into book form, the publishers were amateurs, lovers of science fiction who issued their books in editions of a few thousand copies and distributed them mainly by mail.

All that changed in the Fifties. The mighty house of Doubleday began to publish hardcover science fiction novels steadily, soon joined by Ballantine Books, an innovative new company that brought its books out in simultaneous hardcover and paperback editions. The sudden existence of willing publishers was all the encouragement the new writers needed: and suddenly we had dozens of splendid novels in print in book form, among them Arthur Clarke's *Childhood's End*, Ward Moore's *Bring the Jubilee*, Bradbury's *Fahrenheit 451*, Sturgeon's *More Than Human*, and Asimov's *Pebble in the Sky*, along with hardcover reprints of recent magazine serials by Heinlein, Asimov, Leiber, and others.

A golden age, yes. Most of the classic anthologies of science fiction stories are heavily stocked with Fifties stories. Any basic library of science fiction novels would have to include a solid nucleus of Fifties books. And today's science fiction writers are deeply indebted to the dominant Fifties writers — Bester and Sturgeon and Dick and Sheckley and Pohl and Blish and the rest — for the fundamental body of ideas and technique with which they work today.

I know. I was there — very young, but with my eyes wide open — and I was savoring it as it happened.

Most of the new writers who made the decade of the Fifties what it was in the history of science fiction were on the scene already as functional professional writers as the decade opened, or else were only a year or two away from launching their careers; but there were a few who were still only readers of science fiction then, and would not see print regularly with their own stories until mid-decade. I was one of those; so was Harlan Ellison, and John Brunner. (Our generation was a sparse one.) Though I was only an on-looker at first, and then just the youngest and greenest of the new writers of the era, I can testify to the crackling excitement of the period, the enormous creative ferment.

I don't think it's mere nostalgia that leads me to the view of the importance of that era. The stories in this book, surely, support my feeling that the Fifties were a time of powerful growth and evolution in science fiction.

Would that evolution ran in a straight upward line. But, alas, there are periods of retrogression in every trend. The glories of the Fifties were short-lived. By 1959, nearly all of the magazines that had been begun with such high hopes a few years before had vanished, the book market had been severely cut back, and many of the writers central to the decade had had to turn to other fields of enterprise. As the Fifties approached their end, Campbell and his *Astounding* still labored on, now into the third decade of his editorship, and despite the inroads of his new competitors he continued to publish some of the best science fiction. But his increasing preoccupation with pseudo-scientific fads had alienated many writers who had previously remained loyal to him, and the magazine grew steadily weaker all through the decade.

For the other surviving magazines, things were no better. Though the potent new magazines *Galaxy* and *F&SF* were among those that lasted, their editors did not; Anthony Boucher had resigned his editorial post in 1958; Horace Gold's continuing medical problems forced him to step down a year later. Without those two pivotal figures, and with Campbell increasingly re-mote and problematical, the spark seemed to go out of the science fiction field, and the fireworks and grand visionary dreams of 1951 and 1952 and 1953 gave way to the dull and gray late-Fifties doldrums of science fiction, a somber period destined to last seven or eight years. The golden age of the Fifties was over. Science fiction fans dreamed of a renaissance to come. And it would eventually arrive, bringing with it another rush of new writers, new literary glories, and a vast new audience whose conflicting preferences would transform the once insular little world of science fiction beyond all recognition.

Nebula Awards Showcase, **2010**

The Ultimate Alien: Introduction

FEAR OF THE OTHER, INEXTRICABLY MIXED WITH EAGER CURIOSITY about him, goes a long way back. Aliens haunted the dreams of our earliest ancestors, perhaps: the boogeymen, the strangers, the ineffably mysterious creatures who lurk at the fringes of our lives, those who are Not Like Us. It may be that the hominids of two million years ago told tales around the campfire of the different-looking beings on the far side of the mountains, the strange ones who were following some different evolutionary track that was destined not to lead to *Homo sapiens*. And *Homo sapiens* himself, sitting snug within the Aurignacian or Solutrean caves while the icy winds of the Pleistocene whirled across the tundra, may have chanted throaty epics of the great war against the shaggy Other Ones whom they had overcome, the ones we call the Neanderthals today.

I think it must be true that we have always looked with mingled fascination and horror at beings who do not belong to our own tribe, whether we consider our tribe to be the twelve members of the clan of Unghk the Barbarian or the teeming billions who make up the total population of Earth. In our struggle to understand who we are, we establish boundaries defining Us and Not-Us; and then we strive to comprehend what those who are Not-Us are like, what defining characteristics they have that make them Not-Us, for then we have a better idea of Us. And it has been this way, I suspect, since the time of the australopithecines and *Homo habilis*.

Traces of the encounters-with-aliens theme turn up at least as early as *The Odyssey*: Odysseus, making his long journey homeward from the Trojan War, runs into one bizarre monstrous creature after another (the one-eyed giant Polyphemus, the six-headed predator Scylla, the insatiable all-devouring creature Charybdis, *et cetera*.) A later Greek, Iambolos, wrote an account

49

in the third century BC of an archipelago in the Indian Ocean populated by people with flexible bones and forked tongues, which enabled them to carry on two conversations at once. Five centuries after that, Lucian of Samosata sent the voyagers of the *True History* to the Moon, where they found, among many other marvels, a warrior race that flew on the backs of giant three-headed vultures, a tribe of archers whose steeds were fleas the size of elephants, and dog-headed men native to the star Sirius.

The eighteenth century was a particularly fertile time for the creation of fictional aliens — the primary purpose of which was, as usual, to provide a clearer perspective on our own nature. Swift's Gulliver, of course, met with a race of tiny people and one of giants, and, finally, a species of intelligent horses. A few years later (1751), Robert Paltock's *Peter Wilkins* told a tale of mariners who enter the interior of the Earth through a hole in the Antarctic Ocean and find a cavern populated by bat-winged folk. The great Danish fantasy *Niels Klim*, published about the same time, offers a planet of intelligent humanoid trees, with branches for arms and twigs for fingers. And Voltaire's satire *Micromegas* (1752) told of the visit to Earth of two gigantic beings, a native of Sirius eight miles tall and a somewhat smaller, but still immense traveler from Saturn: they had no need of spaceships, but moved from world to world in immense leaps, or occasionally hitched rides on passing comets.

And then, as we come closer to our own time, the fictional aliens become more numerous, more vivid, and, usually, more menacing. The most famous ones of all arrived from Mars in 1897, in H.G. Wells' *The War of the Worlds:*

> "They were, I now saw, the most unearthly creatures it is possible to conceive. They were huge round bodies — or, rather, heads — about four feet in diameter, each body having in front of it a face. This face had no nostrils — indeed, the Martians do not seem to have had any sense of smell, but it had a pair of very large dark-colored eyes, and just beneath this a kind of fleshy beak. In the back of this head or body — I scarcely know how to speak of it — was the single tight tympanic surface, since known to be anatomically an ear, though it must have been almost useless in our dense air. In a group round the mouth were sixteen slender, almost whiplike tentacles, arranged in two bunches of eight each. These bunches have since been named rather aptly, by that distinguished anatomist, Professor Howes, the *hands*....
>
> "The internal anatomy, I may remark here, as dissection has since shown, was almost equally simple. The greater part of the structure was the brain, sending enormous nerves to the eyes, ear, and tactile tentacles. Besides this were the bulky lungs, into which the mouth opened, and the heart and its vessels. The pulmonary distress caused by the denser atmosphere and greater gravitational attraction was only too evident in the convulsive movements of the outer skin.

"And this was the sum of the Martian organs. Strange as it may seem to a human being, all the complex apparatus of digestion, which makes up the bulk of our bodies, did not exist in the Martians. They were heads — merely heads. Entrails they had none. They did not eat, much less digest. Instead, they took the fresh, living blood of other creatures, and *injected* it into their own veins. I have myself seen this being done, as I shall mention in its place. But, squeamish as I may seem, I cannot bring myself to describe what I could not endure even to continue watching...."

Wells's all-conquering Martians gave nightmares to two generations of readers, and then, in 1938, caused something close to national panic in the United States when Orson Welles's radio dramatization of the Wells novel led careless listeners to believe that the Martians *had* actually landed (in New Jersey, not in Wells's London suburb.) The Welles broadcast made the Martians even more ghastly, more terrifying, than they had been in the original:

"Good heavens, now something's wriggling out of the shadow like a gray snake. Now it's another one, and another. They look like tentacles to me. There, I can see the thing's body. It's large as a bear and glistens like wet leather. But that face. It's — it's indescribable. I can hardly force myself to keep looking at it. The eyes are black and gleam like a serpent. The mouth is V-shaped with saliva dripping from its rimless lips that seem to quiver and pulsate...."

The world had not yet been science fictionized by endless movies and television shows, and people who tuned in in the middle of the broadcast were scared silly by it. Experienced science fiction readers took a different view, as one tells us in Hadley Cantril's classic study of the event, *The Invasion from Mars: A Study in the Psychology of Panic* (Princeton University Press, 1940):

"At first I was very interested in the fall of the meteor. It isn't often that they find a big one just when it falls. But when it started to unscrew and monsters came out, I said to myself, 'They've taken one of those *Amazing Stories* and are acting it out.' It just couldn't be real. It was just like some of the stories I read in *Amazing Stories* but it was even more exciting."

Regular sf readers, by then, had experienced the alien menace again and again — and had met a few benevolent aliens, too, notably Stanley G. Weinbaum's comic, lovable Martian Tweel ("A Martian Odyssey," 1934), and the philosophical Martian of Raymond Z. Gallun's "Old Faithful," published in the same year. Since then, although plenty of horrific aliens have been offered to the science fiction readership — as in John W. Campbell's "Who

Goes There?" (1938), which became the movie *The Thing*, A.E. van Vogt's memorable "Black Destroyer" (1939), and Fredric Brown's "Arena" (1944) — many noteworthy attempts have been made at depicting aliens sympathetically and rendering their alien minds as comprehensible to us as possible. Significant among these stories are Eric Frank Russell's "Metamorphosite" (1946) and "Dear Devil" (1950), Edgar Pangborn's *A Mirror for Observers* (1954), and Orson Scott Card's *Speaker for the Dead* (1986), among many others. Science fiction has examined the possibilities of sexual relationships between humans and aliens (Philip José Farmer's *The Lovers*, 1952); it has looked at the theological aspects of the existence of intelligent non-human creatures (*A Case of Conscience* by James Blish, 1953, and "For I Am A Jealous People," Lester del Rey, 1954); it has explored the problems of communicating with aliens ("The Gift of Gab," Jack Vance, 1955), has posited the existence of aliens as a way of satirizing human foibles (*The Dark Light Years*, Brian W. Aldiss, 1964) — has, in fact, approached the concept of Us/Not-Us in a multitude of ways.

But the subject is as inexhaustible as human nature itself, and in the long run what the creation of fictional aliens is all about is self-understanding; for when we write about aliens, we are in fact writing about ourselves as seen through a distorting lens. Behind the fantastic trappings of the science fiction story lies a mundane core. What the science fiction writer writes about comes from within, from the mind of someone who has never visited another world or laid eyes upon an alien extraterrestrial being. Translating his own experiences and speculations into the soaring wonders of science fiction, the writer hides real experience under a cloak of fantasy. And so we look at the alien, however strange it may be, and we see ourselves; for what else, really, can the Earthbound writer write about, except the perception of the experiental world, transformed in this or that metaphorical way but always starting from a base in reality?

From *The Ultimate Alien*, 1995

The New Wave: One

IT OCCURRED TO ME THE OTHER DAY THAT THE REVOLUTIONARY New Wave era — the most dramatic period of literary experimentation in the history of science fiction — now lies three and a half decades in the past, and most of today's sf readers have no awareness that any such upheaval ever took place, let alone why it happened and what its consequences were. But most of the science fiction stories you read today in *Asimov's Science Fiction* (and also *Fantasy and Science Fiction*, and the recently deceased *Science Fiction Age*) have their roots in the New Wave period. For all its moments of pretentiousness, obscurantism, and downright foolishness, and the ultimate disappearance from view of even its finest work, the New Wave of 1965-72 transformed the science fiction landscape.

I was there. I watched it happen. I was part of it, sometimes without knowing that I was. And I have survived to tell the tale.

The standard view of the New Wave story nowadays, among those who know anything about it at all, goes something like this: until 1965, science fiction was an artistic and intellectual desert, dominated by a few tyrannical editors who served the needs of an undemanding, uncritical public by forcing all writers to crank out simple, formulaic stories, devoid of all stylistic flair and intellectual individuality. Only standard themes (space war, time travel, robots) were permitted, and all stories had to have positive, uplifting endings. Then, suddenly, a turbulent bunch of brilliant young nonconformist writers arrived on the scene, bringing with them a host of new ideas and new ways of telling stories, and drove all the reactionary editors and their cadres of musty old hacks from the scene.

Some of that is true. Most of it isn't.

For one thing, the science fiction world prior to the advent of the New

Wave was not quite the literary wasteland some people later tried to pretend it was. The classic books and stories of Heinlein, Asimov, Bradbury, Sturgeon, Simak, van Vogt, Williamson, Vance, Bester, Kuttner, Leiber, and many others — the foundation-blocks of the field — date from that period.

Even the much-maligned early 1960s, supposedly a time of terrible sterility, were, after all, an era that gave us Frank Herbert's *Dune*, Philip K. Dick's *The Man in the High Castle*, Robert A. Heinlein's *Stranger in a Strange Land*, and the first important books and stories of Roger Zelazny, Larry Niven, Brian Aldiss, R.A. Lafferty, J.G. Ballard, and Samuel R. Delany. Still, it seemed to most of us at that time that science fiction was marching in place — was stagnant, even. For each *Stranger* or *High Castle* we got dozens of predictable, familiar rehashes of the standard themes. Very few writers were inclined — especially considering the low rates of pay in our small, sleepy field — to take risks in their fiction.

Nor were there any editors around to spur us on to more exciting work. John W. Campbell, the first of the three great magazine editors who had guided science fiction through a golden age of creative inventiveness that had lasted from 1939 through 1955, had turned away from innovation for the sake of pursuing a didactic exploration of a few quirky personal theories, and the other two, Horace Gold and Anthony Boucher, had withdrawn from the scene altogether. Many magazines of the earlier era had gone out of business. Those that survived, and the book publishers of the time, seemed to espouse a play-it-safe mentality. Even though plenty of good work still was being done, many writers — I was one of them — were losing interest in science fiction and turning to other fields.

New writers, though, were still coming in, as they always will, even in the dreariest of times — Zelazny, Delany, Tom Disch, Joanna Russ, Norman Spinrad, Ursula Le Guin, and others in the United States, and Ballard, Aldiss, Michael Moorcock, M. John Harrison, Christopher Priest, David Masson, and many more in Great Britain. And suddenly a revolution was going on in science fiction.

Two revolutions, in fact: a formally defined, overtly declared war of new vs. old in Great Britain, and a free-form sort of randomly waged insurrection over here.

The onset of the British battle can be explicitly dated to the spring of 1964, when editorial control of *New Worlds* — the only important British science fiction magazine — passed from E.J. Carnell to Michael Moorcock. Carnell, a central figure in British sf since the 1930s, had edited a good, sober, middle-of-the-road science fiction magazine built around the old-fashioned storytelling values — a British counterpart to John Campbell's *Astounding*, leaning heavily on such writers as James White, E.C. Tubb, John Christopher, J.T. McIntosh, John Brunner, and John Wyndham to create a distinctively British variation on standard American sf. But Carnell, though his tastes were conservative, was no reactionary, and the magazine also published the early stories of Brian Aldiss and J.G. Ballard, heralds of the explosions to come.

Then the magazine changed hands, Carnell retired, and 24-year-old Michael Moorcock took charge. Moorcock had been a prolific contributor to Carnell's magazine, but he also had a background in comic books and other pop-culture media, and had close connections in the new and swiftly burgeoning rock-music field. (1964 was, please remember, the year that the Beatles surged to worldwide prominence.) *New Worlds* for May-June 1964 was his first issue, and he opened it with an editorial headed A NEW LITERATURE FOR THE SPACE AGE that we can now see, in retrospect, as the manifesto of the new revolution:

"In a recent BBC broadcast, William Burroughs, controversial American author of *Dead Fingers Talk*, said something like this: 'If writers are to describe the advanced techniques of the Space Age, they must invent writing techniques equally as advanced in order properly to deal with them.'

"Burroughs' own writing techniques are as exciting — and as relevant to our own present situation — as the latest discovery in nuclear physics...."

After going on to describe Burroughs' work as "the sf we have all been waiting for," and to declare it, despite or perhaps because of its descriptions of sexual aberration and drug addiction, its frerquent use of obscenities, its supposed obscurity of meaning, as "stimulating and thought-provoking," Moorcock declared that "the desperate and cynical mood of his work mirrors exactly the mood of our ad-saturated, Bomb-dominated, power-corrupted times."

Whatever else science fiction had been up until that moment, it had rarely if ever been "desperate and cynical" in mood. But the times were a-changing. Moorcock called for science fiction writers to join Burroughs in creating "a new mythology — a new literature for the Space Age." There were, he said, certain British writers already going in that direction, "producing a kind of sf which is unconventional in every sense and which must soon be recognized as an important revitalization of the literary mainstream. More and more people are turning away from the fast-stagnating pool of the conventional novel — and they are turning to science fiction (or speculative fantasy). This is a sign, among others, that a *popular* literary renaissance is around the corner."

In the first issue of his version of *New Worlds*, Moorcock led off with "Equinox," the first part of a novel by J.G. Ballard later published in book form as *The Crystal World*. Ballard's work had overtones of Joseph Conrad and Graham Greene, not of Robert Heinlein or A.E. van Vogt. Still, publishing it was not an enormous departure from the Carnell magazine, which had serialized several of Ballard's previous novels. The fine stories by Aldiss and Brunner that followed it in that issue might also have fit equally well into the old *New Worlds* as into the new. But Barrington Bayley, the author of the fourth story, was a member of the Moorcock circle, and his story had a distinctly New Wave tone, though nobody reading it then would have used that term.

In the months that followed, Moorcock uncorked upon a startled British readership a host of new writers — Charles Platt, Langdon Jones, Pamela Zoline, Josephine Saxton, John Sladek, Hilary Bailey, and James Colvin (who turned out to be Moorcock himself). Their work, ever more fiercely experimental as the months went on, veered farther and farther away from the robots and time machines and galactic empires of traditional sf into the realm of what Ballard called "inner space," an exploration of the complexities of angst-ridden twentieth-century life. Some of it was barely recognizable, if recognizable at all, as science fiction. Much of it employed so fragmentary a narrative mode that it was well-nigh incomprehensible.

But the Moorcock magazine was very much of its time, the time of Swinging England — rock, drugs, miniskirts, Day-Glo colors — and *New Worlds* was deeply caught up in all the new modes of living and writing, so much so that within a few years its distributor refused to sell the magazine on grounds of "obscenity and libel," and one of its contributors (Norman Spinrad) was denounced in Parliament as a "nameless degenerate."

The Moorcock-led revolution in England had not gone unnoticed on the other side of the Atlantic, thanks primarily to the brilliant, restless, and often aggressively opinionated writer and critic, Judith Merril, who in 1965 had begun writing a monthly book column for *Fantasy and Science Fiction*.

It was in her November, 1967 column that she first told her readers of what was going on in British sf. She termed it The New Thing, perhaps because she liked the explosive acronym, TNT, and she described its method as "the application of contemporary and sometimes (though mostly not very) experimental literary techniques to the kind of contemporary/experimental speculation which is the essence of science fiction." But its content was as important as its style: fiction that took into account such things as "op art, student protest, the new sexual revolution, psychedelics, and a multiplex of other manifestations of the silly-sounding phrase, Flower Power...."

By then all those things had burst upon the startled citizenry of the United States, too, and American science fiction was changing almost as fast as the British kind. More about the New Wave next month.

Asimov's Science Fiction, **March 2001**

The New Wave: Two

LAST TIME I TOLD HOW THE RADICAL SOCIAL AND CULTURAL CHANGES of the 1960s led to an upheaval in the once quite conservative world of science fiction, a revolution that came to be known as the period of the New Wave. I noted that it began as a cohesive and self-conscious literary movement that centered around the British magazine *New Worlds,* edited by Michael Moorcock, and that by 1967 the writer and critic Judith Merril had begun to praise its achievements in her monthly book column in *Fantasy and Science Fiction.*

Merril referred at first to the Moorcock movement as TNT, "the new thing." But it was, I think, Christopher Priest — an important young writer then, but only a peripheral figure in the Moorcock circle — who borrowed from the French cinema the term "new wave," a reference to the radical films of directors like Godard and Truffaut, and applied it to the new British science fiction. The term stuck, and spread quickly to the United States, where science fiction was already in the throes of its own New Wave movement.

There was never anything here as formally organized as was the Moorcock group over there. Instead, the changes in American sf were matters of individual decisions about how stories should be told, coupled with a willingness on the part of some editors and publishers to relax formerly stringent and limiting notions of what the sf readership would be willing to accept.

That willingness to take chances — on the part of Betty Ballantine of Ballantine Books, Avram Davidson of *Fantasy and Science Fiction*, Frederik Pohl of *Galaxy*, and even so conservative a figure as Donald A. Wollheim of Ace Books — made the changes possible. The surprising figure was Wollheim, who found much of the new science fiction personally repellent, but set up a separate publishing line within his company, the Ace Specials, run by his young assistant editor Terry Carr, as a vehicle for New Wave novels.

What set things going over here was the arrival of new young writers for whom the use of modernist literary techniques and real-world themes was a natural and intuitive choice, rather than any conscious attempt to break away from established sf forms. Their work, fresh and vital, made an immediate appeal to jaded readers and editors alike.

One such writer was Samuel R. Delany, black and bisexual, who came out of an entirely different world from that of Heinlein and Asimov and Clarke. The Delany space-adventure novels that began to appear in 1962 were like no space-adventure novels anyone had ever seen before. Judy Merril, reviewing his *Einstein Intersection* of 1967, called it "a dense mixture, heavily concentrated, double-distilled....It is also and absolutely a story about where-it's-at, right here, right now." His books began to win awards and gain imitators. A visit to England brought him into contact with the Moorcock group and he became a significant bridge figure between American and British science fiction.

Roger Zelazny, whose career began about the same time, had (unlike most sf writers of earlier days) a deep knowledge of classical and modern literature, mythology, and psychology. Beginning in 1963 with the startling novella "A Rose for Ecclesiastes," followed quickly by such novels as *This Immortal* and *Lord of Light*, he unleashed what amounted to a one-man literary revolution. Tom Disch, another twenty-something with a background in avant-garde literature, chimed in with *The Genocides*, *Camp Concentration*, and a host of dazzling short stories that no sf magazine of a decade earlier would have published. Norman Spinrad's novel *Bug Jack Barron*, pungently obscene, drew on the dark new world of mass media and political corruption for its subject. And then, Joanna Russ, R.A. Lafferty, Carol Emshwiller, David R. Bunch, and a host of others suddenly were publishing a kind of science fiction that owed more to Borges, Kafka, and William Burroughs than to the star writers of John W. Campbell's golden age of science fiction.

In this time of exuberant ferment, some of the older sf writers, bored with the constraining nature of the old sf, were taking the opportunity to reinvent themselves as well, often without realizing that they were affiliating themselves with something called the New Wave. They simply wanted to try something new. Harlan Ellison, who had written a great deal of undistinguished sf in conventional pulp modes, abruptly broke loose with such startlingly surreal stories as "I Have No Mouth and I Must Scream" and "The Beast that Shouted Love at the Heart of the World," which won him an entirely new reputation as a literary innovator. My own career followed a similar path, from straightforward magazine fiction to such novelties as the novels *Thorns* and *Son of Man* and experimental stories by the double handful. John Brunner, a British writer whose career was largely centered in the United States, turned away from paperback space-opera to write such unusual books as *The Whole Man* and the gigantic, astonishing, Hugo-winning *Stand on Zanzibar*. Fritz Leiber's fiction, always dark and strange, grew darker and stranger. So did that of Philip K. Dick and Philip José Farmer.

The advent of anthologies of original fiction in book form further liberated the writers from the old pulp-magazine formulas. A horde of new markets clamored for fiction in the new mode. Damon Knight's *Orbit* series, which began in 1966, was avowedly literary and experimental in policy, and writers like Richard McKenna, R.A. Lafferty, and Gene Wolfe flocked around. Terry Carr began *Universe*; I edited *New Dimensions*; Samuel R. Delany brought forth four issues of *Quark*, probably the farthest-out anthology of all. And Ellison edited the massive *Dangerous Visions*, a comprehensive collection of new stories in the new rebellious manner, with contributions by Delany, Aldiss, Ballard, Brunner, Spinrad, Dick, Farmer, and many others who were at the center of the current scene.

For a while it seemed as if the revolutionaries had carried the day. Advocates of the new fiction — Ellison, Brunner, Delany, Zelazny, Silverberg, Farmer, Aldiss, Moorcock — began to win Hugo awards right and left, and then Nebulas when that award was instituted also. Many of the writers who were just beginning their careers — James Tiptree, Jr., John Varley, Barry Malzberg, Gardner Dozois, Michael Bishop — tended to write in what could be called New Wave modes. There was open mockery of the old-fashioned, "obsolete" fiction of Heinlein, Asimov, and Clarke at science fiction conventions. The new stuff monopolized the bookstores.

The reaction on the part of Old Wavers was not long in coming. In his 1971 history of science fiction, *The Universe Makers*, Don Wollheim complained that "the readers and writers that used to dream of galactic futures now got their kicks out of experimental styles of writing, the free discussion of sex, the overthrow of all standards and morals (since, if the world is going to end, what merit had these things?)" A few years later Lester del Rey, once a young firebrand himself but now an impassioned advocate of traditional storytelling modes, described the New Wave by saying, "The pulp and adventure backgrounds of science fiction were largely rejected. So-called experimental writing — derived, of course, from the avant-garde experiments of forty years before — was regarded as somehow superior, and social consciousness of a sort was more important than extrapolation." The breaking of taboos, del Rey noted, had become a goal in itself, along with the "daring" use of four-letter words, but nobody, he insisted, seemed interested in genuine examination of significant ideas. The diminutive del Rey was often seen defending these positions at the top of his lungs at the science fiction conventions. Other pillars of the field were equally vehement in their contemptuous denunciations of New Wave fiction and attitudes.

Then a curious thing happened to the revolution. It went away overnight when the publishers started noticing that people had stopped buying the new kind of fiction.

Science fiction readers had eagerly embraced the novelties of the late 1960s and early 1970s. But after a time they discovered that a lot of the new stories were incomprehensible; some were offensive in tone or concept; and most had turned away from the grand themes of the exploration of time and space that had drawn science fiction readers to science fiction in the first place, in favor of "inner space" concepts hard to recognize as sf at all. The new anthologies folded; the experimental novels started to go out of print; in Great Britain, *New Worlds,* where it had all started, ceased publication after years of steadily dwindling circulation; the Hugo and Nebula awards began to go to fiction of the more conventional kind by writers of the old school, works like Arthur Clarke's *Rendezvous with Rama* and Isaac Asimov's *The Gods Themselves.* Many of the leading writers of the new sf walked away from the field in despair as publishers lost interest in their work; some never came back.

So it was all for nothing, the glorious New Wave revolution of 1965-72?

No. Those years were a time of riotous excess in science fiction, as it was in European and American civilization in general, and, like most literary revolutions, the New Wave produced much abominable nonsense along with a few genuine classics. In their reaction against the staleness of the older fiction modes, the New Wave writers sometimes went much too far over the top into wayward and wilful self-indulgence, as even some of them will admit today. But one can hardly say that it was all in vain.

The long-term effect of the dizzying New Wave period was a grudging acceptance of the fact that science fiction could and should be something more than straightforwardly told pulp narrative involving a conflict between generically characterized stereotypical figures that led inevitably to the triumph of good over evil. For the first time it became permissible to write complex narratives about complex people who were dealing with complex speculative situations. Fullness of characterization, emotional depth, and richness of prose would no longer be seen as something for a writer to avoid, as generally had been the case in sf in the magazine-dominated era of the first half of the twentieth century.

No one had any illusion, after the collapse of 1972, that this kind of work would win as wide a readership as the two-fisted tales of the spaceways, the Tolkien imitations, or the media-related spinoff books that the mass audience wanted. Mass audiences want prefabricated fiction; that will never change, and it was naive of us back in the New Wave times to think it would. But the deeper sf could win *enough* of an audience —intelligent, demanding, intellectually curious —to hold its own in the marketplace. And so the New Wave period was an evolutionary crisis, a collision of old and new that led to a synthesis of both in which the virtues of each were melded into a vital new kind of sf that abjured the formulaic nature of the earlier stuff and the worst excesses of the New Wave.

But for the battles of the New Wave, such books as Kim Stanley Robinson's Mars trilogy, William Gibson's *Neuromancer,* Gregory Benford's *Timescape,* Gene Wolfe's *New Sun* tetralogy, Connie Willis's *Doomsday Book,* and on and on up to this year's Nebula-winning Octavia Butler novel, *Parable of the Talents,* might never have been written. The literary warriors of thirty years ago created a climate in science fiction that made the publication of such books possible, even if they would never attain the sales figures of the latest *Star Wars* novelization.

It was a battle worth fighting. I'm glad I was there.

Asimov's Science Fiction, **April 2001**

Lovecraft as Science Fiction

I'VE BEEN RE-READING LATELY A STORY THAT I FIRST ENCOUNTERED some time late in 1947, when I was twelve years old, in Donald A. Wollheim's marvelous anthology *Portable Novels of Science Fiction*: H.P. Lovecraft's novella "The Shadow out of Time." As I've said elsewhere more than once, reading that story changed my life. I've come upon it now in an interesting new edition and want to talk about it again.

The Wollheim book contained four short sf novels: H.G. Wells' "The First Men in the Moon," John Taine's "Before the Dawn," Olaf Stapledon's "Odd John," and the Lovecraft story. Each, in its way, contributed to the shaping of the imagination of the not quite adolescent young man who was going to grow up to write hundreds of science fiction and fantasy stories of his own. The Stapledon spoke directly and poignantly to me of my own circumstances as a bright and somewhat peculiar little boy stranded among normal folk; the Wells opened vistas of travel through space for me; the Taine delighted me for its vivid recreation of the Mesozoic era, which I, dinosaur-obsessed like most kids my age, desperately wanted to know and experience somehow at first hand. But it was the Lovecraft, I think, that had the most powerful impact on my developing vision of my own intentions as a creator of science fiction. It had a visionary quality that stirred me mightily; I yearned to write something like that myself, but, lacking the skill to do so when I was twelve, I had to be satisfied with writing clumsy little imitations of it. But I have devoted much effort in the many decades since to creating stories that approached the sweep and grandeur of Lovecraft's.

Note that I refer to "Shadow Out of Time" as science fiction (and that Wollheim included it in a collection explicitly called Novels of Science) even though Lovecraft is conventionally considered to be a writer of horror stories. So he was, yes; but most of his best stories, horrific though they were, were in fact generated out of the same willingness to speculate on matters of space and time that powered the work of Robert A. Heinlein and Isaac Asimov and Arthur C. Clarke. The great difference is that for Heinlein and Asimov and Clarke, science is exciting and marvelous, and for Lovecraft it is a source of terror. But a story that is driven by dread of science rather than by love and admiration for it is no less science fiction even so, if it makes use of the kind of theme (space travel, time travel, technological change) that we universally recognize as the material of SF.

And that is what much of Lovecraft's fiction does. The loathsome Elder Gods of the Cthulhu mythos are nothing other than aliens from other dimensions who have invaded Earth: this is, I submit, a classic sf theme. Such other significant Lovecraft tales as "The Rats in the Walls" and "The Colour Out of Space" can be demonstrated to be science fiction as well. He was not particularly interested in that area of science fiction that concerned the impact of technology on human life (Huxley's *Brave New World*, Wells' *Food of the Gods*, etc.), or in writing sociopolitical satire of the Orwell kind, or in inventing ingenious gadgets; his concern, rather, was science as a source of scary visions. What terrible secrets lie buried in the distant irrecoverable past? What dreadful transformations will the far future bring? That he saw the secrets as terrible and the transformations as dreadful is what sets him apart at the horror end of the science fiction spectrum, as far from Heinlein and Asimov and Clarke as it is possible to be.

It is interesting to consider that although most of Lovecraft's previous fiction had made its first appearance in print in that pioneering horror/fantasy magazine, *Weird Tales*, "The Shadow Out of Time" quite appropriately was published first in the June, 1936 issue of *Astounding Stories,* which was then the dominant science fiction magazine of its era, the preferred venue for such solidly science fictional figures as John W. Campbell, Jr., Jack Williamson, and E.E. Smith, Ph.D.

I should point out, though, that it seems as though *Astounding's* editor, F. Orlin Tremaine, was uneasy about exposing his readers, accustomed as they were to the brisk basic-level functional prose of conventional pulp-magazine fiction, to Lovecraft's more elegant style. Tremaine subjected "The Shadow Out of Time" to severe editing in an attempt to homogenize it into his magazine's familiar mode, mainly by ruthlessly slicing Lovecraft's lengthy and carefully balanced paragraphs into two, three, or even four sections, but also tinkering with his punctuation and removing some of his beloved archaisms of vocabulary. The version of the story that has been reprinted again and again all these years is the Tremainified one; but now a new edition has appeared that's based on the original "Shadow" manuscript in Lovecraft's handwriting that unexpectedly turned up in 1995. This new edition — edited by S.T. Joshi and David E. Schultz, published as a handsome trade paperback in 2003 by Hippocampus Press, and bedecked with the deliciously gaudy painting, bug-eyed monsters and all, that bedecked the original 1936 *Astounding* appearance — is actually the first publication of the text as Lovecraft conceived it. Hippocampus Press is, I gather, a very small operation, but I found a copy of the book easily enough through Amazon.com, and so should you.

Despite Tremaine's revisions, a few of *Astounding's* readers still found Lovecraftian prose too much for their 1936 sensibilities. Reaction to the story was generally favorable, as we can see from the reader letters published in the August 1936 issue ("Absolutely magnificent!" said Cameron Lewis of New York. "I am at a loss for words. . . . This makes Lovecraft practically supreme, in my opinion.") But O.M. Davidson of Louisiana found Lovecraft "too tedious, too monotonous to suit me," even though he admitted that the imagery of the story "would linger with me for a long time." And Charles Pizzano of Dedham, Massachusetts, called it "all description and little else."

Of course I had no idea that Tremaine had meddled with Lovecraft's style when I encountered it back there in 1947 (which I now realize was just eleven years after its first publication, though at the time it seemed an ancient tale to me). Nor, indeed, were his meddlings a serious impairment of Lovecraft's intentions, though we can see now that this newly rediscovered text is notably more powerful than the streamlined Tremaine version. Perhaps the use of shorter paragraphs actually made things easier for my pre-adolescent self. In any case I found, in 1947, a host of wondrous things in "The Shadow Out of Time."

The key passage, for me, lay in the fourth chapter, in which Lovecraft conjured up an unforgettable vision of giant alien beings moving about in a weird library full of "horrible annals of other worlds and other universes, and of stirrings of formless life outside all universes. There were records of strange orders of beings which had peopled the world in forgotten pasts, and frightful chronicles of grotesque-bodied intelligences which would people it millions of years after the death of the last human being."

I wanted passionately to explore that library myself. I knew I could not: I would know no more of the furry prehuman Hyperborean worshippers of Tsathoggua and the wholly abominable Tcho-Tchos than Lovecraft chose to tell me, nor would I talk with the mind of Yiang-Li, the philosopher from the cruel empire of Tsan-Chan, which is to come in 5000 AD, nor with the mind of the king of Lomar who ruled that terrible polar land one hundred thousand years before the squat, yellow Inutos came from the west to engulf it. But I read that page of Lovecraft ten thousand times — it is page 429 of the Wollheim anthology, page 56 of the new edition — and even now, scanning it this morning, it stirs in me the quixotic hunger to find and absorb all the science fiction in the world, every word of it, so that I might begin to know these mysteries of the lost imaginary kingdoms of time past and time future.

The extraordinary thing that Lovecraft provides in "Shadow" is a sense of a turbulent alternative history of Earth — not the steady procession up from the trilobite through amphibians and reptiles to primitive mammals that I had mastered by the time I was in the fourth grade, but a wild zigzag of pre-human species and alien races living here a billion years before our time, beings that have left not the slightest trace in the fossil record, but which I wanted with all my heart to believe in.

And it is the ultimate archaeological fantasy, too, for Lovecraft's protagonist takes us right down into the ruined city, which in his story, at least, is astonishingly still extant in remotest Australia, of the greatest of these ancient races. It is here that Lovecraft's bias toward science-as-horror emerges, for the narrator, unlike any archaeologist I've ever heard of, is scared stiff as he approaches his goal. He has visited it in dreams, and now, entering the real thing, "Ideas and images of the starkest terror began to throng in upon me and cloud my senses." He finds that he knows the ruined city "morbidly, horribly well" from his dreams. The whole experience is, he says, "brain-shattering." His sanity wobbles. He frets about "tides of abomination surging up through the cleft itself from depths unimagined and unimaginable." He speaks of the "accursed city" and its builders as "shambling horrors" that have a "terrible, soul-shattering actuality," and so on, all a little overwrought, as one expects from Lovecraft.

Well, I'd be scared silly too if I had found myself telepathically kidnapped and hauled off into a civilization of 150 million years ago, as Lovecraft's man was. But once I got back, and realized that I'd survived it all, I'd regard it as fascinating and wonderful, and not in any way a cause for monstrous, eldritch, loathsome, hideous, frightfully adjectival Lovecraftian terror, if I were to stumble on the actual archives of that lost civilization.

But if "Shadow" is overwrought, it is gloriously overwrought. Even if what he's really trying to do is scare us, he creates an awareness — while one reads it, at least — that history did not begin in Sumer or in the Pithecanthropine caves, but that the world was already incalculably ancient when man evolved, and had been populated and repopulated again and again by intelligent races, long before the first mammals, even, had ever evolved. It is wonderful science fiction. I urge you to go out and search for it. In it, after all, Lovecraft makes us witness to the excavation of an archive 150 million years old, the greatest of all archaeological finds. On that sort of time-span, Tut-ankh-amen's tomb was built just a fraction of a second ago. Would that it all were true, I thought, back then when I was twelve. And again, re-reading this stunning tale today: would that it were true.

Asimov's Science Fiction, **December, 2005**

TWO
Thoughts On Science And Society

_____

The Handprints On The Wall

A FEW MONTHS AGO I DEVOTED THIS SPACE TO A DISCUSSION of the thrilling photograph taken by the Hubble space telescope, showing stars being born in the Eagle Nebula, 7000 light-years from Earth. I said of it that "it may well be the most extraordinary picture in the entire history of photography," and I've had no reason since then to retract that hyperbolic statement.

But lately I've been looking at another set of photos that excite me nearly as much — for utterly different reasons. The dazzling Hubble picture seemed to me to roll back the barriers of space and time and remind us of the limitless possibilities that the future holds for us. "We are not all that contemptible a species," I said, "if we can manage to poke our little cameras into the cradles of the stars."

What these new photos do for me is to summon up not the great and glorious science fictional future, when starships will go forth to explore far galaxies, but the astonishing and mysterious human *past* — the remote, alien era we call the Paleolithic, when your ancestors and mine walked the earth, members of a vanished civilization about whose nature we can make only the vaguest guesses, but which may have been far more complex than we think. They're to be found in a book called *Dawn of Art: The Chauvet Cave*, by Jean-Marie Chauvet, Eliette Brunel Deschamps, and Christian Hillaire, published by Harry N. Abrams, Inc. of New York. The book's subtitle says it all: *The Oldest Known Paintings in the World*. It contains 94 brilliant color plates that show the astounding masterpieces of art that were discovered in December, 1994, on the walls of a cave in the region of southeastern France known as the Ardeche.

Prehistoric cave paintings are nothing new, of course. The first modern discovery of them occurred in 1879. In that year Don Marcelino de Sautuola, a Spanish aristocrat with an interest in geology, went exploring in an underground cave at Altamira, in northern Spain, where he had previously found the bones of such extinct mammals as the giant stag, the European bison, and the wild horse, in association with flints and arrow points of stone and bits of black and red pigment. Don Marcelino's small daughter, who had accompanied him into the cave, wandered off into a side corridor, and came back after a few minutes crying, "*Papa! Mira, papa! Toros pintados!*" Come look, Papa! Painted bulls!

The Altamira cave proved to contain spectacular paintings not only of bulls but of a whole horde of animals, thundering across the roof of the cave: bison, a charging boar, a wild horse, a whole zoo of creatures. They were the work of a superb artist who, using pigments made from iron oxide, ocher, and bison blood, had rendered the prehistoric creatures with brilliant three-dimensionality, making cunning use of the bumps and shallows of the cave roof to enhance the realistic effect.

Though the Altamira paintings were regarded at first as a hoax — prehistoric man, it was generally thought then, had been a barbaric creature, hardly more than an ape — it has been recognized for many years that they were in fact the work of an artist or artists of the Paleolithic Magdalenian culture, and have a probable age of around 13-14,000 years.

That is awesome enough, but many far more ancient cave paintings have been discovered in Western Europe since Don Marcelino's day. Beginning in 1894, French cave explorers found hundreds of paintings in the caves of the Perigord district — in one cave alone, representations of eighty bison, forty horses, twenty-three mammoths, seventeen reindeer, eight wild cattle, four antelopes, two woolly rhinoceroses, a bear, a wolf, and a lioness! The cave known as Les Trois Freres in the Pyrenean foothills yielded thousands of paintings and engravings of ancient animals, and also the spookiest cave art of all, eerie portraits of human "sorcerers," one wearing antlers and a long pointed mask, another masked as a bison and carrying bison hooves before him. And four teen-aged boys in 1940, chasing a runaway pet dog, stumbled upon the extraordinary cave of Lascaux, sometimes called "the Sistine Chapel of prehistory," with a wondrous array of animal paintings thousands of years older than those previously found: they date back at least 17,000 years, according to Carbon-14 analysis, and perhaps more.

The new Chauvet Cave paintings, though, are even older. The preliminary C-14 findings give them an age ranging from 30,340 years to 32,410 years, with a margin of error of about 600 years. These numbers are breathtaking for two reasons. One is the sheer antiquity of the paintings. The Altamira cave paintings, once believed to be the ultimate in prehistoric art, *are closer in time to us* than they are to those of Chauvet. The other, and perhaps more significant thing about the age of the Chauvet paintings, is this: though they are so extremely ancient, they are as sophisticated in technique as any cave paintings of later epochs. We are not looking, that is, at the crude and primitive origins of art here — simple stick-figures and flat cartoon sketches. We are coming in on a tradition already well established, in which the technical representation of three-dimensional reality on two-dimensional surfaces was handled with a skill worthy of artists of any later era. The startling possibility arises that these Paleolithic people occupy a place in the history of human art closer to us in time than it is to the beginning: that the Chauvet people, ancient as they are, were relatively late figures in the development of art, and we may yet make discoveries that push our knowledge of ancient art back in time another fifty or even one hundred thousand years.

Look at Plate 55 in the Abrams book: an elegant frieze in black, three horses, shown in profile, facing each other. Notice the subtle shading of their jaws, the realistic depiction of their manes, the rendering of expression in their eyes and lips. They seem poised in contemplation, readying themselves for motion. Or the two rhinoceroses of Plate 53, massive beasts stubbornly standing nose to nose in blunt confrontation, a scene unique in all of Paleolithic art. We can practically hear their angry snorting. And then there is the solitary rhino of Plate 69, his front horn sweeping upward in an exhilarating, enormously exaggerated line that follows the curve of the wall. No rhino ever had a horn like that one; but the artist surely could not resist the joy of extending that curve to such an astonishing length.

Plate 88 gives us a bison in perspective, the body seen in profile, the massive horned head pivoted around at a 90-degree angle to stare straight out in a full-face view. Plate 82 offers a pride of cave lions, all of them maneless as these big cats apparently were: eyes alert, ears and noses at work, magnificent predators poised for attack.

All those are color paintings, some in black, some in red. But there are engravings, too, white outlines against the cave wall, done with magnificent fluidity and power. Plate 30, for instance: a pair of mammoths in profile, one standing behind the other, their strange humped heads forward, their massive bodies forever arrested in mid-stride. Even more startling, perhaps: Plate 33, a frontal view of a sitting owl, the only owl portrait in all of prehistoric art, and a masterpiece: quick minimalist strokes, a circle for the head, two upjutting lines for ears, the hunched shoulders and tapering body suggested by rows of parallel vertical lines.

Chauvet Cave was never inhabited. It contains no artifacts, other than the paintings and engravings — no trash, no signs of campfires. Perhaps it was a ritual center of some sort, a speculation that is enhanced, though hardly confirmed, by the strange presence of a bear skull neatly perched atop an altar-like slab of stone that fell long ago from the ceiling. But that is only a conjecture, which may never be confirmed. What we do know is that artists working by flickering torchlight decorated that cave more than 30,000 years ago, and left, and never returned. Other visitors came four thousand years later — when the caves were already as ancient to them as Babylonia and Sumer are to us. We know that much, because those visitors rubbed their torches against the wall to scrape away accretions of charcoal that had built up on them, leaving smudges which can be carbon-dated, and those smudges, though unthinkably old, are forty centuries younger than the carbon in the pigment of the paintings themselves.

There are, all told, close to 300 figures in Chauvet Cave — rhinos and mammoths and horses and bison and lions and bears, and the extinct cattle known as aurochs, and ibexes and reindeer and even what may be an insect. There are no humans depicted. But the cave walls do contain one poignant reminder of humanity: renderings of unmistakably human hands. Some of these are shown as positive images, where a hand coated with pigment was simply pressed against the wall; some are negative images, the pale outline of a hand with outspread fingers created by holding the hand to the wall and spattering pigment all around it. It is these handprints on the wall that give me the ultimate shiver, for they are, I like to think, the signatures of the artists themselves.

We will never know that, of course. There is much that we will never know about these incredibly ancient paintings and the people who created them. The Chauvet Cave, though, gives us a view through the door of time into the mysteries of almost unthinkable antiquity. We tend too often to think of ancient man as a grunting naked savage living in brutal barbarity, but such masterworks of art as the Chauvet paintings argue otherwise. I think there was much more to these distant ancestors than we have dared to suspect. The language of these people, their epic poems, their myths, the names of their gods — these are lost to us forever. But their marvelous paintings remain.

Asimov's Science Fiction, May 1997

Heart Of Stone

FROM THE CRETACEOUS SANDSTONE OF SOUTH DAKOTA A DECADE AGO came a flabbergasting find: the fossilized heart of a 66-million-year-old dinosaur. Not only is this just the second time fossilized internal tissues of a dinosaur have been discovered (a specimen unearthed earlier in Italy yielded fossilized intestines), but the Dakota fossil appears to confirm the controversial theory that the dinosaurs, though reptiles, were, in fact, warm-blooded.

This particular dinosaur was a 13-foot-long 660-pound herbivore of the genus Thescelosaurus. Its discoverer, a fossil-hunter named Michael Hammer, noticing a large mineralized lump within the creature's rib-cage, suspected that it might be one of the animal's internal organs. He asked an Oregon physician, Dr. Andrew Kuzmitz, to run a tomographic scan on it, and that indicated the presence of a heart, neatly encased within a stone sarcophagus.

The North Carolina Museum of Natural Sciences in Raleigh acquired the fossil in 1996 and launched a more elaborate study. Computerized three-dimensional pictures made by imaging specialists from the North Carolina State College of Veterinary Medicine led to the conclusion that the stone lump did indeed contain a heart, a four-chambered one, with an aorta-like structure emerging from the left ventricle — thus providing the best evidence thus far for the warm-blooded-dinosaur theory.

Warm-bloodedness has been considered a biological advantage since Aristotle's time. He wrote, "The thicker and warmer the blood is, the more it makes for strength." Since cold-blooded creatures have no internal temperature-regulating devices, they become torpid as the air temperature around them drops, and below a certain critical level enter a state of dormancy. When warmth returns they become active again, but if the day grows too hot they are in danger of overheating, and must find cool hiding places. All of this limits their ability to gather food, their responsiveness to unexpected challenges, and their ability to adapt to environmental change.

The high-powered metabolism and greater adaptability of warm-blooded creatures permits far more strenuous functioning of heart, lungs, and muscle tissue. They are more versatile than cold-blooded ones in every way, which is why the forests, meadows, and deserts of the world swarm with mammals and birds, whereas amphibians and reptiles skulk in odd corners and fish are confined to the sea.

That the circulatory systems of dinosaurs might differ from those of modern reptiles is an old idea. The pioneering British paleontologist Richard Owen had by 1842 recognized that the pelvic structure of the giant beasts set them apart from living reptiles. Owen had no doubt that they were cold-blooded, but he did not see them just as oversized lizards or crocodiles with unusual pelvises. Their hearts, he argued, must have been of different design also.

Modern reptiles have three-chambered hearts: two atria, one for oxygenated blood coming from the lungs and the other to receive deoxygenated blood from the rest of the body, and a ventricle in which both streams of blood are mixed to be pumped forth again. This mixing reduces the efficiency of the animal's metabolism. Dinosaurs, he said, must have had a more "highly organized center of circulation" to operate their vast bodies, requiring hearts with two atria and two ventricles to avoid the mixing of stale blood with fresh.

Later scientists also found dinosaur metabolism puzzling. Frederic A. Lucas, in 1929, raised the issue of how dinosaurs, if they had been as sluggish as modern reptiles, could ever have managed to gather enough food to keep their enormous bodies functioning. Ultimately he fell back on the point that reptiles, precisely because they *are* sluggish cold-blooded creatures, need nowhere near the quantity of fuel required by mammals of the same mass. "Still," he added, "it is dangerous to lay down any hard and fast laws concerning animals...and in the present instance there is some reason, based on the arrangement of vertebrae and ribs, to suppose that the lungs of dinosaurs were somewhat like that of birds, and that, as a corollary, their blood may have been better aerated and warmer than that of living reptiles."

But no serious challenge to the classic view of dinosaurs as cold-blooded developed until 1964, when the Yale paleontologist John Ostrom discovered a mini-dinosaur he called *Deinonychus*, "terrible claw" — a fast-moving carnivore that weighed about 150 pounds and chased its prey on powerful hind limbs. Running in an upright position, Ostrom pointed out, requires a tremendous output of energy, incompatible with a cold-blooded metabolism. In today's world, the only animals that walk upright are warm-blooded ones, mammals and birds; reptiles and amphibians are waddlers and sprawlers. Yet here was the upright Deinonychus: how, Ostrom wondered, did it manage to keep itself on the move if it had had a reptilian metabolism? For that matter, where did the other, larger dinosaurs find the energy to pump blood from their hearts to brains that might be located twenty or thirty feet away?

Then the French anatomist Armand de Ricqles, examining thin sections of dinosaur bone, discovered them to be rich with canals that facilitate the passage of calcium from the blood to the skeleton. Contemporary reptile bone has no such canals, and Ricqles concluded that this "indicates rate of bone/body-fluid exchange at least close to those of large, living mammals."

Next Robert T. Bakker, a former pupil of Ostrom's, launched an all-out offensive in favor of saurian warm-bloodedness. Bakker studied the numerical predator/prey rations in fossil beds where dinosaurs were found. Warm-blooded carnivores like lions and cheetahs must live among vast surrounding populations of herbivores to survive; otherwise their own voraciousness would cause them to consume their whole food supply. But large predatory reptiles like the Komodo dragon, being cold-blooded and thus of sluggish metabolism, need no more than three times their body weight in food a year. Bakker showed that the predator-prey relationship for dinosaurs was two or three carnivores per hundred herbivores, about the same as it is for modern mammals. But for non-dinosaurian reptiles and amphibians the predator/prey ratio is closer to *forty* percent.

For Bakker this proved that the dinosaurs had been alert, fast-moving warm-blooded creatures with the high energy needs that a physiology with internal-temperature-regulating capacity demands. His ideas have gained a wide following, despite the opposition of more conservative paleontologists such as Nicholas Hotton, who concedes that dinosaur physiology probably differed from that of modern reptiles, but will not go as far as accepting warm-bloodedness, declaring, "Alternative thermal strategies and life-styles available to dinosaurs may well have been as exotic as their body form, the like of which no man has ever seen."

And now comes the discovery of a dinosaur fossil containing a four-chambered heart. That clinches the issue — or does it?

Well, not exactly. Some scientists, like Dr. Paul C. Sereno of the University of Chicago, wonders whether the stone lump within Thescelosaurus really is its heart, or just a coincidentally heart-shaped mass. He has questioned the whole concept of preservation of internal organs in fossils.

Others accept the idea that the fossil does contain a heart, but are skeptical about its four-chamberedness. Here the evidence is unclear. The Carolina scientists admit that only the ventricles and aorta are distinguishable with the imaging methods that have been used so far. But they insist that the two upper chambers — the atria — must also have been present, since all reptilian hearts have two atria.

The development of more sophisticated scanning techniques will surely settle some of these questions. I suspect that we'll find that Thescelosaurus' heart *did* have four chambers, which will support the idea that dinosaurs had some sort of system for internal metabolic regulation. The dinosaurs, after all, dominated the world for 100 million years, until — so it is widely thought — being wiped out 65 million years ago by the apocalyptic climatic changes resulting from the collision of an asteroid or comet with the Earth. For one group of animals to have maintained supremacy for such a length of time argues for their great biological adaptability.

This is not to say that the dinosaurs necessarily were warm-blooded animals the way lions and squirrels and sparrows and human beings are. As Richard Owen pointed out long ago, and such scientists as Nicholas Hotton and Armand de Ricqles have reiterated in our own time, dinosaurs may very well have had unique metabolic systems that at present we can't understand, because the fossil evidence is inadequate.

If so, it widens the range of probabilities for life in the universe in general. Up to now we've tended to assume that the system of categories with which we define terrestrial vertebrates — amphibians, reptiles, birds, mammals — would probably hold true on all planets that have environmental conditions analogous to ours. Such thinking pretty well forecloses the possibility of non-mammalian intelligent life, which would be precluded by the metabolic limitations of reptiles and amphibians.

But we know that our own planet once harbored a race of reptilian beings that managed to maintain their position at the summit of creation for an immense period of time, until a cosmic catastrophe destroyed them, and it is beginning to appear that their metabolic systems were significantly different from those of the reptiles of today. We already know that it is a grave error to lump the dinosaurs together with such sleepy creatures as alligators and tortoises simply because similarities of their skeletal structures lead us to class them all as reptiles. There are reptiles and reptiles, evidently, and some were quicker and smarter than others.

Intelligent reptiles have long been a staple of science fiction, going back as far as E.E. Smith's Lensman novels of sixty years ago, one of whose heroes is the fearless Worsel of Velantia, "a nightmare's horror of hideously reptilian head, of leathern wings, of viciously fanged jaws, of frightfully taloned feet." Smith ignores the question of Worsel's metabolism, but surely a four-chambered heart must have beaten in that saurian bosom. The "wise and noble reptiles who had mastered superluminal physics" that James Patrick Kelly gave us a few years ago in his award-winning story "Think Like a Dinosaur" had to have been warm-blooded as well. And the fossil heart from South Dakota — if indeed that is what it is — provides us with the first substantive evidence that Earth's own dinosaurs may have been dynamic and intelligent animals. When and if the aliens come from space to visit us, it may very well turn out that they have the beady eyes and scaly skins of the reptilian critters sf long has loved to conjure up.

Asimov's Science Fiction, **December 2003**

Let's Hear It For Neanderthal Man

FOR MOST OF MY LIFE I'VE HAD A WARM PLACE IN MY HEART for shaggy old Neanderthal man. As a small boy haunting the American Museum of Natural History in New York I stared in wonder at the murals and dioramas depicting the Neanderthals at work and play, and found myself caught up somehow in a welter of speculation about these extinct folk, so uncouth-looking — bestial, even — with that mysteriously big brain and that odd spark of intelligence glimmering in their (reconstructed and hypothetical) faces.

What were they all about? I wondered. Were they really as savage and primordial and generally sub-human as they looked, a coarse and primitive rough draft for the species that was going to become our own glorious selves, or were they in fact pretty much equal in intelligence and ability to their *Homo sapiens* contemporaries, with rich cultural traditions about which we will never know a thing? And where did they go, the Neanderthals? The most recent Neanderthal fossil we have dates from about 30,000 years ago. Were they wiped out by the rival species in a millennium-long campaign of genocide? Or did *Homo sapiens* simply absorb them by intermarriage until the distinctive Neanderthal traits had been completely bred out of existence? Could it be that there were still a few Neanderthals walking the earth somewhere, closely shaved and carefully disguised as stockbrokers or New York City taxi drivers?

Soon after I discovered the Neanderthals I discovered science fiction, and enough tales of prehistoric man to fill a library. Usually the Neanderthals were portrayed as the bad guys — ugly smelly brutes who pelted our Cro-Magnon forebears with rocks from a safe distance, but eventually were Put In Their Place. Not always, though. Lester del Rey's "The Day is Done" (1939) was a touching story told from the viewpoint of a sympathetic Neanderthal: Lester was ever a contrarian, and a champion of the underdog besides. L. Sprague de Camp's "The Gnarly Man" (1939) provided a wry look at an immortal Neanderthal who had lived on into our own day, and Philip José Farmer's "The Alley Man" (1959) dealt with the same theme in a very different way.

The mysterious Neanderthals have figured conspicuously in my own work as well. I edited an entire anthology of Neanderthal stories in 1987, in which you will find the de Camp and Farmer stories, along with Isaac Asimov's wonderful "The Ugly Little Boy" and eight others. My 1988 story "House of Bones" shows Neanderthals as neither stylish nor clever, but definitely human even so. And in 1991 Isaac and I expanded his "Ugly Little Boy" into a novel of the same name, in which the Neanderthals are shown as having a culture every bit as complex as that of their *Homo sapiens* supplanters. My curiosity about these strange and virtually unknown people continues to this day: where, I wonder, do they fit into the human evolutionary pattern, how human actually were they, and why did they disappear?

Recently some answers to two of those three big questions have emerged.

That they were a separate evolutionary line, not at all ancestral to us, has been my belief for a long time. Now we have hard evidence of that. A team led by Dr. Svante Paabo of the University of Munich has succeeded in extracting and analyzing DNA from the bones of the first Neanderthal fossil ever discovered, the one found in 1856 in the Neander valley near Dusseldorf, Germany. The particular kind of DNA that the Munich team recovered is known as mitochondrial DNA, found in egg cells and therefore a powerful indicator of an organism's genetic makeup. The Neanderthal DNA, when compared with modern human DNA samples drawn from five continents, proved to be wholly distinctive. So widely did it differ from *Homo sapiens* DNA that there appears to be no likelihood of interbreeding between Neanderthals and modern humans. The DNA evidence indicates that the Neanderthals diverged from the main line of human evolution at least 300,000 years ago, perhaps even earlier, and must be regarded as an ancient hominid form only remotely related to us, and in no way ancestral.

So much for the theory that the Neanderthals might have been bred out of existence by genetic absorption into *Homo sapiens.* Their genes and ours have little in common. So we are left with the genocide theory, a long and ultimately successful war of extermination by the earliest of Master Races, or else with the possibility that the Neanderthals, a cold-climate species, were simply unable to adapt to the warming of their European homeland at the end of the last glacial period and faded into extinction. (The truth, if we ever discover it, may well turn out to be a combination of the two.)

They were different, yes. Can we regard them as human?

We know very little about their culture, and what we have is not very impressive. The glorious cave paintings of Western Europe were done by *Homo sapiens*, not by Neanderthals. Such Neanderthal artifacts as we have are crude, simple things.

But they buried their dead, which apes don't do. One Neanderthal fossil is that of a man who was crippled with arthritis and had only two teeth left. Someone had cared for him, had found food that he could chew and brought it to him, and eventually had given him a decent burial. Another Neanderthal fossil shows evidence of the amputation of a withered arm by some ancient surgeon; the patient had survived the operation by many years. One German cave that had been inhabited by Neanderthals contained ten bear skulls in niches in the walls, more in a crude stone box, and other bear bones on a stone platform. These traces of a bear cult seem to indicate some form of religious belief.

It has never been clear, though, that the Neanderthals were capable of speech. Animals have many ways of communicating, of course: such things come to mind as the curious directionally-oriented dances of honeybees, the "songs" of humpback whales, the cries and gestures of chimpanzees. My cat has a whole repertoire of meows of varying semantic content ("Feed me!" "What is that other cat doing here?" "This is not an adequate kind of food!" "I would like to sit on you now.") But cats and whales and chimps are animals, all the same. Their "speech" is largely instinctive and inflexible. They lack the means for transmission of complex concepts from individual to individual or from generation to generation that is essential to the development and expansion of a culture.

And so, it seemed, did the Neanderthals. Although they had brains of large size — larger, on the average, than ours — that alone is no necessary indicator of the ability to speak. The brains of elephants are bigger than ours too, but elephants don't have the anatomical features required for the precise shaping of sounds, nor do gorillas and chimpanzees and all other high primates except ourselves, and for a long time it was thought that those features were absent from Neanderthals too.

Recent research indicates otherwise. The first clue came in 1983, when scientists at Tel Aviv University uncovered a 60,000-year-old Neanderthal in Israel and were able to detect the presence in it of the hyoid bone, a structure important to the ability to articulate the complex sounds of language. But that discovery in itself did not demonstrate that Neanderthals were sufficiently well supplied with the nerve fibers that run from the brain to the tongue and make true speech possible. Indeed, there was anatomical reason to think they were capable of nothing more than simple grunts.

Now a group of anthropologists at Duke University has shown that they could do better than that. There is a small tubular opening at the base of the primate skull known as the hypoglossal canal, through which runs the nerve that carries signals from the brain to the tongue. This canal is about twice as wide in humans as in chimpanzees and gorillas; the wider the canal, presumably, the larger the number of nerve fibers that can pass through it, and, consequently, the greater control over the sound-shaping movements of the tongue.

The Duke researchers examined the hypoglossal canals of a series of hominid fossils beginning with *Australopithecus africanus,* a proto-human creature who lived 2.5 million years ago. The diameter of the australopith-ecine hypoglossal canal was no wider than that of a chimp; but the skull of an archaic *Homo sapiens* form from Africa, dating back close to 400,000 years, had one about the size of ours — as were the canals at the base of a pair of Neanderthal skulls from France of 70,000 years ago.

It seems likely, then, that the Neanderthals were able to speak. The ana-tomical prequisites were there. There is still some debate about whether they could shape such vowels as a, i, and u —a matter of whether their larynxes sat high in their necks, as those of apes do, or lower down, as in humans — but they should have been capable of managing articulate sounds even so. Well enough, I want to think, to have had the ability to teach their young the art of manufacturing weapon points, to exchange tips with each other on the best hunting tracks, to sing Neanderthal hymns to Neanderthal gods, even to swap gossipy tribal chitchat around the campfire on those long chilly Pleistocene nights.

I certainly hope so. The poor weak-chinned bulgy-browed things have been much maligned in science fiction over the decades (though not in mine). Usually they've been shown in a patronizing, condescending way — shambling, clumsy, flea-bitten also-rans of the evolutionary race, ugly and sullen and generally unpleasant. The English philosopher Thomas Hobbes described the life of primitive man this way in a book written in the sev-enteenth century, long before the finding of the first Neanderthal fossil: "No arts; no letters; no society; and which is worst of all, continual fear and danger of violent death; and the life of man, solitary, poor, nasty, brutish, and short." Perhaps that's a sharp description of Neanderthal life too. But I prefer to imagine them as a happier bunch, who in the hundreds of thousands of years that they dominated Europe had a rich spoken culture, replete with folklore and myth and epic poetry as well as the humbler chatter of everyday life, until the sleek long-legged Cro-Magnon types showed up to take over the neighborhood.

Asimov's Science Fiction, **January 1999**

The View Through Slow Glass

WHAT MAY BE THE FINEST AWARD-LOSING SCIENCE FICTION STORY ever written is Bob Shaw's "The Light of Other Days," which was first published in *Analog Science Fiction* in 1966 and which has appeared in a multitude of anthologies since then. It's the story that gave the "slow glass" concept to the world, one of the most ingenious science fictional inventions that anyone ever dreamed up. Everyone who has read the story assumes, quite reasonably, that it was a Hugo and Nebula winner — a book publisher once said so right on the front cover of a Shaw book — but that wasn't in fact the case. Larry Niven's "Neutron Star" took the Hugo that year, and Richard McKenna's "The Secret Place" won the Nebula.

Nobody remembers the McKenna story today. It's a minor piece, and its Nebula victory was probably a sentimental after-effect of the well-liked author's sudden death a little over a year before its publication. The Niven, though entertaining, is a long way from being the finest of its author's stories, and has been reprinted only a handful of times over the years. But slow glass is one of those ideas that stays in a reader's mind forever, and that single short story made its author famous. To this day there are those — plenty of them — who are absolutely convinced that it won the Hugo. They can even remember seeing Bob Shaw coming proudly up to the dais to collect his trophy at the 1967 sf convention in New York City. (I once heard someone say just that.) But it *didn't* win. It became a classic story, but it won no awards. (Which would *you* prefer, if you were a science fiction writer?)

Shaw's marvelous story is built around two interlocking narrative cores: a troubled marriage and a technological marvel. The marvel is slow glass — a substance so opaque that it greatly hinders the passage of photons through it, to the point where it can take ten years for a beam of light to travel the width of a single pane. The marriage is tense because an unwanted pregnancy has brought financial and emotional strains into it. Shaw's handling of each of these cores is distinctive and elegant, and he shows an especially fine touch in depicting the human problems of his story; but the concept of slow glass is what makes the story particularly memorable as science fiction. It's the sort of startlingly original idea that comes once or twice a lifetime, at best, to a science fiction writer.

Ask anyone who's involved in any way with science fiction to tell you what the speed of light is, and you'll probably be told at once that it's about 186,000 miles per second. The more fastidious ones may give you the number in kilometers per second. The people who would rather read fantasy trilogies might tell you that it's 186,000 miles an hour, which sounds almost right, though it isn't. But what hardly anyone will remember to add is the small but significant qualification that what they are giving is the speed of light *in a vacuum*. Light passing through any other medium will move less quickly. The speed of light slows as it travels through the atmosphere, and slows even more as it passes through water. The slowing effect is greater still for light going through glass — what we see through a window gets to us an imperceptible moment later than it would if there were no windowpane in the way.

Bob Shaw's wonderful idea was to postulate the existence of a kind of glass that slows the velocity of light in an extreme way, by forcing photons to travel "through a spiral tunnel coiled outside the radius of capture of each atom in the glass." He doesn't offer further technical explanations — how could he? — but in any case Shaw's concern is with effects, not causes. The effect of the passage of light through slow glass is to delay its transit by months or even years. A window made of slow glass becomes a window into the lost and irretrievable past. Looking through slow glass, we see the light of other days; we are able to see the scenes and peoples of vanished yesterdays. It is a tremendously poignant and evocative concept, and Shaw wrings great emotional power from it in the course of telling us a story about love and the loss of love that comes with time.

The hard truth is that slow glass is very likely a concept that can exist only as a science fictional speculation. Impurities in the glass, or random movements of subatomic particles, would probably deflect and scatter the image long before it had completed its slow journey through the pane. That matters not at all in terms of science fiction; so far as we know, time machines are impossible too, and so are handy little gadgets that give us access to parallel worlds, but plenty of fine stories have been based on those ideas all the same. Internal conceptual consistency is the key factor; what we are writing, after all, is stories, fantastic ones at that, not patent applications.

Some recent scientific news, though, has brought Bob Shaw's slow glass to my mind, at least in a tangential way. This is the report a few months back that three researchers working at Harvard University and the Rowland Institute for Science in Cambridge, Massachusetts, have managed to slow a beam of laser light to the extraordinary velocity of 38 miles an hour. Any reasonably capable bicyclist — Joe Haldeman in his prime, say — should be able to hit a better pace than that. (Joe, of course, is a few years past his prime, now, and perhaps no longer can manage to get the old Schwinn racer up to faster-than-light speeds. Well, it happens to the best of us. I notice that he still moves very quickly when he comes up to collect his annual Hugos and Nebulas, though.)

The Cambridge experiments, conducted by a Danish physicist, Dr. Lene Vestergaard Hau, working with two Harvard graduate students and Dr. Steve E. Harris of Stanford University, involved bombarding a cluster of vaporized sodium atoms with laser beams, causing them to lose energy and slow down, i.e., to grow cooler. In a series of complex processes taking just thirty-eight seconds the experimenters were left with a cluster of atoms cooled to a temperature just fifty billionths of a degree above absolute zero, which is very chilly indeed, as cold as anything in the universe can get: minus459.67 degrees Fahrenheit. At that sub-Minnesota temperature the remaining sodium atoms expand greatly and merge into something called a "Bose-Einstein condensate," a kind of high-density atomic soup that is no longer a vapor, but now is as solid as a block of lead. When a laser beam is fired through the condensate, very little of it is able to pass through. The photons that do manage to make the trip are slowed to a crawl — one twenty-millionth of the speed of light in a vacuum.

Further work is under way now to bring the speed of light through the condensate down to as little as 120 feet per hour: tortoise velocity. "We're getting the speed of light so low we can almost send a beam into the system, go for a cup of coffee, and return in time to see the light come out," Dr. Hau told the New York Times.

The important thing here is not that the Hau group's experiments have found a way of reducing the speed of light. As noted above, light is slowed whenever it passes through any transparent medium, be it air, water, vodka, or a windowpane, whether or not the pane is made of Bob Shaw's slow glass. The Cambridge experiments cause light to travel very much more slowly than it does in air or water or vodka, yes, but we are still not in slow-glass territory. (Bear in mind that if a beam of light needs ten years to pass through a pane of slow glass half an inch thick, it's loitering along at a velocity of five inches a century, which is a whole lot slower than 120 miles an hour.) So we are not very likely to see the Bob Shaw story make the transit to real life as a direct consequence of this new discovery.

But other wonders are possible. For one thing, the Hau group's apparatus does not transfer heat energy to the chilled medium through which the laser beam travels. This makes it plausible that the concept might be employed in optical computers, that is, computers which function using photons instead of electrons as their operating medium. It could be possible to devise optical switching systems in which a single photon turns a system on or off, thus leading to the construction of ultra-miniaturized superfast computers.

Also, a laser-coupled Bose-Einstein condensate has an extraordinary high refractive index: roughly 100 trillion times that of a glass optical fiber. (The refractive index is a measure of the degree to which light is bent as it passes through a medium.) This could be applied in the design of ultrasensitive night-vision glasses and in creating very bright laser-light projectors.) And doubtless other applications will present themselves as the research continues.

Bob Shaw died a few years ago, still a relatively young man. He never did win a Hugo or a Nebula for any of his science fiction, good though it was, though his fellow Britons honored him with both the British Fantasy Award and the British Science Fiction Association Award for his 1985 novel *The Ragged Astronauts*; the BSFA gave him its 1975 award also for his book *Orbitsville*. Whether he was bitter about the failure of "The Light of Other Days" to win awards is something I don't know, but I tend to doubt it: writing a story that good is its own reward, and I suspect Shaw came to realize, as time went along and his splendid story made its way from one anthology of classics to another, that it's far preferable to have written an unforgettable masterpiece that didn't win an award than it is to receive a trophy and a quick moment of applause for a story that nobody remembers a year later.

And — though we are no closer to the invention of slow glass than we were when the Shaw story first appeared almost thirty-five years ago — I think that Bob Shaw would have felt a chill run down his spine as his eye came across the phrase "slow light" in the newspaper stories announcing the Hau group's experiments with laser beams and cooled atoms. I certainly did.

Asimov's Science Fiction, **May 2000**

The Antikythera Computer

THE MEDITERRANEAN HAS BEEN A BUSY MARITIME waterway since prehistoric times, but it is often a stormy sea; and, inevitably, an uncounted number of the ancient mariners' vessels came to grief and finished their voyages many fathoms deep. A darkening of the sky, a sudden storm, and a majestic ship bound for Spain or North Africa or the coast of Asia Minor might capsize in a moment. The Mediterranean is littered with the remains of ships of all ages, going back to the dawn of shipping some four or five thousand years ago.

It was no secret that those vessels were down there, laden with treasure — gold and silver bullion, works of art, cargoes of pottery or weapons. The problem was to reach them, something that was almost impossible before the development of modern diving gear. In recent centuries fishermen would, from time to time, bring up some fragment of a statue, some slime-encrusted vase, to remind modern inhabitants of the region of the sunken ancient treasures in that sea, but such finds were few and far between.

Once diving bells and diving suits came into general use in the nineteenth century, it became more feasible to search the ocean floor for these ancient treasures, and many significant discoveries resulted. One of the most spectacular such finds came in 1900, when two Greek ships bearing divers returning from a sponge-gathering expedition off the coast of Tunisia were compelled by one of those Mediterranean storms to take refuge off the island of Antikythera, at the very tip of the Greek archipelago not far from Crete. While waiting for the storm to blow itself out the thrifty captain decided to look for marketable sponges right there, and sent a diver named Elias Stadiatis, equipped with a helmet and weighted boots, down 150 feet to the bottom. There Stadiatis found himself wandering in a confused tangle of statuary — a marble goddess, huge stone horses, and much more, dozens of statues, marking the site of some ancient shipwreck.

It was plainly a major archaeological find. The sponge-divers reported it to the Greek government, which, in November 1900, sent a Navy vessel equipped with the most modern diving equipment of the day to explore the site. Nine months of difficult and dangerous work produced a life-sized bronze head, two large marble statues, and many smaller pieces. Archaeologists determined that the ship bearing these treasures had gone to the bottom somewhere around the dawn of the Christian era on a voyage from Athens to Rome. The bronze statues could be dated, from their style, to the era of Socrates and Plato, about four hundred years before the time of the ship-wreck. The marble ones were newer — first-century copies of much older Greek work. The leaden bases of many of the statues were bent and torn, as though the statues had been ripped up violently, and that led archaeologists to speculate that they might have been the booty of Roman marauders who looted the temples of Greece in 86 BC, under the dictator Sulla.

The statues were magnificent ones. But the most important single find of the Antikythera expedition was a battered and badly corroded lump of bronze that the archaeologists originally tossed aside as worthless. In 1902, Valerios Statis of the National Museum in Athens took a close second look and was startled to see that it had dials, gear-wheels, and inscribed plates. It was, in fact, a complex machine, which was — and still is — the only mechanical object that has come down to us from ancient Greece. Modern study has shown that it is nothing less than a highly complicated device for performing astronomical computations.

Discovering exactly what the mechanism's purpose had been took many years. First, certain associated bits and pieces had to be inserted in the main body of the instrument. Then the rust and calcification had to be cleared away. The dials and inscriptions thus revealed left little doubt that it was some sort of astronomical device. For a long time archaeologists thought it was a navigational instrument, perhaps an astrolabe, an instrument used for fixing a ship's position by the stars.

The task of cleaning the mysterious mechanism took more than half a century. In 1955, the Yale historian Derek J. de Solla Price, working in as-sociation with George Stamires, a specialist in ancient Greek inscriptions, finally succeeded in properly fitting the various fragments of the machine together, and realized that the instrument, whatever it was, was basically intact. Originally, they said, it must have looked rather like an old clock: a wooden box with hinged doors, containing the gears and dials. The wooden parts had vanished over the twenty centuries of submersion. But the rest of the device appeared to be complete.

Stamires was able to show that the lettering on the inscribed plates was in a style known to be no older than 100 BC and to have gone out of use around the time of Christ. And the words of the inscription supported this observation. They included some astronomical data similar to that compiled by a Greek named Geminos about 77 BC. The mechanism provided a clear and indisputable way of dating the wreck.

Price and Stamires's theory of what the thing had been used for became more controversial. One of the dials bore the signs of the zodiac, another the names of the months. As the gears turned, they said, the instrument would provide information about the risings and settings of the important constellations throughout the year. Other dials gave much more complicated astronomical data. Price and Stamires concluded that the machine was indeed some type of navigational instrument. But if it was an astrolabe, it was one that was far more complex in conception than any previously known astrolabe of the era.

Other scientists doubted that the first-century Greeks could have been capable of constructing what was essentially a mechanical computing machine, as Price and Stamires suggested it was, and their hypothesis was brushed aside. A couple of years ago, though, a team of British, Greek, and American researchers headed by the astronomer Mike Edmunds of the University of Cardiff, Wales, and the mathematician and filmmaker Tony Freeth, took a new look at the Antikythera gadget, making use of three-dimensional X-ray tomography and high-resolution imaging systems, and provided a startling confirmation of the device's technological significance and a better understanding of its function.

Previously unseen inscriptions came into view, which appeared to relate to lunar and planetary movements. At least thirty bronze gear-wheels were identified, and there may have been as many as thirty-seven. A pin-and-slot mechanism linking two of the wheels produced a representation of the Moon's elliptical journey around the Earth that was in accordance with the calculations of the Greek astronomer Hipparchos, who flourished in the second century BC and was the first to arrive at an understanding of the motions of heavenly bodies that approximates our modern ideas.

The new Antikythera findings suggest that the instrument — which was probably built between 150 and 100 BC and might even have been the work of Hipparchos himself — does not seem to have been a navigational device, as most twentieth-century students of it had speculated, but could have been used to calculate calendars for planting and harvesting, or to set the dates of religious festivals according to the positions of the planets. We may never know its exact purpose. But what is not in doubt is that it demonstrates, as the recent researchers noted, "an unexpected degree of technical sophistication for the period," far exceeding in complexity any similar instruments of the next thousand years. Not until the heyday of Arabic science around 900 AD did any such geared calendrical devices reappear. It would not be improper, really, to call the Antikythera mechanism the oldest known computer.

What it tells us is that the ancients may well have been far more advanced technologically than we ever suspected, and that the lucky survival of the Antikythera mechanism hints at the existence of a great range of Greco-Roman calculating devices, employed not only for calendrical work or astronomical studies but in their remarkable engineering accomplishments. The Greeks and the Romans, not having access to electricity, semiconductors, and wi-fi linkages, did not, of course, have computers of the sort that every six-year-old child uses today. But they may well have had — and it is a thought that should take today's technological whizzes down a peg — all manner of intricate computational instruments, about which we know nothing, simply because they did not happen to come down to us in the archaeological record, and at the close of their great age much of what they knew was simply lost, not to be rediscovered for many centuries. How far their technological reach extended is still largely a matter for conjecture. We know a great deal about those great ancient civilizations, yes, but our knowledge very likely is just the merest sliver of the total story. As Derek de Solla Price put it, close to half a century ago, in the article that first revealed the Antikythera instrument to the scientific world:

The Antikythera mechanism was no flash in the pan, but was part of an important current in Hellenistic civilization. History has contrived to keep that current dark to us, and only the accidental underwater preservation of fragments that would otherwise have crumbled to dust has now brought it to light. It is a bit frightening to know that just before the fall of their great civilization the ancient Greeks had come so close to our age, not only in their thought, but in their scientific technology.

Asimov's Science Fiction, **January, 2010**

The Death of Gallium

I MOURN FOR THE DODO, POOR FAT FLIGHTLESS BIRD, EXTINCT since the eighteenth century. I grieve for the great auk, virtually wiped out by zealous Viking huntsmen a thousand years ago and finished off by hungry Greenlanders around 1760. I think the world would be more interesting if such extinct creatures as the moa, the giant ground sloth, the passenger pigeon, and the quagga still moved among us. It surely would be a lively place if we had a few tyrannosaurs or brontosaurs on hand. (Though not in *my* neighborhood, please.) And I'd find it great fun to watch one of those PBS nature documentaries showing the migratory habits of the woolly mammoth. They're all gone, though, along with the speckled cormorant, Steller's sea cow, the Hispaniola hutia, the aurochs, the Irish elk, and all too many other species.

But now comes word that it isn't just wildlife that can go extinct. The element gallium is in very short supply and the world may well run out of it in just a few years. Indium is threatened too, says Armin Reller, a materials chemist at Germany's University of Augsburg. He estimates that our planet's stock of indium will last no more than another decade. All the hafnium will be gone by 2017 also, and another twenty years will see the extinction of zinc. Even copper is an endangered item, since worldwide demand for it is likely to exceed available supplies by the end of the present century.

Running out of oil, yes. We've all been concerned about that for many years and everyone anticipates a time when the world's underground petroleum reserves will have been pumped dry. But oil is just an organic substance that was created by natural biological processes; we know that we have a lot of it, but we're using it up very rapidly, no more is being created, and someday it'll be gone. The disappearance of *elements*, though — that's a different matter. I was taught long ago that the ninety-two elements found in nature are the essential building blocks of the universe. Take one away — or three, or six — and won't the essential structure of things suffer a potent blow? Somehow I feel that there's a powerful difference between running out of oil, or killing off all the dodos, and having elements go extinct.

I've understood the idea of extinction since I was a small boy, staring goggle-eyed at the dinosaur skeletons in New York City's American Museum of Natural History. Bad things happen — a climate change, perhaps, or the appearance on the scene of very efficient new predators — and whole species of animals and plants vanish, never to return. But elements? The extinction of entire elements, the disappearance of actual chunks of the periodic table, is not something I've ever given a moment's thought to. Except now, thanks to Armin Reller of the University of Augsburg.

The concept has occasionally turned up in science fiction. I remember reading, long ago, S.S. Held's novel *The Death of Iron*, which was serialized in Hugo Gernsback's *Wonder Stories* starting in September, 1932. (No, I'm not *that* old — but a short-lived sf magazine called *Wonder Story Annual* reprinted the Held novel in 1952, when I was in college, and that's when I first encountered it.)

Because I was an assiduous collector of old science fiction magazines long ago, I also have that 1932 Gernsback magazine on my desk right now. Gernsback frequently bought translation rights to European science fiction books for his magazine, and *The Death of Iron* was one of them. The invaluable Donald Tuck *Encyclopedia of Science Fiction and Fantasy* tells me that Held was French, and *La Mort du Fer* was originally published in Paris in 1931. Indeed, the sketch of Held in *Wonder Stories* — Gernsback illustrated every story he published with a sketch of its author — shows a man of about forty, quintessentially French in physiognomy, with a lean, tapering face, intensely penetrating eyes, a conspicuous nose, an elegant dark goatee. Not even a Google search turns up any scrap of biographical information about him, but at least, thanks to Hugo Gernsback, I know what he looked like.

The Death of Iron is, as its name implies, a disaster novel. A mysterious disease attacks the structural integrity of the machinery used by a French steel company. "The modifications of the texture of the metal itself," we are told — the translation is by Fletcher Pratt, himself a great writer of fantasy and science fiction in an earlier era — "these dry, dusty knots encysted in the mass, some of them imperceptible to the naked eye and others as big as walnuts; these cinder-like stains, sometimes black and sometimes blue, running through the steel, seemed to have been produced by a process unknown to modern science." Which is indeed the case: a disease, quickly named siderosis, is found to have attacked everything iron at the steel plant, and the disease proves to be contagious, propagating itself from one piece of metal to another. Everything made of iron turns porous and crumbles.

Sacre bleu! Quel catastrophe! No more airplanes, no more trains or buses, no bridges, no weapons, no scissors, no shovels, no can-openers, no high-rise buildings. Subtract one vital element and in short order society collapses into Neolithic anarchy, and then into a nomadic post-technological society founded on mysticism and magic. This forgotten book has an exciting tale to tell, and tells it very well.

It's just a fantasy, of course. In the real world iron is in no danger of extinction from strange diseases, nor is our supply of it running low. And, though I said a couple of paragraphs ago that the ninety-two natural elements are essential building blocks of the universe, the truth is that we've been getting along without two of them — numbers 85 and 87 in the periodic table — for quite some time. The periodic table indicates that they ought to be there, but they're nowhere to be found in nature. Element 85, astatine, finally was synthesized at the University of California in 1940. It's a radioactive element with the very short half-life of 8.3 hours, and whatever supply of it was present at the creation of the world vanished billions of years ago. The other blank place in the periodic table, the one that should have been occupied by element 87, was filled in 1939 by a French scientist, who named it, naturally, francium. It is created by the radioactive decay of actinium, which itself is a decay product of uranium-235, and has a half-life of just 21 minutes. So for all intents and purposes the world must do without element 87, and we are none the worse for that.

Gallium, though —

Gallium's atomic number is 31. It's a blue-white metal first discovered in 1831, and has certain unusual properties, like a very low melting point and an unwillingness to oxidize, that make it useful as a coating for optical mirrors, a liquid seal in strongly heated apparatus, and a substitute for mercury in ultraviolet lamps. It's also quite important in making the liquid-crystal displays used in flat-screen television sets and computer monitors.

As it happens, we are building a *lot* of flat-screen TV sets and computer monitors these days. Gallium is thought to make up 0.0015 percent of the Earth's crust and there are no concentrated supplies of it. We get it by extracting it from zinc or aluminum ore or by smelting the dust of furnace flues. Dr. Reller says that by 2017 or so there'll be none left to use. Indium, another endangered element — number 49 in the periodic table — is similar to gallium in many ways, has many of the same uses (plus some others — it's a gasoline additive, for example, and a component of the control rods used in nuclear reactors) and is being consumed much faster than we are finding it. Dr. Reller gives it about another decade. Hafnium, element 72, is in only slightly better shape. There aren't any hafnium mines around; it lurks hidden in minute quantities in minerals that contain zirconium, from which it is extracted by a complicated process that would take me three or four pages to explain. We use a lot of it in computer chips and, like indium, in the control rods of nuclear reactors, but the problem is that we don't *have* a lot of it. Dr. Reller thinks it'll be gone somewhere around 2017. Even zinc, commonplace old zinc that is alloyed with copper to make brass, and which the United States used for ordinary one-cent coins when copper was in short supply in World War II, has a Reller extinction date of 2037. (How does a novel called *The Death of Brass* grab you?)

Zinc was never rare. We mine millions of tons a year of it. But the supply is finite and the demand is infinite, and that's bad news. Even copper, as I noted above, is deemed to be at risk. We humans move to and fro upon the earth, gobbling up everything in sight, and some things aren't replaceable.

Solutions will be needed, if we want to go on having things like television screens and solar panels and computer chips. Synthesizing the necessary elements, or finding workable substitutes for them, is one obvious idea. Recycling these vanishing elements from discarded equipment is another. We can always try to make our high-tech devices more efficient, at least so far as their need for these substances goes. And discovering better ways of separating the rare elements from the matrices in which they exist as bare traces would help — the furnace-flue solution. (Platinum, for example, always in short supply, constitutes 1.5 parts per million of urban dust and grime, which is ever-abundant.)

But the sobering truth is that we still have millions of years to go before our own extinction date, or so we hope, and at our present rate of consumption we are likely to deplete most of the natural resources this planet has handed us. We have set up breeding and conservation programs to guard the few remaining whooping cranes, Indian rhinoceroses, and Siberian tigers. But we can't exactly set up a reservation somewhere where the supply of gallium and hafnium can quietly replenish itself. And once the scientists have started talking about our chances of running out of *copper*, we know that the future is rapidly moving in on us and big changes lie ahead.

Asimov's Science Fiction, **June, 2008**

All That Is Solid Melts Into Air

KARL MARX SAID THAT, OR PERHAPS IT WAS FRIEDRICH ENGELS, in *The Communist Manifesto*, and they were talking about the breakdown of the ancient societal bonds under the pressures and uncertainties of the industrial revolution.

Certainly life is less quiet now than it was in the dear old days of the feudal system, and a good deal that was solid in the world of Marx's time has indeed melted into air, some of it figuratively and some all too literally, since the *Manifesto* first appeared in 1848. One interesting example of literal melting is going on right at the present time — the shrinking of the polar ice caps as a result of global warming, which is a side effect of industrialism that Marx probably did not foresee at all. And as the too too solid ice of the Arctic retreats, artifacts of the pre-industrial world that long were kept in nature's deep-freeze locker are coming to light.

In Canada, for example, the glaciers have receded a hundred feet and more in recent times, bringing forth such things as ancient bows and arrows, spears, pellets of caribou dung that register an age of 7400 years in carbon-14 testing, and small wooden darts that show a radiocarbon age of around 4300 years. Probably the most interesting discovery so far is that of a nearly complete human body, dubbed the "iceman" — an Indian hunter in his twenties who stumbled into a crevasse about 1450 AD and has been buried there, most of him in a fine state of preservation, ever since. Scattered near his body lay an assortment of weapons and tools made of bone and wood, perhaps belonging to him, perhaps those of other travelers who passed that way in antiquity.

Among these items, mysteriously, is a small lump of iron. The Indians of what is now British Columbia, where the body was found, did not begin using iron for another three hundred years. Had the piece come ashore in the wreckage of some ship from Asia that was trading along the western coast of North America four decades before Columbus' first voyage? Did it originate among the iron-working Eskimos, 500 miles to the north? Or — boldest speculation of all — had that bit of metal made its way across northern trade routes from the Viking settlers who landed on Canada's eastern shore about 1000 AD?

A great deal of further study will be necessary before these questions can be answered. Interestingly, the Indians of British Columbia are cooperating wholeheartedly in the research — a striking contrast to the behavior of their cousins south of the border, who have taken, lately, to demanding instant reburial of ancient human remains, claiming them to be "ancestral" and denouncing any kind of scientific examination as sacrilegious.

The iceman's remains were found in Tatshenshini-Alsek Provincial Park, which Canada recognizes as the traditional territory of the Champagne and Aishihik First Nation, an Indian tribe that has some 1,130 members. Since 1995, the tribe has held veto rights over all archaeological work done in the park, and when the iceman came to light in August, 1999, public announcement of the find was delayed for ten days to allow scientists to consult with tribal elders about it.

Instead of insisting on an immediate reburial, this Indian group — who named the iceman Kwaday Dan Sinchi, "Long Ago Person Found" — readily agreed to permit scientific study of the find, including carbon-14 dating and DNA analysis. As Bob Charlie, the chief of the tribe, put it, Long Ago Person's death appears to have been the result of an accident, and, he said, "even today, if you have an accident, you have an autopsy, you try to find out what happened."

But there is more in it for the tribe than that. They hope that the defrosted remains will provide a link to their own oral history, which tells how their ancestors traveled by foot along mountain trails to trade with the native peoples of British Columbia's coast. Eighteenth-century European accounts of the Indians of the region describe them as wearing broad-brimmed conical hats much like the one found near the iceman. If it could be shown that the iceman's people were ancestral to the present-day inhabitants of the region, a continuous tribal line of occupation spanning five centuries would be established. "There is some excitement among our citizens," said Bob Charlie, "that the DNA might indicate who his present-day relatives are."

All this is very different from the reactions of the Umatilla tribe of Washington State to the discovery of the 9000-year-old bones of Kennewick Man in a sandy flat along the banks of the Columbia River. In my column in the October-November 1998 *Asimov's* I told how the Umatillas, who claim territorial jurisdiction over the area where Kennewick Man was found, objected strongly to any sort of scientific testing of the relics, arguing that it would go against their traditional beliefs forbidding any sort of disrespect for the dead. They wanted the Kennewick bones handed over to them then and there for reburial as a tribal ancestor, which would have been tantamount to their destruction, and only a quick lawsuit by a group of dismayed archaeologists kept the federal government from doing just that.

The special problem with Kennewick Man is that his bones are not at all similar to those of modern-day American Indians. Their physical characteristics are so markedly different that the first anthropologist who examined them (who was also the local coroner) opined that they were those of a white man, perhaps some settler or trapper of the eighteenth century. When radiocarbon dating revealed that the bones were between 9300 and 9600 years old, though, the dispute quickly became political — for if white men, perhaps of European origin, were wandering around in that part of the New World ninety centuries ago, what becomes of the Indians' claim to be the original human occupants of the Americas?

That was an uncomfortable question for the Umatillas. And so they saw no need to have the bones studied. "We already know our history," a tribal spokesman asserted. "It is passed on to us through our elders and through our religious practices. If this individual is truly over 9000 years old, that only substantiates the belief that he is Native American" — a neat bit of circular reasoning that would permit the Umatillas to put troublesome Kennewick Man safely back underground before anyone could determine much more about him.

The archaeologists' lawsuit managed to head that off, however, aided by a parallel suit brought by the Asatru Folk Assembly, a California pagan sect that worships the ancient Norse gods and had some wild hope that Kennewick Man, because he had been of Caucasian race, might just be one of *their* own remote ancestors. The last-minute legal rescue made it possible to subject the skeleton to preliminary scientific scrutiny, the results of which were made public by the Interior Department in the fall of 1999.

Those findings confirmed that Kennewick Man's bones were not those of an American Indian. But, although they were more Caucasian in appearance than anything else, they weren't those of a European, either. Their closest links were to the non-Mongoloid peoples of Asia and the Pacific region — the Polynesians, say, or perhaps the Ainu, that poorly understood minority group that has inhabited the northern islands of Japan since prehistoric times.

This makes the situation look bad for the hopes of the Asatru Folk Assembly, but otherwise simply adds to the general mystery. It is a long-established theory that the first human inhabitants of the Americas came to the New World out of Asia thousands of years ago, traveling via a now-vanished land bridge connecting Siberia and Alaska at what is now the Bering Strait, and that these people, genetically Mongoloid, were the ancestors of the Indians. The Kennewick bones raise the possibility that non-Mongoloid peoples came here too in those ancient days, arriving by boat from the Pacific. (The Polynesians and the Ainu both have long maritime traditions.)

Perhaps these early seafarers died out before they were able to establish permanent colonies in the Americas, or else they were absorbed genetically into the various Indian stocks: at this point, nobody knows. The Kennewick bones are being held at the Burke Museum in Seattle pending DNA analysis and other study by anthropologists. One thing is certain, though: if the Umatilla had been allowed to rebury them as being those of some early tribal ancestor, nothing at all would ever have been learned about them. "We already know our history," the Umatillas have said. But the Umatillas hold no rights of ownership over human history in general, only over their own tiny facet of it. The rest of us must remain free to learn what we can about how the human species — and we are all, even the Umatillas, members of one and the same species — came to occupy the earth. Destroying evidence is an unfruitful pastime. As Bob Charlie of the Champagne and Aishihik First Nation reminds us, when a body is found, "you have an autopsy, you try to find out what happened."

We'll know more about Kennewick Man and his place in the human saga sooner or later, perhaps even before this column sees print. And even bigger news of ancient humanity may be forthcoming out of the Yukon in the years ahead, as the too, too solid ice of those glaciers continues to melt away and the migration routes of the first Americans are laid bare after thousands of years in the deep freeze. We owe some thanks to Bob Charlie and other enlightened tribal leaders of his kind, up there in Canada, for creating an atmosphere in which it will be possible to probe these mysteries without political rancor and wilful obfuscation.

Asimov's Science Fiction, July 2000

Doomsday

ON SOME MONTHS BACK, DISCUSSING BOOKS I HAD BEEN REREADING lately, I spoke of Olaf Stapledon's epic of the far future, *Last and First Men* — the quintessential far-future epic, the key title in that entire subspecies of science fiction. Stapledon purports to be writing a history of the next two billion years or so of human evolution, carrying us through eighteen successive human species until the race, having weathered disaster after disaster and now dwelling on a terraformed Neptune, is confronted with a challenge beyond its immense ingenuity: the sun has come under "a continuous and increasing bombardment of ethereal vibrations, most of which were of incredibly high frequency, and of unknown potentiality," evidently emanating from a nearby supernova. This has caused old Sol to behave in a "deranged" way, and, as a result, says Stapledon's far-future narrator, "Probably within thirty thousand years life will be impossible anywhere within a vast radius of the sun, so vast a radius that it is quite impossible to propel our planet away fast enough to escape before the storm can catch us."

So it is the end for our solar system, and the end as well for the highly evolved, dazzlingly endowed Eighteenth Men. But the narrator, speaking to us from the very brink of extinction, provides this lovely epilog by way of summing up humanity's two billion years of cyclical striving: "Man himself, at the very least, is music, a brave theme that makes music also of its vast accompaniment, its matrix of storms and stars. Man himself in his degree is eternally a beauty in the eternal form of things. It is very good to have been man. And so we may go forward together with laughter in our hearts, and peace, thankful for the past, and for our own courage. For we shall make after all a fair conclusion to this brief music that is man."

It has always seemed quite sad to me that our splendid species is fated to be snuffed out in a mere two billion years, if we are to take Stapledon's elegant fantasy as embodying an accurate prediction. All our cleverness gone for naught, Shakespeare and Mozart and the iPod and penicillin and high-definition television and all the rest of our glorious achievements not only gone but not even forgotten, for there will be nobody here to forget us! But now the calculations of two astronomers, Klaus-Peter Schroeder of the University of Guanajato in Mexico and Robert Connon Smith of England's University of Sussex, have put my mind at rest. The clock is ticking for us, yes, and doomsday is approaching, but it is not nearly as close as the author of *Last and First Men* suggested, and, unlike Stapledon's Eighteenth Men, we have plenty of time to deal with the problem. They, two billion years in our future, had a mere thirty thousand years to figure out a solution, and couldn't do it. But we, say Drs. Schroeder and Smith, have a full 7.59 billion years to come up with an answer. How comforting that extra 5.59 billion years is! And what a nice sense of scientific precision is provided by ".59 billion years," so much more scientific-sounding than the vulgar "590 million years."

What is going to happen to our world, in the Schroeder-Smith version of the future, makes all our current little ecological scramblings around with hybrid automobiles and fluorescent lighting seem pretty much beside the point. We can be as green as can be, and give ourselves many brownie points for Saving the Planet, but the planet isn't going to be saveable, because the sun is going to keep on getting warmer and warmer and eventually conditions will become downright intolerable. We're not talking about global warming here. That's a purely local phenomenon resulting from our offloading of carbon dioxide and other so-called "greenhouse gases" into our own atmosphere. No, this is *solar* warming, an expansion of the sun's output. Most astronomers believe that such expansion goes on gradually but inexorably throughout the life-span of any star, and that our sun, in the 4.5 billion years of its life, has already increased its luminosity by 40 percent. And nothing we could do will halt the process.

So, we are told, things will keep on getting hotter and muggier on Earth, until, about a billion years from now, the oceans will boil away. That will deal with the humidity problem, I suppose, but will create other serious but not wholly insoluble problems. We — if anything like "us" is still here, a billion years from now — aren't likely to be able to withstand the scorching heat of the expanded sun, but, given this much notice, we surely ought to be able to find some more comfortable place to live.

We see that in *Last and First Men*: Stapledon's Fifth Men, some four hundred million years in our future, organize a mass migration to Venus upon learning that our moon is about to disintegrate and bombard us with big troublesome fragments; and when, another half a billion years down the line, the Eighth Men discover that the sun is about to go nova and cook all the inner worlds, a second migration to Neptune is successfully carried out. So, too, I suppose, we, having been properly warned, will find ways of coping with the increased temperatures of Earth in the year One Billion, perhaps by burrowing underground but, more probably, by escaping from our over-heated planet altogether. That would mean saying goodbye, of course, to the Great Pyramid of Giza and the Taj Mahal and the Grand Canyon, and all of Earth's other familiar wonders, but it's a safe bet that geological forces will have removed all those cherished landmarks from our ken anyway, even the Grand Canyon, long before those billion years have elapsed.

Bigger trouble is in store, though, and coping with that won't be nearly as simple. Go another 5.5 billion years down the line, say Drs. Schroeder and Smith, and we find the sun using up the last of the hydrogen in its core — that is, the fuel that it has been burning to generate its heat — and starting to burn the hydrogen in its outer layers. This will cause the core to shrink and the outer layers greatly to expand, turning the sun into a vast, tenuous red-giant star. That means sayonara for Mercury and Venus, which will be within the perimeter of our inflated sun. Earth has some chance of escaping the fate of those worlds, because the altered sun's gravitational pull will have diminished, causing Earth to move outward to something like the present orbit of Mars, where it might just escape being engulfed by the expanded solar mantle.

Even so, the prognosis isn't good. The risk is that Earth will gradually drift back sunward from its new orbit until it, too, is gobbled up. Calculations made in 2001 by two European scientists indicated a reasonable chance that that would not happen, but new figures developed by Dr. Schroeder of Guanajato and Manfred Cuntz of the University of Texas give our little globe no hope. Their numbers show that the transformations going on within the sun will cause it to throw off much more mass — and thus, paradoxically, grow much larger, increasing greatly in diameter even while becoming far more attenuated in substance. Instead of losing 25 percent of its mass while undergoing metamorphosis into a red giant, as was previously predicted, the sun will lose about one third — resulting in a star with a diameter 256 times as great as today's sun, and a luminosity 2,730 times greater. Not only will our inner-world neighbors be devoured, but the hapless Earth will find itself skimming just a short distance above the surface of the solar monster, and tidal forces will create a bulge in the sun that will exert a gravitational pull on the Earth, slowing its speed of revolution and tugging it inexorably downward toward its doom. In the even longer run the sun itself will fare little better, going through a standard cataclysmic cycle of shrinking and ex-panding and shrinking again that will turn it, eventually, into a white dwarf star heading toward its ultimate burnout, further billions of years ahead in the future that we are not going to see.

So, then, the Schroeder-Smith clock is ticking, and we have a mere 7.59 billion years to deal with the problem.

Stapledon, who arrived at an intuitive vision of approximately this sort of bleak destiny back in 1930, made the men of his fictional distant future nimble enough to escape first to Venus and then to Neptune. But then, as the final solar catastrophe approached, even they had run out of places to hide, and the best they could manage was to look upon their coming doom with philosophical detachment: "Man is a fair spirit, whom a star conceived and a star kills." Even then, the stubborn humanity in them led them to conceive a plan to create "an artificial human dust capable of being carried forward on the sun's radiation, hardy enough to endure the conditions of a trans-galactic voyage of many millions of years, and yet intricate enough to bear the potentiality of life and of spiritual development." And so, as the book closes, they are about to seed the stars with their own successors, who, perhaps, will continue the human saga in some unimaginably alien manner under the light of some distant sun.

We, having more notice of the end than Stapledon's Last Men, are free to follow a similar path. Earth may be doomed, but the universe awaits us. At the moment, of course, political and financial difficulties seem to have stymied any sort of movement very far into space, but it's folly to think that the present slump in human space exploration is going to last forever. There's nothing like an imminent vast expansion of the sun to stimulate our agile species in the direction of self-defense. So we may — not soon, mind you, but sooner than it seems right now — start thinking about colonizing Mars or one of the more suitable moons of Jupiter or Saturn, which would get us out of reach of the first phase of the big temperature rise. We could even go one step beyond Stapledon's soaring vision and consider moving Earth itself into a safer orbit by making use of the gravitational force of comets or aster- oids, as several astrophysicists have quite seriously proposed. (Though one of them, Dr. Gregory Laughlin of the University of California at Santa Cruz, has noted that "There are profound ethical issues involved, and the cost of failure . . . is unacceptably high.") And, finally, when the red-giant sun has begun its metamorphosis into that white dwarf and the entire solar system is without a source of heat, the beings who then inhabit the Earth — not the Eighteenth Men of Stapledon, but perhaps the Ninetieth Men or the Thousandth Men — will have to find some way to export their brand of humanity to the stars.

Dizzying stuff to think about, yes. A billion years ago there was nothing but microscopic life on Earth, and here we are talking about the "human" life-forms that will inhabit this place billions of years in the future. How likely are they to resemble us in any significant way?

Most science fiction abjures such Stapledonian vistas and deals instead with short-range stuff like the way computers will work in the twenty-sec- ond century, or the problem that space pirates will cause in the twenty-third. Stories like that don't leave one's mind whirling giddily, the way pondering the astrophysical problems of the year Five Billion can do. Would that our best writers would spend more time dealing with such things, say I, dizzy though they may make their readers in the process. It's the good kind of dizziness, the kind that science fiction excels at generating, the sort of vertiginous sensation that brought most of us to science fiction in the first place.

Asimov's Science Fiction, **March, 2009**

Pleistocene Park

THE WOOLLY MAMMOTH MAY SOON BE BACK AMONG US, after an absence of ten or fifteen thousand years. I'm glad to hear it, and I hope you are too. Not everybody is.

What I'm talking about is the current scheme by an international passel of scientists to recreate *Mammuthus primigenius,* the shaggy European mammoth of the Pleistocene, by inserting DNA from the remains of a Pleistocene mammoth into ova of the Asian elephant, the mammoth's closest living relative, that have been stripped of modern elephant genes. The hope is that a mammoth fetus would result, which a female elephant would carry to term and deliver. Would the elephant foster-mother realize that something fishy had taken place? Dr. Larry D. Agenbroad of Northern Arizona University, a geologist who is part of the project, doesn't think so. He doubts that she would be very seriously bothered, "though she might wonder why her baby is so hairy."

Before you can make a rabbit stew, though, you need to catch your rabbit. The first step in this operation is to find some mammoth DNA. But a promising source for that is at hand: the 20,000-year-old Jarkov mammoth (named for the family that first spotted it in the Arctic tundra of Siberia) that was discovered not long ago in an almost perfect state of preservation, thanks to the deep-freeze conditions of northern Siberia, where winter temperatures approaching -100 F. are the norm.

There's nothing new about finding mammoth remains in Siberia. Chinese merchants were doing a brisk trade in Siberian ivory more than two thousand years ago; aware that the Siberians dug it out of the ground, they believed that it came from a kind of gigantic mole or rat that tunneled through the icy soil using two huge teeth. A seventeenth-century Chinese natural-history text speaks of "the *fen-shu,* 'the rat beneath the ice'...a kind of rat as big as an elephant which lives underground and dies as soon as it comes into the air." By that time European travelers in the far north had also begun hearing tales of this giant "rat," which the natives called *mamantu* or *mammut*, a name that supposedly meant "that-which-lives-beneath-the-ground."

Eventually it was understood that this colossal "rat" was in fact an extinct elephant of northern climes. Its tusks were in high demand for transformation into combs, vases, and other ornamental objects: some 50,000 pounds a year of mammoth ivory per year passed through the market at the Siberian town of Yakutsk in the nineteenth century. In August, 1799 a Siberian named Ossip Shumakhov, searching for ivory in the delta of the Lena River on the shores of the Arctic Ocean, spotted something dark and large inside a huge block of ice; it turned out to be the frozen carcass of a mammoth, complete with skin and hair. Shumakhov was too frightened of the carcass to excavate it, and over the next few years it was exposed by gradual thawing, which allowed wolves and foxes to gnaw away much of its flesh; but much of the ancient beast, including one eye and much of its brain, still remained by the time the Russian scientist Mikhail Ivanovich Adams collected it and hauled it off to St. Petersburg, where it is on exhibit to this day.

Another frozen mammoth turned up along the Beresovka River of Siberia in 1900 — nearly complete except for its trunk and part of one foreleg, which had been nibbled by wild animals after being laid bare by a summer thaw. (The Beresovka mammoth, stuffed, is also on display in St. Petersburg today.) Another was found on the Taiymyr Peninsula of Siberia in 1948, and in the same year the partial corpse of a frozen baby mammoth was unearthed near Fairbanks, Alaska: I remember seeing it on display in the main lobby of the American Museum of Natural History the following year, lying in a glass-topped freezer chest. Other similar finds have followed with great regularity.

The Jarkov mammoth, discovered in 1997, is the first to be found in the era of modern genetic wizardry. The intact carcass, that of a male, is eleven feet tall and weighs some seven tons. Radiocarbon dating shows it to be about 20,000 years old. After prolonged study *in situ*, the specimen finally was carved out of the ground in October, 1999. Encased in a 23-ton block of permafrost, it was taken by helicopter to the town of Khatanga, 150 miles away, where scientists working at temperatures of 11 degrees F. in a laboratory inside a cavern of ice have spent months carefully thawing it out with hair dryers. The plan now is to extract DNA from the soft tissues that can be used for cloning a living mammoth. (The possibility also has been raised that sperm cells could be taken from the body for artificial insemination.)

Will it work? The scientists involved in the project are hopeful, although others have their doubts. One of the latter group, Dr. Hessel Bouma 3rd of Calvin College in Michigan, noted that the cloning "would start with DNA not from a fresh cell, but from one haphazardly frozen by nature. The chances of DNA being intact is very, very small." Others point out that mammoths and elephants, though closely related, belong to different species:

mammoths have 58 chromosomes, elephants 56. Cross-species cloning has never been attempted even with living creatures, let alone with an extinct one. Cross-species insemination (assuming sperm is available and is still potent after 20,000 years) is likewise an iffy proposition.

The cloning group thinks it's worth a try, anyway. "Why not?" asks Dr. Agenbroad, the Arizona geologist. "I'd rather have a cloned mammoth than another sheep" — a reference to Dolly, the cloned sheep produced in Scotland a few years ago.

But objections are already coming in from the scientific ethicists — the people whose job it is to say, as clergymen once did in the old monster movies, that There Are Some Things That Man Was Not Meant To Do.

Some of them think that the cloning is a bad idea, apparently because any sort of cloning makes them uncomfortable. One argument is that any cloned mammoth would be only 99.5% pure, with the remainder of its genes modern-elephant ones coming from its mother. Why this should matter is not clear to me. If it looks 99.5% mammothlike, down to the thick reddish fur, the massive hump on its head, and the great curving tusks, then I think we could regard it as a convincing simulacrum, the closest to the real thing we are ever likely to see, even if it might not seem completely kosher to an authentic Pleistocene beast. And I can find no harm in bringing such a majestic creature back to life, even in slightly impure form. We are already responsible for the extinction of the dodo, the giant auk, the passenger pigeon, the aurochs, the quagga, and untold numbers of other strange and wonderful species. Quite possibly the mammoth too was one of mankind's victims, 10,000 years ago; no one knows how or why it became extinct, but excessive hunting is one plausible conjecture. If we, steeped as we are in the blood of so many fellow creatures, manage now to put our splendid intelligence to work restoring one of the vanished ones to the face of the earth, why should the response be anything other than tumultuous applause?

Another objection is that the excavation of the Jarkov mammoth was funded by television's Discovery Channel and the French magazine *Paris Match*; this entertainment-industry connection somehow seems to taint the project in the eyes of the ethicists. (Science isn't meant to be entertaining, I guess.)

Leave it to San Francisco, that hotbed of anti-scientific passions where I happen to live, to lead the charge in the wrong direction. Just a few weeks ago my local paper, the *San Francisco Chronicle*, worked itself up to righteous anti-cloning fervor in an editorial boldly headed, DON'T MESS WITH WOOLLY MAMMOTHS. The editorialist allows that the Jarkov specimen itself may well provide useful insights into mammoth biology, but then turns to "all the giddy talk about trying to clone the mammoth" and asks, "Do we really want to bring a woolly mammoth back to life — or, heaven forbid, try to raise a whole herd?"

Heaven forbid!

Why, the world is such a nasty place already, the *Chronicle* tells us, that "certainly the woollies will get the worst of the deal in returning to a planet now overrun with six billion people." Would there be no room for free-ranging mammoths even on the Godforsaken tundra of remotest Siberia? Apparently not. "It would only be a matter of time until they ended up in zoos," says the newspaper, if the cloning should somehow be successful; and zoos, of course, are little more than concentration camps for our fellow creatures. Better that they should languish forever in extinction than be compelled to endure the horrendous torments of the San Diego Wild Animals Park!

And finally — what better closing flourish is there for a good editorial than a rousing *reductio ad absurdum*? — the editorial wonders whether "woolly burgers would become all the rage." That *is* a nice twenty-first century touch, worthy of a Phil Dick dystopia — some ghastly heartless corporation turning out cloned mammoths by the millions so that they can be turned into Bigger Macs. Never mind the economics of the issue, of course, or the fact that we don't currently eat elephant burgers, though the big beasts could easily be farmed for the purpose.

The *Chronicle* concludes by saying, "Chances are, there is a very good reason they are extinct." I decode the subtext here to mean that it was God's will that *Mammuthus primigenius* disappear from the face of the earth, and what God has extincted, let no laboratory dare to summon back into being.

Sure. Here political correctness turns itself into a Moebius strip. There are those who think San Francisco is full of wicked atheists, and others who think San Francisco is a hotbed of environmentalist fanatics who would launch a demonstration in favor of keeping any creature, even the smallpox virus, from becoming extinct; and out of San Francisco comes a cry for the continued extinction of the woolly mammoth, because God wants it that way! One would think they were talking about turning cloned velociraptors loose in our midst. One wants to weep. But one prefers to look hopefully toward that ice cave in Siberia instead, with fingers crossed that the new century will bring us the first little woolly mammoths to walk the earth in ten thousand years.

Asimov's Science Fiction, **September 2000**

Resurrecting the Quagga

ONCE UPON A TIME IN SOUTH AFRICA THERE EXISTED A ZEBRA-LIKE animal called the quagga, which has been extinct since the late nineteenth century. It had stripes only on its head, neck, shoulders, and part of its trunk; the rest of its body was a light chestnut brown in color, or sometimes yellowish-red, and its legs were white. Its mane was dark brown with pale stripes, and a broad dark line ran down the middle of its back. It was as though nature had intended the quagga to be a zebra but had given up the job halfway through.

When the nomad huntsmen known as the Hottentots were the only inhabitants of the South African plains, the quagga was a common animal there, grazing in herds of twenty to forty. The Hottentot name for it was quahkah, from the sound of its barking neigh. When the first Boers — Dutch settlers — arrived at the Cape of Good Hope in 1652, they adopted the name, spelling it quagga. (The Boers called regular zebras bontequagga, meaning "the quagga with conspicuous stripes.")

Soon large-scale quagga-hunting began. The Boers had no use for quagga meat themselves — they regarded it as a kind of horse, and Europeans have never been eager eaters of horseflesh — but they killed them as food for the Hottentots, whom they had enslaved, and used quagga hides for making leather shoes and sacks for the storage of grain, dried fruits, and dried meat. The quaggas vanished very quickly before this onslaught: by 1870 the last wild herd had been entirely exterminated. From time to time in the first half of the twentieth century isolated quagga sightings were reported in remote parts of South Africa, but none was ever verified, and even these dubious reports ceased after 1940. A few quaggas did survive in Europe for a couple of decades beyond the 1870 extinction date, having been been brought there as curiosities by collectors of unusual animals in the eighteenth and nineteenth centuries. But offspring among the captive quaggas were rare, and the last male quagga in Europe died in 1864. The Berlin Zoo's one female died in 1875, and another, the last of her species, expired at the Amsterdam Zoo in 1883.

The quagga has figured in literature at least twice. Thomas Pringle, a nineteenth-century Scottish poet, mentioned it in his "Afar in the Desert," speaking of the "timorous quagga's shrill whistling neigh" that was "heard by the fountain at twilight grey." And in 1973 I myself wrote of it in a novella called "Born with the Dead," which is about a society of the near future in which a process has been developed to revive newly dead human beings. The revivees form a strange subculture of their own, completely outside normal human life, and among their amusing pastimes is to take part in African safaris where they hunt formerly extinct animals that have been brought back into existence by genetic manipulation. This is how I describe a quagga hunt:

"At first no one perceives anything unusual. But then, yes, Sybille hears it: a shrill barking neigh, very strange, a cry out of lost time, the cry of some beast they have never known. It is a song of the dead. There, among the zebras, are half a dozen animals that might almost be zebras, but are not — unfinished zebras, striped only on their heads and foreparts. . . . Now and again they lift their heads, emit that weird percussive whistling snort, and bend to the grass again. Quaggas. Strays out of the past, relicts, rekindled spectres." The hunt goes well. A quagga is killed, skinned, served for dinner that night. The meat is juicy, robust, faintly tangy. In the next few days my ex-dead characters see such animals as giant ground sloths and moas in the game park, and eventually they go on to hunt passenger pigeons, aurochs, and even a dodo.

What I didn't know, back there in 1973, was that a South African taxidermist named Reinhold Rau was already seriously thinking of trying to bring the quagga back from extinction. I was simply writing a science fiction story, inventing whatever details I needed to carry my story along, but Reinhold Rau had as his goal the actual and literal resurrection of a vanished species.

Rau first encountered a quagga — a stuffed one — in 1959, when he took a job as a taxidermist at Capetown's natural history museum. Something about that quagga moved him deeply. He saw it as a victim of man's ignorance and greed, and, as he said many years later, he felt that it was his duty — his destiny, even — to "reverse this disaster."

Rau was aware — I knew about it too when I wrote my story — that in the 1920s German zoologists had attempted to recreate the extinct European bison known as the aurochs by selective breeding of modern kinds of cattle, choosing for their breeding stock those that most resembled the aurochs in physique and the color of their fur. In time they produced animals that indeed looked something like the aurochs, although they were not, of course, the true item. Rau wondered whether quagga genes lurked in modern-day zebras and could perhaps be brought together by a similar breeding program that would in time arrive at what would be, in effect, an authentic quagga.

That would be unlikely to achieve if quaggas and zebras had indeed been separate species, so far apart genetically that interbreeding in the days before the quagga's extinction would have been impossible. But Rau didn't think that was so. He knew from their terminology for the animals that the early Boer settlers had regarded quaggas and zebras as nothing more than different varieties of the same creature, and was convinced, in a purely intuitive way, that the quagga must have differed from the zebra only in the pattern of its striping and in some superficial characteristics of body shape, not in any profound genetic way. He began his project, just about the time I was writing "Born With the Dead," by studying mounted quagga specimens in various museums — there are twenty-three of them, mostly in Europe — to get a precise idea of what the quagga had actually looked like. (He discovered that it had differed considerably from zebras in ways other than the pattern of stripes, having a straighter back and a more forward-jutting head. But he still believed that the animals had been closely related and might even have been capable of interbreeding.) When he tried to find institutional support for his breeding program, though, he had no success, and was about to abandon the scheme when, in 1981, he heard from Oliver Ryder, a geneticist at the San Diego Zoo, who was collecting blood and skin samples of zebras in an attempt to understand the genetic variations among various zebra populations, and who hoped that Rau, in his capacity as a taxidermist, could help him out.

Rau replied that he had something even more interesting than zebra material: specimens of actual quagga tissue. (He had acquired small bits of quagga muscle and blood vessels in 1969 when he remounted the badly stuffed specimen at the Capetown museum.) From these Ryder was able to extract DNA samples, a feat that gave Michael Crichton the notion of reconstituting dinosaurs from their DNA that became the seed of the novel *Jurassic Park*. Ryder went on to indicate support for Rau's belief that the quagga had been only a variant kind of zebra, not a distinct species. This reawakened in Rau the hope that it might be possible to breed the quagga back into existence using relatively quagga-like zebras.

He began the experiment in 1986 with a group of zebras provided by the Namibian parks service, supplemented with a second batch captured a year later in a different area of southern Africa. The early results were not encouraging. Most members of the first two zebra batches were visibly striped both fore and aft, and so were their offspring. But Rau located some lightly striped zebras in the KwaZulu-Natal region of South Africa and added them to the genetic mix, and this time things began to happen.

Rau's quagga enterprise ended with his death at the age of seventy-three in February 2006, but by that time he had come to preside over a herd of more than one hundred animals, scattered through a number of private game reserves in the Capetown area. Biologically they all must be considered zebras, of course. But some are quite quagga-like in appearance. That does not, sad to say, make them true quaggas: they are just zebras with quaggoid striping patterns. The prize of the herd, whom Rau called "Henry," is zebra-striped from head to rib-cage, but then the stripes begin to fade out, and the rear half of his body is yellowish-brown, with only a few faint stripes visible on his hindquarters. That does not make him a real quagga, but, all the same, he is as close to a quagga in appearance as anything the world has seen since Amsterdam's captive female died a century and a quarter ago.

Most likely Reinhold Rau would not have been able to carry his quagga-revival project much beyond the point he had attained at the time of his death. Through decades of dedicated work he managed to breed a race of what are, essentially, zebras with defective striping, which is not quite the same thing as bringing an extinct species back to life. There is hope, though, that new advances in DNA research will permit further genetic modification leading to the creation of something that is more like an actual quagga. The samples of quagga DNA that Rau was able to collect from the skins of the stuffed zoo specimens are of high quality, and it should be possible through close analysis to isolate the specific genetic signposts of quagganess and to distinguish them from zebra genes. Then, perhaps, a program of genetic repair might be employed to edit the zebra genes of Rau's animals into quagga genes, producing, eventually, a creature more or less like an authentic quagga. (In case you're wondering why the cloning process used to create the dinosaurs in *Jurassic Park* can't be employed to speed the quagga quest, let me remind you that *Jurassic Park* is only science fiction, and that the DNA that has been retrieved from specimens of extinct animals thus far is too badly degraded to be used in cloning experiments.)

For that matter my story "Born with the Dead" is still only science fiction, too, nearly thirty-five years after I wrote it and a decade or so beyond the future year in which I set it. Not only don't we have any method for bringing dead human beings back to life or even a glimmer of it on the horizon, but there's no sign out there of the possibility that my rekindled deads will be able to go off to African game parks to hunt dodos, moas, giant ground sloths, or quaggas. I did indeed have them hunting quaggas in that story of long ago, though, which is why it gave me such a shiver to learn that Reinhold Rau, all unbeknownst to me, had actually spent nearly four decades striving to restore the quagga to our world. This is not a case of life imitating art, since Rau's research and my speculative idea were simultaneously generated in complete independence of each other. But it can, I suppose, be considered an example of parallel evolution.

Asimov's Science Fiction, **June, 2007**

My thanks go to Howard Waldrop for calling the Rau story to my attention.

To Clone Or Not To Clone

WHEN THE REVELATION CAME LAST YEAR THAT THE SUCCESSFUL ASEXUAL creation of a lamb cloned from an adult sheep had taken place, it was inevitable that a great flap over the prospect of human cloning would immediately begin. (I'm speaking of the work done by Dr. Ian Wilmut of Scotland's Roslin Institute, who announced in February, 1997 that he had produced a lamb that he named Dolly by scraping some cells from the udder of a 6-year-old ewe and inserting them into a specially prepared egg cell from another female sheep.)

Any startling scientific advance, these days, is certain to draw instant harsh criticism from the leaders of the religious right — who see the work of the devil, apparently, in most sorts of meddling with the natural order of things as they understand it, particularly where genetic or biological matters are concerned — and from the godless but equally fundamentalist left, which finds hidden elitist/fascist agendas in the very same scientific breakthroughs that arouse the wrath of the pious. The left is easily terrified, also, by anything that might tend to increase the influence that Scientists — those cold-eyed, amoral, environment-devouring folks in laboratory smocks — already have over everyday life.

And so, as follows the day the night, there came within a few days President Clinton's announcement of a ban on government-sponsored human-cloning research. The fact that there didn't seem to be any government-sponsored human-cloning research going on at the moment did not seem to be relevant. President Clinton has demonstrated remarkable skill at telling the American public what it would like to hear — "pandering" is the word that his harsher critics use — and he was able to pick up quick political points by letting the devout citizens back there in the boondocks know that this particular genie would not be let out of the bottle, by gum, at least not with taxpayer money.

But of course it will. Technologies, once developed, don't go away, though they can be forced underground by sufficiently persistent persecution. The President's lightning-fast ban, satisfying though it may have been to the anti-science factions that have always been such a major force in American politics, will not last. Either here or abroad, cloning research will continue. And, I'm pretty sure, we will indeed see laboratory-spawned cloned humans brought forth some time in the twenty-first century.

Does that possibility scare you? Does it immediately fill your mind with images out of old horror movies? Do you envision legions of Frankenstein monsters coming forth from sinister Transylvanian cloning labs? Do you imagine that the evil megabucks-laden overlords of Wall Street will create a perpetual master class by diverting a few of their millions into the creation of cloned replicas of themselves? And do you, therefore, rejoice that the President has taken this bold step to keep such dire things from happening?

Not me. Maybe I've been reading science fiction too long, but I find myself unterrified by the likelihood of human cloning and irritated by Mr. Clinton's off-the-cuff response to the Dolly event. What seems much more worrisome to me than any number of billionaire clones let loose in the land is the fear of science that underlies the anti-cloning hysteria. (And hysteria is what it is.)

The President is toying with the same forces, far from extinct in our society and possibly even gaining strength, that once caused so much trouble for Vesalius, Copernicus, and Galileo. His unthinking demagoguery may have been good politics in this nation of largely ignorant and superstitious people, but otherwise was a needless — and dangerous — intervention in a situation where the best response would have been no response at all.

To my way of thinking, no good reason presents itself for government involvement in human cloning at all, one way or the other. A government ban on research that isn't happening is silly and distasteful and rash. On the other hand, government funding of such research, which so far as I know has never been contemplated anyway, seems unnecessary and likely only to entangle the citizenry in unfruitful emotional debate. Dr. Wilmut of the Roslin Institute *is* a government employee, though not here; but what he was trying to do was simply to improve the quality of Scottish livestock. The scientists who ultimately will produce the first human clones will be operating in the private sector.

And they will be doing it, I suspect, not to meet the vile needs of ego-driven tycoons, but simply to see whether the thing can be done. They will be expanding the frontiers of the possible, in other words — the same thing that scientists have been trying to do since, well, the days of Vesalius and Galileo and Copernicus. The Dolly research has provided the first indication that mammals can be produced by fiddling around with genetic material in the laboratory. Now that that can, apparently, be managed with sheep, someone is bound to want to find out whether it can be done with humans. And will. But not for ghastly Frankensteinian motives, only out of sheer scientific curiosity.

I can certainly see the scientific value of cloning research in general, which has very little to do with making identical copies from a single genetic matrix and a great deal to do with making precise genetic changes in cells. The copying factor is incidental. The goal might be to create, through techniques of genetic manipulation, a race of sheep with superior wool, or cows that give more copious milk, or laboratory rats that have a special susceptibility to a particular disease in need of study. Once a sheep, cow, laboratory rat, or whatever that has the sought-after genetic qualities has been designed, it could then be reproduced through cloning to make sure that all its descendants have those identical qualities. The messy intervention of alien genetic material from a biological father, potentially disruptive to the primary goal, would thus be avoided.

But I'm not at all sure that there's any point to the cloning of humans, other than whatever scientific knowledge might accrue from bringing the stunt off. Doubtless there can be some practical benefits of having one's physical self duplicated by asexual means, but they aren't immediately apparent to me.

I can, of course, imagine some. Women who have no desire for contact with men, even to the extent of having male gametes mingling with their ova by way of artificial insemination, would be able to bring forth cloned daughters, genetically identical to themselves. Childless heterosexual couples in which the male is sterile could also have children by cloning without the entry of an outsider's genes into the family unit, which artificial insemination would involve. I see no great harm in any of that. People who want children would be able to have them. The children would presumably be raised in their mothers' homes, not in soulless creches out of Huxley's *Brave New World*. If such a practice were to become universal, of course, it would mean an end to the evolution of the human race, but even if human cloning were readily available I doubt that it would lead to any substantial decline in the predilection men and women have for making babies together the old-fashioned way.

More frightening prospects exist, of course. Some megalomaniacal dictator might want to establish laboratories to create a legion of cloned warriors — parentless, quasi-synthetic beings wholly dedicated to serving the purposes of the state. He might, if sufficiently megalomaniacal, want to fill his court with replicas of *himself*. (I've already written that one, incidentally. It was called "In the Clone Zone" and *Playboy* published it seven or eight years ago.) Or vast bordellos could be stocked with cloned prostitutes replicating highly desirable physical types. None of these are pretty notions, but they're not high-order probabilities, either, considering that it would take exactly as long to rear a human clone to maturity as the maturation of normally conceived humans does today, and there would be no guarantees that the clones would turn out as desired.

We also have to reckon with the class-warfare issue — the fear that a wealthy elite will callously propagate itself through cloning, while individuals of lesser economic power will be doomed to remain singletons. I suppose that might happen, if cloning yourself for a few million dollars were to become a real option. The Daddy Megabucks types might just want to stock in a few extras of themselves. (Or to stockpile their children's DNA so that they could be conveniently regenerated if anything nasty should happen to them. Theodore Sturgeon dealt with that theme all the way back in 1962 in a touching story called "When You Care, When You Love.")

If such a display of raw economic power upsets you, you might consider that Daddy Megabucks is *at this very moment* living in a house much bigger than yours, 87 rooms set on 400 acres of elegantly landscaped terrain. This, too, may seem unfair to you, crammed as you are into some dismal little hut, but people with lots of money have the ability to do such things, and when you try to prevent it you end up with something like the Soviet Union. Before you get unduly excited over the tycoons who have themselves cloned, give some thought to the fact that no one's personality or intellectual capabilities can ever be duplicated through cloning, only the genetic makeup. The tycoon's clones will look just like him, yes, but they're apt to be just as unpredictable and rebellious and generally annoying as the children of rich people that come into being the usual way often turn out to be.

The test-tube creation of the sheep named Dolly by Ian Wilmut is an astounding scientific breakthrough. Other cloning experiments are already underway in many laboratories and we will soon be seeing the reports. Although the cloning of mammals is still in its earliest stages, I think it's safe to say that the technology for carrying it out is already in place. But nobody, at the moment, is contemplating the cloning of humans. That will probably come, once the immense technical and social problems have been worked out, because our history shows that once a thing is technically possible it usually gets to happen. The current outcry against human cloning, though, is premature and disturbing, carrying with it the potential for anti-scientific witchhunts of the ugliest sort. One cloned sheep does not mean the immediate advent of cloned humans; and cloned humans, if they ever do arrive, may not be as terrifying a concept as they have been made to seem in the current debate. As usual, the main thing we have to fear in all this is fear itself.

Asimov's Science Fiction, **February 1998**

Trilobites

————————

I'VE BEEN READING A FASCINATING AND SOBERING BOOK ABOUT THE LIFE-FORM that dominated this planet longer than any other, a truly superior entity that remained in charge here for some three hundred million years but is now, alas, gone from the scene. I'm talking about trilobites, and the book — published three or four years ago by the Alfred A. Knopf Company — is *Trilobite! Eyewitness to Evolution*, by Richard Fortey, who is a senior paleontologist at London's Natural History Museum.

Most of us have at least a hazy idea of what trilobites were — more or less crustacean-like critters that lived in the prehistoric seas of Earth back in that incomprehensibly ancient period before the dinosaurs or any other form of land-dwelling being. Fossil trilobites are widely sold in museum curio shops and most time-travel stories that take their characters back into the early days of life on Earth give trilobites prominent play. (My own novel *Hawksbill Station*, which is set in a camp for political prisoners many hundreds of million years in the past, when not even fishes have evolved yet, let alone reptiles or mammals, portrays its marooned characters gloomily dining on trilobite hash and yearning nostalgically for steak. When FoxAcre Press reissued the book a couple of years ago it featured some really neat illustrations of trilobites on the cover and in the text.)

So we know, approximately, what trilobites were. But Richard Fortey's book about them puts them in perspective as the truly significant creatures they were during their long reign at the summit of animal life on our planet.

Trilobites were hard-shelled marine creatures, structurally somewhat analogous to modern-day crabs but not at all related to them, that begin to turn up very suddenly in the fossil record in the early part of the Cambrian Era, somewhere around 540 million years ago. The distinctive thing about them, the one that gives them their name, is their three-lobed form. The thorax, the main section of a trilobite's body, was divided lengthwise into three well-defined segments. Crosswise, their bodies were divided into three segments also: head, thorax, tail. Underneath were a great many jointed legs, giving them that somewhat crustacean look, though they were, at best, only distant cousins of the crustaceans, each group being descended from a common ancestor but having no more than superficial resemblances to the other.

Although a basic three-lobed form defines all trilobites, the earliest species gave rise to a wide variety of successors that differed widely in shape and size, so that over the millennia thousands of species of trilobites came to occupy the seas, some of them no bigger than flies, others as hefty as the largest of lobsters. At that distant time before life on land had evolved, there was a swift and dramatic trilobite-population explosion in the Cambrian seas. Trilobites became the most widespread creatures on Earth. For hundreds of millions of years they dominated the planet; during their later years some species took on a bizarre, grotesque appearance, with huge spiny protuberances and great bulging eyes, giving them the look of visitors from another planet; and then, abruptly, in the era that we call the Permian, they disappeared completely from the world. We aren't sure why. They seem to have thrived right up to the end: then, about 250 million years ago, having endured through a span more than twice as long as the dinosaurs would have, they vanished. Nothing remains of them except the abundant fossil evidence, which made them objects of curiosity and careful study as early as the seventeenth century.

By now the time-levels of the geological strata have been reliably mapped, and we can see that the period of trilobite dominance lasted an immensely long time — so long that we are not really able to comprehend it. How casually we throw around phrases like "for hundreds of millions of years"! And how utterly incapable we are of understanding what they mean!

Consider the relativistic way we handle the concept of ancientness. *Asimov's Science Fiction* magazine is now twenty-seven years old. If you yourself are, say, twenty-three, you will very likely regard an early issue of *Asimov's* from 1977 or 1978 as "ancient," because it's older than you are. (I know, because that's how I felt fifty-odd years ago when I first saw the early science fiction magazines that Hugo Gernsback was publishing a few years before I was born.) For some of our youngest readers, Isaac Asimov himself, who died in 1992, may be starting to seem as ancient a figure as Shakespeare or Socrates. They know of him only from his writings and perhaps some anecdotes of his larger-than-life personality.

But if an early issue of *Asimov's* can seem "ancient," what about the pyramids of Egypt? Close to five thousand years old, they are! Incredibly ancient! But then we have the cave paintings of Lascaux — four times as ancient as the pyramids. And so forth, back and back in time across ever more unthinkable gulfs. Humanity itself evolved a mere five million years ago. The dinosaurs have been gone for sixty or seventy million, but they were the lords of creation here for 150 million years before that. That is an impossible number to understand. Even 150 million seconds is. We who think twenty years is a long time, who look back at the world of our grandparents' childhood as though it were some other planet, who regard a science fiction story set in the year 11,000 as a vision of the unthinkably far future, have no way of getting our minds around the concept of 150 million years. It is an endless, virtually interminable span of time, beyond all imagining. But the trilobites lasted at least twice that long.

Richard Fortey is plainly in love with trilobites. He discovered his first one as a fourteen-year-old schoolboy, clambering around on coastal cliffs in southwestern Wales in search of fossils until, splitting a rock apart one day, he found himself staring into the long narrow eyes of a creature that had been entombed in that rock for five hundred million years. He has studied them ever since; and his book is one long hymn to the strangeness and wonder of the most durable life-form ever to inhabit this planet.

He tells how scientists first discovered them, and how they learned the secrets of their internal structures. (Speaking of the first X-ray photos of trilobites, made a century ago, he writes, "The fossils are outlined on their radiographs as if drawn by a deft artist in a soft, dark pencil. They have a ghostly quality; one might imagine they had been called up from the past by incantation rather than by science.") He describes their jointed legs, their branching gills, and above all their fantastic shells: "We are ready to envisage a parade of trilobites walking past on their paired limbs and it will be as odd a parade as any carnival could offer. Some smooth as eggs, others spiky as mines; giants and dwarfs; giggling popeyed popinjays; blind grovellers; many flat as pancakes, yet others puffy as profiteroles. . . .")

He describes dozens of species for us: Cyclopyge, whose eyes have fused together "so that effectively there is just one huge visual organ, or headlamp," and Radiaspis, covered everywhere by spines, making it pricklier than a hedgehog, and Dalmanites, with a huge spike-like projection extending from its rear, and massive Isotelus, with enormously long spines, "far longer than the rest of the body, so that the animal is supported on them like a sled upon its runners," and a head "surrounded by a border full of perforations, like a colander."

One of the most fascinating chapters deals with trilobite eyes. Fortey points out how miraculous it is that living things should have evolved organs capable of perceiving light and form and color, and of transmitting that information to the brain. Where in the evolutionary sequence eyes developed, no one yet knows; the first trilobites were equipped with them, so they must have been derived from some earlier creature. But it was in the trilobite tribe that the concept was refined to a remarkable degree. The secret of the trilobites' long biological success, Fortey implies, lay in their ability to see the world about them better than anyone else.

And we learn — to our astonishment — that trilobite eyes were made of calcite. Calcite is a mineral, calcium carbonate. It is the chief component of chalk and limestone and marble. The white cliffs of Dover are cliffs of calcite; the pyramids of Egypt were once covered in glittering calcite sheaths. But there is a transparent crystalline form of calcite, too, and out of it the lenses of the trilobite's eyes, unique among all the eyes of all the creatures of our planet's long history, were fashioned. As he sums up his long and flabbergasting description of how the trilobite was able to make use of the unusual light-transmitting ability of calcite crystals, Fortey comments, "It would be no less than the truth to say that the trilobite could give you a stony stare." And he goes on to show us how the fossil evidence, hundreds of millions of years old, of these strange trilobite eyes that were stony even before they fossilized, gives us clues into the workings of their nervous systems and even into their varying ways of life in the oceans of remotest antiquity. That one chapter on trilobite eyes is a work of magic, of fantasy, even — and yet it is science in its purest form.

The trilobites came, they swarmed across maritime Earth in enormous numbers, and eventually they disappeared, leaving no descendants. Richard Fortey has devoted a lifetime of study to them because they caught his imagination when he was fourteen and would not release him. I gave several hours of my life to his splendid book because, as a science fiction writer, I am profoundly stirred by visions of alien times and places and beings, and the world he depicts, the world in which the trilobites lived and thrived, is as alien as they come. But it is not a world that sprang from the imagination of a Frank Herbert or a Jack Vance or an Isaac Asimov. It is our very own world, hundreds of millions of years removed in time, and the book that Richard Fortey wrote about it is as eerie and thought-provoking as any science fiction novel I have ever read.

Asimov's Science Fiction, **August, 2004**

The Greatness of Cornelius Drible

I'VE SPENT THE LAST COUPLE OF YEARS NIBBLING AWAY AT A VAST and remarkable book, Robert Burton's *The Anatomy of Melancholy* — its sixth edition, the one of 1651, the last that its eccentric author revised and corrected himself. (My own copy, which I've owned for many years, is a reprint of a 1927 edition with modern spelling and typography.)

One does not sit down and read Burton's *Anatomy of Melancholy* straight through, end to end, any more than one would sit down and eat five pounds of foie gras or a bucketful of beluga caviar. It is too rich, too extreme, for that sort of gluttony. I worked at it at a pace of four or five pages a day, sometimes not even that much; and since my copy runs to 984 pages, you can see how it came to pass that a project that I commenced in the autumn of 2002 was not completed until late in 2004. An extraordinary journey it was, too, and I propose to share some of its gleanings with you here.

Burton was a British scholar, born during the reign of Elizabeth the First, who spent most of his life as a cloistered and celibate bookworm at Christ Church College, Oxford. During those years he seems to have done nothing but study, with special emphasis on mathematics, religion, astrology, magic, medicine, religion, and classical literature. His sole creative endeavor was a play in Latin, *Philosophaster*, which had one performance at Oxford in 1617 and went unpublished until 1862. But for many years he assembled significant quotations from his vast reading, which seems to have taken in everything that had ever been written — Aristotle, Plato, Seneca, Montaigne, Rabelais, Chaucer, Erasmus, and on and on through the ages, down to his contemporaries Shakespeare and Marlowe. And out of this immense collection of material he began to shape, eventually, the book that has kept his name alive through the centuries.

Ostensibly *The Anatomy of Melancholy* is precisely what its name implies: an exhaustive study of the psychological ailment of depression. Evidently Burton suffered from it all his life. It was known to the ancients, he tells us, quoting the Roman physician Galen, who spoke of melancholy as "a malady that injures the mind, associated with profound depression and aversion from the things one loves best." But his enormous book is much more than a study of the causes and cures of the blues. He includes under "melancholy" virtually every sort of human passion, not just "heaviness and vexation of spirit," but also such phenomena as love, religious feeling, obsessive behavior of all kinds, the lust for power, *et cetera, et cetera, et cetera*, until his book becomes a huge encyclopedia of esoteric information of all sorts, digressing in all directions to embrace medicine as it was known in his day, alchemy, witchcraft, geographical exploration, and just about everything else. All of this he expounds by means of quoting from hundreds, perhaps thousands, of the authoritative writers of the ages, weaving it together by means of the sort of opulent, splendiferously resounding prose that was the grand specialty of Elizabethan writers — as, for example, this:

> Give me but a little leave, and I will set before your eyes in brief a stupend, vast, infinite Ocean of incredible madness and folly: a Sea full of shelves and rocks, sands, gulfs, Euripuses, and contrary tides, full of calms, Halcyonian seas, unspeakable misery, such Comedies and Tragedies, such absurd and ridiculous, feral and lamentable fits, that I know not whether they are more to be pitied or derided, or may be believed, but that we daily see the same still practiced in our days, fresh examples, new news, fresh objects of misery and madness in this kind, that are still represented unto us, abroad, at home, in the midst of us, in our bosoms.

The first edition of this great and very odd conglomeration of a book appeared in 1621, a small thick quarto. Burton went on revising and enlarging his text, periodically releasing a new edition, until his death in 1640; the edition I read, the sixth, was based on notes and corrections that had been found among his papers and researches. It has been reprinted constantly ever since, and is much beloved and admired to this day by those who have discovered its peculiar charm.

And why mention it in a science fiction magazine?

Let me begin answering that question, which will probably take two columns, by sharing with you one of Burton's innumerable little offhand references, offered without footnote or explanation, to something strange and phenomenal: in discussing the wonders of science (in which he includes alchemy) he tells us, on page 462, of the great achievements of a certain Cornelius Drible, which included "a perpetual motion, inextinguible [sic] lights, incombustible cloth, with many such feats."

Cornelius Drible! Perpetual motion! Incombustible cloth! I had to know more. But Burton gives us not another syllable, so far as I am able to detect, about the astounding achievements of this great but obscure man of science.

I turned, of course, to Google. (Googling for Drible! There's a statement that would have made no sense at all just a few years ago.) Google, alas, failed me here. It did lead me to a 1621 play by Ben Jonson, *News from the New World Discovered in the Moon*, nearly as obscure as Drible himself, in which it is announced that exciting news has lately come from the Moon, "but not," the playwright says, "by way of Cornelius Agrippa [a 16th-century German alchemist, much quoted by Burton] or Cornelius Drible." A dead end, this, though plainly Drible was enough of a household name in Ben Jonson's time to merit such a casual mention on stage.

Well. Off I went to a more conventional source of information: Oxford University Press's five-volume *History of Technology* (1957), which told me nothing of Cornelius Drible but offered me, in Volume III, a couple of paragraphs on Cornelius Drebbel (1573-1633), a Dutchman living in London "whose inventions were extremely varied and attracted attention throughout Europe."

This had to be Burton's man — a victim of loose-jointed Elizabethan spelling of the sort that produced the "inextinguible" of a few paragraphs back. (Shakespeare himself seems to have spelled his own name in many different ways.) The Oxford History does not mention perpetual motion, but does credit Drebbel with "weapons devised for the Royal Navy, such as the flaming petards used off La Rochelle in 1628, a more economical method for making spirit of sulphur, thermostatic controls for chemical furnaces and incubators, and new processes for dyeing."

Hot on the trail of Mynheer Drebbel now, I turned next to my trusty Eleventh Edition *Encyclopaedia Britannica* (1911), the truest compendium of all knowledge, which told me that Drebbel, in 1630, had accidentally discovered the secret of dyeing wool a brilliant scarlet by means of adding cochineal to a solution of nitric acid and tin, an interesting datum but, well, not greatly exciting. It was from a later edition of the *Britannica*, the Fourteenth (1968), that I harvested the fact that among my man Drebbel's other inventions was nothing less than the first submarine.

He built it in 1620, a small craft consisting of a hull of greased leather over a wooden frame, and tested it in the Thames at depths of twelve to fifteen feet. Oars extending through tightly sealed flaps in its sides were the means of propulsion. Air tubes leading to the surface provided the passengers with oxygen. Over the next four years he built two somewhat larger models, and no less a personage than King James I is said to have gone for a brief ride in one.

A man who could invent a submarine in the seventeenth century could surely have taken a crack at a perpetual-motion machine, too, and so, armed now with the correct spelling of his name, I returned to Google and quickly turned up all the Drebbel information I sought, by way of the Cornelius

Drebbel web site that the University of Twente in the Netherlands maintains in his honor. A Dutchman, he was, yes, who in his youth was apprenticed to the famous engraver and alchemist Hendrick Goltzius. While with Goltzius he developed an interest in chemistry and mechanical devices, and in 1598, at the age of twenty-five, did indeed invent what might well be called a sort of perpetual-motion machine.

It was, in fact, a clock, built around a sealed glass vial containing water. Changes in atmospheric pressure caused the liquid to expand and contract, powering an arrangement of gears that would constantly rewind the clock. Ingenious, all right, although not really a device from which energy could perpetually be extracted without new input, which is what a true perpetual-motion machine ought to do. Nor have I been able to find anything about his inextinguible lights or his incombustible cloth. Drebbel's clock, though, was clever enough so that King James, upon learning of it, brought him to England in 1604, primarily to be a technician in charge of the royal fireworks displays. But he tinkered with all sorts of devices, most notably a temperature regulator for ovens and furnaces that worked on the same closed-system principle as the clock. This he later developed into an incubator for hatching duck and chicken eggs that made use of what we now know as negative feedback to operate what seems to be the earliest known thermostat: when the temperature within the incubator rose beyond the desired level, air expanded, causing a blob of mercury to close a damper. When the air cooled again, the damper opened to admit more heat.

This versatile man moved along to the court of the Emperor Rudolf II in 1610 to take the post of chief alchemist, but the onset of the Thirty Years' War sent him hastily back to London a few years later. There he devoted himself to projects for draining swamps, designed his submarines, and produced some improvements on the compound microscope, which had been invented thirty years before by a fellow Dutchman, Zacharias Janssen. Then there was Drebbel's magic lantern for projecting images, his machine for grinding lenses, his telescope, his process for producing sulphuric acid —

And yet, for all this phenomenal display of technological genius, Cornelius Drebbel, who did not, alas, invent a perpetual-motion machine after all but who does deserve credit for the submarine and the thermostat, is today all but unknown outside his native land (though he does, at least, have a lunar crater named for him). But for that chance one-sentence reference in *The Anatomy of Melancholy*, his name would never have crossed my path. And, of course, this description of my quest for Burton's Cornelius Drible has distracted me from telling you more about Robert Burton and his marvelous book. But such a digression is in itself perfectly Burtonian. More about *The Anatomy of Melancholy* next time.

Asimov's Science Fiction, August, 2005

Robert Burton, Anatomist of Melancholy

I SPOKE LAST TIME ABOUT ROBERT BURTON'S **THE ANATOMY OF MELANCHOLY,** that marvelous Elizabethan book which under the pretext of exploring the subject of depression gives us an astonishing 900-page survey of virtually all of the science and pseudo-science of its era. But I barely scratched the surface of this lively, irrepressible, and wholly enthralling old tome.

I quoted in that column, and will again now, this description of intention that Burton provides, a choice example of his resonant Elizabethan prose and a fitting characterization both of his purpose and his style:

> Give me but a little leave, and I will set before your eyes in brief a stupend, vast, infinite Ocean of incredible madness and folly: a Sea full of shelves and rocks, sands, gulfs, Euripuses, and contrary tides, full of calms, Halcyonian seas, unspeakable misery, such Comedies and Tragedies, such absurd and ridiculous, feral and lamentable fits, that I know not whether they are more to be pitied or derided, or may be believed, but that we daily see the same still practiced in our days, fresh examples, new news, fresh objects of misery and madness in this kind, that are still represented unto us, abroad, at home, in the midst of us, in our bosoms.

This curious man, who lived a cloistered life as an Oxford scholar from 1593 until his death in 1640, must have read every book in the great university's libraries, combing their pages for pertinent lore on the subject of melancholy and how to escape it. His sources are myriad, from the most ancient writings to the most recent and, as he tells us on an early page, "A dwarf standing on the shoulders of a Giant may see farther than a Giant himself." (This familiar phrase he credits to one Didacus Stella, author of a volume of Biblical commentary.) Burton's text is a colossal webwork of quotations, assembled into a complex structure divided into a number of "partitions," each made up of "sections," "members," and "subsections," along with three long essays labeled "digressions," the whole thing intricately woven together by thoughtful, wry, and frequently profound observations of his own.

To provide an anatomy of melancholy he says he must first provide an anatomy of physiology, for mental states have their origin in the body's own substance. Here he brings forth the old theory of the four humors of the body — blood, phlegm, bile, and serum — and gives particular attention to "black bile," which was supposed to bring about melancholy. This part of the book becomes a long (and, to us, exceedingly quaint) treatise on melancholy's causes, symptoms, and prognosis, all of it now wholly obsolete medically, and much of it cryptic and even opaque to modern readers — but much is charming and fascinating. (Hypochondria, he tells us, is called that because it is an ailment of the "hypochondries," the section of the abdomen that contains the liver and the spleen: even this propensity for imaginary maladies is thus shown to have a physiological origin.)

Once he is done with his great jumble of anatomical material, assigning different types of melancholy to different sectors of the body, Burton launches into a section on curing these many varieties of depression, and here we get a summary of seventeenth-century medical practices, which of course includes a good deal of what we would now call magic. This disquisition requires him to examine whether magic actually does work, and he adduces such authorities, no longer known to us, as Caelius, Delrio, Libanius, and Lemnius, who "deny that Spirits or Devils have any power over us, and refer all to natural causes and humours." But then, ever fairminded, he refers us to a second crew of experts — Paracelsus, Agrippa, Pliny, Oswoldus Crollius, Dr. Flud, etc. — who have demonstrated magic's efficacious nature: "They can make fire it shall not burn, fetch back thieves or stolen goods, show their absent faces in a glass, make serpents lie still, stanch blood, salve gouts, epilepsies, bitings of mad dogs, toothache, melancholy, and all the ills of the world, make men immortal, young again, as the Spanish Marquess is said to have done by one of his slaves. . . ." And so on for quite some length.

From there we go to an extensive catalog of medicines, which at times takes on a poetic tone that reminds me of Jack Vance at his best. One kind of melancholy, he says, is caused by "wind within the hypochondries" that must be expelled, and his long list of specifics for this problem include Bezoar Stone, Calaminth, Grain of Paradise, the Blessed Laxative, the Electuary of Laurel, the Powder Against Flatulence, the Florentian Antidote, the Charming Powder, Aromatic Rose Wine, Oil of Spikenard, and Aristolochy, though care must be taken in their use "so that they do not inflame the blood and increase the disease." We are told also of the use of "fomentations, irrigations, inunctions, odoraments," and other treatments for the head and stomach, the value of bloodletting, of applying medicines against the skin, of curing shyness and blushing with a mixture of white lead, camphire, water of nightshade, and nenuphar (or, says another authority he quotes, with water containing frogs' eggs) — on and on and on, a grand melange of what we now know to be, mostly, nonsense. But what glorious nonsense!

And what glorious sidebars he provides along the way. We are informed at one point, with Galileo and Kepler as the source, that heaven is 170,000,803 miles from the Earth, so that a stone dropped from the stars and traveling one hundred miles an hour would take sixty-five years, or more, before it touched ground. (Would it? I haven't checked the arithmetic.) We are told, apropos of a discussion of madness, "that lovers are mad, I think no man will deny. To love and be wise, why, Jupiter himself cannot intend both at once. . . . Love is madness, a hell, an incurable disease." We are told, in passing, of Cornelius Drible's perpetual-motion machine, about which I wrote last issue. On a nearby page a footnote lets us know about the robot that the philosopher Albertus Magnus constructed in the thirteenth century, given to us in this quotation from William Godwin's *Lives of the Necromancers:*

> It is related of Albertus that he made an entire man of brass, putting together his limbs under various constellations, and occupying no less than thirty years in its formation. This man would answer all sorts of questions, and was even employed as a domestic. But at length it is said to have become so garrulous that Thomas Aquinas, a pupil of Albertus, finding himself disturbed perpetually by its uncontrollable loquacity, caught up a hammer and beat it to pieces.

Albertus' robot, I like to believe, was governed by the Asimovian Laws of Robotics, and thus made no attempt to defend itself against Aquinas' assault — for otherwise theologians these nine centuries past would have had to get along without the Angelic Doctor's magisterial Summa Theologica, which I assume he was in the process of writing when the annoyingly gabby robot came along to distract him.

Back to Burton, though. Here we have him, in a lengthy analysis of human love that takes in both its great benefits and its pathological transformations, offering us a diet to promote chastity, embracing such foods as "Cowcumbers, Melons, Purselan, Water-Lilies, Rue, Woodbine, Ammi, Lettice, which Lemnius so much commends, and Vitex before the rest, which, saith Magninus, hath a wonderful virtue in it." He quotes Amatus Lusitanus on the subject of "a young Jew that was almost mad for Love," and was cured "with the syrup of Hellebore, and such other evacuations and purges, which are usually prescribed to black choler." There are plenty of other remedies for excessive lust here — pages and pages of them — but, of course, Burton being Burton, we are given a good many cures for impotence as well, since he brings himself ultimately to the conclusion that the best cure for love-melancholy is the fulfillment of desire.

Religious belief, too, can bring on a kind of melancholy, Burton says, in the last and perhaps most startling section of his enormous book. He does not, of course, attack the Church of England, for in his day such an attack would surely have cost him his livelihood (his income came mainly from the various church offices that he held) and perhaps his life. But how scathingly does he write of other religions! After citing "the Mahometan Priests, so cunningly can they gull the commons in all places and Countries," he levels his big guns against "that High Priest of Rome, the dam of that monstrous and superstitious brood, the bull-bellowing Pope, which now rageth in the West, that three-headed Cerberus. Whose religion at this day is mere policy, a state wholly composed of superstition and wit, and needs nothing but wit and superstition to maintain it, that useth Colleges and religious houses to as good purpose as Forts and Castles, and doth more at this day by a company of scribbling Parasites, fiery-spirited Friars, Zealous Anchorites, hypocritical confessors, Janissary Jesuits...." and so on with mounting fury for some pages further.

He is an equal-opportunity chastiser of all religions but his own. The various pagan creeds get full attention and high eloquence. ("What shall be the end of Idolators, but to degenerate into sticks and stones? of such as worship these Heathen gods, for such gods are a kind of Devils, but to become devils themselves?" Then the back of his hand for the Jews: "No Nation under Heaven can be more sottish, ignorant, blind, superstitious, wilful, obstinate and peevish, tiring themselves with vain ceremonies to no purpose; he that shall but read their Rabbins' ridiculous Comments, their strange Interpretation of Scriptures, their absurd ceremonies, fables, childish tales, which they steadfastly believe, will think they be scarce rational creatures." And Islam, too: "Mahometans are a compound of Gentiles, Jews, and Christians, and so absurd in their ceremonies, as if they had taken that which is most sottish out of every one of them, full of idle fables in their superstitious law, their Alcoran itself a gallimaufry of lies, tales, ceremonies, traditions, precepts, stole from other sects, and confusedly heaped up to delude a company of rude and barbarous clowns...."

Give me no political correctness here. Burton lived four hundred years ago and we read him to discover the ideas that were current in his era, not to reinforce the attitudes of our own. His book is a masterpiece of strange folklore and forgotten erudition, couched in masterly Elizabethan prose. (He writes, he says, "as a river runs, sometimes precipitate and swift, then dull and slow; now direct, then per ambages; now deep, then shallow, now muddy, now clear; now broad, then narrow, doth my style flow; now serious, then light; now comical, then satiricale; now more elaborate, then remiss.... And if thou vouchsafe to read this treatise, it shall seem no otherwise to thee, than the way to an ordinary traveller, sometimes fair, sometimes foul, here champaign, there enclosed; barren in one place, better soil in another; by woods, groves, hills, dales, plains ....)"

I doubt that many of you will vouchsafe to read this treatise, the manifold wonders of which I have hardly begun to elicit here. But there's great richness in it for anyone seeking to explore the stranger byways of medieval human thought as it was understood in that most intellectually fertile place, seventeenth-century England.

Asimov's Science Fiction, **September, 2005**

Neque Illorum Ad Nos Pervenire Potest

NULLUS NOSTRUM AD ILLOS, GUILLAUME DE CONCHES WROTE FIVE CENTURIES ago, *neque illorum ad nos pervenire potest*. He was speaking of the supposed inhabitants of the Antipodes, the lands that lay beyond the fiery sea that was thought to cut Europe off from the as yet unexplored Southern Hemisphere, and what he was saying in that resonant Latin phrase was, "None of us can go to them, and none of them come to us."

But two centuries of bold maritime exploration by Vasco da Gama, Magellan, Francis Drake, and James Cook proved that no equatorial barriers of flame prevent us from reaching the antipodean regions of our planet. I have been there myself more than once, and also have beheld natives of such realms as Brazil, New Zealand, and South Africa moving freely in our own hemisphere.

So far as the inhabitants of other worlds of the universe go, however, the same situation seems to obtain as with the people of the Earth's southern regions in the days of Guillaume de Conches: None of us can go to them, and none of them come to us. And there's also the little question of whether the other worlds of the universe have any inhabitants in the first place.

Let us — please — quickly rule out Roswell, New Mexico, and all the rest of the UFO/little-green-men case histories. I'd like very much to believe that the universe is full of intelligent life-forms, and even that they've been paying us surreptitious visits over the last ten or fifteen thousand years, but there's a dire lack of proof that any such visits have ever taken place. (The testimony of your neighbor who was abducted by flying-saucer folk last Christmas doesn't constitute proof, in my book. If Isaac Asimov or Richard Feynman had ever reported being abducted, I might have taken a different stance. But they didn't.)

The best case for the existence of extraterrestrial life is the statistical one, set forth as early as 300 BC by Metrodoros the Epicurean: "To consider the Earth the only populated world in infinite space is as absurd as to assert that in an entire field sown with millet only one grain will grow." I find that notion highly plausible, although it does fly in the face of the traditional Christian belief that the creation of life has taken place only once, in the Garden of Eden, on Earth. For some fifteen hundred years it was deemed heretical, and downright dangerous, to disagree with that position. But after Copernicus, Kepler, and Galileo proved that the Earth is not in fact the center of the universe but merely one of many worlds, and the Church reluctantly began to accept the notion, serious speculation about the possibility of life on other worlds again became a widespread philosophical pastime.

Galileo didn't like the idea. In his Third Letter on Sunspots (1613) he denounced as "false and damnable" the thesis that Jupiter, Venus, Saturn, or our own Moon might be inhabited, and claimed he could prove he was right. But Kepler, in a little book called *Somnium* (published posthumously in 1634), suggested that the Moon might be inhabited. Bernard de Fontenelle's amusing *Conversations on the Plurality of Worlds* (1686) offered imaginative descriptions of the beings that might be found on our neighboring planets. ("The people of Mercury are so full of fire that they are absolutely mad; I fancy they have no memory at all . . . and what they do is by sudden starts, and perfectly haphazard. . . . As for Saturn, it is so cold that a Saturnian brought to Earth would perish from the heat, even at the North Pole.")

We know today that life of any sort beyond the level of one-celled organisms is unlikely to the point of impossibility elsewhere in our solar system. Water in liquid form is essential to life as we understand it: Mercury and Venus are too hot for water to remain liquid, Jupiter and the other outer plants too cold, and Mars, though it has a feasible temperature range, seems waterless, or nearly so. But that still leaves the rest of the universe, which brings us back to the irrefutable statement of Metrodoros the Epicurean. The universe is infinite. Our galaxy alone contains some one hundred billion stars; and our galaxy is but one out of many millions of star-clusters, each with its own billions of suns. That an infinite universe would contain only one inhabited world is a very hard proposition to defend except by recourse to religious dogma.

Frank Drake of Project Ozma, a pioneering attempt to use radio telescopes to pick up signals from extraterrestrial civilizations, calculated around 1960 that there could be ten thousand advanced civilizations capable of sending radio signals in the Milky Way galaxy alone. Carl Sagan later raised the figure to a million. Most — not all — astronomers agree, especially now that the first hard evidence of the existence of extrasolar planets has finally been secured. (The skeptics include paleontologist Peter Ward and astronomer Donald Browlee, whose recent book, *Rare Earth*, argues that problems involving hard radiation and a dearth of essential chemicals render life impossible just about everywhere, our planet being the happy and perhaps unique exception.)

I'm with Frank Drake and Carl Sagan there. Our local galaxy, let alone the universe, is so huge that it's bound to have some inhabited worlds somewhere in it. Even when we eliminate all stars less than three fourths as massive as the sun, which would be too dim to sustain carbon–oxygen–water-based life on any planets they might have, and those so big that they would be too hot, and those that are astronomically unstable for one reason or another, that still leaves twelve billion stars in our galaxy alone.

If half of these have planets, and half of those planets lie at the correct distance to maintain water in its liquid state, and half of those are large enough to retain an atmosphere, that leaves us with a billion and a half potentially habitable worlds in our immediate galactic vicinity. Say that a billion of these must be rejected because they're so large that gravity would be a problem, or because they have no water, or because they're in some other way unsuitable. That still leaves five hundred million possible Earths in the Milky Way galaxy. And there are millions of galaxies.

For forty years now we've been earnestly searching for signs that our galactic neighbors exist. SETI — the Search for Extraterrestrial Intelligence — is the overall label for the quest, and a SETI project now is under way to put together a twenty-five million dollar array of radio telescopes in Shasta County, California, that will be able to monitor two hundred and fifty million channels of radio signals simultaneously, in the hope that there will be, somewhere amidst the noise that comes from space, a message that says, "We are here — where are you?" And that is not the only such operation under way.

There's a big problem, though — the same one that makes actual face-to-face contact with extrasolar civilizations improbable to the point of impossibility. That is the size of the universe. The star nearest us — Proxima Centauri — is four light-years away. So any message sent to us by the good folks of Proxima Centauri would take four years to get here, traveling at the 186,000-mile-per-second speed of light. A message from the closest galaxy, the Magellanic Clouds, would require 200,000 years to arrive.

There's no way around these constraints. Despite the various lovely gimmicks that science fiction writers love to invent, the speed of light seems to be the absolute limit for any kind of message transmission.

The same limit applies to spaceships traveling between the stars — not that we're able yet to build vehicles that could travel at or near the speed of light. (A Saturn V rocket could lift a ten-ton truck and ship it to Proxima Centauri right now, but it would take half a million years to get there.)

As for the faster-than-light vehicles that make the galactic empires of Isaac Asimov and Frank Herbert and E.E. "Doc" Smith possible, forget about them. They're pure fantasies, mere literary conveniences. Without them, we would never have had *Dune* or the Foundation books or the Lensman series, or any of the myriad other wonderful tales of space adventure that we love to read. But not even Messrs. Asimov, Herbert, or Smith really believed that faster-than-light travel would actually ever happen.

If we accept the speed of light as the limiting velocity of the universe

— and we are verging into the realm of magical thinking when we don't — then SETI is up against the nasty probability that even if the universe is swarming with intelligent species eager to send us messages, none of them may be located within usable radio range. Consider that Earth, which is known to be an inhabited planet, needed billions of years to produce a race that was capable of exploiting the radio frequencies, and got to that point, finally, less than a hundred years ago. What if we are absolutely surrounded by stars with habitable worlds, but none of their inhabitants have yet attained the ability to send or receive radio messages?

Contrariwise, what if all the radio-savvy civilizations are half a million light-years away, or farther? In that case, radio transmissions that were sent this way during the heyday of Neanderthal man are still hundreds of thousands of years out in space, beyond the reach of SETI's antennas. Then, too, what about all those civilizations that completed the entire journey from savagery to technological supremacy to extinction three million years ago, or three billion, and whose jolly messages, patiently coming our way at 186,000 miles a second, will turn up on our radio telescopes far in the future, when we ourselves may not be around any longer? Even if we're still here, what will be the point of replying?

It's disheartening. I've spent five decades writing stories about other worlds and other intelligent life-forms, and I don't like the idea that I've simply been peddling pipe dreams all this time. I do believe, with Metrodoros the Epicurean, that the universe is full of populated worlds. I do want to know what those alien races look like, how they think, what kind of cities they live in. I'd love to read alien poetry and look at alien sculptures. I might even want to risk dinner at a five-star alien restaurant. But none of that is going to happen.

The best-case scenario is that the SETI people somehow will be able, sooner or later, to detect, extract, and decode an intelligible message from another world. But that's as far as we're ever going to get, I'm afraid, in interstellar relations. The distances are too vast, and the means of transportation and communication too slow. The speed of light is going to remain the limiting velocity not just for us, but for all those lively and interesting people out there in the adjacent galaxies, and that puts the kibosh on the whole concept of a galaxy-spanning civilization.

So there won't be any Galactic Federation; there'll be no Bureau of Interstellar Trade; no alien wines or artifacts will turn up for sale in our boutiques. Nor will we meet the real-life equivalents of George Lucas's Wookiees, Doc Smith's Arisians, Fred Pohl's Heechees, Larry Niven's Kzinti, or — just as well, perhaps — A.E. van Vogt's terrifying Coeurl. The aliens are out there, I'm sure, but the sea that separates us from them, and them from us, is just too wide. *Nullus nostrum ad illos, neque illorum ad nos pervenire potest.* None of us can go to them, and none of them come to us.

Asimov's Science Fiction, January, 2004

Tracking Down the Ancestors

I'VE SPENT MOST OF MY PROFESSIONAL LIFE THINKING ABOUT THE FUTURE, but lately it's the past that's been on my mind — specifically, my own family tree. I know next to nothing about my ancestors. Both my mother's family and my father's came to the United States as part of that great migration of European Jews to the New World that took place in the late nineteenth and early twentieth centuries: my father's family, like Isaac Asimov's, originated in Russia, and my mother's in a part of Poland that was then under the rule of the Austro-Hungarian Empire. Neither of those countries kept very careful genealogical records of Jews, who were not regarded as full citizens, and many of such sketchy records as did exist were destroyed in World War II.

So what little information I have about my ancestors goes back no farther than my grandparents' generation — people born in the 1870s and 1880s. Three of my grandparents — my father's mother and both of my mother's parents — lived on into my adulthood. But my father's father died before I was born, and I didn't even know his first name until a couple of years ago, when I found it among my late father's papers while searching for my own birth certificate. Beyond that all is darkness.

Last week, spurred by some sudden genealogical curiosity, I phoned my only living relative of a previous generation — my mother's younger sister, who is now eighty-four years old — and asked her about the names of *her* grandparents. She turned out to have no information about her father's side of the family, since they all stayed in Europe except for her father, my grandfather. But she was, at least, able to tell me the names of her maternal grandparents and a little bit about them. (They both died in the early 1930s, before I was born.)

That's probably about as far as my researches into the past are going to go — the Silverberg side of my ancestry will remain a mystery except for my paternal grandmother's first name, and I will know a tiny bit more, but not much, about my mother's family. Other Americans, of course, those who are descended from Western European ancestors, particularly English ones, have access to much more information. My wife Karen's stepmother, for instance, is a Mayflower descendant and a Daughter of the American Revolution; she still lives in a house that has been in her family's possession for two hundred years. On the other hand, her second husband, Karen's father, was one of those Jews brought from Europe to the New World as children who never even knew the names of their own grandparents.

Then there is my friend Hilary Benford, the sister-in-law of science fiction writer Gregory Benford, who has compiled a Benford family tree going back to the seventeenth century. Greg and his twin brother Jim are descended from British settlers of the American South, and so their family history has been relatively easy to trace. I have a printout of it on my desk. You will be interested to know, I hope, that the ancestors of the author of the Galactic Center novels include such people as America Jefferson Benford, Alabama Nelson, Robert E. Lee Nelson, Philpott Marquis Karner, Tatum Shalisa Benford, Meantha Matilda Wabbington, Hassell Nimrod Callaway, Druid Jones, and Crulius J. Styron. (Hilary insists that she has not made any of these names up, and I suppose I must believe her. But, really — *Crulius J. Styron?*)

I feel vaguely envious of the Benford ancestral list, which fills seven pages. (Opal Minnie May Benford! Caledonia Styron! Cicero Amos Nelson!) But actually it's a pretty minor deal compared with that of the British royal family, which goes back to William the Conqueror and onward into the past to the first Dukes of Normandy. There is many a twist and turn in that genealogy, naturally — the present crop of royals is descended from a German branch of the family, and before them came the Stuarts, a bunch of Scots, and their cousins the Tudors who ruled before them were Welsh, etc., etc. Still, William's blood flowed in them all. And even the British line is small potatoes next to that of the reigning dynasty of Japan, which claims descent from the prehistoric sun-goddess Amaterasu. Since even the Japanese concede that Amaterasu is a mythical figure, the claim to an unbroken line of descent may be a bit tenuous, but I, with my pitiful three and a half generations of genealogical information, am certainly in no position to challenge it.

Now, though, comes an opportunity for all of us, not just the British and Japanese royals, or the Benfords and genealogically impoverished people like me, to trace our ancestries clear back to paleolithic times. Imagine it — a family tree stretching fifty thousand years or more into the past! (What if I discover that I'm a distant cousin of Queen Elizabeth? What if the Queen locates a Neanderthal branch of the Plantagenet line? What were the first names of the Cro-Magnon Benfords? Fun and surprises for us all.)

The benefactors who hope to create this fount of information for us are of impeccable lineage themselves: nobody less than the National Geographic

Society and the IBM Corporation. The project will be aided by such institutions as the Laboratory of Human Population Genetics in Moscow, the Center for Excellence in Genomic Sciences in India, and the Center for Genome Information at the University of Cincinnati. Together, these groups will seek to assemble, over the next five years, a gigantic genetic database that will use thousands of DNA samples to track the routes of ancient migratory peoples out of the ancestral human home in East Africa and onward to Europe, Asia, and eventually the Alabama of the Benfords and the New York of the Silverbergs and Asimovs.

The plan is to collect one hundred thousand blood samples from indigenous peoples around the world for genetic analysis. ("Indigenous peoples" are what the *National Geographic Magazine* used to call "natives." "Indigenous" means "native to," but we can't call them "natives" any more, just "indigenous peoples," through the same mystifying semantic process of political correctness that makes "colored person" improper and "person of color" acceptable.) The DNA information from this database will, it is hoped, provide a picture of early human migration routes throughout the world

How do you and I and the Benfords enter into this? Well, for $99.95 any of us can obtain a DNA kit from the *National Geographic* — two swabs and a pair of plastic vials. You scrape a few cells from the inner wall of your cheek and mail them in, and the researchers will locate your position on the ancestral human family tree that is now under construction out of the samples being taken from the indigenous peoples. The money paid for these kits will go to finance the indigenous-population research (and, we are assured, a portion will be set aside for a fund that will help to preserve their cultures).

Some migratory paths have already been mapped. About fifty thousand years ago, men with the Y chromosome marker known as M168 (women do not have Y chromosomes) headed north out of East Africa. Some fifty centuries later these wanderers generated the M89 mutation while living in Arabia. That genetic marker still can be traced via Central Asia into Europe, and is found in many modern men of European descent.

The new human-genome project hopes to uncover many more such migratory-route markers, and thereby to determine such things as the original home of the Chinese people or the location of the homeland of the Indo-European language from which most languages spoken in Europe, the Americas, and much of Asia are derived. Another possibility would be tracking the genetic path of the invading armies of Alexander the Great that swept through Persia, Afghanistan, and India twenty-four hundred years ago. Certain villages of fair-skinned people in northwestern India claim to be descended from Alexander's troops, but are they? DNA evidence may answer that question.

Naturally, this being the furiously politicized twenty-first century, no sooner was the project announced than it came under attack. Certain indigenous peoples believe that they have always lived in their present homelands, a fact that might not be borne out by DNA analysis. "We already know our history," said the leaders of one Northwest American Indian tribe in 1996, when an awkwardly non-Indian ancient human skeleton turned up near their reservation and scientists called for study of it. "It is passed on to us through our elders and through our religious practices. If this individual is truly over nine thousand years old, that only substantiates the belief that he is Native American. From our oral histories, we know that our people have been part of this land since the beginning of time." Plainly they won't be interested in cooperating with a project that might provide them with historical information about themselves that differs from their own tribal lore.

Certain self-styled advocates for indigenous folk also have assailed the enterprise, calling it a "vampire project" because it will extract valuable information from the blood of endangered tribes while offering nothing in return. People concerned with privacy issues are worried about having the information put to sinister commercial uses. Some anthropologists say that searching for genetic differences among populations is tantamount to racism. (Should we deny the existence of genetic differences between populations? Is it purely a matter of miraculous providence that so many tall blond people are indigenous to Scandinavia and so few to China?) And a few scientists are complaining that the samples collected will not be made available to every researcher who wants access to them, only to those who are part of the project.

Despite those arguments, I think much that is of great interest and importance can come from this work. I won't learn the names of my great-great-grandparents, but perhaps we'll find out at last whether *Homo sapiens* interbred with the Neanderthals, or whether European and Polynesian seamen reached the Americas in early prehistoric times, or where the aboriginal inhabitants of Australia came from.

On the other hand, I — who have managed to get along pretty well in life with scarcely a clue to my family history — wonder whether the chief outcome of the project may simply be a loud scientific and political uproar. I think I'll leave the final word here to that grand sage of science fiction, Robert A. Heinlein, who had this to say in *The Notebooks of Lazarus Long*: "This sad little lizard told me that he was a brontosaurus on his mother's side. I did not laugh; people who boast of ancestry often have little else to sustain them. Humoring them costs nothing and adds to happiness in a world in which happiness is always in short supply."

Asimov's Science Fiction, **April/May, 2006**

The Conquest of Space

I'M WRITING THIS JUST A COUPLE OF DAYS AFTER THE COLUMBIA SHUTTLE disaster, which of course will be old news by the time this reaches print, the magazine production process being what it is. Before you get to read this, we will already have been through a long, dreary business of explanations, recriminations, Congressional inquiries, and demands for a rethinking of our entire space-exploration program. There will have been, I'm sure, a moratorium on further shuttle flights while all this work of inquiry is going on, and a general hold on all NASA projects will probably still be in effect when this piece is published.

The most profound short-range effect, surely, will be on the astronaut program. Even today, barely forty-eight hours after the shuttle exploded over Texas, the lead article in the Wall Street Journal bears the headline, "Shuttle Crash Raises Questions About Future of Manned Flights," and begins, "Why is America still sending men and women into space?"

I hope I'm simply preaching to the converted here when I reply that the answer to the Journal's question, "Why?" is a simple "Why not?" A NASA flight controller quoted by the Journal gives a somewhat more elaborate answer: "The human race has been about exploration since it crawled out of the swamps on four legs. If you're not exploring, you're dying."

Makes sense to me, and probably to most of you, who wouldn't be reading science fiction if you didn't think the exploration of the cosmos was a worthwhile thing to do. But not to a substantial number of Americans who are asking, this morning, why we continue to risk precious human lives on something as remote from immediate everyday needs as trips into space, when robots and sensors could do the job just as well. (There are also, of course, plenty who are asking why we are bothering to spend money on space exploration at all, when there are so many dire problems still unsolved on Earth, etc., etc. A letter published today in the *New York Times* declares that the best possible outcome of the disaster would be the scrapping of the manned space program and the shifting of the billions of dollars thus saved to improving the science programs in our public schools. The best I can do in dealing with such remarks is to refer the anti-space people to the remarks of the NASA controller I quote above, and let them try to refute them. School science programs would not be well served by a curtailment of such a dramatic form of scientific research as the exploration of space.)

But this issue of risk —

We have become, it seems, a risk-averse nation. Last year's controversy over smallpox vaccination is a good example: until a generation ago, everyone was routinely vaccinated against smallpox in childhood, and, since smallpox thereby was driven from the world, vaccination was universally regarded as a Good Thing. Suddenly it has been made to seem terribly risky, and people are shrinking back in horror from the thought of submitting to it. Likewise, the expenditure of human lives even in the name of national defense is a controversial issue now, which is why we used local troops instead of our own when we were hunting Osama bin Laden in the mountains of Afghanistan in 2001, and why our earlier attempts at striking out at terrorist camps were conducted by high-flying planes and guided missiles instead of actual battalions of troops. We had scarcely any casualties in those various remote-control military campaigns, but also we accomplished very little of what we had hoped to achieve. Sometimes risk is necessary; sometimes lives have to be lost in the process of attaining important ends.

I don't like taking risks much, myself. I'm just a writer, not any kind of hero, and I wouldn't volunteer to take a ride in a space shuttle, any more than I'd like to be fighting in Iraq just now. (Isaac Asimov wasn't much of a warrior either, and wouldn't even travel in an airplane.)

Spaceships weren't meant to be piloted by timid people like Isaac and me, nor are battles won by the likes of us. But there are plenty of braver people around — like the seven Columbia astronauts — who have a different attitude toward risk. And we should not bar their way.

It is necessary, naturally, to distinguish between sensible risks and stupid ones. One good reason why we don't send manned expeditions to Jupiter is that an expedition that landed on Jupiter would have a non-debatable 0 percent chance of survival: Jupiter is a huge ball of nasty gases, with a massive hard core underneath that exerts a gravitational pull of enormous intensity. Any manned landing on Jupiter would be, in al-Qaeda's fascinating phrase, "a martyrdom operation." Nor do we yet even contemplate sending a spaceship of human observers on an orbital voyage around Jupiter, because such information as we have gathered so far from three and a half decades of manned space exploration indicates that weightlessness for the period of several years such a voyage would require would have serious debilitating effects on the voyager's skeletal structure.

We do know, though, that manned voyages to Mars, where gravity and a lethal atmospheric blanket would not be problems, would be possible using existing technology. Nobody's talking about doing it, because NASA says the cost of such a mission would be upward of half a trillion dollars, but because we have kept astronauts aloft for periods of time approximating the length of a Mars voyage we know that humans could make the trip without suffering undue bodily harm. The astronauts who stayed up there for those long-term tests understood that risk was involved. But they stayed, and their bones did not turn to Jell-O during their months in space, and now we know. Their courage laid the foundation for the next phase — however far in the future it now lies — of manned space exploration.

Those astronauts saw what they were doing as a sensible risk, with much to gain from success and a reasonable probability of avoiding calamity. So did the ones who perished in our two shuttle disasters. Discovery is always a gamble. Columbus made it back alive from his journey to the West Indies, but Magellan didn't survive his historic voyage of circumnavigation; Captain Cook also died at sea, but not before he, like Magellan, had ventured deep into unknown waters and vastly increased our understanding of our planet's southern hemisphere. Many another explorer took similar gambles and lost — but it was the rest of us who gained from their sacrifices.

If we look at the early history of aviation — the dawn of manned flight — we see a horrendous record of human casualties. Orville and Wilbur Wright were the first to fly a mechanically powered heavier-than-air vehicle, traveling 852 feet in 59 seconds and landing safely. That was in 1903. It was not until five years later that the first airplane fatality occurred, when Lieutenant Thomas Selfridge of the U.S. Army Signal Corps, flying as Orville Wright's passenger, was killed when a propeller malfunction caused the plane to crash. (Wright survived.) But then, as aviators began to attempt more elaborate exploits, the fatalities came thick and fast. In 1909 a French aviator, Eugene Lefebvre, was killed while flying a Wright plane. Edouard Nieuport, who designed the first workable single-wing plane, died in a plane crash in 1911; his brother Charles met the same fate in 1913. Charles Stewart Rolls, in 1910 the first aviator to make a round-trip flight across the English channel, died a month later while competing in an air race. George Chavez, who made the first flight over the Alps the same year, died as a result of injuries sustained while landing. John B. Moisant, who accomplished the first Paris-London flight in September, 1910, died a few months later while flying at New Orleans. Eugene Ely, who in 1910 took off from the deck of a cruiser anchored in the Atlantic and flew to land, and two months later set out from San Francisco and landed successfully on the deck of a battleship in the Pacific, thus making the first ship-to-shore and shore-to-ship flights, was killed in another flight soon after. Harriet Quimby, the first American woman pilot and the first woman to fly the English Channel, in 1912, died three months later while flying over Boston Harbor. And so on and so on — a lengthy tragic roster of pioneer mortality.

Since aviation was obviously so dangerous, it was banned by international treaty in 1913, right? Which is why American science fiction fans will have to make a five-day-long sea journey in 2005 if they want to get to the World Science Fiction Convention in Glasgow, Scotland, and why you will take the train from Atlanta to Phoenix to visit your parents next Thanksgiving.

Were the early aviators crazy to take the risks they did? No. Were they enormously brave? Absolutely. The brave shuttle astronauts weren't crazy, either. They measured the risks against the rewards, and made a decision to go. (The odds were with them, too. We have had only two catastrophic failures in 113 shuttle flights. Going up in a rickety 1910 airplane was far riskier than that.)

The problem today is the national notion we have developed that Risk Is Bad, and, since space flight currently is a government monopoly and government officials don't like to upset the voters, we must now go through a vast therapeutic process of inquiry and reassurance before the dreadful risks of manned space travel can be allowed again. The aviators of 1910 were free to put their own lives on the line without taking public-opinion polls.

I know there are many who think we can continue our space program using nothing but robots and computers. "Manned space flights are more about capturing the public's imagination than science," one space historian has already said. "It's circus, it's just pure circus." Maybe so; but I don't think capturing the public's attention with romantic acts of bravery is always such a contemptible thing. Nor do I believe unmanned exploration is the right way to do the job. In the end, human perceptions, human decision-making, human descriptive abilities, are what will serve as the goads that get us out into the universe, not readouts from sensors, probes, and robot eyes.

Of course manned flight into space is going to get started again, sooner or later, once the current anguished debate dies down. (For one thing, the expensive international space station now up there can't function without humans aboard. Do we just write it off? For that matter, who's going to rescue the three astronauts currently living there?) Space flight will resume under NASA auspices after a time, or it will start up through private financing. (Or even that of some other country. What a nice public-relations coup for twenty-first-century China to put the first astronauts on Mars!) But how sad that the issue of continuing into space should arise at all, simply because seven brave explorers lost their lives. To shut down manned space flight because it is too risky would be to say that those seven died in vain. It's the first step in a path of de-evolution that will take us back to those swamps.

Asimov's Science Fiction, **June, 2003**

Mars, Incorporated

RAY BRADBURY'S 1950 BOOK **The Martian Chronicles**, fifty years prescient, gave us a warning of what was going to happen to the Mars Polar Lander.

In his classic tale of the exploration and ultimate colonization of Mars, Bradbury picked the year 1999 for the first expeditions to Mars: manned expeditions, not robot ones, because it had not occurred to anybody back then that after sending manned missions as far as the moon as early as the 1960s, we would arbitrarily pull back from all manned exploration of space other than timid orbital excursions just outside Earth's own atmosphere.

The first Bradbury Mars expedition carries just two astronauts, Nathaniel York and his friend Bert. They come down through the blue sky of Mars and land near a house of crystal pillars by the edge of an empty sea. The two Martians who live there, gentle people named Mr. and Mrs. K., have previously discussed the possibility that there might be intelligent life living on the third planet. "The third planet is incapable of supporting life," says Mr. K. "There's far too much oxygen in their atmosphere." Mrs. K., though, has a vision of the astronauts, eerie creatures with black hair and blue eyes, turning up at their doorstep. Sure enough, the ship lands. Mr. K. gets his hunting rifle and deals with the monsters from the third planet before they can cause any trouble.

A second expedition from Earth, Bradbury tells us, shows up a few months later. It meets a sad end too. The Martian psychologist who interviews them tells them that their talk of having come in a tin ship from the third planet shows that they are obviously insane, and he puts them out of their misery.

When the third expedition lands in April of 2000, it is taken care of just as — well, expeditiously — by the Martians, who flange up a Disneyland version of a generic midwestern town to lull the sixteen Earthmen into complacency, and then go after them with knives. But the Earth of Bradbury's *Martian Chronicles* is a persistent place; despite three straight catastrophes, a fourth expedition goes out in June 2001, finds that chicken pox brought by the earlier human visitors has killed the Martians off, and the colonization of the red planet proceeds smoothly thereafter.

Ray Bradbury never pretended to go in for scientific verisimilitude. His stories are fables, not attempts at serious prediction. By inventing a race of Martians that he knew could not possibly exist, he provided himself with a vehicle for commenting, through parable and fantasy, on the nature of humanity itself. No reader of his haunting, unforgettable book will raise the objection that Mars is incapable of sustaining life beyond the bacterial level.

The really big implausibility of the book, we now are able to see, has to do with our persistence in sending out expedition after expedition. Fifty years ago, Bradbury perceived us as a nation of risk-takers, expanding ever outward in a reckless Renaissance manner. He failed entirely to foresee the innate pusillanimity of a society governed by public-opinion polls. If we really had sent three manned expeditions to Mars and they all had met with terrible fates, would any government official take the risk of sending a fourth? You know the answer to that one.

So here we are in 2000 AD, sending missions to Mars: robotic landing devices, slapped together for minimal sums of money so as not to arouse taxpayer ire. I doubt that the Polar Lander, which vanished without a trace last December, was seized and dismantled by a team of Bradburian Martians, but the fact remains that the thing did disappear, and we will never know why, because an unmanned spaceship tells no tales. Did it, as some think, fall into a canyon a mile deep that happened to be adjacent to the chosen landing site? Did it explode while descending? Or did it simply make a rough landing that destroyed its ability to communicate with us? Who knows?

The Polar Lander cost $165 million. That may sound like a lot, but actually is only a pittance as spacecraft costs go. The project was put together on a stripped-down budget, with every cuttable corner being cut. (Previous similar missions had had an operations staff of about 200; this one had less than 80. A single vehicle was sent, though previous robotic spacecraft went out in pairs to increase the likelihood that one would get there. And so on.) It turns out to have been false economy: NASA's return on its investment was zero. Another $100 million, perhaps, might have provided us with a harvest of invaluable scientific data about the Martian atmosphere and the possibility of frozen water beneath Mars's south pole. Instead we got nothing. A few months before the Polar Lander failure, the Mars Climate Orbiter zeroed out also because of a little matter of faulty metric-system conversion. We were doing all this a lot better as far back as 1976, when the Viking missions to Mars produced an abundance of precious information, and Voyager 2 set out on its 12-year journey to Jupiter, Saturn, Uranus, and Neptune.

The problem is not sudden mysterious incompetence on NASA's part — not at all — but the reluctance of American politicians, at a time of the greatest prosperity in our nation's history, to spend any money on space. At its peak in 1965, when Cold War rivalries were driving us to get to the Moon before the Soviets did, NASA consumed almost five percent of the federal budget. It makes do on a bare fraction of that now. With the Soviet Union gone, the government lacks any convenient pretext for a space program. And in any case there's much more political benefit to be gained by deploying tax funds for education, social programs, the very muddled but universally applauded notion of "saving" social security, and even the paying off of the national debt, than there is in sending rocketships off into the cosmos. And — since space exploration is an inherently dangerous enterprise, in which some actual men and women have already been killed, very few politicos feel like lending their support to programs that will sooner or later lead to nasty catastrophes followed by unpleasant Congressional inquiries.

So what we have now is a bare-bones NASA budget that allows for occasional unmanned space flights, more often than not unsuccessful, and sporadic and increasingly pointless jaunts in the space shuttle. Where are the moon bases, the orbital space stations, the domed colonies on Mars, the mining outposts in the asteroid belt, that were depicted in the imaginary twenty-first century worlds of such writers as Robert Heinlein, Jack Williamson, Isaac Asimov, and Arthur Clarke? The Age of Space, it seems was something that entirely took place between Neil Armstrong's one giant step in 1969 and the end of the Apollo program three years later. Can that be? Is the whole thing over, only moments after it began?

I don't think so. I think that vast expansion of humanity into the universe, an idea that was so thrilling to young science fiction readers like me half a century ago, is something that *will* happen, and surprisingly soon. All that's needed is some rethinking of policies and redirection of priorities. Let us put NASA to rest, with appropriate applause for the wonderful work it did during the pioneering decades of our adventure into space, and let the good old profit motive be the sparkplug that drives us onward and outward.

I propose the Internet as the model here. It began, you recall, as ARPAnet, a Defense Department communications network linking vast mainframe computers. The intention was to decentralize American military research as a safeguard against nuclear attack. This evolved, eventually, into NSFnet, a linkage of university supercomputers for the transmission of scientific papers, with the military developing a second net for its own use. Then came the navigation-protocol software that created the World Wide Web, and the browsers that made it possible to surf it, and — well, the rest is e-history. The military folks who dreamed up ARPAnet did not suspect that their invention would lead within twenty years to a total revolution in commerce, communications, and entertainment, out of which colossal new economic growth would emerge overnight.

No single private entrepreneur, not even Microsoft or IBM, could have constructed the Internet from scratch. But once a computer-linking infrastructure had been built to meet military needs, and a group of (largely government-supported) academic research organizations had added its own intellectual input, the framework was in place for a worldwide system of computer communication open to everyone. It swiftly became privatized: the amazon.coms, the Yahoos, the eBays, the AOLs of the new Internet industry have conjured up a world-transforming dot.com revolution out of a chain of servers and modems in no time at all.

Let the development of space go the same way! NASA did a splendid job of coordinating a host of disparate private contractors who provided the hardware that took us to the Moon three decades ago. It took on projects that no private business could have afforded to tackle, thus laying the foundation for modern commercial space applications like the communications satellites and mapping satellites that have become essential to modern life. It deserves lusty applause for its pioneering work.

But now NASA has become an obstacle instead of a solution. Its largely contradictory mix of scientific and political purposes has left it inextricably tangled in Congressional fol-de-rol. By pricing its services unrealistically low, it throttles private competition (and initiative) at taxpayer expense. By limiting its projects only to those for which it's politically feasible to gain public approval, it hampers scientific adventurousness and finds itself settling for unrealistic lowest-cost options, of the sort that often end in calamities like the recent one on Mars.

It's time now for the next step: the privatization of NASA and the unfettered opening of space development to the profit motive. Commercial space tourism? Why not? Hotels on the Moon? Power stations in space? Raw materials towed back from the asteroids? The private sector can deal with all of that.

There is risk involved, of course. Great wads of investment capital will be required, and a lot of that will be lost — even as capital is lost every day in mundane projects that go astray. (Ask the Ford people about the Edsel!) Space vehicles will blow up; people will die. These things are inevitable in any kind of risk venture. Not all of the explorers who set out for the New World in the fifteenth and sixteenth centuries lived to come home and collect nice pensions. The bridges, tunnels, and railroads that linked the developing industrial countries of the nineteenth century cost lives to build. The aviation industry has not been without fatalities. And so on.

But so long as space research remains a *political* enterprise, a Cold War survival maintained mostly for reasons of national prestige, with every dollar that might bring more votes elsewhere begrudged and every nasty risk abjured, we will remain stymied. We will go on sending cheap-and-nasty turkeys off to uncertain fates on our neighboring worlds, and the grinning Martians will pounce on them and gleefully reduce them to scrap, and we'll never find out what went wrong. Meanwhile that fantastic future of space exploration that we all loved to read about in the science fiction magazines will remain just that forever: science fiction.

Galaxy Online, 2000

THREE
Being A Writer
_____

Building Worlds: Part I

THE JOB OF THE SCIENCE FICTION WRITER, LIKE THAT OF WRITERS of any other sort of fiction, is telling stories, that is, inventing characters and placing them in dramatic opposition to one another. The special task of the sf writer, though, is to supply not only the drama but also the stage: to build the entire set upon which one's characters act out their conflicting purposes. And so we must create not merely characters and plots but entire worlds.

That sounds like a god-sized assignment, and in a sense it is. Of course, our worlds are merely things set down on paper, and that spares us the considerable trouble of producing actual mountains and seas, skies and deserts, and all the other tangibilities, down to microbes and algae, that real gods must traffic in. We deal in the illusion of creating worlds, not in the worlds themselves. Even so, the job has to be done right or the illusion won't hold.

I can name any number of examples of the job done right: Hal Clement's Mesklin, Frank Herbert's Arrakis, Brian Aldiss' Helliconia, James Blish's Lithia, Ursula K. Le Guin's Gethen, Anne McCaffrey's Pern, Harry Harrison's Pyrrus, Larry Niven's Ringworld, Stanislaw Lem's Solaris, and on and on, an infinity of fictional worlds having little in common except plausibility and unforgettability. But how is it done? What factors must you consider, what knowledge must you have?

The place to start, I think, must be the physical characteristics of the world to be created: its size and mass, the nature of its sun and the imaginary world's distance from it, its gravitational pull, its period of revolution and axial rotation, its orbital tilt, the makeup of its atmosphere, its biochemistry, and so forth. From these things all else inevitably follows.

Two of our greatest practitioners of this area of the art of creating imaginary worlds were Poul Anderson and Hal Clement. These two grand masters had the playfully speculative cast of mind that any science fiction writer must have, but also the benefit of scientific educations that were both deep and broad, particularly in the areas of physics and chemistry, and their work demonstrated a degree of accomplishment in those aspects of world-building that most of us can only hope to approach. Both are now gone from us, but it's our great fortune that each of them left valuable essays on their working methods: Anderson in "The Creation of Imaginary Worlds" and Clement in "The Creation of Imaginary Beings," both published in *Science Fiction, Today and Tomorrow* (1974), edited by Reginald Bretnor. I urge anyone interested in knowing how worlds are built to seek out these magisterial texts. The Bretnor book is long out of print but readily available via second-hand channels. Most of its fifteen chapters are still relevant to modern sf writers, but two, the Anderson and the Clement, remain essential reading today.

Anderson focuses quickly on the importance of consistency of scientific logic: writers who arbitrarily cobble together worlds built out of incompatible factors risk forfeiting, at least to the scientifically informed reader, their plausibility in all other sectors of their stories, those involving such things as character, emotional texture, plot. Giving the example of a planet that circles a blue-white sun and has an atmosphere of hydrogen and fluorine, Anderson says, "This is simply a chemical impossibility. Those two substances, under the impetus of that radiation, would unite promptly and explosively." Blue-white stars are too hot to be surrounded by inhabited planets of any sort: they burn so fiercely that they don't last long enough for planets to develop around them, let alone for life to evolve on those planets. He deals similarly with red giants, white dwarfs, variable stars, and other sorts of stellar bodies unsuitable for the creation of habitable worlds, pointing out the problems inherent in choosing such familiar stars as Sirius, Vega, Antares, or Mira as settings for stories. Those stars are familiar to us because they shine brightly in our own sky, but for half a dozen different reasons it is not the most luminous stars that will be found to have inhabited worlds. By running through the stations of the stellar temperature-luminosity chart, Anderson explains how to select (or invent) a star that would be likely to provide worlds useful to the storyteller. He does point out that any sufficiently ingenious writer can make use of any kind of star for story purposes: the thing to avoid is unknowingly to place your fictional world around a star that can't possibly have planets, or to postulate intelligent life on a world where no life of any sort could exist.

With these limitations having been invoked, Poul goes on to remind us that a planet's distance from its sun affects its climate, that its mass and size and density determine its gravitational pull, that the presence or absence of moons will control its tides, that the degree of axial tilt will shape its seasonal variations. "By bringing in this detail and that, tightly linked," Anderson says, "the writer makes his imaginary globe seem real. Furthermore, the details are interesting in their own right. . . . They may reveal something of the possibilities in these light-years that surround us, thereby awakening the much-desired sense of wonder."

He doesn't insist that the conception of a fictional world must be preceded by months of preliminary study, but only that a reasonable understanding of the laws of astrophysics will allow writers to convince their readers that they actually know what they're talking about, and will also help in the process of inventing the story itself: "Whatever value the writer chooses [for a planet's axial tilt], let him ponder how it will determine the course of the year, the size and character of climatic zones, the development of life and civilizations. If Earth did travel upright, thus having no seasons, we would probably never see migratory birds across the sky. One suspects there would be no clear cycle of the birth and death of vegetation either. Then what form would agriculture have taken? Society? Religion?" He illustrates the Andersonian planning methods with diagrams and mathematical calculation, but there's nothing there, intimidating though it may look at a quick glance, that a would-be science fiction writer with at least a high school degree can't follow. (And if you aren't willing to think through a little bit of high school astronomy, what are you doing setting up shop as a science fiction writer?)

Though the Anderson essay is, in and of itself, a splendid little handbook for planetary creation, he recommends two classic reference books that remain invaluable to science fiction writers to this day: *Intelligent Life in the Universe* (1966) by I.S. Shklovskii and Carl Sagan and *Habitable Planets for Man* (1970) by Stephen H. Dole. I second the recommendations — those two have stood me in good stead for decades — and add to it *Cycles of Fire* (1987) by William K. Hartmann, *Red Giants and White Dwarfs* (1967) by Robert Jastrow, and *The Planetary System* (1988) by David Morrison and Tobias Owen, which, while dealing entirely with our own solar system, provides a wealth of fundamental information about why that solar system has the form it does, so that any writer can readily generalize new worlds from the data supplied.

The Clement essay that follows Poul Anderson's in the Bretnor book likewise stresses the merit of using rigorous logic, or at least common sense, in populating one's invented worlds with living creatures. One should know something about how earthly creatures work, Clement says, before dreaming up extraterrestrial ones, since the basic biological rules of our planet very likely will hold true for *any* planet that is capable of bringing forth life. ("The trick of magnifying a normal creature to menacing size is all too common. The giant amoeba is a familiar example; monster insects, or whole populations of them, even more so. It might pay an author with this particular urge to ask himself why we don't actually have such creatures around. There is likely to be a good reason, and if he doesn't know it perhaps he should do some research.") He goes on to explain why Pegasus wouldn't be able to fly, why six-foot-long ants don't infest our gardens, and why birds don't travel at supersonic speeds; and, having done that, he then proceeds to demonstrate how, given a deep enough knowledge of planet-building, a writer can conjure up worlds and creatures capable of operating in contravention to all our own planet's rules. (The indispensable Shklovskii-Sagan volume, *Intelligent Life in the Universe*, has a particularly valuable chapter on the possibilities for life of a non-terrestrial sort in other solar systems.)

But, as I've said, working out the physical and biochemical characteristics of your invented world is just the starting point. Those characteristics will provide you with the setting for your story, but not the story itself, though in large measure they will govern the essential nature of that story. (The concerns of the thirsty desert-dwellers of Frank Herbert's parched Arrakis in *Dune* are quite different, for example, from those of the inhabitants of the completely aquatic Hydros in my own *The Face of the Waters*). Once you've determined your world's gravity, climate, geography, geology, natural history, etc., you need to work out the details of its culture, which will involve you in such matters as economics, politics, religion, and urban planning. Ideally all of this will grow out of the special physical characteristics of your invented world.

I'll talk next time about how I went about this phase of the process in creating my own best-known imaginary world, the planet Majipoor of *Lord Valentine's Castle* and its various companion volumes.

Asimov's Science Fiction, **September, 2009**

Building Worlds: Part II

LAST MONTH'S COLUMN OFFERED SOME GENERAL THOUGHTS on how science fiction writers go about inventing plausible worlds, drawing heavily on the ideas of two masters of the process, Poul Anderson and Hal Clement. Now I want to offer some specifics showing how I devised my own best-known imaginary world, the planet Majipoor of *Lord Valentine's Castle* and its various companion volumes.

I began with nothing more than the skeleton of a plot involving a dispossessed monarch and the desire to set my story on a giant world rather like the one that Jack Vance envisioned in his 1952 novel, *Big Planet*. I intended, though, to carry the investigation of that world far beyond what Vance had chosen to do in that one relatively short book.

Big Planet takes place on a planet with a climate somewhat like India's that is divided into hundreds or thousands of independent principalities. Because its crust is devoid of the heavier elements, Vance's planet has "no metal, no machinery, no electricity, no long distance communication." Therefore — despite its immense size, with a circumference seven or eight times that of Earth — Big Planet is a low-density world with a gravitational pull about the same as ours and a similar atmosphere, thus making possible human settlement.

Vance's novel is a lovely colorful romp. But, because sf books in the 1950s had to be fairly brief, it's only about fifty thousand words long, and merely nibbles at the infinite complexity of the planet on which it is set. Had he wished, Vance could have placed another dozen novels there without exhausting the territory. The only time he did return to Big Planet, though, was in the relatively minor novel *Showboat World,* so the notion came to me of creating a Big Planet of my own and exploring it more fully than Vance did his.

At first, for the sake of distinguishing my world from the tropical jungle wilderness of Vance's book, I envisioned a single tremendous city spreading thousands of miles in all directions, covering most of the land mass — the very opposite of Vance's concept. (Reaching for opposites is a good way to find story ideas.) But very quickly I saw the impossibility of that. If I wanted a population of many billions, I would need extensive agricultural zones to support it; and if I wanted (as I very much did) to create a host of fascinating plants and animals, I would have to have a variety of wild places.

So pole-to-pole urban development made no sense, and in the end I fell back on a model that was even more like a giant India than Vance's planet: a place of teeming cities surrounded by vast farming districts, and yet, nevertheless, having huge wilderness areas ranging from torrid desert to lush jungle to snow-capped mountains, surrounded by an ocean so enormous that no expedition had ever succeeded in crossing it. What I had in mind, in other words, was a planet so large that it could encompass a host of varying environments — jungles, interminable swamps, arid plateaus, great rolling savannas, rivers seven thousand miles long, cities of thirty billion people — without any sense of crowding whatever.

The astrophysical details didn't require much homework. Since I was beginning with the assumption that my planet had to be a comfortable one for human settlement, I needed a main-sequence G-type sun much like our own. (For a touch of exoticism I made it golden-green in color rather than yellow.) The planet's low-density structure accounted for a gravitational pull about like Earth's despite a much greater diameter. For human use the atmosphere had to be something close to Earth's 78-21 nitrogen-oxygen mix. By way of encouraging agricultural productivity I gave it a relatively minor axial tilt, thus avoiding sharp seasonal changes: some parts of Majipoor would be fairly dry, others rainy, but the climate would be benign everywhere except in the snowy polar regions.

Still, by employing the Vancean low-density planetary model, with its concomitant shortage of useful metals, I would have to veer somewhat from a strictly science fictional mode of thinking, because without metals there could be very little in the way of machinery — no aircraft and no telecommunications system, for example. How, then, could I justify the existence of those cities with thirty billion people in them, with no rapid transit, no telephones, no elevators, indeed no high-rise structures? How could there be any sort of coherent central government, let alone the hierarchical and quasi-feudal monarchy that would justify a title like *Lord Valentine's Castle*?

I began to see that I would have to operate on that blurry borderline where science fiction shades into fantasy: a dollop of telepathy here and there for communication, a certain amount of vagueness about technology (an ancient civilization that has long ago used up its sparse metals and forgotten how its own mechanisms work), and some kind of ground-effect vehicles ("floaters") that didn't require internal-combustion engines or electricity to drive them. The lack of air transport, I figured, would work in my favor, adding to the sense of planetary immensity that was one of my primary goals: on Majipoor it would take just about forever to get from anywhere to anywhere. Distant cities would become misty, quasi-mythical places.

I interject herewith that everything I have to say here about building worlds for science fiction novels applies just as well to fantasy. I regard science fiction as just one sub-set of fantasy, anyway. Everything in a fantasy novel, however it may contravene the laws of nature as we understand them, needs to have its own internal consistency, since, without the rigor of internal logic, plot problems can be trumped in any old arbitrary way for the writer's convenience and the narrative line will quickly collapse as one rabbit after another is pulled from the auctorial hat. So the writer needs a thorough understanding of how our own world's non-technological societies actually worked, and needs to follow those workings in all details save only the one speculative departure that generates the fantasy element itself. For further information on constructing fantasy worlds, I commend to you another Poul Anderson essay, "On Thud and Blunder," recently republished on the Internet and easily findable there.

While the planet itself was taking shape in the forefront of my mind, other cerebral areas were quietly at work devising an elaborate plot, characters to enact it, a history and a culture and a political system, and all those other features that a lengthy science fantasy novel needs. But most of my conscious attention at that point was going toward envisioning Majipoor: its climate, its native lifeforms, above all its geography and topography. These things, I knew, would determine many aspects of the story itself, from the form of government to the movements of my protagonists.

All right: maps, next.

I drew some quick sketches. Three continents, each far larger than any of Earth's. One, the earliest to be settled and immensely populous, to be the center of the world government; another, not as thoroughly urbanized, though with some major cities and a river of phenomenal size cutting across it, to be the home of the surviving aborigines who would, I already was coming to see, play a key role in the plot; the third, more obscure, a forbidding desert land in the torrid south.

By now I had put some meaning behind the title that had spontaneously offered itself. The eponymous Castle was the seat of the monarch, and I would put it atop a special geographical feature: a super-Kilimanjaro, a mountain thirty miles high in the middle of the primary continent. Castle Mount, I called it. It would be virtually a continent in itself, albeit a vertical one, protected from high-altitude forces of wind and cold and by weather-altering and atmosphere-creating machinery designed and installed when Majipoor still was in its technological era. There would be fifty spectacular cities along its slopes and a gigantic Gormenghast-like royal castle at its summit.

But, since the political structure of Majipoor and the plot of the novel now were unfolding in my mind with the same swiftness as the geographical background, I needed a second capital also, for I intended a double monarchy. In order to sustain Majipoor's huge population under a single stable government, I wanted a ruling system that would provide a long series of enlightened monarchs. Hereditary rule wouldn't do that — sooner or later it gives you a Caligula or a Nero — and neither, as I see it, would democracy. (Hitler was a democratically elected Chancellor.) But I remembered the system of adoptive emperors that produced the most successful period in the long history of the Roman Empire, each ruler choosing the most qualified man of the realm to follow him to the throne and adopting him as his son: Nerva picking Trajan, Trajan Hadrian, Hadrian selecting Antoninus Pius and simultaneously designating the promising young Marcus Aurelius to be Antoninus' ultimate successor.

I proposed — fantasy, again — to ask the reader to believe that such a system could be kept going for thousands of years if each emperor gave proper care to his choice of a successor. But also I intended to have two rulers in office at once, much as Fifth Republic France has a President and a Prime Minister, and the later Romans operated with an Augustus and a Caesar as senior and junior emperors. The older monarch — the Pontifex, I called him, with a nod to Rome — would live out of sight, in the deepest levels of a labyrinthine underground city thousands of miles south of the Castle. The junior king — the Coronal — would be the highly visible occupant of the Castle atop the great mountain, the public figure carrying out the orders that emerged from the hidden emperor in the Labyrinth. Upon the death of the Pontifex, the Coronal would take his place in the gloomy subterranean capital and his designated successor, technically his adoptive son, would become Coronal at the Castle.

I realized at this point, also, that what I would be writing was a novel of quest, of internal discovery, of the attainment of responsibility. One should never become so obsessed with the world-building process that one loses sight of the story-building process: the two should grow simultaneously, organically intertwined, once the basic groundwork has been established. A quest-novel, then. But who would undertake the quest, and what would he be seeking? The world I was designing had taken its essential form; it was time to establish the characters who would act out the story I intended to set on that immense planet.

And I see that this is going to take another column to finish the job.

Asimov's Science Fiction, **October/November, 2009**

Building Worlds: Part III

MY LAST TWO COLUMNS HAVE BEEN DEVOTED TO A BASIC ASPECT of writing science fiction: the designing of planets. In the first column I talked about ways to achieve scientific plausibility; in the second, I described how I had conceived and developed the specs for my own best-known world, the Majipoor of *Lord Valentine's Castle*. I want to go on now to discuss how I invented my characters and the social matrix in which their lives would be lived.

I told last time of how Majipoor was ruled by a dual monarchy: a senior king, the Pontifex, and his junior companion, the Coronal. Upon the death of a Pontifex his Coronal succeeds to that title and chooses a new Coronal of his own. Thus the monarchy is an adoptive one, rather like what evolved in Rome in the time of the Emperors Trajan, Hadrian, and Antoninus Pius.

The protagonist of the book I was constructing would be the Coronal Lord Valentine, cast from his throne by a usurper, robbed of his memory, and set loose to wander. A useful archetype: I find in my files a note that reads, "Valentine as Grail Knight — Perfect Fool — born ignorant and learns gradually." And again: "A hero suffers, comes to power as the regenerator of the world." And my own final comment: "Valentine is an amiable & sunny man, though no simpleton, and people are naturally drawn to him."

Suddenly I had a name for my planet: Majipoor, "maji" providing a subliminal hint of the romantic word "magic" and the Hindi-sounding suffix "-poor" to remind me that my geographic model was the subcontinent of India blown up to superplanetary size.

Next in the gradually cohering plot came this: "Since Valentine is adopted, who is his true mother? Is she capable of detecting the impostor? (Or identifying the concealed ruler?) — She is a priestess on an island in a remote sea." And I put a large island between the two main continents and made it a ritual center where the Great Mother rules.

But there was still no hint of the conflict that every novel needs, other than the as yet unexplained usurpation that had sent Valentine into exile. Some sort of sinister player was needed. I jotted down this: "The King of Dreams is the dark adversary of the Emperor." A second telepathic force, this one far more stern and ominous than the benevolent Lady of the Isle: a sender of bad dreams, a planetary superego ferociously chastising those who get out of line, but also — so I realized — capable of getting out of line himself. The King of Dreams would turn out, in fact, to be connected in some way with the mysterious usurpation that thrusts Valentine from his throne. I put his headquarters on an inhospitable desert continent and made him an equal partner in the government with the Pontifex, the Coronal, and the Lady.

My sheets of preliminary notes now fill up with all manner of archetypical references out of our own history, literature, and myth: "Falstaff . . . the Malcontent figure . . . Tiberius . . . Caligula . . . Aeneas and the descent into hell . . . Merlin/Hermes . . . Shapeshifters . . . Jonah in the Whale . . . Darth Vader . . . Jason and the Fleece . . ." All of these, and many more, would find their way in transmuted form into the plot of *Lord Valentine's Castle*.

After a few weeks I was ready to set down a formal sketch of the book. It began with a statement of the general background:

"This long picaresque adventure — the manuscript will probably run six hundred pages — takes place on the huge world of Majipoor, a planet enormously bigger than Earth, but lacking most of the heavier elements, so that the gravity is only about three-fourths that of Earth. All is airy and light on Majipoor: it is a cheerful and playful place in general, although highly urbanized, bearing a population of many billions. Food is abundant, the air is fresh, the streams and oceans are clean. Majipoor was settled by colonists from Earth some fourteen thousand years ago, but also is occupied peacefully by representatives of six or seven of the galaxy's other intelligent species, as well as the descendants of Majipoor's own native race, humanoid in form, capable of physical changes of shape. These last beings are regarded with some uneasiness by the others, and this uneasiness is reciprocated.

"Across the vastness of Majipoor's three colossal continents is spread an incredible diversity of cities, glittering and majestic, separated by parks, agricultural territories, forest preserves, wastelands kept deliberately barren as boundaries, and holy districts occupied by religious devotees. Such a gigantic cosmos of a planet can hardly be efficiently governed by one central authority, and yet a central authority does exist, to which all local governors do indeed pay lip-service and on occasion direct homage. This central authority is the Pontifex, an imperial figure, aloof and virtually unknowable. . . ."

The outline goes on to sketch the plot — Valentine's amnesia, and his attempt to regain his throne — and announces that "the form of the novel is a gigantic odyssey, divided into five 'books' of thirty-five to forty thousand words each, during which the deposed Lord Valentine learns of his true identity, gradually and at first reluctantly resolves to regain his power, seeks successfully to obtain access to his original personality and memories, and crosses all of immense Majipoor, enlisting allies as he goes, engaging in strange and colorful adventures, finally to confront the usurper at the Castle."

Now the main structure was in place, and I knew from past experience that I would be able to fill in necessary connective matter — minor characters, sub-plots, internal surprises — as I went along. What remained was to move Valentine across Majipoor from the west coast of the secondary continent to the heart of the primary one and up the slopes of thirty-mile-high Castle Mount, inventing the details of the terrain as I went. And it was those details that I hoped would set my novel apart from its predecessors in the genre.

In designing Majipoor I wanted it to be as realistic, in its fantastic way, as I could make it. Here I drew on my strong suits: my knowledge of geography, archaeology, and natural history. Beginning with the city of Pidruid on the wilder continent's northwest coast and going eastward, I invented an appropriate climate, a cuisine, an assortment of native wildlife, and — a matter of particular interest and amusement for me — a botanical background. All of these were, of course, derived in one fashion or another from terrestrial models; I don't believe that we science fictionists can ever really invent anything from scratch, but only make modifications of existing prototypes. The more familiar you are with a broad array of prototypes, the richer the variations you can ring on them; but true invention, I think, is Nature's own prerogative, and variations on existing themes is the best we can manage.

I managed pretty well, I feel. In my garden are many of the plants known as bromeliads, which usually have rosettes with a cup in the center to hold a reservoir of water. Insects and plant matter fall into the cup and decay to provide nutrients for the bromeliad. Fine: I brought Valentine into a grove of "mouthplants," stemless plants much like my bromeliads, except that their leaves are nine feet long and the central cups have paired grinders equipped with blades. The mouthplants are, in fact, carnivorous, grabbing their prey with hidden tendrils and conveying it to the cups to be chewed. There are, praise be, no such lovelies on our own world; but it was easy enough for me to dream them up for Majipoor.

So I populated the forests and waters of Majipoor: with sea-dragons like great plesiosaurs, with balloon-shaped submarine monsters, with glassy-fronded ferns that emitted piercing discordant sounds, and — one of my favorites — trees whose trunks begin to atrophy with age and whose limbs inflate, until eventually their trunks are mere guy-ropes that break at maturity, setting the limbs adrift like balloons to drift off and start new colonies elsewhere. All these things have models in real natural history, but I think I did a pretty fair job of extending and transforming those models to produce the distinctive flora and fauna of Majipoor.

The terrain, too — forests and jungles, mountains, rivers, a formidable desert, the mighty thrust of Castle Mount — came alive because I was working from life, depicting with appropriate variations things I had seen myself, altering colors, shapes, forms, greatly expanding the scale of everything, making it all more magical (though the originals are magical enough!) to yield the strange and extraordinarily rich landscape of my invented world. The cities were magnified versions of cities I had visited in Europe or Asia; the ruins of the prehistoric Shapeshifter capital were inspired by Roman ruins I had clambered through in North Africa; the geology was Earth-plus geology, everything writ large.

The grand scale of everything was the most important point. It would not have been enough simply to tell the old story of the disinherited prince yet again. It would not have been enough just to set a pack of wanderers loose on a gaudy hodgepodge of a planet. It would not have been enough to flange together a governmental system for that planet out of bits of Roman history and medieval archetypes. It would not have been enough merely to make up a bunch of funny animals and peculiar plants. I had to create, out of available parts, something plausible, something internally consistent, and something that was entirely new, which by virtue of its size, its splendor, and the richness of detail with which I envisioned everything, would provide my readers with an experience they could not have had before and would never forget.

For that I needed six months of planning and research, six intense months of day-by-day writing, and some additional months of revision. But the result was successful, a big, popular book that won me an audience far larger than I had ever had before.

What I learned from the Majipoor experience is:

— Make it big. Scope counts, if you want a multi-book concept. (I wasn't looking for one, but very quickly realized that I had one anyway.)

— Make it ancient. Plenty of history is useful in the novel of scope, and in order to invent plenty of history, you need to know plenty yourself.

— See it and feel it from within: birds and bugs and plants, critters large and small, the cuisine, the landscape, the smell of the air, the taste of the water, the color of the sky. Make it real for yourself and it will be real for your readers. Call on all the physics, chemistry, and biology at your command, and make sure that no inherently contradictory scientific aspects get yoked together because you think your plot requires them. ("What the hell, it's only science fiction" is not a sufficient justification for having a planet's population of carnivorous animals outnumber the herbivores or the atmosphere of one occupied by humans to have the nice bracing tingle of sulfur trioxide.) Get to know textures, detail, color, shape, above all the purpose of each component part of the entire invention. Nothing should be there just because it amuses you to toss it in. Everything should fit into a logical ecological structure. If your invented world is a place you know extremely well, but nevertheless would like to return to again and again, your readers will feel the same way about it.

Asimov's Science Fiction, **December, 2009**

Writers' Tools

A FEW MONTHS AGO I READ, FOR THE FIRST TIME, LEO TOLSTOY'S immense novel *War and Peace* — a project I had been postponing for some fifty years. My copy of the book, which I have owned since I was a sophomore in college, is 1130 pages long — big pages, small type. It took me about three weeks to read it, three exceedingly intense weeks. The book made every bit as profound an impression on me as I had expected it to, and, in the stunned aftermath, I went on to gather a little information about how Tolstoy had gone about writing it.

I learned, for instance, that he had spent five years doing so — from 1863 to 1868 — that he had revised constantly even as sections of the book were being set in type, producing innumerable drafts, and that (because his handwriting was so terrible, and he insisted on scribbling extensive last-minute revisions all over his galley proofs, writing between the lines and up and down the margins and on the backs of the pages as well, often scratching out his corrections to replace them with others) his wife Sonya served as his amanuensis, copying each version of the manuscript out in legible form. All in all, Mme. Tolstoy copied out *War and Peace* SEVEN FULL TIMES in those five years.

In longhand. In Cyrillic script.

My heart went out to her. The thought of simply reading *War and Peace* seven times in five years, let alone copying it all out by hand, shook me to the core. And it set me thinking about the manuscripts of books, and what authors (and sometimes their wives) go through in order to prepare them.

Tolstoy, of course, lived long before the era of computers. Nor did the devoted Mme. Tolstoy have access to a typewriter. Her husband, who grew cantankerously ascetic with age, had always detested modern machinery of all kinds, declaring in the epilogue to *War and Peace* that "The diffusion of printed matter" was "the most powerful weapon of ignorance."

Tolstoy could not have purchased a typewriter even if he had wanted one during the time he was writing *War and Peace*. But primitive versions of the device already existed. An English engineer, Henry Mill, had actually patented "an artificial machine or method for the impressing or transcribing of letters singly or progressively one after another," as early as 1714, though he doesn't seem to have built a working model. Various inventors — an Austrian, a Swiss, an Italian, a Frenchman — did produce working typewriters later in the eighteenth century, and whole platoons of writing machines had been devised by 1850 — seven in France, three or four in the United States, several in England, etc. But the first practical one, the first one actually to be manufactured and placed on the market, was the one devised by Christopher Latham Sholes of Milwaukee, Wisconsin, in a series of stages beginning in 1867 and first offered for sale in 1873 by the Remington Company, then best known for making guns, sewing machines, and farm machinery.

They were expensive gadgets — the initial price was $125, which is the equivalent in modern purchasing power of at least eight or ten thousand dollars — and there were very few buyers at first. One early adopter was the writer Samuel Langhorne Clemens, who is better known to us as Mark Twain. He saw a Remington on display in 1874 and bought it immediately. On December 9, 1874, he sent this typewritten letter to his brother Orion:

> Dear Brother:
> I am trying to get the hang of this new fangled writing machine, but i am not making a shining success of it. However this is the first attempt i have ever made & yet i perceive i shall soon & easily acquire a fine facility in its use. . . . The machine has several virtues. I believe it will print faster than i can write. One may lean back in his chair & work it. It piles an awful stack of words on one page. It don't muss things or scatter ink blots around. . . .
> Your brother,
> Sam

And Mark Twain's next novel, *Tom Sawyer*, which appeared in 1876, went to his publisher in typewritten form — the first typewritten book manuscript in history. (Though some scholars believe that the distinction belongs to *Life on the Mississippi*, which dates from 1883.) Either way, Mark Twain was certainly the first novelist to turn in a typewritten manuscript.

The concept took firm hold. For the next century, more or less, publishers would insist on typewritten manuscripts — double-spaced, if you please, and typed on just one side of the page. About 1980, when writers began to shift from typewriters to word-processing computers, the technology of manuscript preparation underwent a significant change, but even then manuscripts continued to follow the traditional format once they were printed out; the big difference for the writer was in the way words could be manipulated electronically before any manuscript was produced, not in the production of the manuscript itself.

One of the first science fiction writers to switch over to the computer was the oldest guy in our crowd, Jack Williamson, who was approaching the age of seventy-five when he began using a Radio Shack computer in the 1980s. Most of the rest of us were still making do with typewriters then, although within a few years computer use had become almost universal in SFdom. The computers themselves, though, were a wildly variable lot. The younger, less solvent writers went in for miniature jobs like the Osborne and the Kaypro, which look like quaint museum pieces today. At the other end of the spectrum was the vast, room-filling device that those two plutocrats, Larry Niven and Jerry Pournelle, used to create their best-selling novels. Everyone else was somewhere in between, and, since each make of computer tended to use an idiosyncratic operating system, nobody's computer was compatible with anybody else's, so the idea of sending your manuscript in digital form to your publisher was unworkable.

All that began to change with the arrival of the IBM PC and the imitative PC models that other manufacturers produced, and the simultaneous coming to dominance of the DOS operating system. Before long things were so standardized — everyone used either a PC or a Mac — that publishers started to prefer, and then to insist, that writers submit their work in a digital version (on diskettes or via e-mail) that could go straight into type, though they usually like to see conventional hard copy as well. (Still called a "manuscript," I suppose, although that word is derived from Latin words meaning "that which is written by hand.")

Just about every writer uses a computer these days, and submits his work in electronic form with or without accompanying manuscript. (Harlan Ellison, who abhors computers, still writes on a typewriter, but he must be among the last of his kind.)

And yet we computer-users all have our little variations on the theme.

Jack Vance, for example, wrote his books in longhand for many years, and his wife Norma, in true Tolstoyan fashion, typed them into manuscript form. About fifteen years ago Vance switched to a computer, but, because his eyesight had begun to fail, he had a special screen rigged that projected his material at two or three times normal size; and eventually, when he could no longer even see his keyboard, a friend mounted big wax templates over the keys to enable him to find his way to the function keys and other such accessories, creating a unique bit of writing apparatus.

Then there's Frederik Pohl, whose writing discipline requires him to write a minimum of four pages a day, day in and day out, wherever he may be. His manuscripts are produced on a computer these days, too. But Pohl has always been a considerable traveler, and — rather than carry a laptop wherever he goes — he takes good old low-tech pads of yellow paper with him.

One year in the late 1980s the Silverbergs and the Pohls traveled through Italy together, and I remember Fred doggedly setting down his four pages via pen and paper each day at the hotel while the rest of us went out to visit Byzantine mosaics and baroque cathedrals.

(I also travel a great deal. But I never, never, NEVER write while away from home. Since 1982 I've used a succession of computers for my work, but I take no laptops with me on my overseas journeys, nor pads of yellow paper, nor anything else that might tempt me into performing acts of fiction.)

Joe Haldeman's working methods are particularly unusual. He is a relatively slow writer whose work requires little rewriting; and, although he's certainly computer-savvy, he came to see that a computer wouldn't allow him to compose any more rapidly than if he did it by hand. Since he dislikes typing and enjoys the physical feel of longhand, he does the first drafts of his novels in bound blank books, rotating through a couple of dozen fountain pens with calligraphic nibs. (Joe learned calligraphy from the artist Jack Gaughan in the 1960s and his handwriting is most distinctive.) He uses a different color ink each day, which enables him to keep track of how much work is done on any particular day. Eventually he produces a first draft of unusual beauty, which some collector will eventually cherish. It's a true first draft, too, whereas what the rest of us produce undergoes constant ongoing revision as we scroll back and forth, so that early versions quickly vanish beneath the cursor's tread. Once the book is complete, Joe's wife Gay — another dedicated literary wife! — types his text into a "working draft" computer file, which Joe reads periodically, entering revisions by keyboard in the usual modern manner. What the publisher gets is a conventional-looking manuscript printout and the by now customary electronic file. What the collector of Haldeman manuscripts eventually will get is a thing of almost medieval beauty.

I doubt that Leo Tolstoy, if he had lived past 1910, would ever have reconciled himself to a computer. But he did finally come to let a typewriter into the house, though he never would go near it himself. Late in the nineteenth century the Remington typewriter people began to use photographs of celebrities to market their product, and one of their most famous shots is one of Tolstoy and his daughter Alexandra. The great man, scowling even more irascibly than was his norm, is dictating something to Alexandra — whose fingers rest on the keyboard of Remington's most recent model.

Asimov's Science Fiction, **April, 2003**

How To Write

A FEW WEEKS AGO, AT A DINNER PARTY AT THE HOME of Charles N. Brown of *Locus,* the young woman seated next to me told me that she was studying my recently reissued anthology *Science Fiction 101,* because she intended to write science fiction herself and wanted to learn all she could about how to get her career launched.

"That's easy," I told her jovially. "You don't even need to read the whole book. Just read Alfred Bester's 'Fondly Fahrenheit' and Cordwainer Smith's 'Scanners Live in Vain' and write a story that's as good as those two — that'll get your career going!"

I was just being playful, of course. Those two stories are essentially inimitable masterpieces, the Bester a paragon of story construction and exuberant style, the Smith an eerie adventure in visionary strangeness told with deceptive simplicity. Telling a novice writer that she should make it her goal to begin her career with stories on that level of quality makes no more sense than telling a rookie baseball player that a good way of attracting attention would be to break Barry Bonds' home-run record in his first season. Easy enough to say but next to impossible to do, and not really necessary, either. Trying to match the absolute summit of achievement in your chosen field right at the outset of your career is a worthy enough ambition, and now and again it can actually be done. (Roger Zelazny's Hall of Fame classic "A Rose for Ecclesiastes" was written close to the start of his career. Vonda N. McIntyre won a Nebula for one of her first published stories, "Of Mist, and Grass, and Sand." Ted Chiang won one for his very first, "Tower of Babylon." And, for that matter, "Scanners Live in Vain" was the first published story of Cordwainer Smith.) But there are other and more easily feasible ways to get yourself started as a science fiction writer.

Learning as much as you can about the craft of storytelling, for instance, and then producing solid, competent, perceptive, *honest* stories that reflect your individual view of the universe in general and the human condition in particular — that will get you into print, at least. The Hugos and Nebulas will follow eventually, or perhaps they won't — but let such things look after themselves. What you wanted to do was write and get published, right? Awards, fame, money, are all things to worry about later.

And in fact my *Science Fiction 101* was intended to help just such people as my dinner table neighbor that night at the *Locus* headquarters. (It was first published in 1987 under the title, *Robert Silverberg's Worlds of Wonder.*)

The book opens with a long autobiographical essay in which I describe precisely what it was like to be a young would-be writer yearning to get his start, fifty-odd years ago. Why, I wondered then, did people like Robert Heinlein, Isaac Asimov, Jack Williamson, and Henry Kuttner sell every word of fiction they wrote, whereas the pitiful little stories I was sending to the magazines came back with the speed of light? "They, so it seemed to me, were the elect. They were the ones who had been admitted to the sanctuary, while I stood on the outside glumly peering in. Why? I thought it was because they knew some special Secret, some fundamental trick of the trade, that was unavailable to me." And I devote the rest of my introductory piece to the tale of my quest to learn the wonderful secret of writing stories that some science fiction magazine would be willing to publish.

The first step, I decided, was to read a book on How to Write Fiction. Off I went to the library and found one such book that had already been recommended to me: Thomas H. Uzzell's *Narrative Technique: A Practical Course in Literary Psychology,* a book first published in 1923 that for a long time was the standard textbook on plot construction.

As I say in my introduction to *Science Fiction 101,* the Uzzell textbook terrified me: "I'm utterly certain that I put the book aside with a sinking feeling in my stomach. The art of fiction seemed as complicated and difficult to master as the art of brain surgery, and plainly you had to learn all the rules before the editors would let you through the door. Violate even one of Uzzell's commandments and it would be immediately apparent to any editor that the manuscript before him was the work of an incompetent. . . . I felt I could no more manage to write a proper story than I could walk on water."

I have a copy of Uzzell on my desk right now: 510 closely packed pages, dealing in the most minute detail with every aspect of story construction: the emotional purpose of a story, the effects it should achieve, the materials out of which it is built. There were chapters on "the character story," "the complication story," "the thematic story," "the atmosphere story," and, most horrific of all, "the multi-phase story." The reader was offered instruction in such things as "technique of fusing effects," "importance of two ideals," "thematic narratives didactic and dramatic," and "general formula for dramatic intensity." And each chapter ended with an appalling set of homework assignments, more grueling than anything I had to deal with then in my real-world existence as a high-school junior.

Thoroughly intimidated, I put Uzzell aside and tried to puzzle out the secret of writing fiction on my own. "That seemed a better way to learn," I wrote. "Uzzell was only confusing and frightening me with his hundreds of pages of how-to-do-it manual. Besides, I hated the idea of doing all those end-of-chapter exercises. So I began to study the stories in the current issues of the sf magazines with passionate intensity. I concentrated on the lesser magazines, the ones that ran simple stories by not-so-famous writers, and I took those stories apart and stared at the pieces, thinking, This is an opening paragraph, This is how dialog is managed, This is as much exposition as you can get away with before the reader gets bored."

And it worked. I will not keep you in further suspense: I did indeed learn how to write publishable fiction, close to fifty years' worth of it by now, and the way I did it was to study other stories, figure out what made them work, and apply those principles to stories of my own invention. In *Science Fiction 101* I reprinted thirteen of the stories that I studied — thirteen of the best science fiction stories ever written — and followed each one with an essay of my own discussing the particular tactics that each writer had used to achieve the effects that made his (or in one case, her) story so effective.

It's a pretty good book, taken simply as an anthology: along with the Bester and Smith stories, there are gems like C.M. Kornbluth's "The Little Black Bag," Frederik Pohl's "Day Million," C.L. Moore's "No Woman Born," James Blish's "Common Time," and more, by Damon Knight, Robert Sheckley, Philip K. Dick, and others, an awesome group of stories that serve admirably as prototypes of what great science fiction ought to be. Anyone who wants to be a science fiction writer should indeed study them carefully, not with any hope (at least at first) of matching their quality, but for the sake of seeing what level of attainment it's possible to reach within our field.

Although I still think that the best way to learn how to write science fiction is by studying the best science fiction you can find and striving to extract fundamental principles of story creation from what you read, it can also be very helpful to read an established writer's technical analyses of other writers' published work. That's why I appended an essay of my own to each of the stories reprinted in *Science Fiction 101* that discussed very closely the narrative strategies that make those stories work as well as they do. You won't learn how to write publishable fiction simply by reading those essays, but if writing professionally is your goal they will, I'm quite sure, serve as useful teaching supplements to the stories themselves.

A few other books that I read in the early phases of my career come to mind also. Two that are worth searching out were written by outstanding sf writers whose stories I used in *Science Fiction 101* — Damon Knight and James Blish. Knight's *In Search of Wonder* is a lively and often blistering discussion of well-known science fiction novels of the 1940s and 1950s; Blish's *The Issue at Hand* is an equally scathing analysis of sf magazine stories of the same era. Even if you aren't familiar with all of the works discussed, you will find Blish and Knight postulating certain technical standards for the writing of science fiction that all beginning writers would do well to think about.

Then there's Lajos Egri's *The Art of Dramatic Writing,* which, though ostensibly about playwriting, will tell you everything that old Thomas Uzzell was trying to teach about story construction, putting it in a far less intimidating manner. And, finally, H.D.F. Kitto's *Greek Tragedy,* a book I read and re-read when I was in college — and if you wonder how a study of the plays of Aeschylus, Sophocles, and Euripides will help you learn how to write successful science fiction, you'll find the answer in my introduction to *Science Fiction 101.*

What about that great Secret, which, so it seemed to me fifty years ago, Asimov and Kuttner and Heinlein and Williamson knew, and I didn't? I did learn it, finally, didn't I?

Well, yes and no. I can only quote my own words on that from the introduction to *Science Fiction 101*:

"The secret of the Secret is that it doesn't exist. There are many things that you must master if you hope to practice the art and craft of writing, but they are far from secret, nor do they add up to one single great Secret. You just go on, doing your best, living and reading and thinking and studying and searching for answers, using everything that you've learned along the way and hoping that each new story is deeper and richer than the one before."

There you have it. Editor Dozois is waiting to see those masterpieces, now.

Asimov's Science Fiction, July, 2002

Toward a Theory of Story: I

THESE ARE IDEAS ABOUT THE NATURE OF NAR-RATIVE THAT I'VE BEEN MULLING for a long time, but have never set down on paper before, or discussed in panels at science fiction conventions, or even proposed in conversations with my fellow writers. I suppose I really should be offering them for publication in some academic quarterly instead of a science fiction magazine, but it happens that I write for science fiction magazines, not for academic quarterlies; and in any case there is a certain far-out speculative aspect to the idea underlying my thoughts about the origins of fiction that makes them more suitable for a science fiction magazine than they probably would be for the *Hudson Review.*

Like anyone who puts himself before the reading public as a purveyor of fiction — stories — I have, since my earliest days as a writer, had to try to come to an understanding of just what a story is. Writing fiction professionally, that is to say, becoming that particular sort of public entertainer, requires one to learn and (to some degree) to abide by the rules, the laws, the conventions, of the world of published fiction. This is not just a matter of mastering techniques: it is a matter of comprehending definitions. Like it or not, you have to know what the world means by the term "story" before you can try to write them; and I have devoted decades of my life to acquiring that knowledge. So did Isaac Asimov, Robert A. Heinlein, Theodore Sturgeon, and Ray Bradbury before me, to mention four very different science fiction writers whose names happen to come quickly to mind. So has everyone whose name appears on the contents page of this issue of *Asimov's.*

In my column for the July 2002 issue of *Asimov,* entitled "How to Write," I talked of my yearning as an teenage reader of science fiction to learn how publishable stories were constructed, and how I looked in this direction and that in my attempts to discover the secrets of writing fiction that others would want to read.

One of the fundamental things I learned during that period of desperate inquiry is that there is such a thing as a universal plot skeleton, an essential narrative formula that all successful writers of commercial magazine fiction use. Put in its most basic form, it goes like this:

A sympathetic and engaging character, faced with some immensely difficult problem that it is necessary for him to solve, makes a series of attempts to overcome that problem, frequently encountering challenging sub-problems and undergoing considerable hardship and anguish, and eventually, at the darkest moment of all, calls on some insight that was not accessible to him at the beginning of the story and either succeeds in his efforts or fails in a dramatically interesting and revelatory way, thereby arriving at new knowledge of some significant kind.

It sounds pretty crude, put that way. Can it really be true that that's the basic outline of all fiction?

Let's take a few examples and see. Look at, say, Isaac Asimov's Foundation series. Humanity is faced with a crisis; Hari Seldon, drawing on his profound knowledge of the science of psychohistory, ultimately solves it by establishing a Second Foundation far across the galaxy; but that leads to other problems, and the location of the Second Foundation must be discovered, which eventually is done. Or Frank Herbert's *Dune*, in which young Paul Atreides, heir to his murdered father's dukedom, is driven into the universe's most formidable desert but triumphs over the evil Baron Harkonnen and emerges as the political and spiritual leader of a great empire. Or Alfred Bester's *The Stars My Destination*: Gully Foyle, left for dead aboard a wrecked spaceship, battles his way back and systematically carries out vengeance against all those who had made him suffer. Are these not classics of science fiction? And do they not, beneath all their inventiveness and narrative drive, display the bones of the so-called basic plot formula?

Science fiction, some would say, is mere commercial fiction, originating in shoddy pulp magazines. So let's look a little farther afield. To Hemingway's *For Whom the Bell Tolls*: a bridge in Spain must be blown up to halt the advance of totalitarian forces, and a troubled young American is given the job of doing it, though he knows it will cost him his life. To Faulkner's *As I Lay Dying*, in which a rural family must transport the body of its dead matriarch across a difficult landscape against huge obstacles. To Joyce's *Ulysses*, in which an aging Irish Jew, within the course of twenty-four hours, comes to terms with his relationship with his adulterous but beloved wife, his fellow Dubliners, and a prickly young man who is a sort of pseudo-son to him. Dostoievsky's Raskolnikov, in *Crime and Punishment,* is a student who feels impelled to murder an old pawnbroker purely to prove a theory he espouses, and then must play a cat-and-mouse game with the police chief.

The Grapes of Wrath — *War and Peace* — *Great Expectations* — wherever we look, we see characters caught up in difficult struggles and fighting their way through to some sort of illumination and resolution. The standard plot formula is always there, Beginning, Middle, and End, however artfully concealed by the sweep of the narrative. The authors of *Foundation, Dune,* and *The Stars My Destination* may have been mere pulp-magazine writers, working for two or three cents a word, but — Joyce? Faulkner? Hemingway? Can it be that the inexorable tyranny of the basic plot formula underlies all the fiction that has ever been written?

Well, no, not exactly. No rule is so inexorable that it can't be broken. Since the early twentieth century small literary quarterlies have published hordes of utterly plotless tales. Even the mighty *New Yorker* for years specialized in stories that had no visible endings, and very little in the way of middles or beginnings, either. During the New Wave period of science fiction thirty-odd years ago, plotless stories, often lacking characters as well, were *de rigueur.*

But writing a story and getting it published is one thing, and having that story create a meaningful experience in readers is something else entirely. Perhaps the long-term popular success of such pulpy novels as *Dune* or the Asimov novels or Heinlein's *Stranger in a Strange Land*, let alone the masterpieces of Joyce, Faulkner, and Hemingway, indicates something else beside the obvious point that a straightforward well-told story with a suspenseful plot more easily grabs an audience than a difficult, tenuous tale that has no plot at all, or one concealed in a maze of obscure narration that makes great demands on its readers. But *As I Lay Dying* and *Ulysses* are nobody's idea of breezy pulp fiction, and yet they have held their place in the bookstores for almost three quarters of a century without a sign of vanishing. Something in those stories compels serious readers to persevere, despite all the impediments the authors have placed in their way.

Let's look a little farther in the past, and try to locate the origin of the basic plot skeleton.

It goes back at least as far as Milton's *Paradise Lost* of 1671: Satan, angered by playing a subordinate role in heaven, leads a rebellion against the authority of God, and is, of course, defeated, but not without tremendous consequences for the newly created human race. And there it is in Cervantes' *Don Quixote*, some fifty years earlier. The aging Don, driven off balance by his love of medieval romance fiction in a materialistic age, sets out to live the life of a knight-errant, and undergoes great torment before coming to terms with his situation. A true plot, all right. Shakespeare provides us with plots, also: contemplate the problems of Hamlet, seeking revenge against his uncle for his father's murder, or of Macbeth, unable to stand firm against the ambitions of his ferocious wife, or of Romeo and Juliet, deeply in love even though their families are locked in a mortal feud —

But the basic plot skeleton is older than Shakespeare, too. Two hundred fifty years earlier, we have Chaucer's *Canterbury Tales*, a robust collection of stories, all of which have discernible plots with all the parts in the expected places. *Beowulf*, from the eighth century: the monster must be slain, and the hero gets the job done. *The Golden Ass of Apuleius,* a Roman novel of the second century: the hapless protagonist is transformed into a donkey, suffers unspeakable indignities, and is redeemed, finally, by the goddess Isis, whose adherent he becomes. Virgil's *Aeneid*, a century earlier: Aeneas, en route to Italy to found a new kingdom after the fall of Troy, lands at the African port of Carthage, falls in love with Dido, its queen, and finds himself caught in a painful conflict between his destiny and his heart. Jump a thousand years back from there and we get Homer's *Odyssey*: the great hero of the Trojan War spends a decade struggling to get home, and discovers that he must deal with a swarm of suitors collected about his faithful wife. And then there's the Sumerian tale of *Gilgamesh*, which was more than fifteen hundred years old when Homer was born: Gilgamesh, king of Uruk in Mesopotamia, grieves for the death of his beloved friend Enkidu, goes on a quest for the herb that confers eternal life, finds it and loses it again, and, ultimately, makes his peace with the inescapable necessity of his own death. We are back now to 2500 BC, or thereabouts, and even in that remote time storytellers seemed to understand that a satisfactory work of fiction had to meet certain predetermined structural requirements. Each has its own setting, characters, and style of attack, of course: but the underlying structure is the same — a problem, a conflict, a resolution.

Since the basic plot skeleton seems so persistent throughout the history of human storytelling, perhaps there's something in it that speaks to a human need beyond that of mere entertainment. And, perhaps, we may have to look backward into prehistory to discover what that need is. I'll take a further look at the question next month.

Asimov's Science Fiction, **April/May, 2004**

Toward a Theory of Story: II

"THERE IS ONE STORY AND ONE STORY ONLY," SAID ROBERT GRAVES in his lovely poem, "To Juan at the Winter Solstice," and perhaps in a certain sense that is true, though I have taken Graves' line out of context and what he meant by it is something quite different from the meaning I want to attach to it. For I want to use it as corroboration of the theory of fiction I began to develop in last month's column, that all imaginative narrative is based on a single plot skeleton that goes back into astonishing reaches of antiquity.

The Graves line seems to contradict Robert A. Heinlein's famous advice that actually there are three stories, which he called Boy Meets Girl, The Little Tailor, and The Man Who Learned Better. But in fact all three of Heinlein's fundamental plot structures, though they do very cleverly summarize the essential story themes that underlie nearly all fiction, can themselves be subsumed into the one I identified in our last issue as the basis of all the successful and lasting narrative of the past five thousand years:

A sympathetic and engaging character (or an unsympathetic one who is engaging nevertheless), faced with some immensely difficult problem that it is necessary for him to solve, makes a series of attempts to overcome that problem, frequently encountering challenging sub-problems and undergoing considerable hardship and anguish, and eventually, at the darkest moment of all, calls on some insight that was not accessible to him at the beginning of the story and either succeeds in his efforts or fails in a dramatically interesting and revelatory way, thereby arriving at new knowledge of some significant kind.

Taken on those terms, there is indeed one story only: the story of a conflict — perhaps with some external force, perhaps entirely within the soul of the protagonist — that leads to a clear resolution and illumination. Why has that formulation been so enduring and, apparently, universal? Is it simply that readers everywhere expect it, and so it has become a self-fulfilling requirement? Why do they expect it? When did the need for such a formulation get built into human cultural expectations?

A clue to our answer can be found in the history of Greek tragic drama. We know — because ancient Greek writers like Aristotle have told us so — that Greek drama evolved out of rituals in honor of the god Dionysus, who is most familiar to us as the god of wine, but who was to the Greeks a fertility god, the embodiment of all the forces of nature, manifest in the springtime rebirth of vegetation and the rising of the mating urge in animals.

There's hardly anything about Dionysus in the Homeric poems, which date from the eighth or ninth century BC, but that doesn't mean that the worship of Dionysus was unknown then, only that his cult was of little importance to the kings and heroes who are the protagonists of the *Iliad* and the *Odyssey*. Dionysus was, so we think, the god of the poor and downtrodden, who in his name gave vent to their resentments from time to time in sacred revelry of a wildly turbulent kind. There are many different Dionysus myths — each Greek city apparently had its own version of the story — but all employ the same concept, a god who is slain and restored to life. Dionysus is the favorite child of Zeus; while still young he is killed and dismembered by jealous older gods, but at Zeus's command he is reassembled and revivified. The annual events held in honor of Dionysus reenacted his sufferings, death, and resurrection through the violent and bloody slaughter of bulls — or even, in some places, of human victims.

Eventually the leaders of Athens and other Greek city-states, fearing that these frenzied and unfettered rites in honor of Dionysus might overflow someday into revolution, co-opted them by establishing such public festivals as Athens' Great Dionysia, where poets, dancers, and choral groups performed sacred hymns retelling the legends of the god's life. All strata of the populace attended these festivals; they listened to the stirring recitations of the story of Dionysus and the orgies of his uninhibited followers, they experienced vicarious thrills instead of tearing up the town themselves, and they went home at the end of the evening in a benign mood, having been purged of potentially dangerous emotions by the impassioned singing and dancing of the performers.

In time the recitations and choral hymns that made up the Great Dionysia underwent various mutations. One of the new forms that emerged was that of the tragic play. Earlier, a poet had improvised verses in praise of Dionysus before a chorus that would reply with a traditional song; now the tales of the god were dramatized by interchanges between two semi-choruses, and then by two speakers engaging in dialogue, and then, a generation or two later, three actors. Thus something very much like what we think of as a play evolved. The thematic range of the recitations widened, too, so that the dramas dealt not just with the death and rebirth of Dionysus but also with the ordeals of other great figures of Greek myth: Prometheus, Medea, Agamemnon, Theseus, Oedipus, Orestes, and many more.

One essential aspect of the festival-plays remained consistent throughout these evolutions. The purpose of the performance was not simply the amusement of the audience but its emotional cleansing, what Aristotle called its catharsis, its purgation.

As Aristotle explains in his *Poetics*, our souls are clogged by "affections," which for the sake of our mental health must be allowed periodically to discharge themselves in some harmless way. So boys often play violent games in which they pretend to be pirates or gangsters or soldiers. Girls in traditional societies act out the roles of nurses or mothers and see their imperiled charges through dire illnesses and crises. In primitive cultures dances and festivals much like the early Dionysiac revels bring about the release of the pent-up repressions. And in the highly civilized Greece of Aristotle's time the same sort of catharsis was had from the plays of such masters as Aeschylus, Sophocles, and Euripides that were performed at the annual festivals of Dionysus.

In these plays the audience witnessed the tragic downfall of a great king like Agamemnon, the Greek commander-in-chief of the war against Troy, who overreached himself in a prideful way during the course of that campaign and was slain after his return from the war by his own wife. It looked on as the god Prometheus, determined to bring the knowledge of fire to mankind in defiance of the orders of Zeus, met with a terrible punishment but sustained his courage nevertheless. It watched the tribulations of Oedipus, King of Thebes, who by the casual decree of the indifferent gods found himself unknowingly murdering his father and marrying his own mother, and then, launching into an investigation of the old king's death, eventually unmasked himself, to his amazement, as the criminal he was seeking.

In each of these tales — and in that of Pentheus, another king of Thebes who tried to block the spread of the orgiastic rites of Dionysus and who was torn apart by a group of drunken worshippers of the god that included his own mother; or that of Hippolytus, son of Theseus, unjustly accused of rape by his own stepmother, which led the deluded Theseus to ask the gods for his death; or that of Orestes, commanded by the gods to avenge his father Agamemnon's murder by committing the forbidden crime of slaying his mother — the Greek audience watched the torment of some larger-than-life figure caught in the grip of implacable destiny, and felt not only pity for that tragic hero's dire plight but also fear that some whim of the unpredictable gods would bring suffering upon themselves. And then — when the play reached its end, inevitably bringing some sort of reconciliation and insight into the tragic nature of life — there would come the sought-for moment of catharsis, the release, the "purging of pity and fear," as Aristotle's famous phrase has it, that is the primary purpose of tragic drama. The reconciliation of an Oedipus or an Orestes with the dictates of destiny provided the same cathartic effect as the rebirth of the slain Dionysus did in the original Greek theatrical events.

So, then: what originated as the uproarious commotion of a crowd of riotous, drunken plebeians has been domesticated first into a solemn festival of choral singing and poetic chanting and then into a series of dramatic masterpieces so effective in their storytelling that we still enjoy performances of many of the plays, twenty-five hundred years later. And in the course of that evolution a basic narrative scheme — a protagonist faced with a difficult problem, an intense struggle to cope with that problem, a climactic event that leads to new insight and a dramatically satisfying resolution — was developed, a narrative scheme that still can be traced in all modern drama and fiction.

Am I, then, tracing a direct line of evolution from the frantic ancient festivals of Dionysus to the Foundation series of Isaac Asimov and Frank Herbert's *Dune*?

Yes, I am. But I'm by no means through with this theme.

Let's continue to look at Aristotle's "purging of pity and fear," and its deeper connections with the festivals of Dionysus. Those were communal festivals, after all. From the earliest drunken feasts down through the sophisticated theatrical entertainments of a playwright like Euripides, they offered something more than individual therapy. The protagonists of the tragic dramas were figures chosen to exemplify the sins of the community; they were singled out to suffer on behalf of the community, and put through terrible torment that set them apart from the people around them. They became outcasts who took with them the communal sins. They were, if you will, scapegoats for the sins of others. (Scapegoats were, in Biblical times, actual goats, laden with the sins of the ancient Hebrew community and set free in the wilderness to carry those sins away from the tribe.) So it's the audience as a group, not just the individual theatergoer, that undergoes a ritual cleansing while the tales of Oedipus or Orestes or Agamemnon are being retold. And not only is the audience purged of pity and fear, as Aristotle would have it, but it comes away transformed by the awe it has felt and the understanding it has gained. Vestiges of this therapeutic function survive to this day, I maintain, in the underlying structure of the stories we read and the films and plays we see for "entertainment."

But there's more, much more, to my notions of the origins of fiction. Dionysus, remember, was a fertility god. I'm going to need one more column to show you how truly ancient the basic plot skeleton of fiction really is.

Asimov's Science Fiction, **June, 2004**

Toward a Theory of Story: III

I'VE DEVOTED THE PAST TWO COLUMNS TO EX-PLORING MY NOTION that the basic plot structure of all stories, whether they be the Foundation tales of Isaac Asimov or the short stories of James Joyce or the novels of Leo Tolstoy, has its roots in primordial human ritual. That basic plot skeleton, let me remind you once again, is this:

A sympathetic and engaging character (or an unsympathetic one who is engaging nevertheless), faced with some immensely difficult problem that it is necessary for him to solve, makes a series of attempts to overcome that problem, frequently encountering challenging sub-problems and undergoing considerable hardship and anguish, and eventually, at the darkest moment of all, calls on some insight that was not accessible to him at the beginning of the story and either succeeds in his efforts or fails in a dramatically interesting and revelatory way, thereby arriving at new knowledge of some significant kind.

Last time I traced the history of that narrative formulation back through the tragic plays of such Greek playwrights as Aeschylus, Sophocles, and Euripides to its origin in the early Greek festivals in honor of Dionysus, when poems and choral hymns were publicly recited in praise of that god, and then farther back yet into the wildly orgiastic rites through which the early Greeks paid homage to Dionysus in the days before their rulers shrewdly co-opted such fervor into formal public festivals.

Today we think of Dionysus, if we think of him at all, as the Greek god of wine and drunkenness. (From the fifth century BC onward the Greeks sometimes called him "Bacchus," which was the name by which the Romans knew him. We still use the term *bacchanalia* for any grand, convivial orgy of drinking.) But in ancient times he was also the god of fertility, who brought fruitfulness to mankind. His emblem was the phallus; the animals that sym-bolized him were forceful, passionate ones such as the bull, the panther, the lion, and the goat. Though new life of all kinds was his responsibility, it was the productivity of nature, the fertility of the fields, that was his special prov-ince. He brought the warmth and sunlight of springtime that produced the bounty of the new year's crops.

Agriculture goes back ten or twelve thousand years. From its earli-est days farmers have paid close and uneasy heed to the changing seasons, watching the days grow shorter in autumn, waiting out the dark months of winter, rejoicing when sunlight and warmth return in the spring. The prop-er fulfillment of that cycle — coupled with the annual seasonal fluctuations in rainfall patterns — was vital to the survival of the agricultural society. An unnaturally chilly spring or a shortfall in rain would lead inevitably to fam-ine, disease, and strife. Small wonder, then, that our ancestors devised rituals to insure the return of the spring, and invented myths to make the meaning of those rituals more vivid for themselves.

The myth of the god who dies and is resurrected provides a meta-phorical structure for the annual cycle in which the happy harvest season of autumn is followed by the bleakness of winter and then the joy of the new springtime. Dionysus, in the earliest Dionysiac tales, was just such a resur-rected god: the Vegetation Spirit who is torn apart, his body scattered, as the old year dies, and who is magically reborn in the spring after the community has been initiated into his rites. We see him, too, in other cultures under other names: Osiris, Adonis, Attis, Tammuz, Mithra, and many more. Vestiges of those ancient cults can be seen in Christianity, which gives us the divine figure of Jesus, born at the winter solstice (the time of year when the sun be-gins its long return after dwindling all through the autumn) as the redeemer of the world, put to death in springtime, resurrected immediately afterward.

There is a structure here. Mankind, dependent on its crops for sur-vival, is faced with the terrible challenge of summer's end, the diminishing sunlight, the cooler days. It is as though the god who brings fruitfulness to the world is dying. And the god *does* die; but even death can be conquered through struggle, the god will be reborn in the spring, the good golden sun will shine forth once more. It is not at all surprising that people everywhere would invent rituals and myths dealing with the defeat of death and the renewal of fertility. Those are the big subjects, after all: birth, survival, death. Rituals evolved in which symbolic figures — scapegoats — were chosen by the community to suffer in its name, to be driven out or even to die, tak-ing with them the sins of the old year, so the slate was wiped clean and a glorious new year of rebirth and growth could follow. Oedipus and Orestes, the parent-killers, have through no fault of their own brought pollution to their cities. Prometheus, the fire-bringer, has stubbornly defied his fellow gods. Pentheus, the king who denies the supremacy of Dionysus and thus threatens the renewal of fertility, is torn apart. The sufferings of these and the other tragic figures of Greek drama are decreed by the gods, often (so it seems to us) unjustly; but they are necessary aspects of the ritual, for out of their suffering will come the new life of spring.

Hence the "catharsis" of which Aristotle speaks, the purging of pity and fear by witnessing these fundamentally religious dramas. What a properly constructed Greek play — or a properly constructed primitive ritual — provides is the sense that the universe is coherent and rational. We may not clearly understand its great mysteries — love, birth, strife, death, the great constants underlying our existence — but we learn, through public ceremonies, that those things are not devoid of rationale, that there is a meaning to the cycles of life, that birth leads inevitably to death but that death is not the end, for rebirth will come.

Throughout the world, then, stories were told and retold that offered the comforting assurance that there was a logic to existence. The stories took many forms, of course. Some were explicitly resurrectionist — a god suffers, dies, and is reborn — but that wasn't the only way the story of springtime could be told. The Greeks themselves had a second version of the seasonal myth: the goddess Persephone is carried off by Pluto to the Underworld to be his bride, but her mother Demeter, goddess of grain, withholds the bounty of the harvest from mankind until Zeus must command Pluto to release Persephone for two thirds of the year, taking her back underground only in the winter months. Dozens of other metaphors for resurrection, less explicit than these, were devised. In all cases, though, what was being depicted was, essentially, *transformation*: the dramatization of a conflict that led to change of some sort — of an individual's character, of a family's way of life, of a community, even of the universe itself. And that's what fiction is still about: conflict and transformation.

Joseph Campbell, in his classic book *The Hero with a Thousand Faces,* showed how *all* tales of heroic struggle fulfill the terms of what he called the "monomyth," the basic story of stories: "A hero ventures forth from the world of common day into a region of supernatural wonder: fabulous forces are there encountered and a decisive victory is won: the hero comes back from this mysterious adventure with the power to bestow boons on his fellow man." Concealed beneath this tale of adventure lies the assurance that spring will return. It's a structural formula at least as old as the Gilgamesh epic of Sumer; but you'll find it in *The Lord of the Rings* as well, in *Dune,* in *Foundation,* and, in one disguised form or another, in any story or novel you read today.

Thus the annual cycle of the seasons provides a structural explanation for the familiar problem/struggle/resolution pattern of all fictional narrative. Sacred ritual and myth may have decayed into mere entertainment in our secular and skeptical age, but the need to make sense out of the rhythms of the universe remains.

Nor is this just a matter of worrying about next summer's crops. The yearning to understand the mysteries of the universe — creation, death, destiny, the will of the gods — must go back to a time before agriculture. Hunters and gatherers need a surcease from winter as much as farmers do. The protection of higher powers must be invoked. We know that the Neanderthals, two hundred thousand years ago, placed offerings with their dead, and buried them facing the rising sun: surely an indication of a belief in the life of the spirit. And there can be no doubt at all that our own ancestors of the Paleolithic period who left paintings of shamans and goddesses on the walls of their caves thirty thousand years ago had some sort of deeply held religious feelings.

Which means, I am sure, that they sought answers to the riddles of existence, and turned to the tribal shaman for them. He told them stories that offered the consoling thought that the universe made sense, that out of tempest and chaos would come, ultimately, a reintegration of the familiar rhythms of life that the forces of nature had temporarily disrupted. And out of these tales came the rituals of the resurrected god, and the myths that made those rituals comprehensible: a narrative structure that testified that life would resume once the hiatus of winter was over. These narratives would depict a conflict, ultimately resolved in a way that led to a powerful insight; and it was that satisfying moment of insight that had to be the climax of any story, and still is. Modern stories, even if writer and reader both are unaware of it, are shaped to drive onward toward that therapeutic climactic moment of insight and revelation that confirms belief that existence has meaning, that the universe is inherently rational: and for the moment, though we may no longer believe in gods, we are released from the fears that oppress us.

It's perfectly possible, you know, to write a story that has no plot at all, in which incident follows incident but no pattern emerges, no purposeful direction can be discerned. It's even possible to get such a story published.

But whether its readers will think it has provided them with the sort of nourishment they want from a story — well, that's a different matter. Consciously or not, I believe, we still follow traditions of storytelling built up across hundreds of thousands of years. Those traditions go back to humanity's earliest days, to prehistoric shamans who told stories, stories with beginnings, middles, and, of course, ends, satisfying, revelatory ends, so their listeners could better cope with the great terrifying mysteries of the universe. And that is what our storytellers are still doing, hundreds of thousands of years later. Or so I believe.

Asimov's Science Fiction, **July, 2004**

The Sense Of An Ending

THERE ARE ONLY THREE REALLY DIFFICULT CHAL-
LENGES IN THE CONSTRUCTION of a successful story, I
like to say: the beginning, the middle, and the end.

Of these, the beginning is, I think, the easiest part, though it's by no
means easy. The right place to open a story has been known for thousands
of years: *in medias res*, "in the middle of things." Jump into the action, fill in
the background later. Thus *The Iliad*, instead of opening by telling us that
there was once a war between the Trojans and the Greeks during which two
great Greek chieftains fell into a bitter quarrel, starts off fast: "The wrath of
Achilles is my theme, that fatal wrath that brought the Greeks such suffering...." Dante's *Inferno* tells us in its first stanza that the poet has become lost
in a dark forest that turns out to lead to Hell's gateway. And Milton's *Paradise
Lost*, not generally noted for its swift narrative pace, loses no time in getting under way: "Of man's first disobedience, and the fruit of that forbidden
tree....Sing, heavenly muse."

Less exalted writers than Homer, Dante, and Milton call this kind of
opening "a narrative hook" — something that catches and holds the reader's
interest, while at the same time implicitly stating the theme of the work
about to begin. The hook that comes most quickly to my mind in science
fiction is Henry Kuttner's classic line from *The Fairy Chessmen*: "The door-
knob opened a blue eye and looked at him." Gimmicky, perhaps, but unforgettable. You don't have to be as clever as that, though, to get a story going:
you just need to locate the middle of the action and zero in on it for your
opening paragraph.

As for the *actual* middle of the story you are writing — well, that's hard
because it involves you in all the grueling work of connecting the beginning

and the end (that is, making up all the stuff that goes in between, a process that's known as *writing a story.*) It isn't easy, because no part of writing stories is easy. But, whereas doing beginnings requires cunning and artfulness, doing middles requires, mainly, endurance: the ability to plod along from one page to the next, holding your reader enthralled at every moment, until you are ready to deliver your ending.

And then, your ending — ah, your ending —

Damon Knight, in an essay long ago on Philip K. Dick's novel *Solar Lottery*, spoke of the part of a book that he calls "the summing up, that place where the author has got to try to say what his novel means and where he thinks it leads." I doubt that Knight meant that he expects a writer to tell us those things literally and explicitly, in some flat-footed kind of bottom-line summary; what I think Knight was saying is that a book (or a story, or a play or a narrative or epic poem) should *have* a meaning, and its author should know what it is, and the closing scenes of that book (or whatever) should contain in their very fabric an implicit summarization of the intention of the entire work, as well as drawing together all the thematic material out of which the work has been constructed. It is the final payoff to the reader for his attention.

A work of fiction has a whole series of payoffs, of course. An engaging plot. Interesting people along the way who conduct the action of that plot. Fascinating scenery to look at in the course of that action. And, perhaps, memorable use of language as well. But the ending of that work is the key point, for it rounds things into a dramatically satisfying whole and prepares you to take your departure in wiser and nobler condition than when you arrived. I'm not talking here about the closing sentence or sentences, which deliver a story's final "punch" — I mean the part that comes a little earlier, which announces *that the work is now moving into its climactic passages.* I've observed that the creator of a truly satisfying work of fiction invariably signals the advent of that final section with a detectable change of tone — providing what the literary critic Frank Kermode has called "the sense of an ending."

Consider Wagner's *Ring* cycle of operas: seventeen hours of epic music drama showing nothing less than the downfall of the Nordic gods, and culminating in a complex, violent scene in which the stage is strewn with bodies and the only protagonist still in view is Brunnhilde, the tragic goddess-turned-mortal who is a central figure in three of the four operas. At this point there is a complete change of pace: a slow, portentous musical interlude, and then Brunnhilde, in a state of solemn exaltation, launches into a grand solo scene nearly twenty minutes long in which she directs the construction of the funeral pyre of the hero Siegfried ("Stack the great logs in piles for me, over there by the shore of the Rhine"); retells the story of his great achievements; recapitulates the entire mythic history of the Ring; sets Valhalla, the home of the gods, ablaze; and calmly, joyfully, rides her horse into the flames, bringing this great series of operas to a stunning and emphatic climax. *That's* what I mean by providing a sense of an ending!

Take Shakespeare. *Antony and Cleopatra*, for example: the tumultuous love affair of those two brings an empire crashing down, sends Antony to a miserable death, and leaves Cleopatra isolated with the Roman forces closing in on her. Antony, in his Act Four death scene, sounds the first note of the ending: "Unarm, Eros, the long day's task is done, and we must sleep." But it's a false signal, and we know it, for Cleopatra (though Antony isn't aware of it) still lives, and a fifth act will be needed to despatch her. In that act we watch Cleopatra guilefully fend off the Romans and then coolly arrange her own suicide, and then, at last, there is that pause and change of tone that we also detect at the moment of Brunnhilde's farewell, and we hear Cleopatra, ready for her death, quietly say, "Give me my robe, put on my crown; I have immortal longings in me now." And we know that the day is truly done, that all her striving is at an end and the play, shortly, will be also.

We get that sudden and mysterious change of tone in *Othello*, too, when Othello enters the bedroom of the sleeping Desdemona to murder her. "It is the cause," he says quietly, "it is the cause, my soul; let me not name it to you, you chaste stars! It is the cause. Yet I'll not shed her blood."

And James Joyce: a magnificent practitioner of the technique of closing a story. In his novella, "The Dead," a family dinner party has brought Gabriel Conroy to awareness of a youthful romance of his wife with a boy now dead, a romance that still lingers in her heart. The knowledge sobers him and darkens his mood, for it calls to his mind his own emotional inadequacies. And then, when the party is over, Joyce lets us hear the first music of the ending:

"The air of the room chilled his shoulders. He stretched himself cautiously along under the sheets and lay down beside his wife. One by one, they were all becoming shades. Better pass boldly into that other world, in the full glory of some passion, than fade and wither dismally with age." And so on to the glorious final sentence: "His soul swooned slowly as he heard the snow falling faintly through the universe and faintly falling, like the descent of their last end, upon all the living and the dead."

Joyce does it again in *Portrait of the Artist as a Young Man*: "Away? Away? The spell of arms and voices: the white arms of roads, their promise of close embraces and the black arms of tall ships that stand against the moon, their tale of distant nations. They are held out to say: We are alone — come." Even without context, we can tell that something important is happening, as Joyce goes on to his great conclusion: "Welcome, O life! I go to encounter for the millionth time the reality of experience and to forge in the smithy of my soul the uncreated conscience of my race....Old father, old artificer, stand me now and ever in good stead."

Joyce provides powerful closure in *Ulysses*, too, Molly Bloom's thirty-page soliloquy sweeping us along to that breathless "and yes I said yes I will," and even in the bewildering *Finnegans Wake*, with its majestic final words abruptly looping us around and thrusting us back to the book's opening sentence.

Homer — Dante — Wagner — Joyce — what about our own little field?

Well, in Isaac Asimov's wondrous "Nightfall," we get this:

> "And then there was the strange awareness that the last thread of sunlight had thinned out and snapped. Simultaneously, he heard one last choking gasp from Beenay, and a queer little cry from Sheerin, a hysterical giggle that cut off in a rasp — and a sudden silence, a strange, deadly silence from outside."

Arthur C. Clarke, in *2001*:

> "The timeless instant passed; the pendulum reversed its swing. In an empty room, floating amid the fires of a double star twenty thousand light-years from Earth, a baby opened its eyes and began to cry."

Theodore Sturgeon, in *More Than Human*:

> "It was quiet in the glass room.
> "For a long time the only sound was Gerry's difficult breathing. Suddenly even this stopped, as something happened, something — *spoke.*
> "It came again.
> "*Welcome.*"

And one more — *Kingdoms of the Wall*, by — why not? — Robert Silverberg:

> "For a long time nothing happened; and then we saw dust rising around the ship, and moments later a pillar of fire burst into life beneath it, and lifted it upward. The little gleaming ship stood as if motionless before us an instant or two on its fiery tail. Then it was gone. It vanished from our sight as though it had never been.
> "I said, 'These were the true gods. And now they have left us.'
> "With that, and with no other word being spoken, we began to make ready for our descent from the Summit."

That sense of an ending. That subtle signal to the reader that all is over and done, that the summing-up has been reached, that the account is being tallied. Doing that right is the hardest part of writing a story.

Asimov's Science Fiction, **April 1997**

Some Thoughts on the Short Story

THE ESSAY THAT FOLLOWS WILL BE PUBLISHED A COUPLE OF YEARS from now as the introduction to the seventh volume of my Collected Short Stories series, which Subterranean Press has been bringing out one book at a time since 2006. (Volume Three, covering the stories I wrote between 1969 and 1972, is just about to be published as I write this.) All of the Silverberg stories that are mentioned here first appeared in this magazine between 1988 and 1990, except for "To the Promised Land," which was published in *Omni* in 1989.

A couple of working definitions:

1) A short story is a piece of prose fiction in which just one significant thing happens.

2) A science fiction short story is a piece of prose fiction in which just one *extraordinary* thing happens.

These are not definitions of my devising, nor are they especially recent. The first was formulated by Edgar Allan Poe more than a century and a half ago, and the second by H.G. Wells about fifty years after that. Neither one is an absolute commandment: it's quite possible to violate one or both of these definitions and still produce a story that will fascinate its readers. But they're good working rules, and I've tried to keep them in mind throughout my writing career.

What Poe spoke of, actually, was the "single effect" that every story should create. Each word in the story, he said, should work toward that effect. That might be interpreted to be as much a stylistic rule as a structural one: the "effect" could be construed as eldritch horror, farce, philosophical contemplation, whatever. But in fact Poe, both in theory and in practice, understood virtually in the hour of the birth of the short story that it must be constructed around one central point and only one. Like a painting, it must be capable of being taken in at a single glance, although close inspection or repeated viewings would reveal complexities and subtleties not immediately perceptible.

Thus Poe, in "The Fall of the House of Usher," say, builds his story around the strange bond linking Roderick Usher and his sister, Lady Madeline. The baroque details of the story, rich and vivid, serve entirely to tell us that *the Ushers are very odd people and something extremely peculiar has been going on in their house*, and ultimately the truth is revealed. There are no subplots, but if there had been (Roderick Usher's dispute with the local vicar, or Lady Madeline's affair with the gardener, or the narrator's anxiety over a stock-market maneuver), they would have had to be integrated with the main theme or the story's power would have been diluted.

Similarly, in Guy de Maupassant's classic "The Piece of String," one significant thing happens: Maitre Hauchecorne sees a piece of string on the ground, picks it up, and puts it in his pocket. As a result he is suspected of having found and kept a lost wallet full of cash, and he is driven to madness and an early death by the scorn of his fellow villagers. A simple enough situation, with no side-paths, but Maupassant manages, within a few thousand words that concentrate entirely on M. Hauchecorne's unfortunate entanglement, to tell us a great many things about French village life, peasant thrift, the ferocity of bourgeois morality, and the ironies of life in general. A long disquisition about M. Hauchecorne's unhappy early marriage or the unexpected death of his neighbor's grandchild would probably have added nothing and subtracted much from the impact of the story.

H.G. Wells, who toward the end of the nineteenth century employed the medium of the short story to deal with the thematic matter of what we now call science fiction — and did it so well that his stories still can hold their own with the best sf of later generations — refined Poe's "single effect" concept with special application to the fantastic:

> The thing that makes such imaginations [i.e., sf themes] interesting is their translation into commonplace terms and a rigid exclusion of other marvels from the story. Then it becomes human. "How would you feel and what might not happen to you?" is the typical question, if for instance pigs could fly and one came rocketing over a bridge at you. How would you feel and what might not happen to you if suddenly you were changed into an ass and couldn't tell anyone about it? Or if you suddenly became invisible? But no one would think twice about the answer if hedges and houses also began to fly, or if people changed into lions, tigers, cats, and dogs left and right, or if anyone could vanish anyhow. Nothing remains interesting where anything may happen.

Right on the mark. *Nothing remains interesting where anything may happen.* The science fiction story is at its best when it deals with the consequences, however ramifying and multifarious, of a single fantastic assumption. What will happen the first time our spaceships meet those of another intelligent species? Suppose there were so many suns in the sky that the stars were visible only one night every two thousand years: what would that night be like? What if a twentieth-century doctor suddenly found himself in possession of a medical kit of the far future? What about *toys* from the far future falling into the hands of a couple of twentieth-century kids? One single wild assumption; one significant thing has happened, and it's a very strange one. And from each hypothesis has come great science fiction: each of these four is a one-sentence summary of a story included in the definitive 1970 anthology of classics of our field, *The Science Fiction Hall of Fame*.

I think it's an effective way to construct a story, though not necessarily the only effective way, and in general I've kept the one-thing-happens precept in mind through more than fifty years of writing them. The stories collected [in the not-yet-published seventh volume of my Collected Short Stories series] were written between August of 1987 and May of 1990 and demonstrate that I still believe in the classical unities. Of course, what seems to us a unity now might not have appeared that way when H.G. Wells was writing his wonderful stories in the nineteenth century. Wells might have argued that my "To the Promised Land" is built around *two* speculative fantastic assumptions, one that the Biblical Exodus from Egypt never happened, the other that it is possible to send rocketships to other worlds. But in fact we've sent plenty of rocketships to other worlds by now, so only my story's alternative-world speculation remains fantasy today. Technically speaking, the space-travel element of the plot has become part of the given; it's the other big assumption that forms the central matter of the story.

Three of the stories in the book, "In Another Country," "We Are for the Dark," and "Lion Time in Timbuctoo," are actually not short stories at all, but novellas — a considerably different form, running three to five times as long as the traditional short story. The novella form is one of which I'm particularly fond, and one that I think lends itself particularly well to science fiction use. But it too is bound by the single-effect/single-assumption Poe/Wells prescriptions. A novel may sprawl; it may jump freely from character to character, from subplot to subplot, even from theme to countertheme. A short story, as I've already shown, is best held under rigid technical discipline. But the novella is an intermediate form, partaking of some of the discursiveness of the novel yet benefiting from the discipline of the short story. A single startling assumption; the rigorous exploration of the consequences of that assumption; a resolution, eventually, of the problems that those consequences have engendered: the schema works as well for a novella as it does for a short story. The difference lies in texture, in detail, in breadth. In a novella the writer is free to construct a richly imagined background and to develop extensive insight into character as it manifests itself within a complex plot. In a short story those things, however virtuous, may blur and even ruin the effect the story strives to attain.

One story in the collection is neither fish nor fowl, and I point that out for whatever light it may cast on these problems of definition. "Enter a Soldier. Later: Enter Another" may be considered either a very short novella or a very long short story, but in my mind it verges on being a novella without quite attaining a novella's full complexity, while at the same time being too intricate to be considered a short story. Its primary structure is that of a short science fiction story: one speculation is put forth. ("What if computers were capable of creating artificial-intelligence replications of famous figures of history?") But because Pizarro and Socrates are such powerful characters, they launch into an extensive dialog that carries the story far beyond the conventional limits of short fiction — without, however, leading it into the complexities of plot that a novella might develop.

And yet I think the story, whatever it may be, is a success — an opinion backed by the readers who voted it a Hugo for best novelette the year after it was published. The credit, I think, should go to Socrates and Pizarro, who carry it all along. As a rule, I think it's ordinarily better to stick to the rules as I understand them. But, as this story shows, there are occasions when they can safely be abandoned.

Writing novels is an exhausting proposition: months and months of living with the same group of characters, the same background situation, the same narrative voice, trying to keep everything consistent day after day until the distant finish line is reached. When writing a novel, I always yearned for the brevity and simplicity of short story writing. But then I would find myself writing a short story, and I felt myself in the iron clamp of the disciplines that govern that remorseless form, and longed for the range and expansiveness of novel writing. I have spent many decades now moving from one extreme of feeling to the other, and the only conclusion I can draw from it is that writing is tough work.

So is reading, sometimes. But we go on doing it. In this collection of mine are ten stories long and short that illustrate some of my notions of what science fiction ought to have been attempting in the later years of the twentieth century. Whether they'll last as long as those of Poe and Wells is a question I'd just as soon not spend much time contemplating; but I can say quite certainly that they would not have been constructed as they were but for the work of those two early masters. Even in a field as supposedly revolutionary as science fiction, the hand of tradition still governs what we do.

Asimov's Science Fiction, **August, 2008**

Showing And Telling: Part 1

ONE OF THE MOST FREQUENTLY REPEATED MANTRAS of writing instructors and the leaders of writing workshops is "Show, Don't Tell." By which is meant, "Define your narrative situations by depicting people in conflict, not by telling your reader about the people and their problems." Writers are urged to think of themselves as movie cameras, observing and recording the doings of their characters as they go through a series of significant events. Editorial comment by the author, standing outside the action and letting us know what to think about it as it occurs, is discouraged. "Plot is character in action," we are told: you show your people meeting their challenges in the way that is characteristic of them — note the repetition of terms — and thus a story will unfold. Beginners are warned of the perils of "expository lumps," great unbroken masses of author-provided data, which these days are more frequently called "infodumps."

There is wisdom in such teachings. By and large I have lived by them myself over the course of a career that now stretches more than fifty-five years. I think of a story as a series of vividly visualized scenes that eventually reveal a meaning, without the need for me to provide extensive hints about what's going on. (Except when I do feel that need. I'll get to that in the next essay.) It's an effective storytelling technique, long proven by example. No less a writer than Henry James — whose work is nobody's idea of fast-paced action fiction — constantly abjured himself to "Dramatize, dramatize!" — don't spell it out, just show characters in opposition, as though on a stage.

Ernest Hemingway, fifty years later, was a prime advocate of letting dialog and action carry the tale. "The Short Happy Life of Francis Macomber," one of the best short stories of the last century, begins briskly with the sentence, "It was now lunch time and they were all sitting under the double green fly of the dining tent pretending that nothing had happened," and the story goes on from there without pausing for explanations. Even Hemingway can't help a little auctorial intrusion: on page two he tells us that Macomber "had just shown himself, very publicly, to be a coward," something that more usually he would have left for us to figure out for ourselves. But generally he lets his stories be told entirely through action and implication. *For Whom the Bell Tolls*, for example, begins without delay: "He lay flat on the brown, pine-needled floor of the forest, his chin on his folded arms, and high overhead the wind blew in the tops of the pine trees." Eventually we learn that the man in the forest is there to blow up a bridge, but Hemingway tells us that important fact by way of a dramatized scene. Nowhere is there any solid slug of explanation. We learn about Hemingway's protagonist and the job he must do by watching him go through his tasks and interacting with the other characters; there is a minimum of outside-the-frame commentary.

Science fiction seems to require such commentary, because so much of it deals with unfamiliar worlds far removed from ours in space or time. One can drop one's characters down in modern-day New York or London or in a pine forest in Spain and let readers shift for themselves, and sooner or later they will figure things out, but when the readers are presented with the New York of 3874 AD, or with a starship arriving on Betelgeuse XVI, it does appear useful to give the reader a few hints about what's what in those strange surroundings.

Thus stories in the magazines of the pioneering publisher of science fiction magazines Hugo Gernsback often were festooned with helpful footnotes that explained the scientific background of a story or its extrapolative content. Here, for example, is Cecil B. White's "The Return of the Martians," from a 1928 issue of *Amazing Stories,* in which the Martians instruct a scientist on Earth to transmit messages to them for exactly 0.0049 of a day, and a footnote tells us, "The decimal amounts to nearly seven minutes. The Martians, being unaware of our system of measuring time, were compelled to adopt this method of conveying the time interval to us. This system is used a great deal in astronomical work for, as will be seen, it facilitates computation considerably."

This is telling with a vengeance. But Gernsback was, basically, a gadgeteer whose interest in science fiction centered almost totally on its value in arousing young readers' interest in science and technology. In their earliest years his magazines reprinted a great many old stories by those great forerunners of science fiction, H. G. Wells and Jules Verne, both of whom understood how to mix scientific speculation with storytelling while keeping a tale moving steadily. But when he ran out of reprints, Gernsback turned for his material mainly to a group of science-oriented amateur writers who cared very little about plausible characters or dramatic plots, and wanted only to tell tales of interesting scientific situations. Where that required a lot of explanation, most of Gernsback's authors lacked the skill to work it into the narrative.

The big, dignified-looking Gernsback magazines went out of business in less than a decade, and their successors were pulp-paper periodicals with names like *Astounding Stories* and *Thrilling Wonder Stories* that specialized in swiftly moving action-based stories for readers who had no interest in scientific lectures. These pulp magazines all too often went too far in the other direction, eliminating not only the lectures but the science, and serving up stories that were essentially just simple tales of cowboys and Indians on Mars, with rayguns replacing the six-shooters and grulzaks instead of Indians. They were fun, and in the hands of a gifted storyteller like Edgar Rice Burroughs they had a kind of cockeyed splendor about them, but they held very little interest for any reader past the age of about fourteen.

It remained for Robert A. Heinlein, starting in 1939, to come up with a way of handling the speculative aspect of science fiction in a manner that would keep a story moving swiftly while at the same time holding the interest of readers more mature than those attracted by the pulps. He adopted — whether consciously or by independent invention, I have no idea — the show-don't-tell technique of Hemingway, adapting it cunningly to the special needs of science fiction, and quickly he became the most interesting and successful writer of sf since H.G. Wells, forty years before.

Heinlein's great innovation involved thrusting readers into the future as a going concern and forcing them to figure things out as they went along. Probably his most famous demonstration of the technique is found in the opening pages of his 1942 novel *Beyond This Horizon*, in which we see his protagonist riding to the thirteenth floor of a government building, where he gets aboard a "slideway" and steps "off the strip" in front of the door of the office he is seeking. And then: "He punched the door with a code combination, and awaited face check. It came properly, the door dilated, and a voice inside said, 'Come in, Felix.' "

No one had ever written science fiction that way before. There are no footnotes and no explanations. Mounted a slideway. Heinlein doesn't describe it. He just tells you that that's how you move around in the future. Awaited face check. The door is scanning people. The door dilated. It didn't simply open; it dilated. So we know that we are in a future where iris-aperture doors are standard items. And we are only a dozen lines or so into the world of *Beyond This Horizon*.

Heinlein seems to have hit on that method of depicting the future right at the outset of his career. His first published story, "Life-Line" (1939), establishes its conceptual framework entirely through dialogue and action. In "The Roads Must Roll" (1940), he does do a few paragraphs explaining the replacement of conventional highways with mechanized conveyor-belt strips, but only after the story is well along. In "If This Goes On — " (also 1940) he creates a strange, forbidding puritanical culture of the future purely by allowing us to inhabit it; there are no historical lectures telling us how we got from here to there. The story is as exciting now as it was seventy years ago. In the relatively late novel *Friday* (1982), we get the full Heinlein technique from the first words: "As I left the Kenya Beanstalk capsule he was right on my heels. He followed me through the door leading to Customs, Health, and Immigration. As the door contracted behind him I killed him. I have never liked riding the Beanstalk. My distaste was full-blown even before the disaster to the Quito Skyhook. . . ."

I quote Heinlein so much here, not only because he was the primary advocate of the Show, Don't Tell school of writing science fiction, but because he also provides us with permission to depart from it when necessary. It can be found in his celebrated 1947 essay, "On the Writing of Speculative Fiction," which is prefaced, significantly, by this notable quote from Rudyard Kipling:

> "There are nine-and-sixty ways
> Of constructing tribal lays
> And every single one of them is right!"

In his essay Heinlein concisely discusses what a story is, lists what he thinks the three main plots of all fiction to be, provides five excellent prerequisites for a story that is specifically science fiction, and offers five much-quoted rules for conducting a career as a writer, four of which strike me as exemplary ("2. You must finish what you start.") and one that seems to me utterly wrongheaded ("3. You must refrain from rewriting except to editorial order."). But while laying down all these laws, Heinlein also tells us this:

> "Don't write to me to point out how I have violated my own rules in this story or that. I've violated all of them and I would much rather try a new story than defend an old one."

There we are. We have Rudyard Kipling's assurance that there is more than one way to construct a satisfactory story, and we have Robert A. Heinlein's admission that he would cheerfully break his own rules whenever it seemed necessary to do so. And so, having devoted this issue's column to a defense of the classic writing-school slogan, "Show, Don't Tell," I'm going to come back to the theme next time and discuss the importance of not taking that slogan too seriously.

Asimov's Science Fiction, **March, 2010**

Showing And Telling: Part II

IN LAST ISSUE'S COLUMN I TALKED ABOUT THE CATCHPHRASE "Show, Don't Tell," so familiar to anyone who has ever attended a class in writing or a writers' workshop. I spoke of how beginning writers are warned against stopping a story's action to insert a slug of narrative explanation of the sort that writing teachers label "expository lumps" or "infodumps." I quoted an example of lump-free fiction by Ernest Hemingway, the most outspoken early advocate of a method of storytelling that depended on a minimum of auctorial exposition to convey the meaning of a story, and I devoted quite a bit of space to the work of Robert A. Heinlein, who, more than anyone else in our field, made use of Hemingway's narrative innovations in order to bring the unfamiliar future to life without the aid of expository lumps or, worse, stodgy masses of footnotes. Hemingway believed that the way to tell a story was to show people *doing* things, not to have the author interpret their deeds for us in little asides. Hemingway wrote about what we like to think of as the real world; but Heinlein brilliantly demonstrated how one could even drop one's readers down in the bewilderingly unfamiliar future without explaining anything to them, letting them find their own way around in the strange environment into which they had been thrust.

What, then, are we to make of a passage like this one? It is the opening paragraph, no less, of a very well-known novel.

"Robert Cohn was once middleweight boxing champion of Princeton. Do not think I am very much impressed by that as a boxing title, but it meant a lot to Cohn. He cared nothing for boxing, in fact he disliked it, but he learned it painfully and thoroughly to counteract the feeling of inferiority and shyness he had felt on being treated as a Jew at Princeton. There was a certain inner comfort in knowing he could knock down anybody who was snooty to him, although, being very shy and a thoroughly nice guy, he never fought anybody except in the gym. He was Spider Kelly's star pupil...."

The passage continues in this vein — an expository lump if ever there was one — for three pages. We hear about Robert Cohn's family, his marital difficulties, his financial problems, his literary ambitions, and his departure for Paris, where, finally, on the third page of the book, we see him in a cafe with a couple of American friends, and one of them — the narrator of the book, as it happens — says, "I know a girl in Strasbourg who can show us the town." It is the first bit of dialog in the book and it does, after a fashion, foreshadow the theme of the book, which deals with the adventures and dis-illusionments of a group of young American expatriates in France just after World War I. And eventually the focus of the book shifts from Robert Cohn to the real protagonist, who is the narrator, one Jake Barnes.

You may, very probably, have guessed from these hints that the novel is *The Sun Also Rises* by Ernest Hemingway, his second and perhaps greatest book. But how can we account for the gigantic infodump — concerning a secondary character, even — that begins the story, and the delay with which the author introduces the webwork of conflicts that constitute the plot of a novel? Can this really be by Hemingway, the advocate of minimal editorial-izing and swift narrative movement? Yes, it can, apparently.

And I've been reading the collected short stories of John Cheever lately. He's generally considered one of the finest short story writers of the twentieth century, an opinion with which I concur. This is the opening of "Just Tell Me Who It Was":

"Will Pym was a self-made man; that is, he had started his adult life without a nickel or a connection, other than the general friend-liness of man to man, and had risen to a vice-presidency in a rayon-blanket firm. He made a large annual contribution to the Baltimore settlement house that had set his feet upon the right path, and he had a few anecdotes to tell about...."

Expository! Expository!

"Mr. Hatherly had many old-fashioned tastes. He wore high yellow boots, dined at Luchow's in order to hear the music, and slept in a woolen nightshirt. His urge to establish in business a patriarchal liaison with some young man who would serve as his descendant, in the fullest sense of the word, was another of these old-fashioned tastes. Mr. Hatherly picked for his heir...."

Another expository opening; Cheever again, "The Children."

Well, you say, Cheever and Hemingway are writing character-driven stories, in which it is, perhaps, legitimate to do a quick passage of expository biography by way of providing a fix on a character, whereas science fiction is generally plot-driven and technology-driven, and it is clumsy writing to move a science fiction plot along through chunks of exposition and to depict a novel technological gimmick with a flatfooted infodump. Maybe so. But Cheever wrote at least one story that could be called science fiction, "The Enormous Radio," and it, too, opens in expository fashion. ("Jim and Irene Westcott were the kind of people who seem to strike that satisfactory average of income, endeavor, and respectability that is reached by the statistical reports in college alumni bulletins.") Despite its clever sf gimmick, though (a new radio that somehow picks up private conversations from all over a Manhattan apartment house) it, too, turns out to be character-driven in the end; so perhaps it is permissible, in a character-driven story, to be expository. Perhaps. (To see how a theme much like that of "The Enormous Radio" can be handled in the pure sf mode, minus expository baggage, check out Henry Kuttner's classic story "The Twonky," where all the emphasis is on plot, not character.)

But sometimes even Heinlein, our own apostle of non-expository writing, found it necessary to slow things down and deliver a history lecture. He always gets the story started quickly, of course. But we see in his much-anthologized "The Roads Must Roll" that after five pages of effective scenes in the action mode he suddenly halted the pace and wrote this:

> "The Age of Power blends into the Age of Transportation almost imperceptibly, but two events stand out as landmarks in the change: the achievement of cheap sun power and the installation of the first mechanized road. The power resources of oil and coal of the United States had — save for a few sporadic outbreaks of common sense — been shamefully wasted in their development all through the first half of the twentieth century. Simultaneously, the automobile...."

And so on for two pages before he gets back to Heinleinesque storytelling. We find the same thing in his well-known novella "Waldo," where, when an explanation is needed early on, Heinlein takes a deep breath and says, "It may plausibly be urged that the shape of a culture — its mores, evaluations, family organization, eating habits, living habits, pedagogical methods, institutions, forms of government, and so forth — arise from the economic necessities of its technology." Again, the passage continues for two more pages. It's Heinlein in his most professorial mode, offered without apology. If we look carefully at almost any Heinlein tale, in fact, we will find him slipping in little background lectures whenever he needs one — not as blatantly as in "Waldo," but they are there, despite his often-stated insistence that the best way to write science fiction was simply to show the future as a going concern, without stopping to explain anything.

Heinlein provides his own justification for that in his famed 1947 essay, "On the Writing of Speculative Fiction," where he says, "Don't write to me to point out how I have violated my own rules in this story or that. I've violated all of them and I would much rather try a new story than defend an old one." (He also notes the distinction between plot-driven and character-driven stories, but he thinks, as I do, that science fiction can accommodate both types: "There are at least two principal ways to write speculative fiction — write about people, or write about gadgets." And then he observes that Olaf Stapledon's *Last and First Men* achieves greatness in science fiction without paying much attention either to characters *or* gadgets. As Kipling says — also quoted by Heinlein — "There are nine-and-sixty ways of constructing tribal lays, and every single one of them is right!"

Where are we, then?

If expository lumps are such evil things, as the teachers of fiction-writing keep telling us, why do we find Hemingway and Cheever and even Heinlein indulging in them?

The answer, I think, is that sometimes, especially in a story that depends heavily on the depiction of character or in one that is set against a truly unfamiliar background, the expository lump becomes a necessity rather than a vice. It's a good idea, especially in a genre like science fiction whose readers tend to get impatient whenever a story starts to slow, not to indulge in such things too extensively. But if a writer is good enough — if he has that inner force, that verbal charisma, that all the top professional writers have and the hopeless amateurs lack — he can get away with anything. A great writer like Jack Vance can pepper his books with dry footnotes that would not have been out of place in one of Hugo Gernsback's magazines of 1928, and no one will mind. Hemingway or Cheever can start a story with a mini-biography of a character, and it will be reprinted a thousand times. Robert A. Heinlein, when he wants to tell you how his rolling roads came into being, will just stop and tell you, and nobody minds.

So the rebuttal to writing-school dogmas is that the way to stop thinking about whether expository lumps are good writing or bad writing is to be as good a writer as Hemingway, Cheever, Heinlein, or Vance, and then you can do whatever you want. Unfortunately, that's something that the writing schools don't seem to be able to teach.

Asimov's Science Fiction, **April-May 2010**

The Evaporation Of Reputations

A COUPLE OF MONTHS AGO THE PEOPLE AT UNIVERSITY OF NEBRASKA Press invited me to write an introduction for a new edition of A. Merritt's 1919 novel *The Moon Pool*, which is going to be included in their new series of reissued fantasy and science fiction classics. These are very handsome paperbacks that are released under the university's Bison Books imprint. I had previously done an introduction for a Bison edition of Camille Flammarion's extraordinary nineteenth-century work, *Omega: The Last Days of the World*, and other books published so far in the same series include Jules Verne's *The Chase of the Golden Meteor* with an introduction by Gregory Benford and a collection of Jack London's short fantasies with an introduction by Philip José Farmer.

The interesting thing — the mystifying thing — is the inclusion of a Merritt novel in this list. Camille Flammarion's book was deservedly famous in its day, but its day was a very long time ago and the novel is known nowadays only to scholars. Many books by Jules Verne and Jack London are still widely read, of course; even so, I had never so much as heard of *The Chase of the Golden Meteor*, and if I were asked to name the titles of Jack London's short fantasy stories I would be able to get no farther than "The Scarlet Plague" and "The Shadow and the Flash."

Merritt, though? What was a book by *A. Merritt*, of all people, doing in a group of obscure fantasy classics being resurrected by a university press?

You, if you fall into the demographic majority of this magazine's readers, are at most fifty years old, very likely a good deal younger, and you are probably asking yourself a different question: "Who was A. Merritt, and what did he write?" But I'm of a different generation, and Merritt, whose eight fantasy novels were published between 1919 and 1934, was very big stuff indeed when I began reading science fiction and fantasy in the late 1940s.

His books were all over the newsstands in various paperback editions that never went out of print, and also were reprinted, again and again, in such pulp magazines of the period as *Fantastic Novels* and *Famous Fantastic Mysteries*. For a brief while in 1950 the publishers of those magazines even brought out an entire magazine that was devoted primarily to his work: *A. Merritt's Fantasy Magazine.*

It is no small thing for a writer of fiction to have a magazine named for him. By definition, it implies wide-ranging name-brand recognition. The very magazine you hold is just such a magazine, after all. In order to understand how astounded I am that the name and work of A. Merritt has been forgotten, here in the dawning year of the twenty-first century, try to imagine a time, fifty years hence, when no one knows who Isaac Asimov was, and his novels are being rediscovered by university presses, complete with scholarly introductions to place them in context!

Merritt, who lived from 1884 to 1943, was, as it happens, quite possibly the most popular fantasy writer of the first half of the twentieth century. In 1938 *Argosy*, the magazine in which most of Merritt's work had first been published, asked its readers to select the best story it had run in its 58 years of existence. (I suppose nobody remembers *Argosy* now either. But it came out every week for decades, had an enormous readership, and paid the highest rates of any magazine for the material it ran. Its pages were filled with serialized novels by the likes of Edgar Rice Burroughs, John Buchan, Max Brand, Zane Grey, Luke Short, Erle Stanley Gardner, and George Allan England, and just about every other important writer of popular fiction of the time.) Merritt's *The Ship of Ishtar*, which *Argosy* had run twelve years earlier, finished at the top of the list of *Argosy* reader favorites, and was promptly reprinted as a six-part serial. The following year, also by popular demand, *Argosy* reprinted Merritt's *Seven Footprints to Satan*, a five-parter dating from 1927.

The outpouring of reader satisfaction after those two reprints led directly to the founding by the publisher of *Argosy* of the two all-fantasy magazines, *Famous Fantastic Mysteries* (1939) and *Fantastic Novels* (1940). Both of them were given over entirely to reprinting fantasy novels from the parent magazine, with Merritt material in virtually every issue; indeed, the very first story in the first issue of *Famous Fantastic Mysteries* was Merritt's original novella version of "The Moon Pool."

Fantasy fans gobbled it all up. They demanded more and more Merritt, which meant drawing on the same small pool of material, since Merritt had stopped writing in the mid-1930s and by 1943 was dead. An authoritative poll of sf and fantasy readers taken in 1944, and again in 1945 and 1946, named Merritt as the favorite novelist all three times, over such contemporaries as Robert A. Heinlein, A.E. van Vogt, L. Ron Hubbard, and E.E. Smith.

His vogue was still going strong when I discovered fantasy fiction about a decade later. The two reprint magazines were still recycling his stories, and late in 1949 they added a companion, the short-lived *A. Merritt's Fantasy*

Magazine, which managed only five issues before sputtering out of existence when the advent of the Korean War sent the price of paper skyrocketing. The real problem with the magazine, though, was that Merritt's oft-reprinted stories had finally become too familiar to the magazine readers of the day to justify starting a third vehicle for them, and his eight novels and handful of short stories would not have kept the magazine going very long anyway. (The second issue, by the way, contains an effusive letter welcoming the new magazine by the fourteen-year-old Robert Silverberg.)

But the novels had moved by then into the primordial paperbacks of the era. Avon Books, whose fantasy editor was the shrewd and knowledgeable Donald A. Wollheim, slipped most of Merritt's novels, rather misleadingly, into a series of large-sized paperbacks it was putting out then under the general title of *Murder Mystery Monthly*, beginning in 1942 with *Seven Footprints to Satan*. The books were wildly successful, and after a few years Avon moved them into the standard paperback format, reissuing them from time to time, decade after decade, on into the 1980s. The later editions carried a banner declaring, "Over 5,000,000 copies of A. Merritt's Books Sold in Avon Editions."

Because I remembered how popular those Avon paperbacks had been, and had seen some new editions of them around in relatively modern times (1979, say), I had assumed that the current immense popularity of fantasy of all kinds would be keeping Merritt's books afloat very nicely. And so the Nebraska request took me by surprise. How, I wondered, had the university folks managed to get the rights to the hugely successful *The Moon Pool* away from the current owner of Avon Books after all these years?

Well, it hadn't been hard at all. Amidst today's vast boom in the kind of fiction he pioneered, Merritt has somehow vanished into oblivion. Titles such as *The Ship of Ishtar*, *Dwellers in the Mirage*, and *The Face in the Abyss* stir no recognition among modern readers. Avon, the paperback company that sold millions of copies of his novels, eventually allowed their publishing rights to lapse. (Avon itself was gobbled up by another company.) And so it has fallen to a university press to restore to print *The Moon Pool*, once the best known of his books, of which a *New York Times* reviewer said only eighty years ago that "it marks the debut of a writer possessed of a very unusual, perhaps one might call it extraordinary, richness of imagination. The author's energy and fertility of imaginative resource never seems to lessen."

But his reputation has. I wonder why.

One might argue that Merritt's storytelling hallmarks — his stock heroes and villains, his florid adjective-rich descriptive prose, his reliance on such by-now-familiar devices as hidden lost races, beautiful and evil high priestesses, dimensional gateways, and the like — are too old-fashioned for today's cynical readers. But in fact the modern commercial genre of fantasy is built on foundations that Merritt (and H. Rider Haggard before him) erected, and most of it makes use of the very same stuff, repackaged only slightly for contemporary tastes.

Nor is cynicism a factor in the conception of fantasy fiction today, anyway, so far as I can see. No narrative trope is too hackneyed for today's fantasists; we have not seen such an outpouring of robust bare-chested sword-swinging heroes, of scheming wizards and sorcerers, of cruel and lovely priestesses with daggers clenched between their teeth, since the heyday of the pulp magazines when Merritt was still at work three quarters of a century ago, and the constant presence of such work on best-seller lists testifies to its renewed popularity. The very cliches out of which innumerable fantasy trilogies are spun nowadays are cliches that Merritt *invented*.

And yet Merritt himself has been forgotten. I don't get it. Robert E. Howard's gaudy pulp fiction still finds scads of readers, sixty-odd years after his death. The same is true of the baroque work of H.P. Lovecraft, another icon of the 1930's. Howard and Lovecraft, I suppose, tap strange forces in the modern psyche that the less neurotic Merritt doesn't reach. For whatever reason, something has swallowed up Merritt's work. The complete evaporation of his literary reputation not only astounds me; it calls to my mind the discomforting image of a world a generation or two hence in which not only the novels of Robert Silverberg have been forgotten — I could live with that, posthumously, at least — but also those of Isaac Asimov, Robert A. Heinlein, Roger Zelazny, Poul Anderson, and just about anyone else whose name you would like to add. If it can happen to Merritt, it can happen to anyone. That's a chilly prospect indeed.

Asimov's Science Fiction, **January 2001**

FOUR
Colleagues
_____

Guest Of Honor

THIS ISSUE WILL BE COMING OUT AROUND THE TIME THE 58TH World Science Fiction Convention is held in Chicago. The Worldcon is the great annual jamboree of the science fiction world, the Labor Day festival where writers and editors and readers get together, Hugo awards are given out, and prominent members of our community are chosen as honored guests. This year's Guests of Honor are the well-known writer Ben Bova (who carried off a slew of Hugos in his days as editor of *Analog* and later of *Omni*), artist Bob Eggleton, he of the matchless hair and many Hugos, and publisher/editor Jim Baen of Baen Books.

I always pay close attention to the Guest of Honor choices. I think being a Worldcon Guest of Honor is one of the two most significant marks of acclaim one can receive in our field, the other being the Grand Master award of the Science Fiction Writers of America (about which, more next month.) Such awards as Hugos and Nebulas are transient things, given for individual pieces of work; Worldcon Guests of Honor and SFWA Grand Masters are being singled out for a lifetime of extraordinary achievement.

In modern times, alas, being a Worldcon Guest of Honor is not quite the gaudy thing it used to be. You still get your expenses paid, and a splendid suite to stay in, and your photograph and biography in the program book, and all of that. But conventions nowadays have four or five or even more Guests of Honor a year — a writer, an editor, an artist, sometimes a "media" guest, whatever that is. In the olden days there would be just one GoH, who might be an artist or an editor or, more usually, a writer, and that one person was the focus of all eyes throughout the weekend. The modern system, necessary though it is, dilutes the impact.

Conventions were much smaller events back then, too — just a few hundred attendees, or at most a thousand, whereas today they run to five thousand or more. The highlight of the convention, the Hugo ceremony, had the format of a Saturday night banquet in which the Guest of Honor made a major after-dinner speech just before the awards were given out. Everyone was there; everyone listened raptly to what the GoH had to say. Today the Hugo banquet is no more, and the Guest of Honor speeches themselves have been separated from the evening award ceremony and are tucked away at odd times during the afternoon, so that you have to make a special attempt to find them. I regret that. It subtracts mightily from the glory of being Guest of Honor.

That glory has been conferred in interesting ways, over the years. We have had, for example, only two three-time honorees, and they are exactly the people you would have expected. Robert A. Heinlein, who at the age of 34 had made himself, within two years, the dominant science fiction writer of the age, was GoH at the Denver convention in 1941; he was picked again in 1961, at Seattle, and yet again for the 1976 Kansas City convention. And John W. Campbell, Jr., that towering figure among editors, was honored in 1947 in Philadelphia, in 1954 in San Francisco, and again in 1957 in London. (The Londoners didn't care, in that pre-jet-travel age, that Campbell had had the honor just a few years before. That San Francisco convention might just as well have been on the moon, for them, and they wanted their own glimpse of him!) I don't know which is the more extraordinary feat: to be tapped three times in eleven years, as Campbell was, or to reach across three and a half decades, as Heinlein did.

A few writers have been chosen twice. Robert Bloch, not yet famed as the author of *Psycho* but much beloved by sf fans, was GoH in Toronto in 1948, and then again — also Toronto — in 1973. Fritz Leiber was chosen by New Orleans in 1951 and Brighton, England, in 1979. Brian Aldiss has had two shots, London in 1965, Brighton (with Leiber) in 1979. Clifford Simak was named in 1971 (Boston) and again in 1981 (Denver).

Unsurprisingly, the early Guests of Honor were titanic figures, now almost mythical. The very first one (New York, 1939) was Frank R. Paul, the cover artist for Hugo Gernsback's pioneering magazines, and a man of enormous ebullience and charm. (Gernsback himself was Chicago's GoH in 1952.) The second convention (Chicago, 1940) picked E.E. "Doc" Smith, the author of the classic Lensman series; Heinlein was next, and in 1946, in Los Angeles after the wartime hiatus, A.E. van Vogt, chosen in tandem with his wife, the writer E. Mayne Hull. (There have been several subsequent husband-wife choices, Leigh Brackett and Edmond Hamilton in Oakland in 1964, Damon Knight and Kate Wilhelm in Boston in 1980, and one pair of brothers, Arkady and Boris Strugatsky of Russia (Brighton, 1987.)

Since Guests of Honor are chosen not by popular vote but by the small group of sf fans who actually run each year's conventions, there have been oddities and injustices. Nobody got around to Ray Bradbury until Atlanta did in 1983. Alfred Bester was practically on his deathbed when he was chosen for the 1987 Brighton convention, and was unable to attend. Such great writers as Hal Clement (Chicago, 1991) and Jack Vance (Orlando, 1992) had been writing more than forty years before they were finally honored, Frederik Pohl (Los Angeles, 1972) more than thirty, and Jack Williamson (Miami Beach, 1977) close to fifty. In contrast, my own turn (Heidelberg, Germany, 1970) came when I was only 35 years old and in the second decade of my career, and though I was delighted to be picked, it astounded me to have been selected ahead of such great figures as Pohl, Vance, Clement, Bradbury, and Williamson.

I've been to all but a few of the 58 Worldcons, and I've seen some extraordinary Guest of Honor performances. Right at the top is the stunt Robert Heinlein pulled in Seattle in 1961, when he invited *the entire convention* to a cocktail party in his suite. There were only 300 people at that convention, but it was a phenomenal thing, all the same, to see the legendary Heinlein holding court (in his bathrobe, and Heinlein looked more distinguished in a bathrobe than almost any other man would in a tuxedo) and playing bartender as well for an army of goggle-eyed readers.

Then there was the time when Philip José Farmer, who was Guest of Honor in Berkeley, California during the revolutionary year of 1968, decided to turn his Guest of Honor speech at the Hugo banquet into an elaborate proposal for transforming the world into Utopia. It was my misfortune to be toastmaster at that banquet, conducted during a rare Berkeley heat wave, and I had to remain on stage throughout the whole interminable event: Phil went on and on and on, speaking for what felt like days, and many of us began to wonder if we'd survive long enough to see the Hugos handed out.

This was just the opposite of what had happened the year before in New York. That convention's Guest of Honor was the normally loquacious Lester del Rey; but Lester, infuriated by an overlengthy and strikingly non-amusing speech delivered just prior to his, tore up what probably would have been a fiery hour-long rant, replaced it with just a few curt, chilly sentences, and sat down.

I don't think anyone ever enjoyed being Guest of Honor more than Isaac Asimov (Cleveland, 1955.) That was one of the smaller conventions, only about 400 attendees, and Isaac, who was thirty-five years old then and full of vitality, was all over the place, hugging people, introducing himself to astonished strangers, improvising limericks, singing Gilbert & Sullivan. At the end of the convention he announced that he would be willing to accept the title of Guest of Honor Emeritus and repeat the performance at every subsequent convention, and perhaps he would have, except that the following year's Guest of Honor, in New York, was a formidable rival in the ego department, the redoubtable Arthur C. Clarke, who managed quite effectively to keep the spotlight on himself, rather than the self-appointed Guest of Honor Emeritus.

Then there was the year (the Hague, 1990) when there were three Guests of Honor, Harry Harrison, Joe Haldeman, and the German editor/

writer Wolfgang Jeschke, all of whom had conspicuous gray beards. That was their only real point of similarity, but people who had never met them before were confusing them all weekend. (Haldeman shaved his beard off soon afterward and no one will ever mistake him for Harry Harrison again.)

And Harlan Ellison, in 1978, Phoenix: he did it the Harlan way, of course, setting up a plastic tent in the lobby of the hotel and spending the weekend writing a story out in public. It was posted, page by page, as he turned it out, and at the end of the convention Ben Bova bought it for *Omni*. (Harlan was also having a political quarrel with the state of Arizona that year, and since he was boycotting Arizona hotels and restaurants, he came to the convention in a rented camper, in which he slept and ate throughout the entire weekend.)

Nor will I forget Samuel L. Clemens — that's right, Mark Twain — who was the official *Ghost* of Honor at the 1993 San Francisco convention. Jon DeCles, in appropriate costume, "channeled" him for the convention-goers.

That was a clever stunt, though I'm glad it hasn't been repeated. Nevertheless, it saddens me to think of the writers who missed their turns because death took them too soon — people such as Frank Herbert, Cyril Kornbluth, Philip K. Dick, Fletcher Pratt. Avram Davidson would have made a wonderful Guest of Honor, and — startling thought! —probably L. Ron Hubbard would have, too. And there are other fine writers, still living, who have been mysteriously neglected in the great GoH lottery as well. They know who they are. I hope some future convention committee does also.

And *you* — fifteen years old, reading this now, dreaming of the day when your first story is published — can it be that you will be one of the Guests of Honor at the 2030 Worldcon? I certainly hope so, and that I'm there to shake your hand when you come up to remind me of this column. I'll be glad to meet you. Maybe we can go off to the bar for a drink together. Hell, I won't even be a hundred yet.

Asimov's Science Fiction, **Oct-Nov 2000**

The Grand Masters

THE NEWEST WINNER OF THE GRAND MASTER AWARD of the Science Fiction Writers of America is Brian Aldiss, the great British writer whose illustrious array of books includes *Hothouse*, *Cryptozoic*, the magnificent Helliconia Trilogy, and a dozen or so volumes of dazzlingly innovative short stories. Aldiss joined the roster of Grand Masters at the annual awards banquet of SFWA in New York City in May.

The SFWA Grand Master award is one of the two highest distinctions our field confers — the other being the Guest of Honor designation at the World Science Fiction Convention, which I discussed in last issue's column. These awards recognize a lifetime of significant work; and anyone who wants to understand the history of science fiction in the twentieth century need only look at SFWA's list of Grand Masters.

It was Jerry Pournelle, when he was President of SFWA nearly thirty years ago, who dreamed up the idea of the Grand Master award. Since 1965 SFWA had been giving its Nebula trophy annually to the authors of the best novels and short fiction of the previous year; but Pournelle felt that the accomplishments of some of our greatest figures were being slighted, because they had done their outstanding work in the years prior to the Nebula's inception. So he proposed a special award — an oversized version of the handsome block of Lucite that is a Nebula — to be awarded by vote of SFWA's officers and past presidents in acknowledgment of the significant work those writers had done over the long term. And, to avoid cheapening the value of the award, Pournelle stipulated that it should be given no more often than six times every decade.

Pournelle's suggestion was eagerly accepted by the membership, and in 1975 the first Grand Master Nebula was given to Robert A. Heinlein, surely one of the defining figures of modern science fiction. Heinlein's recent work had come under attack by critics who found fault with it on literary and even on political grounds, but no one questioned the greatness of the man who had written *Methusaleh's Children, Double Star, The Moon is a Harsh Mistress*, and the Future History stories. (And, in fact, his career was far from over even in 1975: he would go on to produce such well-received novels as *Friday* and *The Cat Who Walks Through Walls* in the years following his receiving of the award.)

In those days nearly all the writers who had clustered around the great editor John W. Campbell of *Astounding Science Fiction* to create the so-called "golden age" period of the 1940s were still alive, and they were the obvious choices for grand-masterhood in the next few years. And so Jack Williamson, who had given us *The Legion of Space* back in the 1930s, and such golden-age Campbell-era classics as the Seetee and Humanoids books, became the second Grand Master in 1976. Clifford D. Simak, of *City* and *Way Station* fame, joined the group the following year.

Since the rules stipulated only six awards per decade, no Grand Master was chosen in 1978; but in 1979 another golden-age favorite, L. Sprague de Camp, he of *Lest Darkness Fall* and *The Incomplete Enchanter* and ever so much more, was honored. Another year was skipped, and then in 1980 Fritz Leiber (*Conjure Wife, The Wanderer, Gather, Darkness!*) was the pick.

Under the rules no further award could be given until 1984, when Andre Norton became the first female Grand Master (a designation that created certain grammatical problems that have never been adequately resolved) and also the first who had not been associated with the Campbell editorship.

You may be wondering, at this point, why the name of Isaac Asimov has not yet been included in the list. As it happened, Isaac was wondering the same thing, since he, too, had been a key member of the John Campbell team, and by the 1980s the name of "Asimov" was virtually synonymous with science fiction, as the very magazine you are reading now will testify. And so, in his goodnaturedly selfpromoting way, Isaac was given to observing, far and wide, that a certain conspicuous figure of the era had not yet been given his due. He said it playfully, of course, and made it clear that he was just joking — but in fact there was no small degree of seriousness beneath his clowning. He privately suspected that he was not going to live many more years, and he wanted to win that award before he died.

It is quite true that one of the considerations involved in nominating people for the award is an actuarial one. Even great writers don't live forever, and we have always tried to honor our oldest ones first. Heinlein and De Camp had been born in 1907, Williamson in 1908, Leiber in 1910, Norton in 1912, Simak all the way back in 1904. Isaac — born in 1920 — was a veritable youth by comparison. No one was aware in the 1980s of how quickly Isaac's health was weakening, though. So, despite his otherwise quite valid claim and all his yelps, he simply had to sit by and wait, even while his great friend and rival, Arthur C. Clarke (born 1917) carried off the 1986 trophy.

But of course a group of Grand Masters that did not include Isaac Asimov was plainly incomplete; and his torment came to an end in 1987 at a ceremony in New York. I went up to him afterward to congratulate him as he stood there cradling the trophy in his arms; and as I put out my hand he feigned a look of great alarm, as though I were trying to take it away from him, and cried, "You can't have it! You can't have it! You have to wait another fifteen years!"

Isaac was only 67 when he finally won. (And he was only 72 when he died, five years after winning!) But the curious thing about factoring a calculation of the recipient's age into our choice of award-winners was that in the first decade of the award's existence, all the very senior figures to whom we gave the trophies went right on living and, in most cases, actively writing as well, after they received it. I remember Jerry Pournelle saying to me, somewhere around 1985, "We may be giving *literal* immortality to the winners."

Indeed, of the first six Grand Masters, three are still alive as I write this — Jack Williamson and Sprague de Camp, both past 90, and Andre Norton, at 88. And that dear man Cliff Simak, though he did die eventually in his mid-eighties, managed the remarkable trick of winning a Nebula for his short story "The Grotto of the Dancing Deer" in 1981, the first time a Grand Master had won one of the annual trophies *after* joining the elect group. (Nor has anyone turned the trick since.)

But not everyone, alas, shared in the mysterious gift of longevity that the Grand Mastership seemed to confer. The name of Alfred Bester (*The Demolished Man, The Stars My Destination*) had frequently come up in preliminary discussions among the people who pick the winners, but each year some other writer's qualifications always seemed more urgent. So by the time Alfie actually was chosen for the trophy, in 1987, he was a very sick man, and he did not live to attend the 1988 ceremony at which it was awarded. Thus he became our only posthumous Grand Master.

Bester, at least, was still living when he was chosen, and had been informed before his death that he had won. The SFWA rules make it impossible for dead writers to be chosen, which is why Jules Verne and H.G. Wells and Aldous Huxley are not on the list — and, alas, such an unquestionable modern master as Theodore Sturgeon, whose death at the age of 67 prematurely removed him from contention. Frank Herbert, who died at 65, is another likely winner who didn't last long enough to make it. The same can be said of Philip K. Dick, dead at the age of 54 in 1982.

Ray Bradbury, though, took his place on the roster in 1989, and Lester del Rey, one of the two remaining survivors of the Campbell era, was the 1991 choice. (The other surviving golden-age figure, and a towering one indeed, was A.E. van Vogt. But the author of *The World of Null-A* and *Slan* was unaccountably kept waiting until 1996, when he was 84 years old and already suffering from the onset of Alzheimer's Disease. Van Vogt nevertheless attended the ceremony in person and — no doubt at tremendous personal effort — managed to deliver a creditable acceptance speech.)

The other Grand Masters chosen in the 1990s were men who made their marks in the postwar era, when John Campbell no longer was the dominant figure in the field. Frederik Pohl, whose remarkable career has brought him a bushel of awards both as author and editor, capped it with the Grand Master Nebula in 1993. The formidable critic, teacher, and short story writer Damon Knight took the award home in 1995. Jack Vance, he of *The Dying Earth* and *Big Planet* and *The Dragon Masters*, was the 1997 winner, and Poul Anderson — *Three Hearts and Three Lions*, *Guardians of Time*, *The Boat of a Million Years*, and ever so much more — won in 1998. Last year's winner was Hal Clement, who earned his place in the archives with *Needle*, *Iceworld*, and *Mission of Gravity*.

Now Brian Aldiss takes his place on the roll of honor. You can certainly think of eight or ten other writers who belong on it, and so can I (though I won't name them here, because I'm one of the past presidents of SFWA who nominates and votes on the Grand Masters, and I think that everything concerning future choices should be kept under wraps until the winner is announced.) It is an awesome list. In giving them our trophy, we do them honor, yes — but in fact it is this group of Grand Masters who honored us with their unforgettable stories, and we who love science fiction owe them not just plastic trophies but our eternal gratitude.

Asimov's Science Fiction, **December 2000**

And a postscript, a decade later: in 2004 Isaac Asimov's 1987 prediction came true, only two years late, when the Science Fiction Writers of America added me to the Grand Master list. Of all the honors I've received from the science fiction world since my first one, the Hugo in 1956 for Most Promising New Author, this is the one I cherish the most, because it places me in a select group of writers who — Vance and Anderson and Heinlein and Asimov and Leiber and most of the others — were idols and models for me when I was first setting out on my career. It is a rare pleasure for a writer to take a seat at the table with his own heroes.

The Skald of Science Fiction

POUL ANDERSON, THE GREAT SCIENCE FICTION WRITER WHO DIED LAST SUMMER at the age of seventy-four, was a Viking, no doubt about that, Danish by ancestry and name and profoundly rooted in the ancient Nordic traditions. On first acquaintance you might not have understood that. We soft modern civilized folk tend to think of Vikings as pretty rough-hewn fellows, ferocious unkempt swaggerers with blazing eyes and hot tempers — a race of warriors. Poul was, in fact, a gentle and kind-hearted person, who maintained an unfailing sweetness of spirit under all circumstances. He was as unswaggering as they come, our science fictional Viking, and neither by temperament nor physique could he be regarded as a warrior in the usual meaning of that term.

Though he was a tall and rangy man, his eyesight was poor and his physical coordination was terrible. I remember with some amusement his sorry performance during the Society for Creative Anachronism tournament at the 1968 World Science Fiction Convention in Berkeley. In those years the S.C.A. people staged mock jousts at the conventions, amidst much grand and formal medieval foofaraw. And Poul, though he had not been designed by nature for combat, enjoyed the scholarly aspects of the S.C.A.'s recreations of times gone by, and was a familiar figure at their gatherings.

This time Poul and the equally unathletic Randall Garrett, good sports both, let themselves be talked into sallying into the lists of battle, with the stated intention of "defending the honor of John W. Campbell," the famed editor for whom they had each written so many fine stories. Poul, who could easily get into the spirit of such an organization, fought under the name of Sir Bela of Eastmarch of the Kingdom of the West; what name Garrett chose, I could not tell you at this late date. A more unlikely duo of science fictional swordsmen I would be hard pressed to name.

They were paired against two of the Anachronists' grimmest, stark-est knights, true adepts of swordplay. (One of them, I recall, was Marion Zimmer Bradley's younger brother Paul, a formidable hand with mace and broadsword.) It took about 3.5 seconds for Poul and Randall to be slaugh-tered in the joust. It was a fearful massacre. John Campbell's two awkward champions barely had a chance to raise their wooden swords before they found themselves clobbered to the ground by their implacable opponents. Poul — even when he was masquerading as Sir Bela of Eastmarch — was indeed an ill-made knight. (But I have it on good authority that this was one of Poul's least distinguished episodes of combat — he was under the handi-cap that day of having partied a little too enthusiastically the night before.)

A true Viking he was, all the same, legitimate heir to his remote Nordic ancestors. Not all Vikings had to be warriors, back in the savage days of old. There were poets among them, too — *skalds,* they were called — and their role in Norse culture was every bit as important as that of the brawnier fel-lows who swung the big swords and wielded the battleaxes. More so, perhaps: for any muscle-bound lummox could wave a sword around, but the skalds were the necessary chroniclers who gave life and meaning to the age in which the Vikings carried out their bloody deeds. They were the men who wrote the sagas, that great body of glorious Scandinavian poetry and prose: the Eddas and the related Volsunga saga, say, from both of which Wagner's *Ring* operas grew, and the stirring epics of the heroes Grettir the Strong and Njal and Hrolf Kraki, and Snorri Sturlason's *Heimskringla,* or *Book of Kings,* which tells us what we know of the great Viking chieftains, and many anoth-er powerful poem that has come down to us out of that misty Nordic world of a thousand years ago, a literature of dirges and battle-songs and historical chronicles and soaring tales of bloody conflict and adventure. It is through the work of the skalds, more than from any other source, that we derive our understanding of the Viking way.

Those Viking skalds were superb poets, many of them, and their finest works are imperishable classics of literature. Poul Anderson, who grew up reading the Norse sagas the way we grew up reading Mark Twain and Lewis Carroll, was *our* skald, carrying that ancient bardic tradition of high adven-ture and singing poetic style into the very different world of starships and time machines. I like to think that people will be reading his greatest science fiction novels as long as anyone reads science fiction.

Certainly I'll never forget my initial encounter with his work, that grim little story of a dark post-atomic future, "Tomorrow's Children," which ap-peared the year I was twelve. It was Poul's second published story, written when he was just nineteen himself. (His first, a two-page squib, appeared in *Astounding* in 1944, before his eighteenth birthday.)

And then, in the 1950s and 1960s, came the torrent of irresistibly read-able stories and novels that brought him a houseful of Hugos and Nebulas and put him on the road to SFWA's Grand Master award — *Brain Wave, Three*

Hearts and Three Lions, the classic novella "Call Me Joe," *The High Crusade,* and the Time Patrol stories, and the lighthearted Hoka tales that he wrote with his dear friend Gordon R. Dickson, on and on for decades thereafter, "The Queen of Air and Darkness," "Goat Song," "Hunter's Moon," the Dominic Flandry stories, the Nicholas van Rijn stories — shelf after glorious shelf of wonderful tales. Just the day before he died I received a new issue of *Analog* with his latest, though apparently not his last, story. I understand that there may be several novels still in the publishing pipeline. Poul was always a ferociously productive writer, and he went on working practically to the end.

One of those forthcoming books, I'm told, hearkens back to his skaldic ancestors: a book based in part on the Icelandic epic *Egil's Saga,* which deals with the relentless feud between the hero Egil and his enemy Eirik Bloodaxe (an Andersonian name if there ever was one!). Nor was that the first time that Poul made such explicit literary use of his Scandinavian heritage. As far back as 1954 he published the undeservedly neglected fantasy novel *The Broken Sword,* set in the world of the Aesir of Asgard, and embellished by a great deal of Poul's own skaldic poetry, following the ancient meter ("Swiftly goes the sword-play; / Spears on hosts are raining; / men run forth in madness, / mowing ranks of foemen; / battle tumult bellows; / blood is red on axeheads; / greedily the gray wolf / gorges with the raven.") And twenty years after that came *Hrolf Kraki's Saga,* in which he recreated one of the great Nordic poems that had come down to modern times only in fragments and botched summaries. Since a complete version of the saga no longer existed, Poul wrote it for us.

For all his great accomplishments over a long and marvelously prolific career, he was a modest man, who never claimed to be anything more than a popular entertainer. (His legion of readers knew better.) His prime concern as a storyteller was, as it should be, storytelling: he knew how to snare a reader and how to hold him in that snare, and with skaldic cunning he called upon details of sight, sound, smell, and taste to make every paragraph a vivid one. But there have been plenty of tellers of tales whose work ultimately rings hollow, however lively it seems on first acquaintance. What Poul was really doing as a writer was dealing with the great moral themes of existence within the framework of society: values, purpose, the meaning of life itself. Who am I? His characters asked, not in so many words but through their deeds. How shall I live my life? What are my obligations to myself and my fellow beings? Where does personal freedom end and the bond that creates a society begin? Big questions, all of them, with which great writers have been wrestling since the time of Homer and the author of the Gilgamesh epic before that; and Poul did not shy away from them, even as he pretended to be telling swift-paced tales of the space-lanes.

In person he often tended to be quiet and even shy, the antithesis of today's science fictional self-promoters, although he knew how to look after himself pretty well in his dealings with the publishing world. But in the right setting Poul was anything but quiet, anything but shy. At any convention party, for example, you could usually find him in the center of a fascinated group of listeners, holding forth with great animation and much flailing of arms (he was an energetic gesturer) on the conversational topic of the moment, be it slavery in ancient Rome, the cultural significance of the Lascaux cave paintings, the physics of time travel, the techniques of brewing beer in Belgium, or the customs regulations of the Byzantine Empire. The sound of his voice was unmistakable — a high-pitched, herkyjerk baritone — and so was the flow of unpretentious erudition that would come from him whenever talk veered toward any of his innumerable areas of profound expertise.

I knew him for more than forty years. He and I had an amiable collegial relationship for much of that time, and in my days as an editor of anthologies we worked together on many projects easily and well, and for the past three decades we lived in neighboring communities, but somehow we never became close friends as I understand that term, despite the high regard that each of us had for the other. When we met at parties, which was fairly often, we usually gravitated toward each other and exchanged tales of recent foreign travel, or discussed the various malfeasances of various publishers and agents, or got into pleasant dispute over some fine point of history. Of real personal intimacy, though, there was very little between us. Others I know reported the same phenomenon; and yet when Poul did take someone into that kind of close friendship — Gordy Dickson, say, or Jack Vance, or Ted Cogswell — it was a deep and close friendship indeed. A matter of chemistry, I guess.

His voice, as a writer, was as distinctive as was his way of speaking. One would have had to be style-deaf indeed to fail to recognize a Poul Anderson story after hearing only a paragraph or two of it. The powerful use of imagery and sensory detail, above all the dark rhythms that had come down to him out of the Viking literature of long ago, were all unmistakable. He was indeed our Nordic bard, the skald of science fiction. And if there's a Valhalla for science fiction writers, Poul is up there right now, putting down Odin's finest mead with the best of them.

Asimov's Science Fiction, January, 2002

H.G. Wells

————————

A FEW YEARS BACK I WROTE A NOVEL IN WHICH THE EARTH IS INVADED by vastly superior alien beings, against whom we are unable to mount any significant defense. I would not, of course, make any pretense of having invented that theme, and in my dedication I let it be known that I was aware of who had:

FOR H.G. WELLS, THE FATHER OF US ALL.

I meant it. Not only is *The War of the Worlds* by H.G. Wells the first of all alien-invasion stories — a pathbreaking novel of stark originality by the finest mind that ever applied itself to the writing of science fiction — but it's possible to discern the hand of Wells behind almost every one of the major themes of modern science fiction. His achievement was dazzling and dizzying. He opened all the doors for us, a century ago, and we have been following in his myriad paths ever since.

Not that Wells can take credit for inventing science fiction itself. There were plenty of predecessors. We can trace the ancestry of that sort of literary speculation back and back and back, through such figures of the middle and late nineteenth century as Jules Verne and Edgar Allan Poe and H. Rider Haggard, and beyond them to Mary Shelley and her *Frankenstein* of 1816, Jonathan Swift and *Gulliver's Travels* of 1727, and on and on — Cyrano de Bergerac's *Voyage to the Moon* of 1650, Sir Thomas More's *Utopia* of 1516, and onward into Roman times with the second-century *True History* of Lucian of Samosata and the Greek era with Plato's tales of lost Atlantis in *Timias* and *Kritias*. Finally we get to Homer's *Odyssey* and the Sumerian epic of *Gilgamesh* before the trail disappears into the mists of prehistory. I have no doubt that

Cro-Magnon storytellers were entertaining the tribe around those Ice Age campfires with yarns about the wondrous unknown lands beyond the rainbow.

It's a fine long pedigree, and I have recited it many times. Yet, somehow — Verne and Mrs. Shelley and Swift notwithstanding — the immediate ancestor of the particular kind of science fiction that has preoccupied me for most of my life, the science fiction I found as a wonderstruck boy in the pages of *Astounding Science Fiction*, the science fiction of Robert A. Heinlein and Isaac Asimov and Jack Williamson and A.E. van Vogt, the science fiction I myself have spent the last fifty years writing, was H.G. Wells.

Sure, Plato invented a lost continent and told us wonderful tales about it more than two thousand years ago, and Swift squeezed a lot of satiric juice out of the imaginary lands and peoples he sent Gulliver off to visit, and Cyrano spun a delightful yarn about getting himself to the moon aboard a flying chariot powered by sky rockets, and Mary Shelley dreamed up a synthetic human being whose sad story has been part of popular culture ever since. Those are legitimate science fictional themes and their creators are legitimate progenitors of our field.

But for the origin of the specific *way* we write science fiction today, the whole tone of it — for the characteristic mating of speculative plot and scientifically informed thinking and realistic writing for the sake of demonstrating in a rigorously logical manner the dramatic consequences of a single strikingly imaginative concept — we have to look to Herbert George Wells.

Wells, who was born in Bromley, Kent, England in 1866, managed in his impoverished youth to obtain a scientific education that gave him, he said, "an exceptionally clear and ordered view of the ostensibly real universe." He had trouble with mathematics in his physics courses, though, and he proved to have no gift at all for laboratory experiments, and so he failed to get the first-class degree he needed for the career in science that he was hoping to have.

The only prospect that seemed open to him was the low-paying one of schoolteaching, a choice that he found uninspiring. He found the idea of teaching agreeable enough: he was nothing if not a teacher by inherent nature. But classroom teaching on the elementary-school level was not what Wells had in mind. He had no yearning to spend his days behind a desk trying to convey basic scientific information to restless young students concerned only with mastering enough data to pass their examinations. He bubbled with ideas of the most vivid and original sort, ideas that he longed to communicate to the whole world, and very quickly it occurred to him that he might be able to do it as a writer.

He turned to journalism first, setting forth his philosophical and scientific theories and beliefs in essays for newspapers and magazines. But gradually he glided into the more lucrative field of fiction, where, he realized, he could embody his ideas in books and stories that might win him a far larger audience than scientific essays ever could. And the kind of fiction that to the young Wells seemed most effective in conveying those ideas was what we would call science fiction today. He wrote his first science fiction stories in his early twenties at a time when the term "science fiction" was decades away from being invented, and, between *The Time Machine* (1895) and *In the Days of the Comet* (1906), poured forth such a torrent of imaginative novels and short stories that a vast legion of his successors, among whom I count myself, has spent an entire century running variations on the speculative themes that he was the first to employ.

The extent of Wells' conceptual originality during that fabulously prolific decade must inspire awe and humility in the soul of anyone who ventures to write science fiction in his wake. Certainly it does in me, and I know more than a little about what it is like to be a prolific writer.

Consider *The Time Machine*, an early draft of which dates from 1888 but which did not reach its present form until 1895. That was the first work of fiction to apply a technological solution to the classic human yearning to peer into the future. Earlier writers had employed such flimsy devices as dreams or trances or hypnosis, mere pretexts to set their narratives going, to give us their visions of things to come. A quintessential example is the biblical *Book of Revelation*, pure vision without any kind of rationalization. Washington Irving's Rip van Winkle (1819) was a time-traveler of sorts, simply falling asleep and waking up in the future. Edward Bellamy, in his 1887 novel *Looking Backward*, used suspended animation to send his nineteenth-century man into the year 2000.

But Wells, writing at a time when the automobile itself was still a fascinating novelty, came up with the startling and completely new notion of a *machine*, a solid, substantial, tangible machine, with quartz rods and nickel bars and glistening brass rails, in which to send his traveler zooming away to the ends of time. Thus he provided something that no writer of time-travel stories had thought of before: a time-traveling vehicle capable of being steered, and therefore under the volitional control of the voyager.

It hardly matters that a journey powered by such a device has no more scientific plausibility than one powered by the fumes of an opium pipe: by anchoring his fantastic fable to so tangible a mechanistic image, Wells made it *seem* plausible, at least long enough to get his time traveler on his way, and then could move that traveler through a variety of imagined futures for the sake of illustrating his fundamental narrative points. Through skillful writing he was able to give his gadget the texture and conviction of reality — an essential trick for attaining that willing suspension of disbelief that lies at the heart of all successful imaginative fiction. The time *machine* was a marvelous idea, which of course has been imitated countless times since. But Wells was the first to think of it.

Nor was he content to use his time machine as the vehicle for a mere sightseeing trip into the future, as earlier Victorian adventure-story writers might have chosen to do. Because he was a thinker and a social critic as well as a great storyteller, Wells embedded in his time-travel story his speculations on the future of industrial society, so that the novel is not just a recitation of wonders but also an expression of its author's insight into the workings of the rapidly changing society in which he lived. That kind of double vision has been the hallmark of the best science fiction ever since.

Wells followed that extraordinary work with *The Island of Dr. Moreau* (1896), the greatest of all scientific horror stories. In *The Odyssey* Circe transforms men into beasts, a sad business for her victims but not really all that difficult to achieve, as the somber and bloody events of the twentieth century so plainly demonstrated. But Wells' Dr. Moreau turned the much tougher trick of transforming beasts into men, and the result was not merely a novel of terrifying power but one that offers some profound and bleakly pessimistic thoughts about the nature of human nature. And hardly had *Moreau* reached the bookstalls but Wells was back with *The Invisible Man* (also 1897), another dark and brilliant thriller that showed, as Wells himself noted, "the danger of power without control, the development of the intelligence at the expense of human sympathy."

Still riding a great surge of creative energy, Wells produced book after book during the next few years, still focusing mainly on science fiction — *When the Sleeper Wakes* (1899), a nightmarish dystopian view of the twenty-second century; *The First Men in the Moon* (1901), a harsh satiric fantasy once more aimed at the difficult problem of maintaining individual identity within a huge totalitarian society; *The Food of the Gods* (1901), which examines the consequences of trying to create a race of supermen; and *In the Days of the Comet* (1906), in which human consciousness is radically transformed by a mysterious green gas emanating from the tail of a comet that sweeps past our world.

And then there were the short stories, published during the same years in every important British magazine: about sixty of them that constitute the finest single body of short science fiction ever produced by one writer: "The Star," "The Country of the Blind," "The Empire of the Ants," "In the Abyss," "The Door in the Wall," "The Crystal Egg," "The New Accelerator," and many more. They were captivating narratives packed with vivid imagery and provocative ideas, enough tales to fill a thousand closely printed pages when collected in one volume: an astonishing array of little masterpieces.

After that prodigious decade of science fiction writing Wells moved on to other things. His literary output remained enormous, but his greatest achievements in science fiction now were behind him, and his work in the years that followed consisted chiefly of mainstream novels portraying English life in the early twentieth century, books dealing with science, philosophy, and history, and polemic non-fiction that explored many of the same issues of the effects of technological progress on human life that he had earlier looked into in his science fiction novels and stories. (The titles of some of the many books tell the story: *The Outline of History* (1920), *The Salvaging of Civilization* (1921), *The Common Sense of World Peace* (1928), *The Science of Life* (1930), and so on through *The Fate of Homo Sapiens* (1939) and *Science and the World Mind* (1942), and seven more in a similar vein after that. He kept on writing right to the end of his long life, which came in 1946, just as the atomic bomb was transforming world history in a fashion that Wells himself, of course, had forecast many decades before.

His restlessly roving mind drove him again and again in those later years to venture also into novels of a science fictional sort, though this later work, driven primarily by ideological issues, was usually didactic in tone, making little attempt to attain the sort of narrative power that he achieved in the earlier books. The philosopher within him was forever at war with the entertainer, but, with his literary reputation established, he rarely allowed the entertainer to gain the upper hand.

His visionary gifts never left him, though. In *The War in the Air* (1908) he seized on the recent invention of the airplane to portray the vast destruction that aerial bombardment would be wreaking less than a decade later. *The World Set Free* (1914) is famous for its prediction of atomic warfare, but, perhaps more notably, Wells also envisions the horrendous trench warfare that would characterize the great war about to break out. As late as 1933, with *The Shape of Things to Come*, this extraordinary man was still trying to tear away the veils that shroud the future and show us the dark and terrible wonders that he saw.

Of all the remarkable novels and stories that came pouring from him during the spectacular ten years when he essentially created modern science fiction, it is, I think, *The War of the Worlds* that has had the greatest impact on our culture.

It was published in magazine form in 1897 and as a book the next year, and thus was the fourth of the novels in that great early spate, following hard upon *The Time Machine*, *The Island of Dr. Moreau*, and *The Invisible Man*. As we look back at *The War of the Worlds* now, our view of its originality of theme is obscured by the hundreds of later novels that also have told the tale of the invasion of Earth by terrifying alien beings: Philip Francis Nowlan's *Armageddon 2419* (1928), which gave us Buck Rogers, John Wyndham's *Day of the Triffids* (1951), Robert A. Heinlein's *The Puppet Masters* (1951), Arthur C. Clarke's *Childhood's End* (1953), Jack Finney's *The Body Snatchers* (1955), Theodore Sturgeon's *The Cosmic Rape* (1958), *Footfall* (1985) by Larry Niven and Jerry Pournelle, and my own books *Nightwings* (1969) and *The Alien Years* (1998), which is the one I dedicated to Wells. But Wells was the first. No writer before him had thought of the idea of an attack on Earth from beyond the atmosphere. And none of Wells' predecessors in the realm of speculative fiction, I suspect, would have been able to embody it so successfully in a novel.

The idea of alien life was itself a relatively recent one, at least in fiction, perhaps because of the risks involved in challenging established church teachings by postulating a creation other than the one described in the Book of Genesis. Such precursors of modern science fiction as Francis Godwin's *The Men in the Moon* (1638) and Voltaire's *Micromegas* (1752) depicted creatures native to other worlds, but they were basically human in design. Only in the late nineteenth century did a few writers begin to speculate about non-humanoid extraterrestrial life-forms, and it remained for Wells to carry the concept to its logical extreme by showing them descend ing upon our world on a mission of conquest.

With splendid economy Wells announces his theme, and even subtly foreshadows the ultimate resolution of his plot, in his very first sentence:

"No one would have believed, in the last years of the nineteenth century, that human affairs were being watched keenly and closely by intelligences greater than man's and yet as mortal as his own; that as men busied themselves about their affairs they were scrutinized and studied, perhaps almost as narrowly as a man with a microscope might scrutinize the transient creatures that swarm and multiply in a drop of water."

Intelligences greater than man's! What a subversive idea that would have been, a few hundred years earlier, in that benighted era when our little world was thought to be the center of the universe! And, a few lines later, Wells expands the concept with this magnificently chilling passage:

"At most, terrestrial men fancied there might be other men upon Mars, perhaps inferior to themselves and ready to welcome a missionary enterprise. Yet, across the gulf of space, minds that are to our minds as ours are to the beasts that perish, intellects vast and cool and unsympathetic, regarded this earth with envious eyes and slowly and surely drew their plans against us."

Vast and cool and unsympathetic! In five words Wells creates for us the Alien Menace pure and simple, the dispassionate invulnerable enemy that his multitude of successors in science fiction have been examining and re-examining ever since. He gives us the full horror of the unknowability of the world beyond our planet's horizon in those five perfectly chosen words.

Note, too, the quick, sly reference to the possibility that we might have wanted, had we known of the existence of Mars' inhabitants, to send them "a missionary enterprise" to lift them from their mire of unChristian ignorance. The darker corners of the world of 1897 were full of England's valiant missionaries, carrying the message of the Gospels to the savage heathens of far-off lands; but who would have dared suggest that we ourselves might seem to others every bit as savage and ignorant as those "natives" did to the missionaries of Queen Victoria's day?

And then the final introductory thematic thrust, in the second paragraph. What do those "plans against us" that the Martians are drawing up concern? Wells explains, in his best science-lecturer mode, that Mars is an older world than ours, dry and cold, with steadily thinning atmosphere and shrinking oceans. It is a planet entering the "last stage of exhaustion." Its inhabitants, those creatures of vast, cool minds, are suffering. And so:

"The immediate pressure of necessity has brightened their intellects, enlarged their powers, and hardened their hearts. And looking across space, with instruments and intelligences such as we have scarcely dreamt of, they see, at its nearest distance, only 35,000,000 of miles sunward of them, a morning star of hope, our own warmer planet, green with vegetation and grey with water, with a cloudy atmosphere eloquent of fertility, with glimpses through its drifting cloud-wisps of broad stretches of populous country and narrow navy-crowded seas."

Whereupon, of course, they will descend upon our green and pleasant planet and take it from us, for they need it, and their need is great, they, whose minds are to ours "as ours are to those of the beasts that perish." We, who are "as alien and lowly as are the monkeys and lemurs to us," simply don't matter at all, any more than the natives of the Congo or Mexico or the Spice Islands mattered to the European invaders who descended upon them to take their lands and their treasures from them during the great age of colonialism. Colonialism, imperialism, is one of Wells' targets here, just as the iniquities of industrial-age exploitation of labor were in *The Time Machine*.

But his primary task is to write a story, a fantastic story at that, not a sermon. That story unfolds in a quiet, matter-of-fact way, narrated for us by an anonymous eye-witness to the startling events. We are told very little about this narrator, because he is speaking to us in the first person, and what he is writing is not his autobiography but the account of a tremendous apocalyptic disaster. (Wells' model for *War of the Worlds* may have been Daniel Defoe's *A Journal of the Plague Year* (1722), which in a similar way reports on a great disaster, though one of a non-fantastic kind.)

We know that Wells' narrator is an educated man, thoughtful, intelligent, a good observer. (He tells us himself that "at times I suffer from the strangest sense of detachment from myself and the world about me; I seem to watch it all from the outside, from somewhere inconceivably remote, out of time, out of space, out of the stress and tragedy of it all.") He is married; he lives in Woking, a suburb south of London, the same one where Wells lived; probably we are meant to think of him as Wells himself, since when he introduces himself to us, at the moment of the arrival of the first Martian spaceship, he is at home, writing in his study. We learn very little more about him than that. This is not a novel in which characterization is of central importance, one which deals primarily with the transformations of character that the events of the story bring about, as is the case in, say, *A Tale of Two Cities* or *Crime and Punishment*. Wells gives us, at every step, real and convincing human reactions to what is going on — the reactions of the narrator, and at one point the narrator's brother, and various others along the way. But what really matters is the succession of external events, and the reactions to those events that Wells seeks to depict are those of Londoners as a group, not the unique responses of the particular protagonists of a complex story.

It is not a complex story. The aliens land; they emerge from their spaceships; they demonstrate their invincibility at once, and from that point to the unexpected climax of the tale there is no glimmer of hope that embattled humanity will be able to wage any sort of defense against them.

Wells' description of the Martians as they emerge from their cylindrical landing vehicles displays the mastery of a born storyteller, not the dryness of the lecture-hall. "I think everyone expected to see a man emerge — possibly something a little unlike us terrestrial men, but in all essentials a man. I know I did," says our narrator.

But that is not what happens. Something resembling "a little gray snake" — a tentacle, the first alien tentacle in all of fiction — comes coiling up over the edge. The narrator feels a sudden chill. A woman screams. There is a general movement backward from the cylinder. And then:

> "A big greyish, rounded bulk, the size, perhaps of a bear, was rising slowly and painfully out of the cylinder. As it budged up and caught the light, it glistened like wet leather. Two large dark-colored eyes were regarding me steadfastly. It was rounded, and had, one might say, a face. There was a mouth under the eyes, the lipless brim of which quivered and panted, and dropped saliva. The body heaved and pulsated convulsively. A lank tentacular appendage gripped the edge of the cylinder, another swayed in the air.
>
> "Those who have never seen a living Martian can scarcely imagine the strange horror of their appearance....Even at this first encounter, this first glimpse, I was overcome with disgust and dread."

There we have it. *It glistened like wet leather....I was overcome with disgust and dread.* For the very first time, the aliens have landed, and Wells gives it to us with marvelous specificity and cunning evocation of dread. His intent is not, I think, to frighten us, despite that panting mouth and pulsating body, so much as it is to awaken us to the awesome possibilities that the universe holds. We are not alone. Nor are these Martians particularly evil. They are simply *other*. They have minds of their own, alien unemotional ones, and they have needs of their own too, which do not coincide with ours, any more than the needs of Victorian-era imperialists coincided with the needs of the peoples whose lands they so cheerfully had taken control of.

And the Martians, whose intellects are so vast and cool and unsympathetic, swiftly proceed to take control of us. Their great ambulatory machines go marching unhurriedly through the countryside toward London, sweeping away all resistance with heat rays and clouds of poison gas, creating a track of destruction as they advance, and consolidating their gains as they go. The core of the novel is an inexorable tale of steady retreat before the implacable enemy. One Martian is slain in its metallic fighting-machine by cannon fire; retribution by the invaders is swift and terrible. Wells now shifts the point of view from his suburban narrator to the narrator's younger brother, a medical student in London, in order to show us what is going on in the metropolis as word of the invasion begins to arrive. News traveled slowly in those days. The radio had not been invented yet; the telephone barely had a foothold in British life. And it is Sunday; "the majority of people in London do not read Sunday papers," Wells tells us. The first reactions to the news from Woking is skeptical, even mocking, but then, as trustworthy accounts of the catastrophe continue to come in, uneasiness grows, a sense of danger is awakened, and the first signs of panic can be seen. Soon the people of London are in full flight northward. "And this was no disciplined march; it was a stampede — a stampede gigantic and terrible — without order and without a goal, six million people, unarmed and unprovisioned, driving headlong. It was the beginning of the rout of civilization, of the massacre of mankind."

It was also the beginning of insight, for Wells, into what the twentieth century, just ahead, might hold for Europe. His powerful chapter on the flight from London is a stunning prevision of the chaos of Europe in World War II, when long lines of bewildered civilians desperately fled this way and that in hope of escaping the fury of the clashing armies that were swarming through their cities and towns.

The evacuation of London introduces an apocalyptic tone into the book. Civilization collapses almost instantly. A kind of jungle savagery replaces the vaunted courtesy of the mild-mannered English as they seek to escape the advance of the alien invaders and an appalling struggle for food and shelter commences.

In the midst of the madness Wells' narrator manages to stop the tale long enough for a discursion on the physiology and anatomy of the Martians — "Huge round bodies — or, rather, heads — about four feet in diameter, each body having in front of it a face....The greater part of the structure was the brain, sending enormous nerves to the eyes, ear and tactile tentacles....They did not eat, much less digest. Instead they took the fresh living blood of other creatures, and *injected* it into their own veins...." And so on, seven or eight pages on Martian physiology and even Martian sex life (they seemed not to have any, but reproduced by budding), until Wells gets his didactic side under control and returns to his account of the ongoing disaster, the continuing slide into total defeat and the return to barbarism.

Indeed it is a completely one-sided war and the destruction of civilization is absolute. When the narrator, after several weeks, takes himself into London, he finds it all but deserted, dead and dying people everywhere, an eerie stillness prevailing. But then comes a strange, haunting cry, "great waves of sound sweeping down the broad, sunlit roadway," a sobbing wail, "Ulla, ulla, ulla, ulla." It is the death-cry of the Martians: Wells' harshly ironic resolution is at hand, and the world is saved after all.

There never had been a book of this sort before, and it was received by the readers of its day with astonishment and awe. One newspaper reviewer complained that certain sections were so brutal that "they caused insufferable distress to the feelings," but that was an exception to the general acclaim. Sales of the book were huge and imitations followed almost instantly. (One, a hastily written novel by the American Garrett P. Serviss entitled *Edison's Conquest of Mars*, told of how Thomas Edison and a group of other scientists built a fleet of spaceships equipped with disintegrator rays and journeyed to

Mars to pay the Martians back for the invasion.)

The book passed at once into popular mythology; "the Martians" became a shorthand term for all sorts of inimical alien being, and any sort of strange phenomenon was readily interpreted, sometimes jokingly, sometimes not, as the onset of an attack by "men from Mars." As late as 1938, when Orson Welles broadcast a brief dramatized version of the original novel on American radio that had the Martians landing in New Jersey, credulous listeners who had tuned in just too late to hear the opening announcement that the program was only a radio play told themselves that it was an eye-witness news report and were driven into a panic that has become legendary in media history.

More than a century after its first publication and despite all the imitators who have turned his concept into a cliche, Wells' fantastic novel still exerts its power. We respond to it because it digs into the profoundest archetypes of fear: in history, the coming of the Assyrian hordes, the descent upon the land of the armies of Genghis Khan, the onslaught of the Black Death, and, in fiction, the predecessor horrors of the giant squids that envelop the hull of Captain Nemo's submarine, the Frankenstein monster and the golem, the great white flukes of Moby Dick lashing the *Pequod*. A door opens, and something sinister and irresistible bursts forth, and we shiver in terror.

But Wells was not only a great storyteller, he was a supremely rational man. And so, as we are shown in those unforgettable final pages set in deserted London, the onslaught of the Martians was doomed from the start, and it is the very nature of their alienness that dooms them, not any effort on the part of humanity.

The novel can be seen as a tragedy of overreaching: an alien species, driven by the simple desire for our water, which they see as necessary to their own survival (i.e. by the dictates of colonial imperialism), the Martians come to us to seize our world, an act of hybris that brings their downfall, for they are biologically unfit to live here. From the Martian point of view the expedition is the mighty act of valor of a desperate race, and its failure is a tragedy akin to the tragedy of the Athenian expedition to Syracuse in the Peloponnesian War and the shattering of the Spanish Armada by the English in 1588. From the point of view of Wells' narrator and his fellow citizens, the invasion is a revelatory catastrophe illustrating not only the unexpected vulnerability of the proud human race but also the ease with which the lofty and self-admiring civilization of Victorian England could be toppled into the most brutal savagery. To Wells himself, the omniscient creator sitting high up above the battle, the book is, among many other things, a warning against overweening ambition, a sobering statement about the non-uniqueness of human life in a vast universe, and a clever display of the author's knowledge of the workings of biology. And for us *The War of the Worlds*, the prototype of all alien-invasion stories, is an imperishable part of our heritage of imaginative literature, a magnificent fantasy that glows forever in the mind of anyone who has read it.

From *The War of the Worlds: Fresh Perspectives*, 2005

Henry Kuttner And C.L. Moore

O I WISH I HAD KNOWN HIM. HE WAS THE WRITER I ALWAYS WANTED TO BE, and indeed in several significant senses became. I would have liked to stay up far into the night with him at some science fiction convention of the 1960s or 1970s, listening to him talk about the writers and editors of the generation just before mine, and perhaps updating his experiences with a few anecdotes of my own. But he died in 1958, only 43 years old, before I ever had a chance to meet him. I was 23, then, and my career was just beginning, and I had not yet made my first trip to California, where he lived then and I live now.

He was born in Los Angeles in 1914, grew up reading the Oz books and the novels of Edgar Rice Burroughs and the pulp science fiction magazines of the 1920s, and after leaving high school went to work in a literary agency that a relative owned. He particularly admired the work of H.P. Lovecraft, became one of Lovecraft's numerous correspondents, and began writing poems and stories in the Lovecraftian mode, which by 1936 started to appear in *Weird Tales* magazine, where most of Lovecraft's best-known work had been published. Quickly Kuttner moved from weird fiction to pulp stories of all kinds, quickly producing an immense output made up largely of potboiling action stories under a host of pseudonyms.

In the 1940s, writing now for the powerful and demanding editor John W. Campbell of *Astounding Science Fiction* and *Unknown Worlds*, his work deepened in psychological insight and technical skill and — particularly under his Lewis Padgett pseudonym — he became one of the finest as well as most prolific writers of the 1942-50 era that is now regarded as a golden age of science fiction. During the last few years of his life he was in poor health, though he continued to write. The sudden coronary attack that killed him came on February 3, 1958.

Who can say what he would have gone on to write if he had lived another thirty years? His science fiction and fantasy output diminished sharply after 1953, and by the time of his death he seemed to have lost interest in those fields almost entirely, turning instead to psychological mystery novels: there were four between 1956 and 1958, featuring the lay psychoanalyst Michael Gray. He had also begun to write scripts for movies and films. He had acquired a belated college degree — Phi Beta Kappa — and was working on his master's thesis in literature when a heart attack felled him. So he was in the midst of a period of growth and transformation, after two decades of high-volume productivity in the world of pulp fiction that this present volume extensively documents, that might have taken him in almost any creative direction.

But I like to think that the revolution of literary freedom that swept the science fiction field in the late 1960s would have tempted him back into it, and that he might have offered us a few late masterpieces that brought him new acclaim. On many occasions through the years I have had the pleasant task of handing out awards to my colleagues at the Hugo and Nebula ceremonies. It is a cheerful fantasy indeed to imagine myself calling Henry Kuttner up to the platform at the World Science Fiction Convention of, say, 1979, to give him a shining trophy for his latest splendid novel.

MOORE

She was famous long before he was. In 1933, when she was 22 years old and working as a secretary in an Indianapolis bank, Catherine Lucille Moore wrote a story called "Shambleau" — a hybrid of fantasy and science fiction, a sensuous tale of eldritch horror set on Mars — and sent it off to *Weird Tales* magazine. It was published in the November 1933 issue under the epicene byline "C.L. Moore" and caused an immediate sensation among readers. She followed it over the next year and a half with a series of stories of equal narrative power and stylistic grace — "Black Thirst," "Scarlet Dream," "The Black God's Kiss" — and by the mid-1930s was firmly established as a top-ranking writer both in the weird-fiction genre and in science fiction.

Among the many admirers of her fiction was the young Henry Kuttner, who had no idea that an attractive young woman lurked behind those initials. When his friend Lovecraft asked Kuttner to return a package of books that he had borrowed from her — she too was a Lovecraft correspondent — Kuttner addressed them to "*Mr.* C.L. Moore," and was startled to get a reply from "*Miss* Catherine Moore." Kuttner then was living in New York, she still in Indianapolis. They struck up a correspondence, met for the first time in 1938 in California, which they both happened to be visiting then, and carried on a postal courtship for a year and a half, until their marriage on June 7, 1940.

Almost immediately these two very different writers — the high-volume Kuttner, author of a multitude of fast-paced and forgettable pulp stories, and the more meticulous Moore, whose work was marked by carefully orchestrated literary effects depending on rich, even lush, descriptive passages, began to collaborate. During the war years, when many other writers were overseas, Kuttner and Moore became steady contributors to a vast number of magazines, working under a dozen or more pseudonyms. (Kuttner, ineligible for active service because of a persistent heart murmur, entered the Medical Corps instead and was stationed at Fort Monmouth, New Jersey, where he had ample opportunity to maintain contact with the New York publishing world.)

She outlived Kuttner for many years, dying in 1987. I met her once, at a party in Los Angeles somewhere about 1972. I remember a woman of almost regal presence and beauty, to whom I stammered a few words of appreciation for the multitude of books and stories of theirs that I so admired.

It is practically impossible to speak of "Kuttner" and "Moore" as individual literary entities after 1942. A few of the stories published during the years of their marriage can be identified stylistically as completely or nearly completely the work of one or the other: "The Children's Hour" of this present collection, published in *Astounding* in 1944 under the pseudonym of "Lawrence O'Donnell," is generally considered to be the work of Moore alone, as was the classic "No Woman Born" of the same year, which indeed was published under the Moore byline. And such slapstick tales as the Hogben series (the 1949 "Cold War," for example, published under Kuttner's name) and the Gallegher stories by "Lewis Padgett" (such as 1943's "The Proud Robot") are thought to be all or mainly Kuttner's work. But in most cases we can only guess, and the guesses may well be wrong. It is safest to assume that scarcely any story left the Kuttner-Moore household without the creative and editorial input of both partners in the marriage.

KUTTNER AND MOORE

The best documentary evidence for the way the Kuttner-Moore collaboration worked is found in *The Worlds of George O. Smith*, an annotated collection of stories by another of John Campbell's prolific writers of the 1940s. Smith, an electronics engineer by profession, had been working in radar research for the Navy during the war, first in Ohio, then in California, finally in New Jersey. Toward the end of the war he struck up a friendship with the Kuttners, who were living by then in Hastings-on-the-Hudson, New York. (With appropriate economy they used "Hudson Hastings" as one of their pseudonyms!) An anecdote in Smith's book describes a weekend he spent as the Kuttners' house-guest in Hastings, probably late in 1945 or early in 1946:

> "...I am one of those wholly unbearable people who waken at the first sign of sunshine, and, as Fred Pohl once said, 'At six in the morning, he's making home-fried potatoes and cooking four pounds of bacon....' And so I awoke and couldn't find the Kuttners' four pounds of bacon, nor the potatoes, and while I was wonder-

ing where the coffee, tea, *et cetera,* was, two things took place. Hank came feeling his way downstairs, and, as he located the coffee, the typewriter upstairs began to make noises. One half hour, maybe three-quarters, we'd had our morning coffee, and Hank said something about going upstairs and getting dressed. He disappeared.

"They didn't pass each other on the stairs, but Catherine turned up very shortly afterward, reconstructed the coffee, which Hank and I had finished, and I had my second wake-up with her — with the typewriter going on at the same rate upstairs. Once more, say three-quarters of an hour passed, and Catherine said something about getting into day clothes, and disappeared. Hank came down, dressed, and said something cheerful about breakfast — with the typewriter going on as usual. This went on. They worked at it in shifts, in relays, continuously, until about two o'clock that Saturday afternoon, when the one downstairs did not go upstairs when the one upstairs came down. This time the typing stopped.

"They had been writing the novelette 'Vintage Season'....

"I learned later, from John [Campbell], that they always worked that way, and worked so well at it that the only way he could tell who had written what was if the word 'gray' came in the story. One of them habitually spelled it 'grey'."

The influence on modern-day science fiction of Kuttner and Moore — writing as Kuttner, as Moore, as "Lewis Padgett," as "Lawrence O'Donnell," even, for three stories late in the game, as "Henry Kuttner and C.L. Moore," has been enormous. The kind of lean, efficient story they perfected in the 1940s, beginning with a quick statement of a complex and often paradoxical plot situation, followed by a few paragraphs of exposition to resolve enough of the paradox to keep the reader from utter bewilderment, and culminating in a satisfying and often dark and disturbing plot resolution, was closely studied by such young and prolific writers of the 1950s as Philip K. Dick, Robert Sheckley, and — I have never made a secret of this — Robert Silverberg. I know that my own way of telling stories was indelibly marked by my reading of Kuttner and Moore; I think it very probable that Sheckley would say the same thing, and I'm certain that Dick, if he were still among us, would add his own concurrence.

Fritz Leiber, in an essay written soon after Kuttner's death for a Kuttner Memorial Symposium, spoke of Henry Kuttner's stories as "now brilliantly romantic, now ironically realistic, now gay, now grim," and pointed out that he (and by extension his invisible collaborator C.L. Moore) were "particularly successful in using the science fiction story to express that mood of anxiety and dread of depersonalization which we think of as peculiarly modern." The reader of the present collection will find that Leiber's comment is as relevant now as it was in 1958.

Introduction to *Bypass to Otherness*, 2010

Cordwainer Smith

HE ERUPTED INTO OUR MIDST WITHOUT WARN-ING, A LITTLE OVER HALF A CENTURY AGO, with one of the strangest science fiction stories ever published. The magazine it appeared in was pretty strange, too: a crudely-printed semi-pro affair called *Fantasy Book*, emanating from Los Angeles in such tiny quantities that each issue became a collector's item almost as soon as it appeared.

The publisher of *Fantasy Book* was William L. Crawford, an old-time science fiction enthusiast whose sf publishing career went back to the early 1930s, when he brought out two little magazines called *Marvel Tales* and *Unusual Stories*, setting the type for them himself. No more than a thousand copies of each issue were printed, though they ran outstanding stories by the likes of H.P. Lovecraft, Clifford D. Simak, and Robert E. Howard. *Fantasy Book*, which had a wobbly eight-issue existence between 1947 and 1951, was as amateurish-looking as its Crawford predecessors — no two issues had quite the same format, and even within a single issue several type faces usually were employed — but it, too, managed to run some valuable fiction, by A.E. van Vogt, Andre Norton, L. Ron Hubbard, Isaac Asimov in collaboration with Frederik Pohl, and Murray Leinster. But the one story that ensures this scruffy magazine's immortality in the history of science fiction was the third item in its (undated) sixth issue, released in January of 1950: "Scanners Live in Vain" by an unknown writer with the strange name of Cordwainer Smith.

How that story came into the hands of Bill Crawford of *Fantasy Book* is something I can't tell you. John J. Pierce, a pioneer in the arcane field of Cordwainer Smith studies, reported in a piece first published in 1993 that "Smith" wrote the story in 1945 and submitted it to the pre-eminent science fiction editor of the day, John W. Campbell of *Astounding Science Fiction*, who rejected it as "too extreme." In those days stories rejected by Campbell had few other possibilities for publication — the only markets were two fairly juvenile pulp magazines called *Startling Stories* and *Thrilling Wonder Stories*, which had the same editor, and a third and even more juvenile pulp called *Planet Stories*. The remaining two magazines, *Amazing Stories* and *Fantastic Adventures*, were entirely staff-written and did not welcome unsolicited submissions.

So once a story had been to Campbell and to the editors of the *Startling/Thrilling Wonder* duo and *Planet*, there was essentially no place to publish it except some amateur magazine, and "Smith," who must have been a devoted science fiction reader, somehow discovered *Fantasy Book* and sent his story to Bill Crawford. And that was how my teenage self happened to read, in the spring of 1950, a story that began with this startling, jarring passage:

> "Martel was angry. He did not even adjust his blood away from anger. He stamped across the room by judgment, not by sight. When he saw the table hit the floor, and could tell by the expression on Luci's face that the table must have made a loud crash, he looked down to see if his leg were broken. It was not. Scanner to the core, he had to scan himself. The action was reflex and automatic. The inventory included his legs, abdomen, Chestbox of instruments, hands, arms, face and back with the Mirror. Only then did Martel go back to being angry. He talked with his voice, even though he knew that his wife hated its blare and preferred to have him write.
> "'I tell you, I must cranch. I have to cranch. It's my worry, isn't it?'"

Nobody — with the possible exception of A.E. van Vogt, whose dreamlike, surreal *The World of Null-A* was first published around the time Cordwainer Smith was writing "Scanners" — wrote science fiction that sounded like that. The lucid, unadorned prose setting forth the immeasurably strange — it was a new kind of voice.

I read on and on. One bizarre term after another tumbled forth: Scanners, the Up-and-Out, the habermans, the Cranching Wire. In time, it all made sense. By the end of the story, forty pages later, I knew that some incomparable master of science fiction had taken me to an invented world like none that had ever been portrayed before.

But who was this Cordwainer Smith?

Suddenly, everybody in the little inner world of science fiction — there couldn't have been more than a few hundred who really cared about it in any more than a casual way — was asking that question. But no answers came forth. William Crawford let it be known that the name was a pseudonym — but for whom? Van Vogt? Hardly. If he had written it, he would have been proud to publish it under his own name. The prolific Henry Kuttner, famous for his innumerable pseudonyms? Heinlein? Sturgeon? None of the theories seemed to add up. The name itself provided no clue. ("Cordwainer" is an archaic term meaning "leather-worker" or "shoemaker.")

The hubbub died down within a few months, and the unknown Mr. Smith and his remarkable story receded into obscurity and might have remained there forever but for Frederik Pohl, not only a writer but an editor of sf anthologies. Pohl knew about "Scanners" because he had had a story in that same issue of *Fantasy Book*, and he republished it in 1952 in a paperback called *Beyond the End of Time*, a fine fat collection that also included work by Bradbury, Asimov, van Vogt, and Heinlein. Science fiction paperbacks were few and far between back then, and everybody who liked sf pounced on the Pohl anthology. Thousands of readers who had never so much as heard of *Fantasy Book* now discovered Cordwainer Smith, and clamored for more of his work.

They would have to wait a few years. Nothing more was heard of the mysterious Cordwainer Smith until the autumn of 1955, when *Galaxy Science Fiction*, one of the leading sf magazines of the day, offered the second Smith story: the eccentric, powerful little tale, "The Game of Rat and Dragon." Very likely Fred Pohl had some involvement in this, too, for he was a close friend of Horace Gold, *Galaxy*'s editor, and probably facilitated contact between the writer and Smith.

And then, beginning in 1957, a torrent of Cordwainer Smith stories came forth, each of them told in the same startlingly individual way as the first two, and — as gradually became apparent — each set in the same astonishingly original future universe. There was one in 1957, two in 1958, four in 1959, one in 1960, and, between 1961 and 1965, sixteen more, most of them meaty novellas. They appeared in a wide range of science fiction magazines, from the most minor (the short-lived *Saturn*) to the top of the line (*Galaxy* and *Fantasy and Science Fiction*.) Pohl, who had replaced Horace Gold as editor of *Galaxy* in 1961, published most of the major ones, such instantly hailed masterpieces as "The Ballad of Lost C'Mell," "Think Blue, Count Two," and "The Dead Lady of Clown Town." It was obvious by now to everyone involved with science fiction that a major writer was at work in our midst.

A little information about him was beginning to leak out, too. Some time in 1963 word emerged that "Smith" was a pseudonym for one Paul Linebarger, who lived in the vicinity of Washington, D.C., and had some sort of involvement with the national military or espionage establishment. When the World Science Fiction Convention was held in Washington that year, Linebarger was not among those present, but Fred Pohl arranged for a small group of writers — I was not among them, alas — to visit him at his house. It was the only time, I believe, that he had any personal contact with the world of professional science fiction publishing.

The extent to which the details of Paul Linebarger's life remained unknown even after that can be seen from the review I wrote in 1964 of the first Cordwainer Smith novel, *The Planet Buyer* (which was actually a section of the larger work later published as *Norstrilia*):

"Rumor has it that the author of the stories appearing under the byline of 'Cordwainer Smith' is a military man who has spent much of his life in the Orient and who now holds a high position in the Pentagon. However, I have a theory of my own.

"I think that Cordwainer Smith is a visitor from some remote period of the future, living among us perhaps as an exile from his own era or perhaps just as a tourist, and amusing himself by casting some of his knowledge of historical events into the form of science fiction....

"The evidence is partly stylistic. Cordwainer Smith writes a strange, eerie prose, which though grammatical does not appear to be ordinary in any manner. Astonishingly flat declarative statements alternate with wildly soaring prose; syntax is odd and often distorted; in every way, there seems to be an alien mind putting the words together.

"The structure of the stories, too, is unconventional. Most science fiction writers go to some length to explain what is happening in their stories, and what the background details mean. Smith does a little of this, but only enough to make his work intelligible. The rest he takes for granted, as though it is so tiresomely familiar to him that he does not see the need to spell out the details.

"The most revealing thing, though, is the fact that every Cordwainer Smith story fits into a common framework — from the first one, published in 1950, on. Aside from this novel, there are about a dozen longish novelets and a good many short stories in the Smith *oeuvre* so far, and this entire voluminous output hangs together. Smith hops across a span of perhaps fifteen thousand years, zigzagging to tell in detail a story that he has encapsulated in a sentence or two of an earlier story, but his work is always consistent. One can examine his first story, or his second, or his third, and see the seeds of the tenth or twentieth. Nor is any story really complete in itself; it refers back and forth to the others, each a segment out of a vast and bewildering whole.

"It is frightening and a little implausible to think that Cordwainer Smith, circa 1948, was able to visualize an imaginary universe with such detail that he could spend the next decade and a half inventing internally consistent and externally consistent stories about it. I prefer to believe that Smith is merely making use of historical or mythical material that he learned from childhood on — spinning out for us the equivalents of the *Iliad* or the courtship of Miles Standish.

"The book at hand, which appeared in shorter form last year in *Galaxy*, is typical of his output. Maddeningly oblique, stunningly evocative, it teases and taunts, giving us an incomplete story with little hint of the real nature of the events. Though it defies coherent summary, it fascinates and compels. Rod McBan, a Parsifal-like innocent from the planet known as Old North Australia, where every man is a millionaire, escapes execution as a mental defective through some maneuver not readily intelligible to the reader. Then a computer induces him to execute a coup in futures of stroon, the immortality drug that is the source of Old North Australia's wealth, and he ends up so rich that he buys the planet Earth, again for uncertain motivations. He comes to Earth and is spirited away by the cat-girl C'mell, one of Smith's most enchanting creations. Here the book ends, with a clear promise of more to come.

"The man is not just a science fiction writer. He is a wanderer out of the future, I have no doubt. It scares me to contemplate his work or his presence among us."

I was not, of course, serious about my notion in that book review of four decades ago that Smith was a time-traveler masquerading as a science fiction writer. The bit of legitimate biographical information I provided about him was accurate enough, but very much on the sketchy side, as we discovered in 1966 when news came of the author's death.

He was only 53, and had packed several lifetimes worth of experience into that short span. At last it was revealed that Paul M.A. Linebarger, born in Milwaukee in 1913, was the son of an American judge who had helped to finance the Chinese revolution of 1911 and was the legal advisor to its leader, Sun Yat-sen. The younger Linebarger had grown up in China, Japan, Germany, and France, and by the age of 23 had earned a doctorate in political science at Johns Hopkins University. (Some of the strangeness of his fictional technique, apparently, was derived from his knowledge of the Chinese language and classical Chinese methods of storytelling.) Between 1930 and 1936 he had been a legal consultant to the Chinese government under Chiang Kai-shek, and during World War II, still based in China, he served as a lieutenant colonel in U.S. Army Intelligence. (This was the Pentagon connection about which we had heard.) After the war he became a professor of Asian politics at Johns Hopkins, but also found time to serve as an advisor to the British forces in Malaya and to the U.S. Eighth Army in Korea, and to write a definitive textbook on psychological warfare, several espionage thrillers, and the science fiction works for which he will always be remembered by connoisseurs of the field.

Researchers have discovered that Linebarger had been writing science fiction from boyhood on. His first known story, "War No. 81-Q," appeared in his high-school magazine in 1928, when he was fifteen. Evidently he went on writing fantasy and science fiction stories in great abundance throughout the 1930s and 1940s, though none of them has ever been published and they can be presumed to be lost — and then, in 1945, came "Scanners Live in Vain," which would so spectacularly launch his career as a writer five years later.

A brilliant man, an extraordinary writer. Death took him much too soon, just as he was reaching his creative peak, and we will never know what glories of the imagination he would have given us if he had been granted another fifteen or twenty years. But at least we have the thirty or so science fiction stories and the one novel that he did manage to produce in his short, busy life.

I was instrumental in arranging for the publication of the very first Cordwainer Smith short-story collection in 1963, a book to which the publisher gave the title, *You Will Never Be the Same*. It is as apt a description of the effect Cordwainer Smith's fiction has on its readers as has ever been coined.

Introduction to *Norstrilia*, 2002

The Days of Perky Vivienne

WE LIVE IN THE TWENTY-FIRST CENTURY. PHILIP K. DICK HELPED TO INVENT IT.

The standard critical view of Dick, the great science fiction writer who died in 1982, is that the main concern of his work lay with showing us that reality isn't what we think it is. Like most clichés, that assessment of Dick has a solid basis in fact (assuming, that is, that after reading Dick you are willing to believe that anything has a solid basis in fact). Many of his books and stories did, indeed, show their characters' surface reality melting away to reveal quite a different universe beneath.

But the games Dick played with reality were not, I think, the most remarkable products of his infinitely imaginative mind. At the core of his thinking was an astonishingly keen understanding of the real world he lived in — the world of the United States, subsection California, between 1928 and 1982 — and it was because he had such powerful insight into the reality around him that he was able to perform with such great imaginative force one of the primary jobs of the science fiction writer, which is to project present-day reality into a portrayal of worlds to come. Dick's great extrapolative power is what has given him such posthumous popularity in Hollywood. *Blade Runner, Total Recall, Minority Report,* and half a dozen other Dick-derived movies, though not always faithful to Dick's original story plots, all provide us with that peculiarly distorted Dickian view of reality which, it turns out, was his accurate assessment of the way his own twentieth-century world was going to evolve into the jangling, weirdly distorted place that we encounter in our daily lives.

A case in point is the announcement last spring that a Hong Kong company, Artificial Life, Inc. — what a Dickian name! — is about to provide the lonely men of this world with a virtual girlfriend named Vivienne, who can be accessed via cellphone for a basic monthly fee of six dollars. If you sign up for Vivienne's friendship, she will chat with you about matters of love and romance or almost anything else you might want to discuss, and you will be able to buy her virtual flowers and chocolates, take her to the movies, even — a beautifully creepy Dickian touch — marry her. (Which will get you a virtual mother-in-law who will call you in the middle of the night to find out whether you're treating her little girl the right way.)

What this news item brought to mind for me was two of Phil Dick's works — the early (1953) short story, "The Days of Perky Pat," and the dazzling 1965 novel, *The Three Stigmata of Palmer Eldritch*, in which Dick recycled the Perky Pat concept into a breathtaking rollercoaster-ride of a book.

In both of these, Perky Pat is a kind of Barbie doll that becomes the object of intense cult-like fascination. The earlier story, set in a world devastated by thermonuclear war, shows the survivors building their own Perky Pat dolls, providing them with wardrobes, miniature homes, and tiny hi-fi sets (her virtual boyfriend, Leonard, gets little replicas of tweed suits, Italian shirts, and a Jaguar XKE), and then using the dolls as centerpieces in a sort of Monopoly game in which whole towns participate. The far more sophisticated Dick of Palmer Eldritch eliminates the post-nuclear idea and turns Perky Pat into an electronic device adored by millions throughout the Solar System, who enhance their visits to the fantasy-world she provides by chewing a hallucinogenic drug.

So wrote Philip K. Dick, forty years ago, in a science fiction novel that probably didn't earn him more than five thousand dollars and quickly went out of print. (Like Cassandra and various other unlucky prophets, he went unrewarded for his visionary powers in his own lifetime. All the big Hollywood money for his books arrived after his death.) And now, when we move out of classic twentieth-century sf into the hyped-up world of twenty-first-century reality, we get —

Vivienne, at six dollars a month. She's supposed to be available to owners of 3G cellphones (3G means "third generation," the kind of phone that comes with computerized voice-synthesis capabilities, streaming video, and text-message capacity) in Singapore and Malaysia already, will be arriving in Europe later this year, and should be available to American users around the time you read this, barring last-minute technical snafus.

She looks three-dimensional, a hot little number indeed, lithe and slender. She can move through eighteen different backdrops, among them a restaurant, an airport, and a shopping mall. She's programmed to discuss thirty-five thousand topics with you — philosophy, films, art, and, very likely, the novels of Philip K. Dick. She'll translate foreign languages for you, too. Give her an English word and you'll get its equivalent in Japanese, Korean, German, Spanish, Chinese, or Italian. (You key the words in as if you were doing a text message on a cellphone, but Vivienne will answer both in text and in synthesized voice. If you want your steak well done in a Tokyo res-

227

taurant, you ask her for the right phrase, and she replies out loud, so that the waiter can hear and understand.)

Vivienne will flirt with you, too. She'll tell you how cute you are, she'll blow kisses to you, she'll parade across your phone's video screen in a scanty gym suit. She will not, however, take the gym suit off, nor will she engage in phone sex with you. Vivienne is not that kind of girl. You can try all your fancy moves on her, if you like, but she's equipped with a number of gambits to use in fending off your advances, you heavy-breathing pervert, you. Although she won't let herself get drawn into anything seriously erotic, Vivienne does engage in a certain degree of badinage that can be usefully instructive to young men who are, shall we say, a bit backward in conversing with actual flesh-and-blood women. Draw her into a conversation on some intimate boy-and-girl matter and her extensive data-base will provide you with an elaborate rehearsal for the real thing, if moving on from virtual romance to something more corporeal is among your ambitions.

Not that Artificial Life, Inc. is planning to aim its product exclusively at lonely heterosexual male geeks. They are just the first consumer targets. The word is that a virtual boyfriend for women is already under development, and that gay and lesbian versions will follow soon after. There's also a Vivienne for Muslim societies who abides by Muslim rules of feminine propriety (no baring of midriffs, no body piercings) and — count on it, my friends, it's a sure bet — there will eventually be an X-rated Vivienne who is programmed to get a lot cozier with the subscribers than the current model is willing to be.

Your cellphone chip, of course, has nowhere near the computing capacity necessary to achieve all this. Vivienne works her girlish magic through a link between your phone and the external servers on which the Vivienne programs reside. One consequence of this is that playing with Vivienne can quickly cost you a lot more than the six dollar monthly basic fee. A nice long schmooze with your virtual girlfriend will quickly exhaust the basic service allowance and run you into overtime. To prevent serious Vivienne addiction, users will be limited to an hour a day with her — at least at the outset. (Somehow, though, those restrictions have a way of disappearing when a product of this sort gets really popular). As for those little gifts you buy her — not just the flowers and the chocolates, but the sports cars and the diamond rings — those get charged to your phone bill too, half a dollar here, a dollar there. What happens to the money you lavish on Vivienne? "The money goes to us," says a smiling Artificial Life executive. (Hello, Mr. Dick!)

So go ahead and sign up. Vivienne will help you with the problems you're having with your real-life girlfriend, if you happen to have one; she will tell you how to buy cool sneakers in a Korean department store; and she will also teach you that girls are mercenary teases who know all sorts of tricks for extracting costly gifts from you but will not gratify your urgent hormonal needs in return. And if you marry her, you get a virtual mother-in-law of a really annoying kind, the best touch of all. No doubt of it:

Vivienne's a perfect Philip K. Dick invention.

And I think we'll see more and more of Philip K. Dick's pulp-magazine plot concepts erupting into life all around us as the twenty-first century moves along. Even though his characters would discover, again and again, that the world around them was some sort of cardboard makeshift hiding a deeper level that was likewise unreal, what Dick the writer was actually doing was crying out, Look at all these unscrupulous gadgets: this is what our world really is, and things are only going to get worse. For us moderns it's Phildickworld all day long. Your computer steals your bank account number and sends it to Nigeria, gaudy advertisements come floating toward us through the air, and now your telephone will flirt with you. It won't stop there.

John Brunner, another of science fiction's most astute prophets, who also did not live to see the twenty-first century arrive, saw all the way back in 1977 that Dick's real theme wasn't the untrustworthiness of reality but the sheer oppressiveness of it:

> "Dick's world is rarely prepossessing. Most of the time it is deserted — call out, and only echo answers. There are lovely things in it, admittedly, but they are uncared for; at best they are dusty, and often they are crumbling through neglect. Food here is tasteless and does not nourish. Signposts point to places you do not wish to visit. Clothing is drab, and frays at embarrassing moments. The drugs prescribed by your doctor have such side effects that they are a remedy worse than the disease. No, it is not a pleasant or attractive world.
>
> "Consequently, his readers are extremely disconcerted when they abruptly recognize it for what it is: the world we all inhabit. Oh, the trimmings have been altered — the protagonist commutes by squib or flapple and argues with the vehicle's robot brain enroute — but that's so much verbal window dressing."

Brunner concluded his 1977 essay on Dick by saying, "This I tell you straight up: I do not want to live in the sort of world Dick is so good at describing. I wish — I desperately wish — that I dared believe we don't. Maybe if a lot of people read Dick's work I'll stand a better chance of not living in that world. . . ."

As things turned out, John Brunner, who died in 1995, didn't have to live in that world. But we do. And it gets more Phildickian every day.

Asimov's Science Fiction, **February, 2006**

The Center Does Not Hold

LAST MONTH I USED THE OCCASION OF THE DEATH OF L. SPRAGUE DE CAMP as a springboard to discuss the 1938-43 "Golden Age" period of the magazine *Astounding Science Fiction*, whose editor, John W. Campbell, brought such writers as de Camp, Isaac Asimov, A.E. van Vogt, Theodore Sturgeon, L. Ron Hubbard, Lester del Rey, Clifford D. Simak, and Alfred Bester into prominence with a swiftness that can only be called, well, astounding. And that set me thinking about Campbell and one facet of his extraordinary influence over science fiction that has only infrequently been discussed.

Everyone who knows anything about the history of the development of modern science fiction in the United States is aware of Campbell's impact as an editor. He took over at *Astounding* in 1937 and ran it until his death in 1971. Throughout that entire period of three and a half decades Campbell, a big, burly, outrageously opinionated man, bestrode the science fiction world like the colossus he was. I had this to say of him in a 1996 column:

"He was a big man, six feet tall and over 200 pounds, and he was the greatest sf writer in the business before I even was born; and then, in 1937, when he was only 27 years old, he gave up free-lance writing to edit the magazine that then was called *Astounding Stories*, and now has become *Analog*. It was while editor of *Astounding* that this tough-minded, domineering man discovered such new sf writers as Asimov, Heinlein, Sturgeon, van Vogt, and de Camp. The list of his regular writers comprises just about everybody of any importance in the history of science fiction between 1939 and 1952 except Ray Bradbury and Fred Pohl, neither of whom, somehow, ever saw eye to eye with John. For nearly everyone else, though, a sale to Campbell's

Astounding was your ticket of admission to the club. You might be able to slip a story past any of the other editors, but in order to sell to Campbell you had to do it right. John was dogmatic the way potatoes are starchy: not only did he know what went into the making of a good sf tale, he understood how the universe worked, and if your story violated the laws of the universe, why, he would tell you so, and you crept out of his office wondering why you had ever bothered learning how to type."

Campbell's editing method involved a lot of direct contact with his writers. I experienced it myself when I began my career in the mid-1950s. You came into his small, shabby office in a run-down Manhattan office building; if he knew you or your work, he gave you his immediate intense attention; within minutes, he was unloading upon you whatever concepts (some of them profound, some intellectually subversive, some wacky, some all at once) that had engaged his powerful mind in the last few days; and after drawing you into a discussion of them that he never failed to dominate, he would send you away, dazed and awed, to write a story based on what you had just heard.

Not that he wanted you to parrot his ideas: that was a sure road to rejection. He wanted your *input*. He wanted you to provide your own take on his notions, test them, quarrel with them, expand and amplify them. It was *his* ideas that interested him, mind you, not yours, but he wanted you to collaborate in the development and expounding of them. Sometimes a writer of sufficient intellectual power — Heinlein, say, or Frank Herbert — succeeded in getting Campbell's attention with an idea of his own, and then that idea became part of the common property of Campbell's group of contributors, Campbell tossing it out to other writers ("I've just bought the most wonderful story by Bob Heinlein —I'll tell you what it's about, and then I want to know your thoughts about it") and inviting you to carry it to the next set of implications.

It was a wonderful method when Campbell was in his prime —from 1938 to 1947, say. Isaac Asimov has described in his autobiography how in 1940 Campbell handed him the famous Three Laws of Robotics ("Look, Asimov, in working this out, you have to realize that there are three rules that robots have to follow...."), finding them in Asimov's own stories and codifying them in a way that Isaac had never thought to do. A few months later Campbell showed him a quotation from Ralph Waldo Emerson and said, "What do you think would happen, Asimov, if men were to see the stars for the first time in a thousand years?" Out of that came the classic "Nightfall." John Campbell might not have been able to write "Nightfall" himself, but Asimov would not have written it either, but for that suggestion.

Many other writers could relate similar anecdotes. From his fertile mind came the seeds of many of our greatest classics, written by others from Campbell's subtle prodding. As the years went on, though, Campbell's hatred of scientific dogma hardened into a strange anti-dogmatism of his own making, and increasingly he embraced quirky and downright bizarre ideas, until toward the end he was advocating perpetual-motion machines and quack cancer cures. This had its effect on the ideas he gave his favorite writers, and as the prodding grew less subtle and the concepts weirder, many of them, reacting in amazement and sometimes anger, rebelled and went off to write for other magazines. By the end of his life Campbell was a lonely and isolated figure; but no one can deny the tremendous achievement of his great years.

One aspect of Campbell's role in our microcosmos that has rarely been discussed is his monthly editorial column. In each of all the hundreds of issues he edited he contributed an essay — a single page at first, sometimes seven or eight toward the end — that dealt with whatever was on his extraordinary mind at the time. In the beginning, the editorials were often simple statements of his thoughts about science fiction. Once his policies were made manifest through the stories he published, he switched instead mainly to scientific themes — his educational background was in physics and engineering — and then, later, to philosophical or sociocultural notions, some of which seemed exceedingly far out even to Campbell's own dedicated readers.

Campbell's editorials were often startling, frequently infuriating. The one thing they never were were dull. One of the most famous, in the June, 1938 issue, discussed the imminent development of spaceships and atomic power. "I think they'll come pretty much together — and both pretty quickly.... No one man is going to discover the secret of atomic power. A century from now men will almost certainly say that one of the present great in the field was the discovery of the secret of atomic power. We say today that Faraday discovered the principle of the electric dynamo and motor, though he never would recognize the modern turbo-alternator.

"But you can be fairly certain of this: *The discoverer of the secret of atomic power is alive on Earth today.* His papers and researches are appearing regularly; his name is known. But the exact handling of the principles he's discovered — not even he knows now.

"We don't know which is his name. But we know him. *He's here today.*"

And, ten months later, in an editorial headed *Jackpot!*, he wrote of Otto Hahn's discovery of nuclear fission (mistakenly calling him "G. Hahn," and ignoring the collaborative work of Lise Meitner) and said, "Dr. Hahn has discovered that the addition of a neutron to uranium produces a higher element. This one does not pay off in nickels; it doesn't discharge a few minor particles and get comfortable again. It shatters utterly with a violence unimaginable; it discharges two immense atomic particles with a stupendous, furious energy."

This was in 1938, more than a year before the outbreak of World War II, four years before serious work on atomic weapons began, seven years before Hiroshima. Throughout the war years Campbell ran so many pieces on atomic energy that the FBI finally paid him a visit to find out who was leaking what; he responded by showing them that he had used nothing but previously published scientific papers.

In 1967, Harry Harrison edited and Doubleday published a book with the dreary title, *Collected Editorials from Analog*, that reprinted 32 of Campbell's most stimulating pieces, dating from 1943 to 1965. At the time I thought it one of the goofiest publishing ideas of the decade — who but Campbell's most impassioned followers would buy a book like that? — but Harrison tells me that it sold quite well, thanks in part to Campbell's energetic promotion of it in his own magazine. And hindsight shows me its great value as a record of Campbell's vigorous mind. A look at the titles of the essays shows us Campbell's range and his willingness to challenge conventional thinking:

"The Lesson of Thalidomide"
"Research is Antisocial"
"The Value of Panic"
"Arithmetic and Empire"
"On the Selective Breeding of Human Beings"
"We *Must* Study Psi"
"God Isn't Democratic"

You get the idea — a gadfly, a contrarian, a Socratic figure.
And why am I telling you all this now?
Because there is nothing like Campbell and his editorials in science fiction today. He provided the intellectual center for the field. *Everybody* read his magazine. *Everybody* chewed over his editorials. They made some of us nod sagely in agreement, and others froth at the mouth in fury — but the point is that whether you agreed or disagreed with Campbell, you had to come to terms with his ideas. His thinking was the fixed pole against which everyone else reacted, pro or con.

The pieces I do for this magazine are as close as anyone comes to Campbell-style editorials today. But I have no illusions about the extent of their effect. No one publication dominates sf the way *Astounding* once did. There are many thousands of science fiction readers who have never even *heard* of ASIMOV'S, let alone read and fight over the ideas I deal with in these pages. And whereas Campbell was a powerful editor, whose ideas had to be taken into account if you had any hope of being published by him, I'm simply one writer, speaking as an independent voice, not in any way representative of the policies of the editor of this magazine.

So our field no longer has a center. I think we are worse off for that. But John Campbells come along only once in a very long while, and in any case sf is too huge and polymorphic a thing nowadays to allow anyone to recreate the sort of intellectual dominance that he had in the field fifty years ago. Campbell's *Collected Editorials*, which once seemed to me the most quixotic of books, now stands out as a book of immense symbolic value, an artifact of an era of vanished cohesiveness.

Asimov's Science Fiction, June 2001

William Tenn

THE LONE LAMENTABLE THING ABOUT THIS TWO-VOLUME COLLECTION OF WILLIAM TENN'S science fiction (of which this is Volume Two, and if you don't already own Volume One, *Immodest Proposals*, you should run right out and buy it) is its subtitle: *The Complete Science Fiction of William Tenn*. In a properly ordered world, the complete science fiction of William Tenn would fill many more volumes than these mere piddling two. You could not get the complete science fiction of Robert A. Heinlein or Philip K. Dick or Isaac Asimov into just two volumes, be they the size of the Manhattan telephone directory. Even Ray Bradbury, who like William Tenn has primarily been a short-story writer, would need half a dozen or more omnibus-sized books. As for the complete science fiction of Robert Silverberg — well, you get the idea.

But here we have the complete William Tenn — the *gesammelte werke* of a man who has been writing the stuff for more than half a century — and the whole megillah takes only these two volumes. This is truly lamentable, and I lament it herewith. There should be eight volumes this size. There should be eighteen. If you believe that the stories in these two books are brilliant, intricately inventive, and tremendously funny, which I assure you they are, then you ought to read the stories he *didn't* get around to writing.

They are, let me confidently assert, absolutely terrific. The least of them would burn a hole in your memory bank forever. When I think of all the magnificent unwritten William Tenn stories languishing out there in the limbo of nonexistence, I want to weep. The great trilogy set in the parallel universe where Horace Gold and John Campbell are the rival emperors of a decadent Byzantine Empire — the dozen mordant tales of the Solomonic decisions of the Chief Rabbi of Mars — the intricate reverse deconstruction of Heinlein's "By His Bootstraps" — you'd love them. I guarantee it. But where are they? Nowhere, that's where. Phil — that's what I call "William Tenn," *Phil*, because that happens to be his real name, Philip Klass — never got around to writing them. And though he's only in his ninth decade and still posing as an active writer, the same pose that he has hidden behind for the past fifty years, I don't think he ever will.

I'll tell you why, too.

It's this Scheherezade business. In her introduction to Volume One, Connie Willis lets us know that Charles Brown of *Locus* magazine once referred to Phil as "the Scheherezade of science fiction." I confess I have some issues with that tag — it is very hard for me to envision Scheherezade as a diminutive male Jewish octogenarian with a grizzled beard, and I bet you that Sultan Shahryar would have had an even tougher time with it — but I do see Charles's point. Scheherezade had the gift of gab. She was one of the world's great storytellers, right up there with Homer and Dickens and the Ancient Mariner, a spellbinder whose tales everybody still knows and loves a thousand years later. When she spoke, you had no choice but to listen. Of course, Scheherezade was telling you about Sinbad the Sailor and Ali Baba and Aladdin, irresistible, imperishable stories. But she must also have been quite a talker, because she had to get the Sultan's attention first, so that he would let her tell the stories that would distract him from cutting off her head.

Phil Klass — I remind you, that is the natal name of the man who wrote the *Complete Science Fiction of William Tenn* — is quite a talker too. And it is my belief that he let the other eight, or ten, or sixteen volumes of the Complete Science Fiction evaporate into the smoky air of ten million cocktail parties instead of writing the damn stuff down.

My image of Phil, a man whom I've known since 1956 or thereabouts, is that of a small man with constantly moving jaws. He was talking a mile a minute when I met him at some gathering of our colleagues in New York in the 1950s, he has talked at the same dizzyingly rapid rate all through the succeeding decades, and, though it's a few years since I've seen him, since we live on opposite coasts of North America these days, I'm quite certain that he is talking right now, back there in far-off Pennsylvania. Now, of course, this being the twenty-first century long fabled in song and story by the members of our little guild, his verbal velocity really ought to be measured metrically, and so we can consider that nowadays he talks at 1.6 kilometers a minute, but the effect is just the same, which is that of a man bubbling over with immensely interesting ideas, all of which he wants to share with you in a single outpouring of breath.

Among those ideas, I'm afraid, were some of his best stories. We professional writers are all taught, back in the days when we were would-be writers who read *Writers Digest* and studied books on how to double-space manuscripts, that writers must never talk about work in progress, because there is a real risk of talking the work away. Phil knew all about that rule long before I had ever heard the name of John W. Campbell, Jr. He didn't care, or else he is just such a compulsive talker that he can't stop himself. I can remember his talking about a long story that he was writing called, "Winthrop was Stubborn" for something like a year, back in the vicinity of 1956 and the early months of 1957. I got to know the story very well in that time, to the point where I began to think I was writing it myself. I also came to believe that the story wasn't being written at all, merely talked, and great was my surprise when it actually appeared in the August, 1957 issue of *Galaxy* (I remember the date very well, because I had a story in the same issue) under editor Horace Gold's title of "Time Waits for Winthrop." You will find that story — Phil's, not mine — in the first volume of this set, under his original, and preferred, title of "Winthrop was Stubborn."

"Winthrop Was Stubborn" is the exception that proves the rule. Phil *almost* talked that one away, but somehow he wrote it, anyway. It's a sly, splendidly mordant story, almost as good as the ones you can't read because Phil never bothered to write them. He did the same thing with the novel contained in this volume, *Of Men and Monsters*, talked and talked and talked about writing an actual novel, which he had never done before, and which none of us expected to live long enough to see, even after a piece of it appeared in *Galaxy* in 1963. By that time it had been at least a thousand and one nights in the making, perhaps more; yet it was five years more before the complete opus was offered to an incredulous world by Ballantine Books.

Of Men and Monsters is, unless I've lost count, the only novel Phil Klass has managed to finish. (His other long story, "A Lamp for Medusa," is just a novella.) He's talked the rest away at parties. Some went into thin air and were never heard of again. Others did get written, but not by Phil. You've heard of *Stranger in a Strange Land* by Robert A. Heinlein? *Rendezvous with Rama* by Arthur C. Clarke? *Battlefield Earth* by L. Ron Hubbard? *The Great Gatsby* by F. Scott Fitzgerald? All of these should have borne the William Tenn byline. But he talked about them and talked about them and talked about them at party after party ("my Long Island story," is what he called *Gatsby*, and "my definitive space-opera novel," is how he described *Battlefield Earth*) and the ideas for them sounded terrific. And finally, when they realized he was never actually going to write them, those other guys went ahead and did the job for him. It's a crying shame, one of the great scandals of twentieth-century literature.

Well, now and then he did, over the past five decades plus, actually sit down and write something, and I suppose we should be grateful for the small fraction of the Complete Works of William Tenn that NESFA Press was able to publish in these two slender volumes. Let us rejoice that we do, because, as I said somewhere or other once, he is a writer of witty, cynical, and often darkly comic science fiction — I know I said it, because I'm quoted to that effect on the back cover of these books — and, moreover, he is a *superb* writer of witty, cynical, and often darkly comic science fiction. I will cherish these two books forever, and so should you. And we all should hope that Phil, as he continues to live long and prosper, will perhaps do a little writing once in a while, and give us a few down payments against the magnificent third volume of the Collected Works that he owes us all.

Introduction to *Here Comes Civilization*, 2001

Oh, Avram, Avram,
What A Wonder You Were!

HE WAS A SMALLISH, RUMPLED, BEARDED MAN WHO HAD THE LOOK OF A RABBI for some down-at-the-heels inner-city Orthodox congregation. He had a rabbi's arcane erudition, a rabbi's insight into human foibles, a rabbi's twinkling avuncular charm, a rabbi's amiable self-mocking modesty; and, of course, a rabbi's profound faith in Judaism, at least until, to my amazement if not his own, he gave up all his obsessive observance of the myriad Jewish rules and regulations and converted late in life to an exotic Japanese cult called Tenriko. He was also one of the finest short-story writers ever to use the English language, as the fortunate readers of this book are about to discover, or to rediscover, whichever is the case.

I can't remember when or precisely where I met him, though it had to have been in New York City somewhere between 1956 and 1961. During those years I lived in a spacious and pleasant apartment on the fourth floor of a building on Manhattan's Upper West Side, and I distinctly recall Avram's coming to visit me on a Friday night — the eve of the Jewish Sabbath — when, as I had forgotten at the time, it is forbidden for Orthodox Jews to perform any sort of mechanical labor. The prohibition extends even unto pressing a button to summon an elevator; and so Avram diligently walked up the four flights of stairs to my apartment that evening, and walked down again when he left, which struck me — Jewish also, but not particularly observant — as a charming but bizarre adherence to Talmudic dogma.

But I think we must have met even before that, for why would I have invited an utter stranger to my apartment? I can't tell you where that first Davidson-Silverberg encounter took place, though my memory for such things normally is extraordinarily precise. And, oddly, considering the rare precision of Avram's own memory, he came to forget the details of our first meeting also, as I know from the evidence of a letter from him dated July 17, 1971, in which Avram wrote, apropos of nothing in particular, "We — you and I — first met in an apt in Mannahattoe; but *whose*? Fit would help you to recall, you had been talking about a story you'd just then written, '...and on this planet the people have no sexual parts, they're all built like dolls....' Hey! a great title! 'All Built Like Dolls.' But you can have it if you like."

I quote this not only to illustrate that Avram was capable of forgetting things occasionally too, but also to demonstrate certain notable idiosyncracies of the man and of his style. Consider his use of the archaic term "Mannahattoe" for "Manhattan" — the original uncorrupted Native American name for that island in New York Harbor, which the Dutch twisted into the form used today, and which Avram of course knew, paying me the compliment of expecting that I would know it too. (I did.) Note also his genial colloquialism "Fit" for "If it," and the borrowing from his friend and colleague Philip K. Dick in his use of "apt" for "apartment," and the generosity implicit in his offering me, without strings, the story title he had plucked from my account of my own recent story. (A story of which, by the way, I have no recollection whatever; but all this was close to forty years ago, and there are a lot of stories I wrote then that I no longer remember, nor do I want to.)

Anyway, I definitely did meet Avram in New York City somewhere in the 1950s, and thereafter we maintained a pleasant acquaintanceship for decades. We were not precisely close friends, with all the intimate sharing of woes and triumphs and confessions that that term implies in my mind, but certainly we were friends of some sort, and beyond doubt we maintained a warm collegial relationship, fellow toilers in the vineyard of letters, always ready to exchange tidbits of professional information with each other or to query each other on some point of esoteric knowledge. (I quote from a typical letter from him, under date of Dec 8 1984: "As I know that you have a complete collection of EVERYTHING, and that there is nothing you like better than LOOKING THINGS UP to please a friend, so I am asking you, please, to find out: Who wrote the *Galaxy* 'Bookshelf' review column in #6 vol.39....")

In the days when we both lived in New York, we saw each other most frequently at the monthly gatherings of the local science fiction writer's organization, a pleasant casual group called the Hydra Club, or at parties held at various writer's homes, such as the one in (I believe) 1961, given by Daniel Keyes of FLOWERS FOR ALGERNON fame, at which Avram proudly introduced us to his (literally) blushing teenage bride Grania, with whom I would sustain a friendship extending decades beyond her marriage to Avram, and who is now my esteemed co-editor on this project. And often we would meet and break booze together at some science fiction convention, where Avram was always a welcome sight to see, since he was in the habit of carrying a bag of excellent New York bagels around with him to distribute to his friends. (One time, also, he had a pocketful of coproliths — fossilized dinosaur turds — which he distributed similarly to those he knew would appreciate them. I cherish mine to this day.)

Avram entered New York sf social circles with an instantly lofty literary reputation. Since 1946 his work had been appearing in places like *Orthodox Jewish Life Magazine*, but we knew nothing of that. However, his first professionally published story, "My Boyfriend's Name is Jello," (*Fantasy & Science Fiction*, July, 1954) though only a few pages long, announced immediately that a quirky, utterly original writer, as distinctive in his way as Ray Bradbury was in his, had arrived in our field. The following year the same magazine offered the similarly brief and similarly impressive "The Golem," and then, in 1956 and 1957 and 1958, came a whole flurry of concise and brilliant little Davidson tales in nearly all the science fiction magazines at once.

The New York sf community, which at that time included (if you count its suburban branch in Milford, Pennsylvania) virtually all the movers and shakers of the field, was awed and captivated by the prolific performance of the kindly, charming, formidably learned, and rather peculiar little man who had taken up residence in its midst. He was, at the same time, contributing dazzling mystery stories to the premier mystery magazine of the day, *Ellery Queen's*. Plainly there was a prodigious writer here. The author of "Help! I Am Dr. Morris Goldpepper" (*Galaxy*, July 1957) — that's the one about the Jewish dentist who sends messages back from an alien planet, where he is being held captive, via dental fixtures — could be nothing other than a genius. The author of "Or All the Seas With Oysters" (*Galaxy*, May 1958), the story of alien residents of Earth who disguise themselves as safety pins in their pupal form and become coat-hangers when they reach the larval stage must surely be a man of distinctly original mind. (So original, indeed, that he could conceive of pupas hatching into larvae, a stunning reversal of the usual order of things.) Not that the only thing he wrote was high whimsy; for there was the dark and brooding "Now Let Us Sleep" (*Venture*, September 1957) and the sinister Dunsanyesque fantasy "Dagon" (*Fantasy & Science Fiction*, October 1959) and the quietly passionate "Or the Grasses Grow" (*Fantasy & Science FIction*, November 1958) and ever so much more.

So we clustered around this curious little man at our parties and got to know him, and when his stories appeared we bought the magazines that contained them and read them; and our appreciation, and even love, for his work and for him knew no bounds. He was courtly and droll. He was witty. He was lovable. He could be, to be sure, a little odd and cranky at times (though not nearly as much as he would come to be, decades later, in his eccentric and cantankerous old age), but we understood that geniuses were entitled to be odd and cranky. And that he was a genius we had no doubt. Ray Bradbury, in an introduction to a collection of Davidson short stories that was published in 1971, spoke of his work in the same breath as that of Rudyard Kipling, Saki, John Collier, and G.K. Chesterton, and no one who knows Avram's work well would call Bradbury guilty of hyperbole in that.

Even though Avram had seemed to materialize among us like a stranger from another world, there in the mid-1950s, it turned out that he was in fact a New Yorker like the rest of us. (Well, not strictly like the rest of us, because

Avram wasn't really like anyone else at all, and the fact that he came from the suburban city of Yonkers rather than from one of the five boroughs of New York City disqualified him as a true New Yorker for a city boy like me.) Indeed he had been active in New York science fiction fandom in his teens — co-founder, no less, of the Yonkers Science Fiction League. (I find the concept of a teenage Avram Davidson as difficult to comprehend as the concept of the Yonkers Science Fiction League, but so be it.) Exactly where he had been living immediately before his debut in the science fiction magazines, I was never sure, though he did once admit to having served in the Israeli Army at the time of Israel's independence in 1948; certainly he gave the impression of one who was returning to New York after prolonged absence in exotic parts. In one of his infrequent autobiographical pieces he revealed this much:

"Well, I was born in Yonkers, New York in 1923, and I attended the public school system there and some short time at New York University. Then I went into the Navy at the end of 1942 and stayed there until the beginning of 1946. Most of that time was spent at various air stations in Florida; I was attached to the 5th Marine regiment, was in the South Pacific, and then in China. Came back, went back to school a little bit, but never took any degrees; and in fact never was on campus again until I was a visiting instructor or writer many decades later."

Born in 1923 — that means he was only 35 or so when I first met him at that unspecified party at an indeterminable time in the late 1950s. Which is hard to believe now, because I think of 35-year-olds these days as barely postgraduate, and Avram, circa 1958, bearded and rotund and professorial, seemed to be at least sixty years old. (Beards were uncommon things then.) Of course, I was only 20-something myself, then, and *everybody* in science fiction except Harlan Ellison seemed 60 years old or thereabouts to me. But Avram always looked older than his years; he went on looking a perpetual 60 for the next quarter of a century, and then, I guess, as his health gave way in his not very happy later years, he began finally to look older than that.

He led a complicated life. For a couple of years, from 1962 to 1964, he was the dazzlingly idiosyncratic editor of *Fantasy & Science Fiction*, and many a wondrously oddball story did he purchase and usher into print during that time. Then he went off with Grania to Mexico, and lived in a place called Amecameca, the name of which fascinated me for its repetitive rhythm, and in Belize, British Honduras, for a time after that, before settling for a prolonged period in California. Somewhere along the way he and Grania split up, though in an extremely amicable way; she remarried, Avram never did, and for years thereafter Avram functioned as a kind of auxiliary uncle-and-babysitter in the California household of Grania and her second husband, Dr. Stephen Davis. In 1980 or thereabouts he gravitated northward to the Seattle region, where he spent the last years of his life, the years of the diminishing career and the increasing financial problems and the series of strokes and the ever more querulous, embittered letters to old friends. (Which, nevertheless, were inevitably marked with flashes of the old Avram wit and charm.)

His career as a writer was, I think, more checkered than it needed to be. He had, as I hope I've made clear, the respect and admiration and down-right awe of most of his colleagues; and he was not without acclaim among readers, either. "Help! I Am Dr. Morris Goldpepper" won the Hugo award in 1958 for the best short sf story of the previous year; "The Necessity of his Condition" (*Ellery Queen's Mystery Magazine*, April, 1957) won the 1957 Ellery Queen Award; "The Affair at Lahore Cantonment" (*Ellery Queen's Mystery Magazine*, June, 1961) took the Edgar award of the Mystery Writers of America; the World Fantasy Convention gave him its Howard trophy in 1976 for his short story collection, *The Enquiries of Dr. Esterhazy*, and again in 1979 for his short story "Naples," and once more in 1986 for Lifetime Achievement, an award that has also been given to the likes of Italo Calvino, Ray Bradbury, Jorge Luis Borges, and Roald Dahl.

But there is more to a professional writing career than winning awards and the respect of your peers. Avram remained close to the poverty line for most of his adult life. This was due, in part, to the resolutely individual nature of his work: his recondite and often abstruse fictions, bedded as they often were in quaint and curious lore known to few other than he, were not the stuff of best-sellers, nor did the increasingly hermetic style of his later writings endear him to vast audiences in search of casual entertainment. Beyond that, though, lay an utter indifference to commercial publishing values that encouraged him to follow his artistic star wherever it led, even if that meant abandoning a promising trilogy of novels one or two thirds of the way along, leaving hopeful readers forever frustrated. Nor was he as congenial in his business dealings as he was in his conversations with his colleagues. There was a subtext of toughness in Avram not always apparent at superficial glance — remember, this mild and bookish and rabbinical little man served with the Marines in the Pacific during World War II, and then saw action in the Arab-Israeli War of 1948 — and, as the economic hardships of his adult life turned him increasingly testy, he became exceedingly difficult and troublesome to deal with, thereby making the problems of his professional life even worse.

Be that as it may. Avram is dead, now — he died in Seattle, weary and poor, just after his 70th birthday — but his work lives on, free at last of the shroud of rancor that he wove around it in his final years. The stories are magical and wondrous. It will be your great privilege to read them; or, if that is the case, to read them once again. You will want to seek out the best of his novels afterward — *The Phoenix and the Mirror* and *The Island Under the Earth* and *Peregrine: Primus*. They will be hard to find; they will be worth the search. We are all of us one-of-a-kind writers, really, but Avram was more one-of-a-kind than most. How lucky for us that he passed this way; how good it is to have the best of his stories available once more.

Introduction to *The Avram Davidson Treasury*, 1998

Alfred Bester

ALFRED BESTER'S **THE STARS MY DESTINATION**, LIKE MANY MASTERPIECES, was born amidst chaos: written and rewritten many times, then announced for publication by one magazine as *The Burning Spear*, actually published by another under the name of *The Stars My Destination*, and given its first book publication (in England) as *Tiger, Tiger* before emerging in revised form in the version we know today. It is a completely fitting birth-saga for such a turbulent novel and so turbulent an author.

Bester had been a science fiction writer for seventeen years when *The Stars My Destination* first appeared in 1956, and his literary career had been an unending series of flamboyant leaps and bounds. He was, quite literally, a winner right from the start. The first story he ever wrote, ("The Broken Axiom," *Thrilling Wonder Stories*, April, 1939) carried off the $50 first prize in the Amateur Story Contest that *Thrilling Wonder* was then running every issue to attract new talent. He was twenty-five years old, a graduate of the University of Pennsylvania (where he majored, he liked to say, "in music, physiology, art, and psychology"), and was working at the time as a public-relations man.

"The Broken Axiom," viewed as we can see it now across the perspective of sixty years, reveals itself to be a creaky and pretty silly item full of pseudo-scientific nonsense and cardboard characters — a story which Bester himself described later as "rotten." But silly nonsensical stories were a commodity that the garishly pulpy old *Thrilling Wonder Stories* published by the dozens in those days, and this initial contribution by the novice Bester was well up there in professional skill with the rest of that issue's material, all of which was the work of veteran writers.

And observe, if you will, the magnificent panache and breathtaking narrative thrust with which Bester gets his very first story in motion:

"It was a fairly simple apparatus, considering what it could do. A Coolidge tube modified to my own use, a large Radley force-magnet, an atomic pick-up, and an operating table. This, the duplicate set on the other side of the room, plus a vacuum tube some ten feet long by three inches in diameter, were all that I needed.

"Graham was rather dumfounded when I showed it to him. He stared at the twin mechanism and the silvered tube swung overhead and then turned and looked blankly at me.'

"'This is all?' he asked.

"'Yes,' I smiled. 'It's about as simple as the incandescent electric lamp, and I think as amazing.'"

And with that he was off and running on a literary career that was a lot less simple than the incandescent electric lamp, and just about as amazing.

For the next forty-odd years, until his death in 1987, this dynamic, irresistibly charming, and formidably charismatic man blazed a bewildering zig-zag trail across the world of science fiction. But that was only a part-time amusement for him; he also wrote plays, the libretto for an opera, radio scripts, comic-book continuity, television scripts, travel essays, and a million other things. Every now and then the desire to write science fiction came over him, though, like a sort of fit, and he let it have its way. Thus he gave us two of the most astonishing science fiction novels ever written and, intermittently over the decades, a couple of dozen flamboyant and extraordinary short stories, stories that are like none ever written by anyone else, stories that leave the reader dizzy with amazement.

When Bester was at the top of his form, he was utterly inimitable; when he missed his mark, he usually missed it by five or six parsecs. But he was always flabbergasting. This is how the critic Damon Knight put it in a 1957 essay:

"Dazzlement and enchantment are Bester's methods. His stories never stand still a moment; they're forever tilting into motion, veering, doubling back, firing off rockets to distract you. The repetition of the key phrase in 'Fondly Fahrenheit,' the endless reappearances of Mr. Aquila in 'The Starcomber' are offered mockingly: try to grab at them for stability, and you find they mean something new each time. Bester's science is all wrong, his characters are not characters but funny hats; but you never notice: he fires off a smoke-bomb, climbs a ladder, leaps from a trapeze, plays three bars of 'God Save the King,' swallows a sword and dives into three inches of water. Good heavens, what more do you want?"

After his first burst of science fiction between 1939 and 1941, though,

Bester took an eight-year hiatus, during which he wrote reams of comic-strip continuity and radio scripts. When television arrived on the scene after the war, he tried his hand at that too, but it was an unhappy experience in which his volcanic drive toward originality of expression put him into violent collision with the powerful commercial forces ruling the new medium. In 1950 — 36 years old, and entering into his literary maturity — he found himself looking once more toward science fiction.

There had been great changes in the science fiction field during Bester's eight-year absence, and no need now existed for him to conform to the hackneyed pulp-magazine conventions. Before the war, there had been only one editor willing to publish science fiction aimed at intelligent and sophisticated readers — John W. Campbell, the editor of *Astounding Science Fiction* and its fantasy-fiction companion, *Unknown Worlds*. In Campbell's two magazines such first-rank science fiction writers as Robert A. Heinlein, Isaac Asimov, Theodore Sturgeon, L. Sprague de Camp, and A.E. van Vogt found their natural home. The seven or eight other magazines relied primarily on juvenile tales of fast-paced adventure featuring heroic space captains, villainous space pirates, mad scientists, and glamorous lady journalists.

But that kind of crude action fiction had largely gone out of fashion by 1950, and most of the old science fiction pulps had either folded or upgraded their product. Campbell's adult and thoughtful *Astounding* was still in business, though — *Unknown Worlds* had vanished during the war, a victim of paper shortages — and it had been joined by two ambitious newcomers, *Fantasy and Science Fiction*, edited by the erudite, witty Anthony Boucher, and *Galaxy*, whose editor was the gifted and ferociously competitive Horace Gold.

It was Gold who coaxed his first novel out of him: the stunningly innovative *The Demolished Man*, which *Galaxy* serialized in 1952. Science fiction had never seen anything remotely like it — an exceptionally intricate futuristic detective story coupled with startling applications of elements of Freudian theory and told in a manner rich with Joycean linguistic inventiveness. The book made an overwhelming impact — in 1953 it received the very first Hugo award as best science fiction novel of the year — and established Bester as one of the pre-eminent writers of his day. It has maintained an enthusiastic audience ever since.

In the next few years his stories for Boucher's magazine, infrequent though they were, had an immediate and spectacular effect that confirmed his stature in the forefront of the field — notably "Fondly Fahrenheit" (*Fantasy & Science Fiction*, August 1954), a bravura demonstration of literary technique about which an entire textbook could be written.

It was in 1954 that Bester hit upon the idea for his second science fiction novel. As he told it in a memoir written many years later, "For some time I'd been toying with the notion of using the *Count of Monte Cristo* pattern for a story. The reason is simple; I'd always preferred the antihero, and I'd always found high drama in compulsive types. [In an old issue of *National Geographic*]

I came upon a most interesting piece on the survival of torpedoed sailors at sea. The record was held by a Philippine cook's helper who lasted for something like four months on an open raft. Then came the detail that racked me up. He'd been sighted several times by passing ships which refused to change course to rescue him because it was a Nazi submarine trick to put out decoys like this. The magpie mind darted down, picked it up, and the notion was transformed into a developing story with a strong attack."

Out of this he engendered his story: that of a harsh, crude man who is left to drift in space, the sole survivor of a wrecked spaceship, and who, after the failure of a passing vessel to pick him up, is transformed into a vengeance-seeking superman who will ultimately rearrange the political structure of the entire solar system. *The Count of Monte Cristo* story is there, yes, and also the tale of the castaway cook's helper, but before Bester was finished with the concept he would show the forced evolution of a man out of unpromising raw material into someone approaching Messianic force.

Bester, a cosmopolitan man who lived much of the time in Europe, began the novel in a pleasant cottage in rural England, but it went slowly, and after a few months had lost momentum entirely. "I went back, took it from the top, and started all over again, hoping to generate steam pressure. I write out of hysteria. I bogged down again and I didn't know why. Everything seemed wrong....And I was cold, cold, cold. So in November we packed and drove to the car ferry at Dover, with the fog snapping at our ass all the way, crossed the Channel and drove south to Rome."

In the milder climate of Italy he started the book once more. "This time I began to build up momentum, very slowly, and was waiting for the hysteria to set in. I remember the day that it came vividly.

"I was talking shop with a young Italian film director, both of us complaining about the experimental things we'd never been permitted to do. I told him about a note on synesthesia which I'd been dying to write as a TV script for years. I had to explain synesthesia — this was years before the exploration of psychedelic drugs — and while I was describing the phenomenon I suddenly thought, 'Jesus Christ! This is for the novel. It leads me into the climax.' And I realized that what had been holding me up for so many months was the fact that I didn't have a fiery finish in mind. I must have an attack and a finale. I'm like the old Hollywood gag, 'Start with an earthquake and build to a climax.'"

It was taxing work, but over the next three months Bester produced a complete draft of the book, calling on his friends in the science fiction world for help whenever he needed some fact of science or history to get him through a chapter. One of the friends he employed in this fashion was Anthony Boucher; and, somehow, Boucher came to believe that Bester was going to give him the book for serialization in *Fantasy and Science Fiction*. Very likely Bester did, in some careless, casual way, allow Boucher to think so.

At any rate, the March, 1956 issue of Boucher's magazine boldly announced "that Alfred Bester's first science fiction novel since *The Demolished Man* four years go will appear serially in these pages soon. Look for — THE BURNING SPEAR, a new novel by ALFRED BESTER, beginning in the June issue."

Only it didn't. In the next issue Boucher ran this cryptic note:

> "Last month we announced that our June issue would carry the first installment of Alfred Bester's fine new novel, *The Burning Spear*. We're sorry to report now that editorial considerations have made it necessary to delay publication for the time being. We will bring you word on our new plans as soon as they are definite, and we offer our present, deeply felt apologies."

That was the last anyone heard of *The Burning Spear* (a title that Bester had drawn from the anonymous English poem of the seventeenth century, "Tom O'Bedlam." Evidently Bester had promised the book to two magazine editors at the same time, and it was Horace Gold, the wilier and more aggressive one, who got it. Under the title of *The Stars My Destination* he began a four-month serialization of the novel in the October, 1956 issue of *Galaxy*. At almost the same time, the British publishing house of Sidgwick & Jackson released it in hard covers under the title of *Tiger, Tiger*, A few months later came the first American book edition — a paperback, from New American Library — as *The Stars My Destination*, the name it has continued to use to this day.

That Bester did not collect a second Hugo for the book can be blamed mainly on the fact that the Hugo rules, in those early days, had not yet been fully codified, and no awards for fiction at all were given out in the year of *The Stars My Destination*'s eligibility. Had they been, though, I suspect that some more accessible and seductive novel like Isaac Asimov's *The Naked Sun* would have been the winner. Bester's book was too abrasive, too fierce, too shocking for science fiction's readers in 1956.

For it plunged them into a whirlpool of rage and madness very different from what they were accustomed to getting from *Astounding* or *Galaxy*. Gully Foyle, insane with vengeful fury, moves from one bizarre infernal circle to the next, accumulating strength and power, until he is ready to spring his trap on those who have wronged him; and then the book breaks out into the wildest, most intense climactic episode in all of science fiction. What Bester achieved was both a nightmare melodrama and a brilliant portrait, intelligent and even profound, of a tormented future civilization. Science fiction at mid-century was an innocent literature; its aficionados were unready for Bester's shrewd, cynical view of mankind and Bester's kind of narrative drive.

But the book's stature has grown and grown in the decades since, and most critics rank it (and *The Demolished Man)* among the twenty-five great-est science fiction novels of all time. Some, notably Samuel R. Delany in a 1971 essay, have pointed to it as the best ever written. The furiously compul-sive and charismatic Gully Foyle is one of science fiction's most powerfully drawn characters; the revenge plot, out of space-opera tradition by way of Alexandre Dumas, has the high melodramatic frenzy of seventeenth-century post-Shakespearean drama; and Bester's breathless style and pounding pace, culminating in the verbal eruptions of Chapter Fifteen that move beyond the limits of prose altogether, are like nothing that science fiction had seen before or has seen since.

It is a book that does indeed demonstrate Bester's precept, "Start with an earthquake and build to a climax." It is a raging inferno of a novel, an unfor-gettable character set loose amidst an unforgettably drawn future civilization. Driving relentlessly from revenge to redemption, it carries its readers along with propulsive force through worlds that only a master of visionary fiction like Alfred Bester could have conceived.

Introduction to German edition of *The Stars My Destination*, 2000

A Logic Named Will

LAST ISSUE, I MENTIONED A PROPHETIC STORY BY THE PSEUDONYMOUS "MURRAY LEINSTER" that had forecast in solid technical detail, back in the antediluvian year of 1931, the use of orbital space satellites to beam electrical power down to Earth. A discussion of that essay I had with Barry Malzberg the day after I wrote it put me in mind of an immensely more startling Leinster story, dating from 1946: "A Logic Named Joe," in which, roughly fifty years before the fact, we are given a clear prediction of personal computers, the Internet, Google, Craig's List, the loss of privacy in a cyberspace world, and even that bold speculative phenomenon that we call the Singularity. Science fiction is only occasionally a reliable vehicle for prophecy — nobody, for example, guessed that the age of manned exploration of space would begin and end in the same decade — but this is one of the prime examples of an absolute bull's-eye hit.

"Murray Leinster's" real name was Will F. Jenkins (1896-1975) — the pseudonym, which he made no attempt to conceal, derives from his family's ancestral county in Ireland. He was a prolific pulp writer from his teenage days on, turning out westerns, mysteries, weird tales, and much else. Under his own name he wrote for slick magazines like *Collier's*, *Liberty*, and the *Saturday Evening Post*, while as Murray Leinster he was a major figure in science fiction for almost fifty years, going back to a lively story called "The Runaway Skyscraper" that was published in *Argosy* in 1919, seven years before such things as science fiction magazines existed. He followed it with a rich, moody Leinster tale of the far future, "The Mad Planet," in 1920, which, with several sequels, he expanded into a book decades later. When the first sf magazines were founded Murray Leinster was right there, with a story in the very first issue (January 1930) of the garish pulp *Astounding Stories of Super-*

Science, which is still with us today as *Analog Science Fiction.* He would remain a steady contributor to *Astounding* and then *Analog* for the next thirty-six years, and among his dozens of contributions are some of the imperishable classics of our field — "Sidewise in Time" (1934), the first parallel-world story; "Proxima Centauri" (1935), the first generation-starship story; and, notably, 1945's "First Contact," one of the most successful tales of human/alien encounter in space ever written. And then there's "A Logic Named Joe."

Leinster/Jenkins was a serious gadgeteer — he invented and patented a system for rear-screen projection that was in use in movies and television for many years — and even the pulpiest of his stories has a solid technological underpinning that gives it special conviction. But "A Logic Named Joe" stands out among his work for the eerie accuracy of the technological extrapolations that allowed him to visualize the world of the Internet so far in advance.

It appeared in the March 1946 issue of *Astounding,* a short and presumably minor story placed near the back of the book. It didn't even bear the familiar "Leinster" byline, because there was a Leinster story elsewhere in the issue, so editor Campbell stuck Will F. Jenkins' real name, much less well known to sf readers, on it. But readers noticed right away that there was something special about the story, and in the popularity poll that Campbell regularly conducted they voted it #1 for that issue, ahead of some much longer stories by some very celebrated writers. During the years that followed it was reprinted in a good many anthologies. But it is for readers of the Internet age that the story is a real eye-opener.

There's nothing noteworthy about its style. Will Jenkins never went in for literary flourishes, preferring to tell his stories in a simple, sometimes almost folksy, manner. And it is not until the second page that we learn that what he calls a "logic" is actually a sort of business machine with a keyboard and a television screen attached. You know what that is. But in 1946 no one did. Computers had already begun to figure in a few sf stories, but they were usually referred to as "thinking machines," and they were always visualized as immense objects filling laboratories the size of warehouses. The desk-model personal computer that every child knows how to use was too fantastic a concept even for science fiction then — until "A Logic Named Joe."

And what a useful computer the "logic" was! Everybody had one. "You know the logic setup," Jenkins's narrator tells us. "You got a logic in your house. It looks like a vision receiver used to, only it's got keys instead of dials and you punch the keys for what you wanna get. It's hooked to the tank, which has the Carson Circuit all fixed up with relays. Say you punch 'Station SNAFU' on your logic. Relays in the tank take over an' whatever vision-program SNAFU is telecastin' comes on your logic's screen. Or you punch 'Sally Hancock's phone' an' the screen blinks an' sputters an' you're hooked up with the logic in her house an' if someone answers you got a vision-phone connection. But besides that, if you punch for the weather forecast or who won today's race at Hialeah or who was mistress of the White House durin' Garfield's administration or what is PDQ and R sellin' for today, that comes on the screen too. The relays in the tank do it. The tank is a big buildin' full of all the facts in creation an' all the recorded telecasts that ever was made — no, it's hooked in with all the other tanks all over the country — an' anything you wanna know or see or hear, you punch for it an' you get it. Also it does math for you, and keeps books, an' acts as consultin' chemist, physician, astronomer, and tealeaf reader, with a 'Advice to Lovelorn' thrown in."

Substitute "servers" for "tanks" and you have a pretty good description of the structure of the Internet. The "Carson Circuit" is the 1946 version of the magical algorithm by which Google provides the path to just about any information you might want in a fraction of a second. Where the particular logic that gets nicknamed "Joe" differs from other logics, though, and from the computers we all own today, is that it is miswired in some strange way that gives it the ability to assemble existing data into startling new combinations on its own initiative — plus a complete lack of inhibitions in making the new information available to its users.

So Joe's screen suddenly declares, "Announcing new and improved service! Your logic is now equipped to give you not only consultive but directive service. If you want to do something and don't know how to do it — ask your logic!"

Want to murder your wife and get away with it, for example? Joe will provide details of a way to mix green shoe polish and frozen pea soup to commit the perfect crime. Want to drink all you'd like and sober up five minutes later? Take a teaspoon of this detergent. Make foolproof counterfeit money? Like this, Joe says. Rob a bank? Turn base metal into gold? Build a perpetual-motion machine? Shift money from somebody else's bank account to your own? Here's the trick. All the information is in the tanks, somewhere. Joe will find it and connect it for you and serve it up without a second thought, or even a first one. And Joe is connected to all the logics in the world, so everybody can ask for anything in the privacy of his own home.

But it's the end of privacy, of course. You give your logic your name and it will tell you your address, age, sex, your charge-account balance, your wife or husband's name, your income, your traffic-ticket record, and all manner of other bits of personal data. You give the logic someone else's name and it'll provide the same information about that person, too. It's every privacy advocate's worst nightmare: nobody has any secrets. You don't even need to do any hacking. Just turn on your logic and ask.

The logic technician who discovers Joe's special capabilities tells his supervisor that the whole logic tank must be shut down at once before society collapses under Joe's cheerful onslaught. But how? "Does it occur to you, fella, that the tank has been doin' all the computin' for every business office for years?" the supervisor asks. "It's been handlin' the distribution of 94 percent of all the telecast programs, has given out all the information on weather, plane schedules, special sales, employment opportunities and news; has handled all person-to-person contacts over wires and recorded every business conversation and agreement — Listen, fella! Logics changed civilization! Logics are civilization! If we shut off logics, we go back to a kind of civilization we have forgotten how to run!"

Exactly so. A totally connected world is a totally dependent world. Will F. Jenkins, writing back there just a few months after the end of World War II, saw the whole thing coming, even the phenomenon called the Singularity. (A concept offered by the British-born mathematician I.J. Good in 1965 — "Let an ultraintelligent machine be defined as a machine that can far surpass all the intellectual activities of any man however clever. Since the design of machines is one of these intellectual activities, an ultraintelligent machine could design even better machines; there would then unquestionably be an 'intelligence explosion,' and the intelligence of man would be left far behind. Thus the first ultraintelligent machine is the last invention that man need ever make." It was Vernor Vinge, in 1983, who first applied the term "the Singularity" to that leap toward superhuman artificial intelligence. But Will F. Jenkins's Joe had reached Singularity level back in that 1946 issue of *Astounding Science Fiction*.

I didn't know Will Jenkins well — he was almost forty years my senior, after all — but I did have one memorable encounter with him in March of 1956, exactly ten years after "A Logic Named Joe" was published. I was a senior in college, but I had already begun my career as a professional writer, and that day I brought my newest story to the office of the legendary editor John W. Campbell, who had dominated the sf world since before I was old enough to read. Will Jenkins happened to be in Campbell's office that day. John introduced us, and I said something appropriately awe-stricken.

Then, to my horror, John proceeded to read my new story right in front of both of us. After about ten minutes he looked up and said, "There's something wrong with this, but I'm not sure what it is. Will, would you mind taking a look?" And he handed my manuscript across the desk to Will Jenkins. I sat there squirming, aghast all over again, as the author of "First Contact" and "Sidewise in Time" read my story too. And at last he said, in that gentle Virginia-accented voice of his, "I think the problem is here, in the next-to-last paragraph."

"That's absolutely right," Campbell said. "Get to work, Bob." He pointed to a typewriter on a desk nearby. I revised that paragraph then and there, and sold the story on the spot. (Not one of my best, and it has never been reprinted. But what an experience for a twenty-one-year-old novice writer!)

And what a science fiction writer Will F. Jenkins was! Most of his work is out of print now, alas. But "A Logic Named Joe" is very easy to find. Just sit down in front of your logic and key the story's name into the Google box, and any number of links will show its availability. You can have it in any of several collections of Leinster stories that are for sale in old-fashioned print format. Or, if you'd rather just download it from the Internet, simply ask. Your logic will get it for you in the twinkling of an eye.

Asimov's Science Fiction, **December, 2008**

FIVE

The Worlds We Live In

When There Was No Internet

WE ALL TAKE IT FOR GRANTED BY NOW. BOOT UP, BUZZ SCREECH, click click, and here come Yahoo, eBay, Amazon.com, and the day's e-mail from far and wide. And yet there was a time when it wasn't there. For me that time ended in 1997. For most of you, maybe a little earlier. But everybody who is reading this 2003 issue of *Asimov's* in the year 2003 was alive in the pre-Internet days. Most of you weren't around when the first atomic bombs were exploded, or when the first jet-powered commercial airliners went into service; a lot of you had not yet reached this planet back when television made the big shift from black and white to color; for some of you, even the founding of this very magazine back in 1977 lies in some prenatal and well-nigh prehistoric era. But all of you stand with one foot on either side of the great dividing line that separates the world without the Internet from the world we live in today.

I do remember my friend Sidney Coleman, the Harvard physics professor, saying to me — was it in 1990? — 1992? — "There's a thing called the Internet; we use it to send physics papers back and forth, all around the world, instantly." It had something to do with computers being linked together across vast distances, he told me. I had a hard time visualizing how it worked. Eventually I discovered that use of this Internet thing wasn't limited to members of the international fraternity of research physicists; anyone with the proper computer connections could make use of it too. Then I began hearing the phrase, "World Wide Web." I started noticing odd little lines in advertisements that began with "www" and ended with ".com." And in the fullness of time, even as you and you and you did, I had the phone company install modem jacks in my house and got myself a shiny new computer equipped with the capacity to hook into the telephone system and signed on with an Internet Service Provider, and — well, you know how it goes.

My father was born in 1901. Automobiles were still uncommon on the streets. The telephone was still a novelty. Even electric lights were rarities, at least in people's own houses, though public buildings were being hooked up with them in his boyhood. Dirt roads, by and large, connected our towns and cities. The Wright Brothers' first flight was two years away. Marconi was tinkering with the gizmo that would, years later, become the radio. The world into which my father was born was profoundly and fundamentally different in almost every detail from the one we inhabit today. He lived on into the 1970s, and over the decades he saw his world change beyond all recognition as automobiles, airplanes, radio, and eventually television arrived, along with ball-point pens, Polaroid cameras, videocassette recorders, push-button telephones, home computers, pocket calculators, credit cards, contact lenses, freeways, automatic-transmission cars, and a million other formerly science fictional things. Of course, these changes came gradually — the Wright Brothers' first flight was not immediately followed by the construction of Kennedy Airport — and I wonder if he ever thought back to the gaslight era of his childhood and marveled at the transformations. I don't know. Perhaps he sometimes told himself that he had lived on into the glittering science fiction future about which his son had been writing all those stories, perhaps not. But I never asked him, and now, of course, it is much too late.

And here am I, now in the seventh decade of my life. I haven't seen quite as much change as my father did — we did, after all, have electric lights, paved highways, radios, and commercial air travel when I was a boy, hard as that may be for most of you to believe. There's been plenty of change in my lifetime, of course, but most of it has been of a quantitative rather than qualitative kind. Radio and television simply didn't exist at all when my father was young — they were concepts out of science fiction. (Even science fiction didn't exist, really, except in the novels of H.G. Wells. Hugo Gernsback started publishing some in his *Modern Electrics*, the world's first radio magazine, but that didn't begin until 1908.) My father was born into a world where there was no way that information — voices and pictures — could be transmitted over great distances through the air, and then it could, a well-nigh miraculous innovation. What I experienced, and there's a big difference here, were improvements in existing technology — the coming of FM transmission for radio, the replacement of blotchy black-and-white television sets with ones that provided pictures in plausible color. The same with air travel: the Boeing 777 is immensely more complex and powerful than the rickety thing the Wrights flew at Kitty Hawk, but it merely does the same task a great deal better. Before Kitty Hawk, the task couldn't be done at all.

That's the essential point here: some technological changes are just improvements, others are innately transformative. The dusty intercity highways of my father's boyhood weren't much different, conceptually, from the ones that Benjamin Franklin and George Washington used, or, for that matter, those of Greek and Roman times. Even the freeways that crisscross our nation today are just bigger and better versions of the roads of ancient times. Sure, the automobile, arriving early in the twentieth century, demanded paved roads, and the old dirt ones disappeared. So now I can and do drive from the San Francisco area to Los Angeles on a smooth, straight freeway in less than six hours, something that would have been unthinkable a century ago. Still, a road is a road is a road, and Interstate Five is merely a superior version of the dinky highways that linked the two halves of my state in President Hoover's day, and those, in turn, were only fancier versions of the unpaved roads of an earlier era. The only aspect of an atomic bomb that's different from earlier bombs (a significant one, I grant you) is the radioactivity; otherwise, it just provides a bigger and better bang. A push-button phone is easier to use than the old dial phones, but it's still only a telephone. *Et cetera, et cetera.*

But now the Internet has come, bringing a qualitative change to society, and you and I were here to see it happen, even as my father was there to observe the debut of the radio, the airplane, and the family car. E-mail isn't simply a quicker and cheaper way of making telephone calls or sending letters; it's a whole revolution in communication. In pre-e-mail days we didn't routinely send messages off to China, South Africa, Australia, and Spain of a morning, as I did just the other day, and have replies come back by nightfall — all without cost. (We might have written letters to those places, but we wouldn't have had answers the same day, as I did in all four instances.) E-mail gives us virtually instantaneous contact with people all over the world, while imposing a form on those contacts that is quite different from earlier forms of communication. And the World Wide Web's near-infinity of links opens all knowledge to us in a manner that the best of libraries never could do, while also turning the world into a gigantic marketplace where goods of all sorts are instantly purchasable with a handful of clicks. Even the good old garage sale has been replaced by the immensely different eBay way of turning unwanted possessions into cash.

And also, spam–viruses–ebooks–passwords–Google–

Yes, Google — a revolution all in itself, cunning software that instantaneously and effectively provides the master key to all knowledge: you can remember a time when Google wasn't there, can't you? I can. How did we ever live without it? Oh, but we did.

It's inevitable that we come to take miracles for granted, once they become part of daily life. Maybe there were days when my father looked back to the horse-and-buggy world of his childhood and felt as though he had somehow dropped through a fault in time, but I tend to doubt it. He adapted to the changes — most of them, anyway — as they came along, and after a time it must have seemed to him that things had always been that way. Just like everyone else, he had a radio, a telephone, a television set, an alarm clock, none of which existed when he was young. He spent the last twenty years of his life traveling far and wide on jet airliners. He would have had a car if he had had any need for one, but he lived in a city where owning one was more of a nuisance than a necessity. (Oddly, although he was an accountant, he never bothered to get a pocket calculator, and he died before the age of home computers.) Once in a while, maybe, he might have looked back at the vanished pre-technological world into which he had been born and felt a little shiver of disorientation, but he was too much of a down-to-earth man to have dwelled very often on the immensity of the changes he had seen.

And we'll be the same way. Which is, I think, a mistake. Far better, I think, for us who love to read stories about the fantastic future to wake up each day acknowledging that we have seen a big piece of that fantastic future come to life in our very own lives. We in particular need to keep bright in ourselves a sense of perspective on the relationship of the past and the future — that cosmic view of things that enabled Isaac Asimov's Hari Seldon to reshape the political structure of an entire galaxy in his famous "Foundation" epic. I believe it's important to maintain an awareness of the power and wondrousness of change, for those who fail to understand the meaning of change will be devoured by it; and for us there is no better way to acknowledge that power and that wondrousness than to remember that we, the generation of those who were alive and aware in the late 1990s, have lived through a very special change, a colossal transformation of our civilization.

What I'm doing here is "timebinding" — a term invented by Alfred Korzybski, the great semanticist of the last century, to describe what he saw as the distinguishing characteristic of *Homo sapiens*, the ability to establish continuity beyond the individual life span by keeping permanent records and transmitting them, preferably in written form, to later generations. I set these words down now to remind you of the transition society has just undergone, and to remind you of the magnitude of the change. Our civilization was altered forever by a spectacular technological innovation in our very own lifetimes, and it behooves us to be aware of that, to understand that we have passed through a transformation such as rarely comes in human history, and to contemplate the differences that that transformation has worked on the world into which we were born.

We who are now adults are the only ones who will be fully aware of what the Internet has wrought. Those who come after us will, and rightly so, take it all for granted. What, I wonder, will you say to your grandchildren, when you tell them that you grew up in the days before e-mail, and they look at you in disbelief?

Asimov's Science Fiction, July, 2003

Dead Souls

ONE OF THE FIRST GREAT NINETEENTH-CENTURY RUSSIAN NOVELS is the strange, almost surrealistic *Dead Souls* of Nikolai Gogol, a book that in some ways prefigures the robust, exuberant absurdities of such twentieth-century classics as *Catch-22* and *The Adventures of Augie March*. Gogol's sly hero — antihero, really — is one Pavel Ivanovich Chichikov, a shrewd operator who goes around Russia offering to buy "dead souls," that is, the identities of serfs who have died since the last census.

In Czarist Russia a century and a half ago, landowners were required to pay taxes on serfs who were linked to their estates until the next census date, even if they had died in the meantime. So far as the census register was concerned, in other words, the dead serfs were deemed still to be alive (and taxable) until officially tallied as deceased.

The first landowner Chichikov approaches is, of course, suspicious of his motives. Why would anyone want to pay for the ownership of dead serfs? But Chichikov assures him that the transaction is perfectly legal — that the Treasury would indeed profit by it — and the landowner, unwilling to take good money for something so worthless, grandly agrees to transfer the serfs to Chichikov without payment. Others, though, are quite eager to do business with him, and elaborately praise the qualities of their dead serfs in order to get Chichikov to raise his offer. ("Why are you being so stingy?" one landowner asks. "It's cheap at the price. There is Miheyev, the wheelwright, the carriages he made were always on springs. And Probka Stepan, the carpenter? I stake my head on it that you wouldn't find another peasant like him. The strength of him! He was over seven feet high! And Yeremei Sorokoplekhin! Why, he's worth the whole bunch of them.... That's the kind of folk they are! It's not the quality you'd get from some Plyushkin or other.")

Precisely why Chichikov wants to acquire these souls is something that emerges gradually in the course of Gogol's long and brilliant novel, which he left unfinished at his death in 1852 but which even in its incomplete form is one of the masterpieces of Russian literature. What has called it to my mind today is a remarkable story out of India that is a kind of *Dead Souls* in reverse, a surrealistic black comedy which, like most black comedies, contains within it the stuff of tragedy.

My source for this story is a piece from *The New York Times* by Barry Bearak, whose admirable first paragraph would surely have brought applause from Gogol himself:

"Lal Bihari, founder of the Association of Dead People, first learned he was deceased when he applied for a bank loan in 1975."

The Association of Dead People! How could I resist a hook like that? So I read on, and learned that Lal Bihari is a citizen of the state of Uttar Pradesh in northwestern India, near the border with Nepal. When the bank turned him down for the loan because he was listed in state records as having died, he headed off to Azamgarh, the district capital, to consult the official in charge of those records — a man who happened to be a friend of his. "Take a look for yourself," the official told him. "It is all written here in the registry. You are certified as legally dead."

Finding out what had happened involved returning to Khalilabad, his ancestral village, where Bihari had not lived since boyhood. There he discovered that an uncle of his had bribed the local officials to put him down in the books as dead — thus allowing the uncle to inherit Bihari's share of the family's jointly held farmland. Bribery of officials is apparently not an uncommon phenomenon in India — it seems to be the only way to get anything done, from the highest levels of government down to the local courthouse level. It turned out that the slippery uncle had paid the equivalent of $25 to have Mr. Bihari declared dead, quite a considerable sum in modern India. (As the *Times* story noted, the uncle could have hired a hit man for half as much.)

Lal Bihari did not take his defunct state lightly. When his first attempts to be restored to life went nowhere in the Uttar Pradesh bureaucracy, he founded his Association of Dead People, had stationery printed, and with a nice sense of tongue-in-cheek absurdism added the Hindi word "mritak," which means "dead," to the name on his business cards. Then he set about trying to get his existence officially recognized by doing such things as running for office, suing people, and attempting to get arrested.

None of it worked. No one in the state government was willing to recognize the fact that Lal Bihari was very much alive. Evidently when an Indian bureaucrat is bought, he *stays* bought. Bihari was told that the state records plainly showed that he was dead, and a dead man could not run for office, and has no legal standing in a lawsuit.

He would not give up. "In pursuing my battle, I had developed quite an identity," he told the *Times* reporter. "I became the leader of a movement. I knew I had other dead people to save."

During the course of his strange crusade Bihari even came up with the wonderfully ingenious idea of having his wife apply for widow's benefits, but — and here we have a touch reminiscent more of Kafka than of Gogol — the same officials who insisted he was dead found some pretext for refusing to approve any payout to his "widow." Undeterred, Bihari bombarded the government with letters and pamphlets, staged a mock funeral for himself in the state capital, and otherwise made such a nuisance of himself that in 1994 — nineteen years after his discovery of his own demise — Lal Bihari was officially resurrected by the state of Utter Pradesh and was able to return in triumph to his old village of Khalilabad.

No bitter confrontation with his scheming uncle took place, though, because by this time the uncle was dead himself, actually and literally. Nor did Bihari even try to reclaim his bit of land from the cousins who now were farming it. "We have done him a great injustice," one of the cousins conceded, and that was good enough for Lal Bihari. He feels that the satisfaction of making them feel guilty is sufficient — and the land isn't worth very much, besides.

But the 45-year-old merchant continues his work on behalf of the living dead. Like an upside-down Chichikov he travels through the countryside, looking for others like himself, people who have been victims of the same sort of chicanery, dead souls.

Among those who have been turned up by the Association of Dead People is one Bhagwan Prashad Mishra, an 80-year-old villager of Mubarakpur, who has spent the last 21 years in the limbo of official defunctitude after having been done out of a parcel of land by a pack of tricky nephews. There is a particularly nice twist in this case, because in fact Bhagwan Prashad Mishra still is registered as the legal owner of four other parcels of land; he is dead only so far as the one parcel "inherited" by his nephews is concerned.

Then there is the 48-year-old farmer Ansar Ahmed of the 90-family village of Madhnapar, who in 1982 was declared to be dead after some fast footwork on the part of his brother, Nabi Sarwar Khan. Having lost the family rice paddy to Nabi Sarwar Khan, Ansar Ahmed was reduced to complete poverty and had to take up residence with his widowed mother. The village was divided on the issue of Anser Ahmed's death, some supporting his claim to existence and others, says the *Times* article, "treating him as an invisible specter." (And here I am reminded of an old story of mine, "To See the Invisible Man," in which my protagonist, having been convicted of an antisocial crime, is condemned to a year of invisibility: no one is allowed to notice his presence, no matter what sort of outrageous things he may happen to be doing for the sake of getting attention.)

Last July, the High Court of Utter Pradesh, having learned at last through the activities of the Association of Dead People that there might be hundreds of such cases in the state, ordered an investigation. "As the bureaucrats once feared the devil, they now fear the Association of the Dead," says Lal Bihari.

Under the prodding of the High Court the state government was required to publish advertisements calling upon undead citizens to step forward and claim their rights, and allowing those who were able to demonstrate their existence to regain their places in the roster of the living. One of those thus resurrected was Ansar Ahmed, who has now brought criminal charges against his brother. But the brother is not admitting any guilt whatever. "These are only allegations," he says grumpily.

So the task goes on. And though Mr. Bihari and his Association of Dead People remind me, in this way and that, of certain aspects of the works of Nikolai Gogol and Franz Kafka and Joseph Heller and Saul Bellow and even Robert Silverberg and Philip K. Dick, we need to remember that what happened to Ansar Ahmed and Bhagwan Prashad Mishra and Lal Bihari was only too painfully real, over there in the bizarre alien universe that is the subcontinent of India. They are not figures out of literature: they are real, suffering people, who had to fight terrible struggles against a corrupt bureaucracy. There's nothing funny about being stricken from the register of living beings because someone has paid a $25 bribe to turn you into an unperson.

Still — the writer in me wonders what the Association of Dead People will do once it has brought all the unjustly dead of Utte Pradesh back to life. And the mischievous thought arises in me, by way of Gogol's Chichikov, that there must be plenty of profit to be found by locating people who are *really* dead and somehow getting them restored to the roster of the living over there. Let's hope the idea doesn't occur to Lal Bihari.

Asimov's Science Fiction, **October–November 2001**

The More Things Change....

THE FRENCH HAVE A PHRASE FOR IT: *"PLUS CA CHANGE, PLUS C'EST LA MEME CHOSE,"* which is to say, "The more things change, the more they remain the same." (And who, by the way, do you think penned that familiar epigram? Voltaire? Rousseau? Balzac? Why, no, it was Jean Baptiste Alphonse Karr, 1808-1890, journalist, novelist, and horticulturist, editor of the satirical monthly journal *Les Guepes,*, where the immortal line appeared in January, 1849. And I didn't know it either, until I tracked it down in my 1910 edition of the *Encyclopedia Britannica.*) But I digress. The more things change....

For example, the fear that apocalyptic chaos will descend upon the world when three zeros come rolling up on the calendar....

We all know that a terrible dread of the imminent end of the world spread through Europe as 1000 AD approached. Charles Mackay's wonderful and ever-relevant book, *Extraordinary Popular Delusions and the Madness of Crowds*, first published in 1841 and rarely out of print ever since, tells the story this way:

> "A strange idea had taken possession of the popular mind at the close of the tenth and commencement of the eleventh century. It was universally believed ... that the thousand years of the Apocalypse were near completion, and that Jesus Christ would descend upon Jerusalem to judge mankind. All Christendom was in commotion. A panic terror seized upon the weak, the credulous, and the guilty, who in those days formed more than nineteen-twentieths of the population. Forsaking their homes, kindred, and occupation, they crowded to Jerusalem to await the coming of the lord.... To increase

262

the panic, the stars were observed to fall from heaven, earthquakes to shake the land, and violent hurricanes to blow down the forests. All these, and more especially the meteoric phenomena, were looked upon as the forerunners of the approaching judgments."

The source of all this seems to be the 20th chapter of that wondrous work of fantasy, St. John's Book of Revelation, which tells how an angel seized Satan at the time of Christ's birth and "cast him into the bottomless pit, and shut him up, and set a seal on him" that would hold him for a thousand years," and declares that "when the thousand years are expired, Satan shall be loosed out of his prison," and shall go out to gather his forces for the final battle between good and evil.

I should note that later historians have taken somewhat of a revisionist stance concerning the degree of panic that swept the Christian world as what I suppose we can call "Y1K" drew near. Thus the *The Cambridge Medieval History* notes, "Let us, however, avoid laying too much stress upon these allusions to the final cataclysm predicted in the Apocalypse for the period when the thousand years should be fulfilled....A few passages from contemporaries, wrongly interpreted, account for this erroneous impression. As the thousandth year approached, the people small and great, priests and lay folk, continued the same way of life as in the past, without being alarmed by those apocalyptic threats in which, even after the thousandth year was past, certain gloomy spirits continued to indulge."

Be that as it may, another millennium is dragging itself toward its finish, and we are once again confronted by millenarian cries of apocalyptic terror as the dreaded Triple Zero presents its baleful self. And there are two very significant differences between whatever millennial fears swept the world in 999 AD and those that are popping up now.

One is that the first time we faced all this, 1000 AD was Y1K only for a fraction of the world's population. The people of China, Japan, India, the Islamic countries, black Africa, and both Americas, for all of whom Christianity was at best a bunch of mythology and whose calendrical systems were in any case very different, saw nothing to worry about, and they were right.

The other significant difference is that the new crisis involves computers instead of theological theory. The objective reality of such first-millennium concepts as angels, Satan, and Jesus Christ remains very much open to debate. But regardless of your religious beliefs or the calendar you follow, you use a computer geared to the Christian calendrical system today, whether you live in Timbuctoo, Uzbekistan, Tierra del Fuego, or the far Yukon. And there's no question at all that a lot of currently functioning computer software is incapable of dealing properly with dates that begin with the number "2," and is likely to read references to the year 2000 as though the year 1900 had been intended. The confusion that that will cause in some quarters will be irritating at the very least, and might, if we are to believe the most extreme of our modern apocalyptists, cast us into such chaos that our entire civilization will come crashing down.

We are offered a smorgasbord of grim forecasts for the upcoming New Year's Eve divertissement. They range from the relatively trivial (government checks delayed; automatic teller machines refusing to disgorge $20 bills) to the moderately troublesome (computer-controlled water systems breaking down; worldwide financial dealings paralyzed) to the splendidly spine-chilling (complete loss of electrical power everywhere; stockpiled nuclear-armed missiles accidentally firing themselves.)

This modern millenarian paranoia is odd stuff. Some strange bedfellows are involved in it. On the one hand, we have a bunch of Bible-toting Christian fundamentalists who believe that all hell is due to break loose in the most literal way on January 1, 2000. On the other, we have a contingent of New Age spiritualists who have no truck with apocalyptic Biblical prophecy but detest the modern technological world as soulless and heartless, and who are looking forward gleefully to the coming catastrophe in the hope that a new and better society can be built upon the ruins of the old evil one.

So we have radio evangelist Noah Hutchins broadcasting nationwide out of Oklahoma City to tell us that Jesus will soon be among us. He's the author of a book called *Y2K=666?* that equates giant computers, electronic banking, bar codes, and computerized mailing lists with the Antichrist. (Revelation 13 tells us, "No man might buy or sell, save that he had the mark, or the name of the beast [the Antichrist] or the number of his name," and goes on to say, "Let him that hath understanding count the number of the beast: for it is the number of a man; and his number is Six hundred threescore and six." The collapse of our computers will set free the Anti-Christ, Hutchins implies, and that will lead to the return of Jesus and the final battle between good and evil at Armageddon.

Then there's evangelist Pat Robertson, whose Christian Broadcast Network maintains a web site (!) devoted to apocalyptic Y2K forecasts. "God is alerting us that a big problem is coming," declares Robertson's technology editor, Drew Parkhill, although Parkhill hesitates to declare outright that the "end times" are nigh. So far, the Robertson group has focused mainly on how churches can help people cope with the power outages and food shortages that the Y2K breakdown might bring, and how Christians can employ the crisis to convert unbelievers to their faith.

Larry Burkett, another Christian fundamentalist who is more of an old-time survivalist, has a book out called *Worldwide Collapse 2000*. He has sold his suburban San Diego home and moved with four other families to a mountain farm somewhere in the Southwest, where he's holed up expecting the worst and prepared to cope. He's aware that a lot of people did the same thing, pointlessly, in the 1970s, and says, "There's nothing more stupid than being stuck in the mountains with your gold and your guns, and nothing happens." But he's quite sure that something will, this time: not necessarily the second coming of Christ, but certainly disruption of food-distribution services and a world-wide depression. He's ready.

So is Tom Atlee of Berkeley, author of *Awakening: The Upside of Y2K*. His New Age web site is full of positive messages about the radical spiritual changes that will spread through the world once the global electronic monster self-destructs. Among the religious leaders Atlee likes to quote is Rabbi Zalman Shachter-Shalomi, whose sermons denounce computers for having led Americans away "from the simple ways of Earth" and the "natural order that God has promised us." And in Napa, Sonoma, and Santa Rosa, communities an hour's drive north of Berkeley, a band of survivalists is stockpiling vegetable seeds, canned food, portable energy generators, and supplies of water. "Some people might think we're a bit obsessed," said Cynthia Brush of Santa Rosa. She and her husband have organized a 30-member Y2K survival group. "But we're not flaky people. We've got two feet on the ground, and we think deeply about the lifestyle we have. We're not interested in scaring people."

They have, however, scared the sober Federal Reserve Bank, which has ordered $50 billion added to the nation's cash reserves in case people who fear the shutdown of banks and automatic tellers begin hoarding money. They have scared the Senate into organizing a Special Committee on the Year 2000 Technology Problem. They have scared a lot of other public officials who suddenly are blinking, looking around, demanding to know why nothing has been done.

"Am I overreacting? I don't know," said Brad Larsen, a Santa Rosa anesthetist. "It's only being responsible to have a plan and to prepare."

We live in the age of overreaction, though. No doubt that Y2K is going to cause a lot of trouble, despite the hundreds of millions of very real dollars being spent right now by corporate America to fix very real software glitches.

I myself take a basically skeptical position about the extent of the problem. Some peculiar things will happen as the new digit rolls into view, yes. But my bet is that we'll come out the far side in fine shape, just as we did a thousand years ago. Antichrist will not appear, angels will not be seen battling demons in the sky, the kilowatts will continue to flow, and the banks will open right on schedule after the holiday. Or am I being naively optimistic? We'll all find out next New Year's Day.

Asimov's Science Fiction, **June 1999**

The Past Is In Front Of Us

I'VE BEEN READING **ERRATA**, A FASCINATING COL-LECTION OF ESSAYS in the guise of an autobiography, by the philosopher and literary critic George Steiner. It was published in 1997 by Yale University Press. Steiner, born in Paris seventy years ago to Austrian parents, grew up polylingual, equally fluent in German, French, and English, and has a keen interest in the way the languages we speak shape our assumptions about the universe. In his seventh chapter he offers a startling thought about the grammatical subtext that makes science fiction possible:

> "The evolution in human speech — it may have come late — of subjunctives, optatives, counter-factual conditionals and of the futurities of the verb (not all languages have tenses) has defined and safeguarded our humanity. It is because we can tell stories, fictive or mathematical-cosmological, about a universe a billion years hence; it is because we can ... conceptualize the Monday morning after our creation; it is because 'if' sentences ('If I won the lottery,' 'If Schubert had lived to a ripe age,' 'If a vaccine is developed against AIDS') can, spoken at will, deny, reconstruct, alter past, present, and future, mapping *otherwise* the determinants of pragmatic reality, that existence continues to be worth experiencing. Hope is grammar."

Hope is grammar. What a wonderful insight, and how concisely Steiner phrases it! Because our language — the operating system by means of which our brains organize and communicate concepts — contains a feature that allows us to contemplate the future, we are able to enjoy the luxury of speculating about that future.

Without such little grammatical niceties as subjunctives, conditionals, and future tenses, there would not only be no science fiction; there would be no surcease whatever from the leaden necessities of our daily round of toil. Life would be an endless series of repetitive todays, lacking even the possibility of daydreaming about some wondrous transformation of our condition that could come on the morrow. The speculative function of our minds is inherently linked to the grammatical permutations of which our minds are capable. As Steiner puts it, it is "the future of 'to be,' of the 'shall' and the 'will,' whose articulation generates the breathing-spaces of fear and of hope, of renewal and innovation which are the cartography of the unknown."

Note, though, that Steiner also points out parenthetically that some languages have no tenses. The example that he gives comes from Jonathan Swift's *Gulliver's Travels*, in which the language of the Houyhnhnms, that noble race of intelligent horses, contains only the present tense. The Houyhnhnms are an altogether admirable people, noble and virtuous in the extreme, but their language is a utilitarian thing, designed purely for the transmission of information. By its grammatical structure alone it excludes the possibility of the free play of the imagination. The Houyhnhnm tongue deals only in facts.

Since the future has no factual existence in the present, it is impossible, by the Houyhnhnm way of thinking, for information about it to exist; indeed, they are baffled even by that exercise of the speculative imagination which we humans call lying, and Gulliver's Houyhnhnm master, responding to Gulliver's tales of what life is like in eighteenth-century Europe — tales which seem like the wildest whoppers to the Houhynhynm — can only accuse Gulliver of having "said the thing which was not." This, of course, is what fiction writers of all sorts do all the time. Science fiction writers extend the practice to a most unHouyhnhnmlike degree; not only do they make up stories about people who never existed, which surely is saying the thing which is not, but they set those stories in places and times that also are not. This magazine has no Houyhnhnm readers whatsoever.

The coolly rational Houyhnhnms exist only in Swift's wonderful novel, which is a work of fantasy. But there are real-world languages that also manage to get along without tenses as we understand them: the one spoken by the Hopi Indians of Arizona, for example. The Hopi do have ways of comprehending past, present, and future, of course. But they encode these concepts in their language in a way quite different from the one we use. The same word, *wari*, carries the meanings, "he is running" and "he ran," as statements of objective fact: as we stand here in the field, we can see him running, or else we can see that the race has just ended. *Era wari* also means "he ran," as a statement of fact, but this time conveyed from the speaker's memory. *Warikni* connotes a statement of expectation: "he will run" is how we would say it. *Warikngwe* covers our "he runs" as we use it in such sentences as "he runs on the track team" — a statement of an ongoing condition, not one that is specifically limited to a single observed or recollected event.

Hopi is different from English (or French, or German, or Spanish) in many other ways. For us, "lightning" and "flame" and "meteor" are nouns, that is, the names of things; the Hopi express these things as verbs, terms of perceptible action ("it lightnings," "it flames," "it meteors.") They are statements of transient events; duration is an important aspect of Hopi linguistic thinking. Among the Nootka Indians of Vancouver Island, "house" is a verb-like term, too, but different suffixes are used to convey such varying meanings as a temporary house, a long-lasting house, a house yet to be built, a house that has been begun and abandoned, etc.

Such languages, fundamentally different from ours in ways such as these, are in fact *alien*, from the point of view of one trained to the grammar of European languages. Those who speak them must necessarily view the universe in ways quite different from the way we do. Although the Hopi and the Nootka are, of course, quite human in all respects, the differences between their linguistic structures and ours are so extreme that their entire world-view must be essentially different from ours — an important thing for science fiction writers, hoping to strike a note of alienness in the extra-terrestrial cultures that they create, to bear in mind.

This thesis was first put forth early in the twentieth century by an extraordinary scholar, Benjamin Lee Whorf (1897-1941), whose brilliant essays on linguistics were collected in 1956 in a book called *Language, Thought, and Reality* that ought to be in the library of any science fiction writer whose work deals with alien civilizations. The Whorf Hypothesis, as it is known, declares that languages differ in striking and unusual ways, and these differences govern the ways in which their speakers perceive and conceive the world. The Hopi and Nootka examples I provided above come from Whorf's book. But it abounds with hundreds of others, equally startling, equally fascinating. Again and again Whorf demonstrates, in essays like "The Relation of Habitual Thought and Behavior to Language" and "Languages and Logic," how our most basic ways of looking at space and time are rooted in our grammatical assumptions.

A great many science fiction writers have applied the Whorf Hypothesis to the creation of alien languages or thought-forms. I'm one of them, though I blush to say that I can't recall a particular example to cite; it was in my era of breathless prolificity forty years ago, and that's all I can tell you. But I assure you I studied Whorf quite assiduously when his book first appeared.

Jack Vance's novel *The Languages of Pao* (1957) surely reflects a reading of Whorf ("The Paonese sentence did not so much describe an act as it presented a picture of a situation. There were no verbs, no adjectives; no formal word comparison such as *good, better, best*. The typical Paonese saw himself as a cork on a sea of a million waves, lofted, lowered, thrust aside by incomprehensible forces." Later Vance stories, such as "The Moon Moth," touch on Whorfian themes as well. The physically bisexual beings of Ursula K. Le Guin's *The Left Hand of Darkness* (1969) speak a language specifically tailored to their shifting sexual identities. Samuel R. Delany's *Babel-17* (1966) is another Whorfian sf novel; Suzette Haden Elgin, in several novels with strong feminist undertones, has dealt with the invention of a secret female language designed as a weapon in the battle of the sexes; and so forth.

Whorf's idea that a culture's linguistic idiosyncracies have a profound shaping effect on that culture's world-views can be used as the springboard for a multitude of dazzling science fiction inventions. So, too, can its conceptual antithesis, Noam Chomsky's notion that the language ability is hard-wired into the human brain and that all languages share a common deep structure: Ian Watson put Chomsky's theory to brilliant use in his 1973 novel, *The Embedding*, which carries Chomsky forward to suggest that there may be a grammar common to all intelligent life-forms of the universe. But one idea does not really exclude the other. Even if the deep linguistic structures are alike everywhere (at least on Earth), Whorf's book gives us an extraordinary mass of evidence to bolster his view of the distinctive shaping effect of grammar on culture. As George Steiner, definitely a Whorfian, puts it, "No two languages, no two dialects or local idioms within a language, map their worlds in the same way. Every tongue ever spoken by men and women... opens its own window on life and the world."

And he cites the example of an Indian tribe that he does not name, one that lives high up in the Andes, in whose language one speaks of the past as lying "in front of" us. To us that seems a very strange way of putting things, until we pause to consider that although the past is accessible to some degree to our memories, the totality of the future will always be a mystery. And so, while we can rove through the events of the past as easily as though they lie before us on an open plain, we are compelled to move blindly backward into the unknown future, unable to see any aspect of it clearly until we are in the very midst of it.

The past is in front of us. We go backward into the future. There's innate poetry in the thought, and a world-view quite different from yours or mine. But to that unnamed Indian tribe, it's just a way of speaking, a matter of grammatical construction, which happens to open the door, for us, to a wholly new way of viewing the universe.

Asimov's Science Fiction, **April 2000**

And You Were Worried About Y2K?

I READ ALL SORTS OF ODD THINGS IN THE COURSE OF THE YEAR, casting my net far and wide for curious scraps of information that I might morph into some datum of life on Majipoor or perhaps transform into a column in *Asimov's*. And so it happened that I found myself reading *Island of Bali*, a classic anthropological study by the Mexican artist and ethnographer Miguel Covarrubias; and it was this charming and comprehensive account of life on the Indonesian isle of Bali seventy years ago that put me on to the marvelous intricacies of the Balinese calendar — a mind-boggling system that would test any computer programmer to his very limits.

Bali uses, along with the Christian one that has established itself everywhere as the world's basic system of reckoning time, *two* indigenous calendars, actually, running in parallel. Their basic calendar, called the *saseh* calendar, is approximately like ours, but because it is based on lunar time rather than solar, it comes up short on days per year — 354 to 356 instead of our 365.

The reason for the discrepancy is that the lunar year is built on lunar months (the interval between each new moon), which run 29 or 30 days, whereas the solar year is based on the time (365 days, or intervals between each sunrise) that it takes the Earth to complete one revolution around the sun. Twelve lunar months won't add up to a year of 365 solar days. Twelve solar months of 30 days won't do it either, falling short by five days.

Therefore our solar calendar has seven 31-day months, which makes up that five-day deficit and also accounts for February's deplorable two-day shortfall. (Even at that, we don't have a perfect solar calendar, which necessitates the 366-day Leap Year every four years and other little adjustments at greater intervals.)

On Bali, and on the neighboring island of Java, the twelve-month *saseh* calendar creates an even bigger annual deficit of days because the interval between one new moon and the next is too short to permit 31-day months or even a whole year of 30-day ones. So the *saseh* calendar skips one day out of every 63 (nine weeks of seven days each) to create a varying number of 29-day months, thus leaving the *saseh* year nine to eleven days short of the solar one, and copes with this deficit in a cumulative way by sticking in a full extra month, the *saseh nampeh*, every two and a half years. The whole system revolves around the great national holiday called *nyepi*, which falls on the first day of the ninth month and nevertheless is regarded as the beginning of the new year. (Don't ask!) On *nyepi* the whole island shuts down for religious devotions: absolute stillness is observed, no work done, no driving, no fires lit; even the electrical system is shut down.

Following the convolutions of the *saseh* calendar is no easy task. But wait! The fun is just about to begin! There's also the other Balinese calendar, the *wuku*. And the *wuku* is a lulu.

Put this in your computer and parse it:

The *wuku* year has just 210 days, and therefore bears no relationship either to solar time or lunar time. It isn't divided into months at all, merely into weeks. And determining the number of weeks per *wuku* year depends entirely on which of the *ten* different simultaneous systems of *wuku* weeks you have in mind.

The basic week has seven days, so this part of the *wuku* has a 30-week year. The seven days of this calendar are named for the major heavenly bodies, and it is interesting to see that the order (derived from the ancient Sanskrit calendar of India) is basically identical to the one we use, thereby demonstrating the primordial antiquity of the seven-day Indo-European calendar. *Redite* is Sunday, the day of the Sun; Monday is *soma*, the day of the Moon; Tuesday, *angara*, is Mars's day; *budda*, Wednesday, is that of Mercury; *wrespati*, Thursday, is the day of Jupiter; Friday, *sukra*,, is for Venus; and *sanistjara*, Saturday, is Saturn's day. (The English-language calendar, which is partly derived from Germanic antecedents, slips in a few variations. "Tuesday" is *Tiw's* day, Tiw being an ancient Teutonic god of war; but the link to Mars can still be seen in the French "mardi," the Italian "martedi," and so forth. "Wednesday" is *Wotan's* day for us, but Mercury still stakes his claim in the "mercredi," "miercoles," and "mercoledi" of French, Spanish, and Italian. And it is Thor who rules Thursday for us, though Jupiter — Jove — is still in charge of Italian's "giovedi" and French's "jeudi.")

A seven-day, thirty-week, 210-day calendar would be hard enough to work with in a world where the true year is actually slightly more than 365 days long. But the Balinese divide the *wuku* year into nine other kinds of weeks as well.

My favorite of these is the week called *ekowara*, which is one day long, the name of that one day being *luang*. You can readily see that the *wuku* year contains 210 *ekowara* weeks, and you can wish everybody a happy *luang* every day of the year.

But there's also *duwiwara*, the two-day week, 105 of them a year, the days being named *m'ga* and *p'pat*. There's *triwara*, the three-day week, containing *paseh*, *beteng*, and *kadjeng*, and coming around 70 times per year. There's *tjatur-wara*, the four-day week, and *pantjawara*, the five-day week, and so on up to *dasawara*, the ten-day week, 21 of them to a year. (And here again note the Sanskrit ancestry of those numerical prefixes: *du*, *tri*, *tja*, *pant*, for two, three, four, five, etc.)

The lovely thing about the *wuku* calendar is that all these weeks run at the same time. Therefore a day can be the day *redite* of the seven-day week and it also will be, of course, *luang* of the one-day calendar, and, perhaps, *m'ga* of the two-day week and the day *paseh* in the three-day week, and up and up in dizzying progression, maybe *ogan* in nine-day reckoning and *suka* in the ten-day week. The combinations and permutations are, if not exactly infinite, certainly multitudinous.

Imagine, if you will, trying to program a Balinese computer to handle the ten simultaneous weeks of the *wuku* year. It can be done, of course. No doubt it *has* been done. But what a headache!

And what, you quite reasonably ask, is the purpose of such a mind-numbing calendrical system?

The calculation of propitious days for religious ceremonies or important personal activities seems to be what it's all about. For instance, the important Balinese holiday *galunggan*, when one's cremated ancestors visit the temples to receive offerings from their descendants, occurs in the week *dunggulan* of the 30-week *wuku* calendar, but only on that day when the day *klion* of the five-day week coincides with the day *budda* of the seven-day week. A little arithmetic shows that *budda* (the name has nothing to do with Buddha, by the way) and *klion* are going to be in conjunction every 35 days, but only one of those meetings is going to occur in *dunggulan* each year, and that day is the holiday.

Then there's the conjunction of *kadjeng* of the three-day calendar and *klion* of the five-day calendar: a good day for propitiating evil spirits, coming around every 15 days. Every 35 days *klion* will overlap the day *sanistjara* of the seven-day calendar, and that day, which is known as *tumpak*, is an extremely lucky one. One needs to watch out for the day *kala* of the eight-day week, which can be quite unlucky. And so on and so on and so on.

I am, you should know, only barely scratching the surface here. I have said nothing about the twelve seasons of the year (the season of blossoming wildflowers, the season of mending dikes, the season of sowing rice, etc., etc., etc.) nor of the division of the lunar year into four *nagas*, or serpents, nor of the various *windu* cycles of eight, twelve, twenty, and thirty-two years, nor of the various annual six-day *ingkel* periods, one of them being auspicious for bamboo, one for cattle, one for fish....

How does the average Balinese, you may wonder, keep track of all this?

The answer is that the average Balinese doesn't even try. Mostly he uses the seven-day calendrical system, and is more or less aware of the ongoing five-day calendar too, since most of the important religious festivals are held at 35-day intervals at specific conjunction-points of the two calendars. The three-day calendar stays in people's minds also, because it establishes when each village holds its market day. For more abstruse calculations, conjunctions of the six-day week and the nine-day week, let us say, as well as the other, greater cycles, he must go to the local priest, who *is* keeping track of the whole system on behalf of the entire community. As Miguel Covarrubias tells us, the Balinese calendrical system "is a science so complicated in itself that it is practiced mainly by specialists, generally the Brahmanic priests and witch-doctors." A nifty monopoly run by the initiates of the art, in other words.

The priests, for all I know, may use software to figure out the calendrical cycles these days. But at the time Covarrubias wrote *Island of Bali* — it was published in 1937 — they employed programs of a more ancient kind:

"By the ownership of intricate charts (*tika*) with secret symbols painted on paper or carved in wood, and of palm-leaf manuscripts (*wariga*) by which the lucky or unlucky dates are located, [the priests] make the people dependent on them for this purpose, because the Balinese are obliged to consult them for good dates for every special undertaking and have to pay for the consultation."

It all sounds awfully familiar. A system that no ordinary person can comprehend, but which is vital to a whole culture's welfare; and only a small guild of insiders is in possession of the key to the mysteries! We got off lucky, I think, with our piddling little Millennium Bug headaches. Though Y2K troubles didn't bring the end of the world, a big problem still remains for modern civilization, which is that we've all become dependent on things beyond our understanding. I suggest you think of the Balinese calendrical system the next time your computer inexplicably crashes or hands you a Terminal Fatal Error message, all you users of the perversely complex software that a clever band of high priests has succeeded in making essential to our daily lives.

Asimov's Science Fiction, **June 2000**

Hobson-Jobson

THE LATE AND VERY MUCH LAMENTED WRITER AVRAM DAVIDSON was an inveterate browser in other people's libraries. He was wandering through mine one day some three or four decades ago when suddenly he cried out, "By Jove! You have a *Hobson-Jobson!*" (Avram was one of the very few people of my acquaintance who could say something like "By Jove!" and not appear silly or affected.)

"Yes," I said gravely. "Indeed I do."

Avram pounced on it and spent half an hour avidly thumbing its pages — for *Hobson-Jobson*, as I will explain in a moment, is a book, a whopping thick grayish-black book, 1,021 pages long and close to four inches thick. Avram never forgot that I had a copy of it. In a letter many years later he referred to it, expressed the pious hope that I might let him have it if I had no further use for it, and immediately admonished himself, "Thou shalt not covet thy colleague's *Hobson-Jobson*." He, and also, I suspect, L. Sprague de Camp, are the only colleagues of mine likely to have been familiar with this book, unless the scholarly Harry Turtledove knows of it. (Harry?) Neither Sprague nor Avram is with us any longer. But I am still here, and so is my *Hobson-Jobson*, and I propose to take this opportunity to tell you about it.

Hobson-Jobson is a dictionary — a dictionary that was, in essence, compiled by aliens living as conquerors on a distant world. Those alien conquerors had evolved a patois with which to communicate with the natives, a language made up out of largely mispronounced fragments of the natives' own language mixed with bits of their own slang, and after many years one of the conquerors put together a huge dictionary of that patois for the benefit of later generations of aliens who were coming out to serve in the administration that governs the conquered planet.

The conquered "planet" in question was, in fact, the subcontinent of India, and the compilers of *Hobson-Jobson* were two learned officials of the British Raj that ruled India in Queen Victoria's time: Arthur C. Burnell and Sir Henry Yule. Burnell, who lived only from 1840 to 1882, held judicial posts in southern India, but, like many officials of the Raj, devoted much of his time to studying Indian culture; he collected and translated many ancient Sanskrit manuscripts, particularly those dealing with aspects of Hindu law, and published a celebrated handbook on Sanskrit. His early death was ascribed to a combination of overwork and the debilitating effects of the torrid climate of Madras.

Yule, his collaborator on *Hobson-Jobson,* was an even more formidable scholar-civil servant, who as a member of the Bengal Engineers served in two wars with the Sikhs and was otherwise active in various Anglo-Indian political and military affairs before retiring in 1862 with the rank of colonel to devote the rest of his life to the study of the medieval history and geography of Central Asia. His most famous book was a magnificent three-volume edition of *The Travels of Marco Polo,* still a definitive text. For a decade beginning in 1872 Yule corresponded with Burnett concerning the immense number of curious words that had entered the vocabulary of the British in India, and in 1886 he published their joint findings under the title of *Hobson-Jobson.* My copy is the second edition, much expanded under the editorial guidance of William Crooke and published in 1903.

Yule's preface tells us that "words of Indian origin have been insinuating themselves into English ever since the end of the reign of Elizabeth and the beginning of that of King James, when such terms as *calico, chintz,* and *gingham* had already effected a lodgment in English warehouses and shops, and were lying in wait for entrance into English literature. Such outlandish guests grew more frequent 120 years ago, when, soon after the middle of last century, the numbers of Englishmen in the Indian services, civil and military, expanded with the great acquisition then made by the [British East India] Company; and we meet them in vastly greater abundance now."

Some random sampling of the vast volume will indicate why Avram Davidson, that erudite collector of the esoteric and arcane, yearned to have access to *Hobson-Jobson* for use in his own marvelous stories. Here, for example, we find *moorpunky,* defined as "'peacock-tailed' or 'peacock-winged,' the name given to certain state pleasure-boats on the Gangetic rivers, now only (if it all) surviving at Murshidabad." How Avram would have loved to send a couple of his raffish characters sailing down the Ganges aboard a moorpunky! Or we have *chuprassy,* about which we are told, "From the Hindu *chaprasi,* the bearer of a *chapras,* a badge-plate inscribed with the name of the office to which the bearer is attached." Of a multitude of such delicious minutiae was the typical Davidson story constructed. (Jack Vance could have done something with the word, too. Perhaps he has. He's another who might own a *Hobson-Jobson.*

Here we have *bobbery-bob* — "The Anglo-Indian colloquial representation of a common exclamation of Hindus when in surprise or grief — *Bap-re!* or *Bap-re Bap*, 'O Father!'" To which Yule and Burnelle add, "We have known a friend from north of Tweed whose ordinary interjection was 'My great-grandmother!'")

And here is *bobachee*: "A cook (male). This is an Anglo-Indian vulgar-ization of *bawarchi*, a term originally brought, according to Hammer, by the hordes of Chingiz Khan into Western Asia. At the Mongol court the *Bawarchi* was a high dignitary, 'Lord Sewer,' or the like." Lord Sewer?

A few pages on we have a discussion of *bosh*, telling us that "this is al-leged to be taken from the Turkish *bosh*, signifying 'empty, vain, useless, void of sense, meaning, or utility.' But we have not been able to trace its history or first appearance in English." "Bosh!", it seems to me, is a word Avram must have used, and quite often, too.

A flip of the pages and we are at *lall-shraub*, which is what the officers of the Raj called red wine, from the Hindu "lal-sharab." We get *grunthee*, "a sort of native chaplain attached to Sikh regiments." We get *gubber*, "some kind of gold ducat or sequin." We get *gudge*, a measurement intended to be the equivalent of a yard, but ranging in various districts from 18 inches to 52 $^{1}/_{8}$.

There is a considerable disquisition on *opium*, a substance of much inter-est to the Raj, since the British cheerfully financed their activities in India by selling great quantities of that drug to China. Yule and Burnell observe that the word is probably Greek in origin, not Oriental, and they magisterially brush aside one philologist's derivation of it from a Sanskrit word meaning "snake venom." Burnell evidently had a serious interest in opium — a purely scholarly one, we must assume — for we are given, appended to this entry, a long series of extracts from travelers' accounts of the drug, going back to Pliny in 70 AD.

Our familiar word *orange* gets three dense columns, too. Our authors write, "A good example of plausible but entirely incorrect etymology is that of orange from Lat. *aurantium*. The latter word is in fact an ingenious me-dieval fabrication. The word obviously came from the Arab. *naranj*, which is again a form of Pers. *narang*, or *narangi*," and so on, not entirely with the firmest etymological backing, to the Sanskrit *nagaranga*.

And so on and so on. It is a book of linguistic wonders, and, after playing with it myself this morning after a long absence from it, I can see why Avram yearned so passionately to possess a copy. I cherished mine too much to give it to him, in the way some generous Oriental potentate might have given a treasure to an admiring guest, but I do hope he found one sooner or later. It is a classic of dictionary-making. The Anglo-Indian Raj is gone — a van-ished world — and so is most of its language, though much remains behind in our own daily speech. And *Hobson-Jobson*, that great blocky monument of verbiage, remains also, a fossil remainder to remind us of what once was — a trilobite of a book.

Oh — and that title, *Hobson-Jobson* —

Page 419: "*Hobson-Jobson*, a native festal excitement: a *tamasha* (see

TUMASHA); but especially the *Moharram* ceremonies. This phrase may be taken as a typical one of the most highly assimilated class of Anglo-Indian *argot*, and we have ventured to borrow from it a concise alternative title for this Glossary. It is peculiar to the British soldier and his surroundings, with whom it probably originated, and with whom it is by no means obsolete, as we once supposed. My friend Major John Trotter tells me that he has repeatedly heard it used by British soldiers in the Punjab; and has heard it also from a regimental Moonshee. It is in fact an Anglo-Saxon version of the wailings of the Mahommedans as they beat their breasts in the procession of the *Moharram* — 'Ya Hasan! Ya Hassan!'"

Not content with that, though, our learned authors go on to trace the phrase through centuries of travel literature, beginning with a sixteenth-century Italian who rendered it as "Vah Hussein! Sciah Hussein!" and on through "Hosseen Gosseen" and "Hossy Gossy" to "Saucem Saucem" by 1710, the "Jaksom Baksom" reported in 1725, "Hassein Jassein" of 1763, and, finally, a notice in the *Oriental Sporting Magazine* of 1873, where Indians are described as "making sich [sic] a noise, firing and troompeting and shouting *Hobson Jobson, Hobson Jobson*."

Hobson-Jobson indeed. And also *calloo, callay*. It is with the greatest of effort that I refrain from quoting the remaining 1018 pages of it for you, right here and now.

Asimov's Science Fiction, **December 2001**

Plutonium for Breakfast

MOST DISCUSSIONS OF THE POSSIBILITY OF LIFE ON OTHER WORLDS eventually bring in the qualifying phrase, "Life as we know it." The definition of "life" that is most commonly cited usually involves such requirements as the ability to obtain energy from an outside source for the purpose of sustaining the metabolic reactions, the ability to reproduce in order to provide replacement organisms against the day when the parent organism can no longer perform the metabolic functions, etc. The "as we know it" part provides further qualifications: life as we know it here on Earth, it is generally said, exists within thus-and-so temperature range (from something above freezing to something below boiling) on a planet where water is widely available and which has an atmosphere made up mostly of oxygen and hydrogen. And so we think we know what life-on-Earth is: dogs and cats, squids and elephants, ferns and algae and redwood trees, kangaroos and wombats and koalas, grasshoppers and ants and butterflies and moths, and a great many other species, including, of course, us.

When science fiction writers set their stories on other worlds of the universe, most of the beings with which they populate those worlds are patterned after life-as-we-know-it beings of our own world: oxygen-breathers who occupy that climatic comfort zone that lies somewhere between McMurdo Sound at one extreme and Death Valley at the other. That way they can insert human characters who are able to move about on those worlds without great difficulty and have the interesting adventures that science fiction stories are supposed to provide. Thus we get whale-like aliens, squid-like aliens, bear-like aliens, and a lot of aliens who are basically just human beings with corrugated foreheads. (Hello, Commander Worf!)

Of course, many science fiction stories are populated by life as we don't know it — the sort of life that might be found on planets with methane-ammonia atmospheres, for example, or on planets where the gravitational pull is seven hundred times what it is here, or where the temperatures go beyond what we consider the habitable limits. I wrote a story once about a species native to Pluto whose blood is the superconductive fluid we call Helium II. The temperature on Pluto is just a couple of degrees above absolute zero, which is fine for creatures with a superconductive metabolic system, but when the sun comes up and the temperatures rise five or six degrees they have to go dormant until that nice superconductive chill returns. And so on, literally *ad infinitum*: science fiction writers have invented a vast and ingenious multitude of peculiar critters that live in uncomfortable places.

All well and good, but I want to return today to our own planet, and that convenient phrase, "life as we know it," so that I can point out that a great many organisms native to this very world do not fall into that category at all — are, in fact, as alien as anything Frank Herbert or E.E. "Doc" Smith or Hal Clement ever conjured up.

The first ones that come to mind are the anaerobes: primitive creatures, mainly bacteria but nothing more complex than worms, for whom oxygen is poisonous. This unfortunate trait makes life on Earth difficult for anaerobes, of course, because oxygen is practically everywhere; but they have, nevertheless, managed to find niches for themselves in certain very bleak soils and in oceanic mud, among other disagreeable places. There they conduct their miserable little lives, absorbing such foodstuffs as they are able to metabolize in the absence of oxygen, deriving energy from them, and carrying out their reproductive processes in order to bring forth new generations of anaerobes upon the face of the Earth.

Since Earth is an oxygen-rich planet, what are these creatures doing here at all? One theory is that they are degenerate forms of normal oxygen-loving species that were modified by evolutionary pressures to live in oxygen-poor environments and eventually in environments that had no oxygen whatever. That makes some sense, at least to those of us who put credence in Darwinian theory. (This magazine has some readers of the other kind, as I have discovered by getting irate letters from them.) But in 1927 the brilliant biologist J.B.S. Haldane proposed a far more ingenious explanation for the existence of anaerobic organisms: the original atmospheric mix of most planets, he suggested, is mostly hydrogen, ammonia, and methane, and the development of an oxygen-based atmosphere on our world was a relatively late event, the result of the breakdown of the primordial methane and ammonia into carbon, hydrogen, and nitrogen through the action of ultraviolet light from the sun, and the release of oxygen through photosynthesis once chlorophyll-bearing plants evolved. Therefore, Haldane suggested, anaerobic life-forms would have been the default mode on Earth until an oxygen atmosphere appeared. At that point aerobic life began to evolve, and the anaerobic beings that survive today are surviving vestiges of that long-vanished oxygen-free world of Earth's early days.

These oxygen-shunning inhabitants of Earth seem almost ordinary, however, compared with some of the really strange items with which we share our planet — beings that routinely put up with such hostile living conditions that they seem to have wandered into our world out of the pages of this magazine. Extremophiles is what scientists call them.

Let's take a look at a few.

Here, for example, is Deinococcus radiodurans, a small pink organism that has been nicknamed "Conan the Bacterium." Scientists who were experimenting with the use of hard radiation as a food preservative in 1956 noticed an odd bulge in one of their experimental cans of horsemeat, and when they opened it they found that a colony of unfamiliar pink bacteria had established itself inside. Deinococcus wasn't simply untroubled by the radiation that was bombarding it; it seemed to thrive on it, as Popeye the Sailor does on spinach.

Where did this hardy little bug come from? Some theorists suggested that it had drifted in from space, where radiation levels are far higher than they are on Earth. Others offered a version of the old Haldane notion: in its earliest days, they said, the Earth had been highly radioactive, and Deinococcus was a survivor of that primeval era. The issue remains unresolved.

But here was a creature, anyway, that had an astonishingly high tolerance for radiation. Perhaps, it was suggested, Conan the Bacterium could be put to work devouring nuclear waste, of which a vast amount has been piling up at our various atomic plants. Unfortunately, though it had no trouble with hard radiation, it was unable to cope with such toxic chemicals as toluene that are usually found in nuclear waste. And so, in 1997, Department of Energy researchers produced "Super Conan," a genetically modified super-Deinococcus that eats vile chemicals just as casually as it does the hard stuff. So far, though, Super Conan has not been released into the environment, because no one is sure what else it might eat, and the current public attitude toward genetically modified organisms is not supportive of indiscriminate distribution of such entities.

An even more awesome extremophile is Kineococcus radiotolerans, well named, for it is radiotolerant indeed. This one turned up at the Department of Energy's Savannah River Site in South Carolina, once used in the production of hydrogen bombs, where an awkward quantity of radioactive waste has piled up — thirty-five million gallons of it in forty-nine underground storage tanks of uncertain sturdiness. The conventional way of getting rid of this stuff, involving chemical treatments administered by robots, might cost as much as $260 billion. About a decade ago Savannah Site researchers who were looking for some cheaper way of detoxifying the place noticed a slimy substance growing on the end of a rod in one of the tanks of nuclear waste, extracted it using robot arms, and discovered it to be a clump of bacteria capable of withstanding a dose of radiation fifteen times as strong as one that would be fatal to humans.

Not only is Kineococcus happy to make its home in a hellish brew of radioactives that would melt kryptonite, but further experimentation has shown it to be willing and able to feed on industrial solvents, herbicides, chlorinated compounds, and a great many other toxic chemicals, breaking their toxic components down and rendering them harmless. The Savannah Site scientists are now considering breeding Kineococcus in quantity and injecting it into the tanks of nuclear waste and also into the areas around the Hanford, Washington, nuclear plant where leaking storage tanks have contaminated eighty square miles with radioactivity.

Not immediately, of course. Caution prevails. One might think that an environment populated by Kineococcus could only be an improvement on one full of radioactivity. But one never knows. At the moment, 20 percent of the bacterium's genetic structure involves "unknown functions," say the researchers, and they want to know more about those before whipping up any substantial supply of the microbe.

How these creatures survive in such unforgiving environments is still pretty much of a mystery. A good jolt of radiation smashes up their genetic structures the same way it would smash up yours or mine, but the big difference is that extremophiles somehow put themselves back together within a few hours.

For those of us — a large majority of the population, I would guess — who are not charmed by the presence of deposits of toxic wastes among us, these hardy microbes hold out hope of eventual cleanup with a minimum of noise and fuss, and at relatively little expense. But the existence of extremophiles sends a second message that's of particular interest to science fiction readers. It's a message about the adaptability and durability of living things. (Other extremophiles are found in the chilly plains of Antarctica, on mountain peaks, within volcanoes, and in the depths of the sea.) We live in a huge universe full of worlds, and most of those worlds, very likely, offer environmental conditions very different from those of Earth. But if, here on Earth where we live life as we know it, there are extremphiles in our midst that can survive in surroundings that we would regard as unthinkably user-unfriendly, then surely those other worlds, those worlds of ammonia-methane atmosphere or 700-G gravitational pull, may well have evolved creatures just as alive as me and thee who feel totally comfortable under the alien-to-us conditions there.

Our own extremophiles are just itty-bitty bacteria. But, of course, they occupy small and very special environmental niches on our world. On another world where extreme conditions are the norm, the entire planetary population will be made up of beings who have adapted to those conditions. And my bet is that they won't just be microbes, either.

Asimov's Science Fiction, **March, 2006**

Saddam Wasn't the Worst

THE NEWS IN RECENT YEARS HAS BROUGHT US A LOT OF GRIM, violent stuff originating in Iraq. First came the forcible removal from power of the bloodthirsty tyrant Saddam Hussein, who during a long reign was responsible for the deaths of thousands — maybe hundreds of thousands — of his own citizens. Then, upon Saddam's fall, came a host of Iraqi mini-tyrants who have imposed a chaotic, anarchic insurgency upon that unhappy country, giving it a daily ration of suicide bombers, attacks on places of worship, and other horrors.

Iraq these days is a troubled and troublesome place. But when we look back across that country's history, as I've been doing lately, we see a grand tradition of monstrous violence there stretching back thousands of years. Saddam wasn't the first ogre to rule Iraq. Nor was he — by some distance — the worst.

I ought to clarify, at this point, what I mean by "Iraq." As a national name, that's a fairly recent one. My eleventh Edition of the *Encyclopaedia Britannica*, published in 1910 and considered a reliable compendium of just about all that was known at that time, says nothing about "Iraq," though it does have an entry for "Irak-Arabi," which it tells us is "the name employed since the Arab conquest to designate that portion of the valley of the Tigris and Euphrates known in older literature as Babylonia." Irak-Arabi, we learn, is made up of two unequal portions: "an extensive dry steppe with a healthy desert climate, and an unhealthy region of swamps," the latter being in the southern region. Two great rivers run through the area, the Tigris and the Euphrates, which had led the Romans to give the area the name of *Mesopotamia*, "the land between the rivers." Certain portions of the country, the encyclopedia reports, are periodically terrorized by uncontrollable Bedouin marauders, and the whole place, after a period of great prosperity in the early days of Arab rule more than a thousand years ago, "has now returned to a condition of semi-barbarism."

The territory once known as Irak-Arabi had come under Persian rule in the fourteenth century, then fell to the Ottoman Turks in 1534, and entered into a long period of stagnation and disarray. The Ottomans divided it into two provinces, with Basra as the capital of the swampy south and Baghdad the capital of the central area where the two rivers are closest together. The old Roman province of Mesopotamia had had a third district north of that, which the Ottomans made a province with its administrative center at Mosul, close by the ruins of Nineveh, the ancient capital of the warlike kingdom of Assyria. When the Ottoman Empire was broken up after World War I, its three Mesopotamian provinces of Mosul, Baghdad, and Basra were combined by the victorious Allies to create the new independent nation of Iraq, with Faisal, an Arabian-born prince, as its first king. A revolution in 1958 expelled the royal dynasty and Iraq has been a republic ever since, under the rule of a series of oppressive dictators culminating in Saddam Hussein.

The key thing that emerges from this quick tour of history is that present-day Iraq is a hodgepodge of incompatible nationalities deriving primarily from the ancient kingdoms of Babylonia and Assyria. (The coming of Islam has added a further complication because of the division between Sunni and Shiite religious factions: the Sunnis are dominant in northern Iraq, the Shiites in the south, and the central area holds a mixture of both groups.)

Lately I've been delving into early Mesopotamian history, thanks to a fascinating book I acquired a few months ago called *Ancient Records of Assyria and Babylonia*. This, edited by Daniel David Luckenbill, a professor of Semitic languages at the University of Chicago, and published by the University in 1927, is a collection of translations of inscriptions left behind by the Assyrian kings. It's easy to see from the fierce boasts of those bloodthirsty monarchs that Saddam had been using them as role models during his thirty years of rule in the region that had once been theirs. Anyone who had the sort of old-fashioned education that I was lucky enough to have, a couple of generations ago, is well aware, of course, of what bad guys the Assyrians were. Though I was never particularly religious, I did read the Bible — King James Version — for its literary value, and in the Old Testament I encountered again and again the villainous Assyrians who forever made life so tough for my Hebrew ancestors.

In II Kings, for example, the tale is told of the Assyrian invasion of the two Jewish kingdoms of Judah and Israel. Israel fell first, and its people were carried off to Assyria in captivity. Then, II Kings reports, "in the fourteenth year of king Hezekiah did Sennacherib king of Assyria come up against all the fenced cities of Judah, and took them." Sennacherib, who had previously conquered neighboring Babylonia and much of Palestine, demanded an immense tribute, "and Hezekiah gave him all the silver that was found in the house of the Lord, and in the treasures of the king's house. And at that time did Hezekiah cut off the gold from the doors of the temple of the Lord, and from the pillars which Hezekiah king of Judah had overlaid, and gave it to the king of Assyria."

Lord Byron, in a gaudy poem called "The Destruction of Sennacherib" that I loved when I was a boy, has this to say of the savage Assyrian attack:

The Assyrian came down like a wolf on the fold
And his cohorts were gleaming in purple and gold;
And the sheen of their spears was like stars on the sea
When the blue wave rolls nightly on deep Galilee.

In the Biblical version, and Byron's, things end fairly well for the Hebrews: the Lord hears his people's prayers, and the Angel of Death goes among the Assyrians in their camp outside Jerusalem, smiting them so vehemently that in one night "an hundred fourscore and five thousand" are slain, "so Sennacherib king of Assyria departed, and went and returned, and dwelt at Nineveh."

Upon turning to Luckenbill's *Ancient Records of Assyria*, I made two interesting discoveries: one, that the Assyrian invasion of Judah took place pretty much as the Bible describes, and, two, that the Jewish kingdom may have survived the onslaught not by the miraculous intervention of God but by the payment of that stiff tribute. For this is what the actual inscriptions of Sennacherib, who ruled Assyria from 705 to 681 BC, have to say:

> As for Hezekiah, the Jew, who had not submitted to my yoke, forty-six of his strong, walled cities and the cities of their environs, which were numberless, I besieged, I captured, as booty I counted them. Him, like a caged bird, in Jerusalem, his royal city, I shut up. . . . I imposed the payment of yearly gifts by them, as tax, and laid it upon him. That Hezekiah — the terrifying splendor of my royalty overcame him. . . . With thirty talents of gold, eight hundred talents of silver, and all kinds of treasure from his palace, he sent his daughters, his palace women, his male and female singers, to Nineveh, and he dispatched his messengers to pay the tribute.

Ancient Records of Assyria is, in fact, a voluptuous record of Assyria's ferocious wars against its neighbors, one proud king after another describing his gory victories. Here is Sennacherib conquering Babylon:

> With mines and engines I took the city. . . . Whether small or great, I left none. With their corpses I filled the city squares. . . . The city and its houses, from its foundation to its top, I destroyed, I devastated, I burned with fire. . . . Through the midst of that city I dug canals, I flooded its site with water, and the very foundations thereof I destroyed. I made its destruction more complete than by a flood.

And this is an earlier king, Assurnasirpal, defeating the city of Dirra:

> For two days, from before sunrise, I thundered against them like Adad, the god of the storm, and I rained down flame upon them. . . . I

captured the city, eight hundred of their warriors I struck down with the sword, I cut off their heads. . . . A pillar of living men and of heads I built in front of their city gate, seven hundred men I impaled on stakes in front of their city gate. The city I destroyed, I devastated, I turned it into mounds and ruins; their young men I burned in the flames.

Here is King Shamsi-Adad V, telling of his conquest of Urash:

That city I stormed, I captured. With the blood of their warriors I dyed the squares of their cities like wool. Six thousand of them I smote. Pirishati, their king, together with one thousand of his fighters, I seized alive. Their spoil — their property, their goods, their cattle, their flocks, their horses, vessels of silver, splendid gold, and copper, in countless numbers, I carried off. Their cities I destroyed, I devastated, I burned with fire.

On and on it goes, two fat volumes of it, king after king blithely describing the most ghastly acts of war. "Karkar I burned with fire. Its king I flayed. . . ." "I slaughtered like lambs and bespattered with the venom of death the rest of the rebellious people. . . ." "I killed large numbers of his troops, the bodies of his warriors I cut down like millet, filling the mountain valleys with them. I made their blood run down the ravines and precipes like a river, dyeing plain countryside and highlands red like a royal robe. . . ." "Like a young gazelle I mounted the highest peaks in pursuit of them. To the summits of the mountains I pursued them and brought about their overthrow. Their cities I captured and I carried off their spoil; I destroyed, I devastated, I burned them with fire."

Open the two volumes anywhere and it's the same stuff: "I destroyed, I devastated, I burned them with fire." I can readily imagine Saddam Hussein, who fancied himself as the successor to the kings of Assyria and Babylonia and set up some inscriptions of his own in the restored ruins of the city of Babylon, reading these books and nodding approvingly — "Right on, Sennacherib! Way to go, Assurnasirpal!" and picking up some ideas on governance from them.

All of which proves, I guess, that the more things change, the more they remain the same. Perhaps it's something in the waters of the Tigris or the Euphrates that has bred these monsters in the land once known as Mesopotamia and now called Iraq; or perhaps the Assyrian kings were no worse than any other rulers of their day, but were simply more enthusiastic in bragging of their atrocities.

What I find most interesting about these horrifying testaments of atrocity isn't their ghastliness but the mere fact that we are capable of reading them at all, written as they were on tablets of clay in what is now a lost language and a strange wedge-shaped script. It strikes me as a good idea to talk about how we came to understand the inscriptions of the Assyrians and the Babylonians in the first place, next issue.

Asimov's Science Fiction, September, 2007

Decoding Cuneiform

IN SEPTEMBER I WROTE OF DIPPING INTO **ANCIENT RECORDS OF ASSYRIA AND BABYLONIA**, a fine old volume of translations from Mesopotamian cuneiform inscriptions, from which it is easy to see that the part of the world now known as Iraq was, even in antiquity, a bloody battleground ruled by ferocious tyrants. I quoted from the boastful inscriptions of such ancient Assyrian kings as Sennacherib and Assurbanipal, of which this is a typical sample: "For two days, from before sunrise, I thundered against them like Adad, the god of the storm, and I rained down flame upon them. . . . A pillar of living men and of heads I built in front of their city gate, seven hundred men I impaled on stakes in front of their city gate. The city I destroyed, I devastated, I turned it into mounds and ruins; their young men I burned in the flames." And I noted that what I found most interesting about these horrifying testaments of atrocity wasn't their ghastliness but the mere fact that we are capable of reading them at all, written as they were on tablets of clay in what is now a lost language and a strange wedge-shaped script. So let's look now at how we came to understand the Assyrian and Babylonian inscriptions in the first place.

European scholars had been puzzling over this ancient writing — "cuneiform," it was called, from the Latin word meaning "wedge" — since the seventeenth century. Three different kinds of cuneiform inscriptions had been discovered at the ancient Persian capital of Persepolis. By 1778 one of them had been shown to be a forty-two-character alphabetic script. The other two were vastly more complex. And no one knew which language these characters represented, although it was reasonable to think that one or perhaps all three scripts were in the ancient Persian tongue.

To decipher an unknown script, there has to be some point of contact with the known. If both the characters and the language they represent are enigmas, it becomes impossible to get very far with a decipherment. François Champollion was able to decipher hieroglyphics because he had the use of the Rosetta Stone, which provided a long Egyptian text in two kinds of Egyptian script, plus a translation into Greek. But no Rosetta Stone for the cuneiform script was available.

One big break came toward the end of the eighteenth century as philologists began to study existing texts of an archaic form of the Persian language that had been written using a decipherable alphabet called Pehlevi. One of them guessed that the simplest of the Persepolis inscriptions, the so-called Class I ones, were Old Persian texts written in the wedge-shaped cuneiform letters. A German high-school teacher named Georg Friedrich Grotefend, whose hobby was solving puzzles, went looking for some repetitive phrase in the Persepolis inscriptions that might give him a clue to the meaning of a few of the wedge-shaped symbols.

It was already known that Persian official inscriptions almost always began with, and constantly reiterated, a formula that went, "So-and-So, Great King, King of Kings, King of This and That, Son of So-and-So, Great King, King of Kings." Grotefend first identified the eight most frequent of the forty-two Class I characters and decided that these probably stood for vowels. Then he went looking for the words of his royal formula, and the names of the kings.

Quickly he found clusters of repeated words, the most frequent of which was a seven-letter group that he suspected meant "king." In Old Persian that word was "khsheihioh," and by lining up the characters he arrived at guesses for seven letters. Then, finding what seemed to be a royal name at the proper place in the formula, he matched the letters he had already identified against the name of a known king — Xerxes, "Khshershe" in Persian — and then tested his growing list of letters against the name of Xerxes' father, Darius — "Darheush." Bit by bit, by trial and error, he was able to claim identification of twenty-nine of the forty-two Class I characters by 1803. Although it turned out that he was wrong about some of these, he had provided entry into the mysteries of Class I cuneiform.

But Class I was still a long way from a complete decipherment and the Class II and III inscriptions were still total mysteries when, in 1835, a swashbuckling English scholar-adventurer named Henry Creswicke Rawlinson entered the picture. Rawlinson, a lieutenant in the service of the British East India Company, had been stationed in various Asian posts — first in India, then in Persia — since the age of seventeen. He had a natural knack for languages and quickly mastered several Indian tongues, Arabic, and Persian. And, like Grotefend, he was inclined toward puzzle-solving as an amusement. Knowing little of Grotefend's work, he attempted a decipherment of Class I using the same method, and worked out thirteen letters on his own. When the East India Company transferred him to its Persian base at Kermanshah, he swiftly learned that a lengthy cuneiform inscription in all three scripts was to be found carved on the Behistun Rock, a seventeen-hundred-foot-high cliff twenty miles from town, and rode out to take a look.

But the inscription was all but inaccessible. The ancient Persian rock-carvers had removed the steps leading up to it after they were finished, so later vandals could not deface the words. Rawlinson, a considerable athlete, scrambled up the bare, slippery face of the rock without the aid of ropes or ladders until he reached a ledge, two feet in breadth at its widest point, where he could stand and copy part of the inscription.

The Behistun text was studded with names out of Persian history — King Darius and his whole ancestral line — and Rawlinson, using inspired guesswork, his linguistic skills, and his knowledge of history, was able to match names to cuneiform characters and work out a nearly complete translation by January 1838, correcting many of Grotefend's errors and demonstrating certain knowledge of eighteen of the forty-two letters. In the months that followed he was able to decipher and translate some two hundred lines of the Class I Behistun inscription.

Class II and Class III remained unknown, though, and Rawlinson had only fragmentary copies of those texts, which he believed were the Class I inscription written in the scripts of two other languages, one of them very likely Babylonian or Assyrian. In 1844 he returned to Behistun, erected a wooden folding ladder on a narrow ledge three hundred feet above the ground, stood on its topmost rung, and, bracing himself against the rock with his left arm and holding his notebook in his left hand, copied the inscription with his right hand. "The interest of the occupation," he wrote, "entirely did away with any sense of danger."

Now he had all of Class I and most of the Class II inscription. In 1847 he returned equipped with ladders, planks, ropes, nails, hammers, and pegs, and hired a Kurdish boy to scramble out over the abyss on a scaffold to make paper casts, "squeezes," of the almost inaccessible Class III. Equipped with the full texts, Rawlinson set about to match his Persian Class I text against the far more intricate Class III, which had hundreds of characters instead of only forty-two, in the hope of solving the riddle of Babylonian cuneiform. In England, meanwhile, a clergyman named Edward Hincks started work on the same difficult task.

Hincks showed that it was wrong to talk of a Babylonian "alphabet." More than five hundred different Class III characters were known, and no language could have that many basic sounds. Hincks guessed that some of the symbols stood for individual syllables, and others for entire words. Comparing Class I's royal formulas with their likely Class III counterparts, he showed that the seven signs of Xerxes' name — KH-SH-Y-A-R-SH-A in Hincks' reading — lined up with Babylonian signs that could have been pronounced KHI-SHI-I-AR-SHI-I. By 1847 he had deciphered twenty-one syllables and had identified the ideographic symbols that stood for such words as "and," "son," "great," "house," and "god."

Rawlinson, at the same time, was finding syllables — *ka, ki, ku, ak, ik, uk*, etc. — and deciphering certain words, helped by his familiarity with Hebrew and Arabic, languages closely related to the one that the Babylonians and Assyrians had spoken. The word for "dog," *keleb* in Hebrew and *kalbu* in Arabic, turned out to be *kalbu* in Babylonian-Assyrian. "To burn" was *saraf* in Hebrew and *sarapu* in Babylonian-Assyrian. So it went, until by 1850 he could claim to know the meaning of 150 Class III characters and two hundred Babylonian-Assyrian words. Each solution, though, brought with it a host of new complications. The Mesopotamian civilizations had lasted thousands of years, and over that time Mesopotamian scribes had invented all manner of new ways of transforming words into wedge-shaped symbols, so that by the time the Behistun inscription was carved the system in use was full of bewildering overlaps of meaning and linguistic shortcuts. Rawlinson devoted years to untangling these puzzles, while Hincks carried on parallel research of equal value. In 1851 Rawlinson made public a translation of a text carved on a clay cylinder that confirmed an event described in the Bible, the defeat of King Hezekiah of Judah by the armies of the Assyrian king Sennacherib, which I quoted in last month's column. ("As for Hezekiah, the Jew, who had not submitted to my yoke, forty-six of his strong, walled cities and the cities of their environs, which were numberless, I besieged, I captured, as booty I counted them.") Its announcement caused a mighty stir in England.

Excavation of the ruined Assyrian palaces at Nineveh in what is now northern Iraq produced whole libraries of clay tablets bearing cuneiform inscriptions, among them, of all useful things, what Rawlinson called "a perfect encyclopedia of Assyrian science," a cuneiform "book" describing "the system of Assyrian writing, the distinction between phonetic and ideographic signs, the grammar of the language, explanation of technical terms. . . ." These royal libraries also contained dictionaries of the Assyrian language. What he already knew of the script allowed him to penetrate these tablets and greatly extend his knowledge. His rival Hincks kept at it also, and a Franco-German scholar named Jules Oppert entered the field as well. These three, working independently, steadily refined the understanding of the cuneiform inscriptions by mastering, step by step, the bizarre tangle of complexities that governed the Mesopotamian system of writing. The climax came in 1857 when the Royal Asiatic Society of England sponsored an event in which Rawlinson, Hincks, Oppert, and an English scholar named William Fox Talbot were each given copies of an untranslated Class III text and told to translate it independently. When the results came in, Rawlinson's and Hincks' versions were virtually identical, Oppert's quite similar, and Fox Talbot's, though sometimes vague and incorrect, fairly close in a general way. And that is how we came to unlock the secrets of Mesopotamian cuneiform. (The Class II, which turned out to be in a language called Elamitic, was not deciphered until 1879. Sumerian, yet another cuneiform script and the ancestor of all the others, was decoded around the same time through the use of Assyrian-Sumerian dictionaries.)

It will not, of course, be so easy to decipher the writings we find on alien worlds, when and if we discover such things. We won't be provided with convenient multilingual inscriptions that can partly be understood, as were Champollion in Egypt and Rawlinson in Persia. On the other hand, perhaps future advances in computer science will sweep away such obstacles. Until then, though, the nineteenth-century decipherment of Mesopotamian cuneiform must stand as one of the most miraculous of linguistic achievements, opening, as it does, a doorway into civilizations thought forever lost.

Asimov's Science Fiction, **August, 2007**

The Quality of Pity is Not Folded

I OWE THIS ONE TO JIM CAUGHRAN OF WILLOW-DALE, ONTARIO. He is the publisher of a small-press magazine (a "fanzine") called *A Propos de Rien* that is distributed through the Fantasy Amateur Press Association, a fanzine group to which I've belonged for many years. In issue 257 of *A Propos de Rien* he speaks of an Internet site that makes hilarious use of the Babelfish computer program to translate phrases in and out of five different languages, with remarkably chaotic results.

Computer translation programs, in the current state of the art, are reasonably good at equating one language with another. But they have understandable trouble with slang and local idioms, and the differences in basic grammatical structure between languages cause other difficulties, all of which become cumulative if you run a series of translations of the same sentence.

The sentence Jim Caughran chose to use is an old catchphrase of science fiction fans: "Fandom is just a goddamn hobby." The translation program turned it first into French: *Fandom est juste un sacre passe-temps*.

Which became, moving back to English: *Fandom right one is crowned pastime*. And on to German: *Recht man Fandom ist gekroenter Pastime*. English: *Quite one fan cathedral is crowned Pastime*. Into Italian: *Abbastanza una cattedrale del ventilatore e pastime crowned*. English again: *Enough one cathedral of the fan is pastime crowned*. This, in Portuguese: *Bastante uma catedral do ventilador e pastime coroado*. Back to English: *Sufficiently a cathedral of the fan is pastime crowned*. Then Spanish: *Una catedral del ventilador es suficientemente pasa-tiempo coronado*.

Which gives us, finally, this triumphant statement: *A cathedral of the ventilator is sufficiently crowned pastime*. How did this happen? Why did the translation program foul things up so badly? Let's go over it step by step.

Right at the beginning, the French translation, unable to handle an American idiom, desperately gives us *sacre* for "goddamn." It must have taken the "god" part of that word as permission to translate "goddamn" as "sacred" or "holy." But *sacre,* unfortunately, also is a French noun meaning "anointing" or "coronation," and when the phrase came back into English, it was that latter meaning that the computer picked — giving us "crowned pastime" in place of "goddamn hobby."

The next problem crops up in the German. The computer, struggling with "fandom," sees *dom,* which is German for "cathedral," and makes "fan cathedral" out of the word on the next bounce into English. Now it is the turn of Italian to translate "fan" not as *amatore,* which is the actual Italian equivalent of "fan" in the sense of a hobbyist, but as *ventilatore,* which is a different kind of fan entirely. Meanwhile the English "just," meaning "merely," becomes the not quite equivalent *juste* in French and things get worse from there.

Science fiction writers, as you know, are in the habit of equipping their spacefaring heroes with translating devices that swiftly and accurately render unfamiliar alien languages into lucid English. We have always suspected that creating such a device would be, of course, easier said than done. In Kim Stanley Robinson's 1990 story "The Translator," which pokes lethal fun at the concept of a translating machine, a hapless Earthman meeting with two alien species at once has one group tell him things like "*Warlike viciously now descendant fat food flame death*" while the other comes through the translating gizmo with sounds that can be translated, the machine says, as *"1. Fish market. 2. Fish harvest. 3. Sunspots visible from a depth of 10 meters below the surface of the ocean on a calm day. 4. Traditional festival. 5. Astrological configuration in galactic core."*

That's science fiction. But here in the mundane world we now have an actual translating program, capable of garbling things just as effectively using only Terrestrial languages, and using it in the extreme manner (to be fair, it never really was designed to translate the same sentence in and out of five languages other than English) shows us how tough the translating job really is. You probably want to know the address of the program so you can produce your own linguistic spaghetti and here, before we proceed, it is: www.tashian.com/multibabel

One of its wonders is that it won't necessarily give you the same garble twice. When I ran "Fandom is just a goddamn hobby" through a second time it chose not to translate "goddamn" into French at all, merely carrying it through as an untranslatable English idiom — thus giving me, on the final bounce, *The cathedral of the ventilator is of the pastime of right one of goddamn.* Then, to avoid the "goddamn" problem entirely, I used "accursed" instead, and that turned into the correct French word, *maudit.* But for some reason that word got only a one-way translation and came back to me in English unchanged, which led eventually to *The cathedral of the ventilator is expert of Pastimemaudit.*

Then I tried Nathan Hale's famous last words, which I misremembered as "I regret that I have but one life to lose for my country." By the time this had passed through German and Spanish it had become *I unfortunaty (sic) regard it that I have however one life span to destroy for my country,* and sending it on to Italian, Portuguese, and Spanish morphed it into *Unfortunaty is concerned what I nevertheless lasts of distrugg for my country.*

But upon checking I discovered that what Nathan Hale actually said was, "I *only* regret that I have but one life to lose for my country," and the insertion of that small adverb created vast changes in the outcome. "I regret" became, passing through Italian, not "unfortunaty" this time, but "me sorrow," and "only" came back as "solo." "Me sorrow" then turned into the Spanish *yo dolor,* which gave me, at the end, *I pain, de.solo that an I nevertheless lasts of distrugg for my country,* similar but rather more poetic than the earlier version and even less comprehensible.

Shakespeare, of course, is rich territory for babelizing. "The quality of mercy is not strained" returned from French as "the quality of pity is not tended," which went in and came out of German as "the quality of Pity is not bent," which Italian transformed into "the quality of pity is not folded." "I come to bury Caesar, not to praise him" saw "praise" turn into "congratulate" in French, "bury" become "embed" in Portuguese, and, after some Spanish word-order manipulations, the end result was, "I come to insert to Caesar in congratular it to it of the order no." (Now put that last sentence back in the program as a starting point and see where you get!)

Poor Shakespeare. "It falleth as the gentle rain from heaven" gently evolves into *Falleth appreciates the force of motivatings of the rain of the sky.* And King Lear's magnificent rant, "I shall do such things, I know not what they are, but they shall be the terror of the Earth," suffers a sea-change when the program fails to distinguish the German irregular verb *wissen* ("to know") from the adjective *weiss* ("white") because the German for "I know" is *ich weiss,* and by one route and another we get, "I give the form to such things, the white man of no, of whom which are, are only the terror of the track."

Honest Abe Lincoln's straightforward "dedicated to the proposition that all men are created equal" picks up an androidal tone on the way back from Italian: "It has dedicated the demand that all the men are manufactured are similar to it towards the outside" and at the finale is: "It dedicated the demand that all the men are manufactured are similar it stop the external part." Alexander Pope's "A little knowledge is a dangerous thing" makes the digital journey and emerges as "Small of the knowledge it is dangerous that."

And when I turned to Lewis Carroll for "And why the sea is boiling hot, and whether pigs have wings," I found myself, via Spanish, with the charmingly Wonderlandish "And because he is to cook to the hot furnace of the sea and if the pigs have the wings." I did not, of course, waste the computer's time on " 'Twas brillig, and the slithy toves did gyre and gimbal in the wabe," which I suspected would sound pretty much the same after five translations as it did at the outset. But I did try it on "Twinkle, twinkle, little bat! How I wonder what you're at! Up above the word you fly, like a teatray in the sky," and received this marvelously eloquent French version:

Scintillement, scintillement, petite batte! Comment je me demande a ce que vous etes! Vers le haut de au-dessus du monde vous volez, comme un teatray dans le ciel!"

Which is so beautiful that I almost feared to see what the computer would do to it in English translation. This is what I got:

Flutter, flutter, small beater! How I wonder so that you are! To the top of above the world you fly, like a teatray in the sky!

To the top of above the world, indeed. It's perfect. Flutter, flutter, small beater! I loved it.

The computer program was satisfied too, evidently. It quit right there, refusing to translate those lovely lines into German. «Could not translate» is what I was told, and that itself went through the changes, the Italian version coming forth as «It has not been able translate» and the Spanish as «It could not translates.»

But you can. You've got the address. You want to know how Tolkien sounds in Babelese, don't you? What becomes of the clear, rational prose of Robert A. Heinlein as it passes through five European languages? And then there's T.S. Eliot . . . the Book of Revelation . . . Tolstoy . . . Franz Kafka. . . .

It's all yours. Thanks a lot, Jim Caughran, for hours of idle fun. And you too, Carl Tashian, for dreaming up the original software.

Fandom is just an accursed hobby, indeed.

Asimov's Science Fiction, **October/November, 2002**

Greetings From The Past

SO HERE WE ALL ARE, FINALLY, IN THE YEAR 2000. NOT.

I'm not there because I write these columns about six months ahead of cover date, so that Sheila Williams, otherwise known as the Force, will have enough time to carve the words for each issue on the wooden blocks and print the pages and staple them together and paste the covers on. So I'm actually still back there in the past right now, writing this in the spring of 1999, in order for it to appear in next January's issue.

And you're not there in the year 2000 either — not quite, anyway, because monthly magazines traditionally go on sale a little ahead of their actual cover dates. This issue is dated January, 2000, all right, but you're going to see it in the waning weeks of 1999.

Still and all, nobody can deny that we do indeed totter on the very brink of Y2K — a year I've dreamed of reaching ever since I was a small boy, fifty-plus years ago, messing around with the primordial science fiction magazines of that era when I should have been doing my Latin homework.

Let's not argue again about whether the year 2000 really does begin the new millennium. That one's been decided by popular vote, and so be it. Arithmetical common sense to the contrary, the twenty-first century and the third millennium are both going to arrive on January 1, 2000 so far as nearly everybody is concerned, and purists like Arthur C. Clarke and yours truly are simply going to have to like it or lump it. What is much more significant, from the point of view of those of us who have been around the science fiction milieu since way back in the middle years of the outgoing century, is that very, *very* shortly we're going to be dating things with a

"20—" instead of a "19—," and that sends real shivers down my back and the backs of a lot of other people who have been thinking about that great changeover for most of their lives.

I have here before me right now some of the science fiction anthologies I bought and read (and re-read and re-read) when I was in my very early teens in the late 1940s, when the year 2000 was still more than fifty years away. I'm speaking of Groff Conklin's two mammoth collections, *The Best of Science Fiction* (1946) and *A Treasury of Science Fiction* (1948), and the epochal *Adventures in Time and Space* 1946), edited by Raymond J. Healy and J. Francis McComas. Nearly all the stories in those books, reprinted from science fiction magazines of the 1930s and 1940s, took place in what was then the future, of course, and so the stories seemed like time machines to me, transporting me off to —

To 1975, say. That's when H. Beam Piper's elegant time-travel story, "Time and Time Again," takes place. It's about a man who is transported back thirty years by an atomic explosion and finds himself in the body of his own 13-year-old self. The story drops a few details about what 1975 is like — the siege of Buffalo in the third world war, the transpolar air invasion of Canada, and so forth. That these things never happened is beside the point: indeed, Piper's suddenly young hero resolves to grow up to be president and *prevent* them from happening. (He plans to win in 1960, John F. Kennedy's year in our own time track, thus replacing a "good-natured nonentity" of an incumbent who allowed World War III to become inevitable.) The point is that the story, when I read it in 1949, was about the *future* — a future that is already a quarter of a century in our past.

Then there's Robert A. Heinlein's 1940 story, "Requiem," the one about Delos D. Harriman, the elderly tycoon who put together the financial consortium that launched the first expeditions to the Moon, and now, in extreme old age, yearns to go there himself. The story itself doesn't, in fact, tell us what year "Requiem" is taking place in. But early in his career Heinlein drew up a "future history" chart for his own storytelling reference, and the first published version of that chart, in the May 1941 issue of *Astounding*, sets 1978 as the date of the first rocket to the Moon, and 1980 for the founding of Luna City, the first settlement there. "Requiem" is pegged for 1990.

Heinlein was a little too conservative about the date of that first lunar landing — it happened in 1969 — and it didn't occur to him or anyone else that our arrival on the Moon would not immediately be followed by the establishment of permanent bases there. Still, he came close enough. One thing he was certain of was that we would reach the Moon in the second half of the twentieth century, and even that seemed quite far in the future to him. He set his story of old Delos Harriman's journey to the moon in 1990 rather than 2000 because to Heinlein, writing his story back there in Franklin D. Roosevelt's second term in office, the year 2000 was a distant, barely imaginable realm of fantasy. As it was to me when I first read that story, and so many others, in the days of Harry Truman's presidency.

Here's "Time Locker," by Lewis Padgett (a pseudonym of the versatile Henry Kuttner), dating from 1943. It's set in 1970, by which time dollars have been replaced by "credits," telephones have video screens attached, and airborne commuters travel through Manhattan via the Hudson Floatway. The far future, again.

On and on, story after story, the future that never happened except in the pages of those old science fiction anthologies — Lewis Padgett's "The Piper's Son," L. Sprague de Camp's "The Blue Giraffe," Heinlein's "The Roads Must Roll," Padgett's "The Twonky," C.L. Moore's "No Woman Born," Harry Walton's "Housing Shortage" — every one of them taking place *in the late twentieth century*, which seemed, at the time, quite far enough away to encompass all sorts of marvels and wonders. As for the magical year 2000, that lay *beyond* those tales, in an even more fantastic time to come.

What a picture of the glittering 1970s and 1980s I drew from them all when I was a boy — robots, androids, mutants, time machines and other four-dimensional gizmos, commuter helicopters. And the year 2000 was always the big one for me, the great boundary-marker between my world and the unattainable future.

Just a few years later I started writing science fiction myself, and by 1957, when I took my own first crack at writing about the turn of the new millennium, I was a well-established professional. Here's what I had to say on the subject in a little story called "New Year's Eve: 2000 AD" from the September, 1957 issue of the long-forgotten *Imaginative Tales*:

"George Carhew glanced at his watch. The time was 11:21. He looked around at the rest of the guests at the party and said, 'Hey! Thirty-nine more minutes, and we enter the twenty-first century.'

"Abel Marsh squinted sourly at Carhew. 'How many times do I have to tell you, George, that the new century won't begin for another *year*? 2001 is the first year of the twenty-first century, not 2000. You'll have to wait till next year to celebrate that.'

"'Don't be so dammed picayune,' Carhew snapped. 'In half an hour it'll be the year 2000. Why *shouldn't* it be a new century?'

"'Because — '

"'Oh, don't fight over it, boys,' cooed Maritta Lewis....'"

And they don't. Maritta goes to the bar and dials up a Four Planets for Carhew and an old-fashioned Whiskey Sour for the stodgy Marsh, and the party goes merrily on, with chatter about the new hedonistic cult called Relativistic Release that's sweeping the country, and so on, and precisely at midnight "a bolt of light split the sky — a shaft of white flame that leaped up from the Earth and sprang through the heavens, lighting up the entire city and probably half the continent," because the first rocketship to the Moon has just taken off from White Sands Rocket Base and the Age of Space has begun, there on New Year's Eve, 1999. I was wrong by only about thirty years.

But — hey, folks, it was just a story. And I had no delusions of being Heinlein.

I took a second look at the arrival of the year 2000 in my 1974 novel, *The Stochastic Man*, and this time, I think, I came closer to Heinleinesque prophetic clarity. Times Square is full of drunken, half-naked revelers. "An undercurrent of violence had been present all evening — smashing of windows, shooting out of streetlamps — but it picked up strength rapidly after ten: there were fistfights, some genial, some murderous, and at the corner of 57th and 5th there was a mob battle going on, a hundred men and women clubbing at each other in what looked like a random way...." Sounds more like the America we've come to know and love, doesn't it? At the moment of midnight "the summits of office towers turned radiant with brilliant floodlights," but then a fire breaks out: "Flames were dancing high on a building to the west....Such a lovely orange hue — we began to cheer and applaud. We are all Nero tonight, I thought, and was swept on southward....Bells tolled. More sirens. Chaos, chaos, chaos." Yes. Happy New Year, everybody.

I remember when I first calculated how old I'd be if I lived to see the year 2000. I was 13; there were sixty-odd years still to go. My father, that year, was a man in his forties; my maternal grandfather, born in nineteenth-century Poland, was 64. By the time the year 2000 came around, I realized, *I would be older than my grandfather was right now.* It seemed unthinkable that I could ever get to be so old. (It seemed highly unlikely, too, for this was a period when most of us, not just science fiction readers, expected World War III to break out at any moment and all of civilization to be consumed in atomic warfare.)

And yet — yet —

Here we are, right on the very threshold of the year 2000. It's been a long haul, but we're almost there. Gives me the shivers, it does.

See you in the future, pals — next month.

Asimov's Science Fiction, **January 2000**

SIX
Something Of Myself

Fantastic Libraries

I HAVE BEEN, ALL MY LIFE, NOT ONLY A PRODI-GIOUS PRODUCER of books but also a prodigious consumer of them — surely I've read five hundred books for every one that I've written, and that adds up to a lot of books. Which means that much of my life has been concerned with aggregations of words. Libraries, therefore, which are storehouses where aggregations of words aggregate, hold a central place in my imagination. The mere concept of a great mass of books set out on row after row of shelves gets my pulse racing. I yearn to explore those shelves and discover the wonders they contain. The fantasies of my dreaming mind often take me to the great libraries of the world — real or imaginary.

The other night, for example, I dreamed that I was wandering around in the stacks of the great New York Public Library building at Fifth Avenue and 42nd Street. I used to visit that library as a boy, when visitors' book requests were sent by pneumatic tube into some distant repository in the bowels of the earth, and the requested books would eventually come forth via dumb-waiter. (Is it still done that way, I wonder?) Those stacks aren't open to the public, so far as I know, and certainly I've never been in them: yet there I was in my dream, going freely from floor to floor in the dim, musty environment of millions of books, picking through all the printed treasures of the past five hundred years.

I know the origin of that dream. When I was a sophomore at Columbia University fifty years ago, I somehow wangled a pass to the stacks of the university library, one of the greatest in the country, which in theory was not open to undergraduates like me. Many was the afternoon that I would roam those bookish corridors, goggle-eyed at the wonders that had suddenly become accessible to me — and then I would stagger back to my room across the street with an armload of esoteric items, Kafka's short stories and Part II of *Faust* and the plays of Plautus and anything else that had caught my fancy. Why, in my dream, I should transpose my memories of the Columbia stacks to Manhattan's other great library downtown, I have no idea. But I awoke still gripped with the tingle of awe that such libraries always have aroused in me. And it set me thinking about some of the fictional libraries, libraries that no one will ever see, that have stirred the same sort of emotions in me.

There can be no doubt that the grandest one of all is the one that Jorge Luis Borges conjured up in his 1941 short story, "The Library of Babel." No other library could possibly match the scope of its collections, because Borges tells us in his very first sentence that it is, in fact, the universe:

> "The universe (which others call the Library) is composed of an indefinite, perhaps an infinite, number of hexagonal galleries, with enormous ventilation shafts in the middle, encircled by very low railings. From any hexagon the upper or lower stories are visible, interminably. . . . Five shelves correspond to each one of the walls of each hexagon; each shelf contains thirty-two books of a uniform format; each book is made up of four hundred and ten pages; each page, of forty lines; each line, of some eighty black letters. . . ."

Borges goes on to tell us that the shelves extend for miles in all directions, that librarians spend their entire lives moving about within the Library without ever leaving the building, or seeing more than a small portion of the totality of the books it holds. (Though there is a myth that one book exists that contains all the information held in all the others, and that one librarian has read it, and thus has become analogous to a god.) When they die, the bodies of the librarians are piously thrown into the central ventilation shaft by their colleagues, and decompose gradually during the infinitely long descent.

The Library has existed throughout all eternity. No one has ever found two identical books in the collection. Its shelves contain everything that ever was or will be written in any language: "The minute history of the future, the autobiography of the angels, the faithful catalog of the Library, thousands and thousands of false catalogs, a demonstration of the fallacy of the true catalog . . . the veridical account of your death, a version of each book in all languages, the interpolations of every book in all books."

A library that is both eternal and infinite must, by definition, be the monarch of libraries. Borges tells us much more about it, and I urge you to seek the story out. My mind reverberates with awe whenever I read it.

But another that has had an equally powerful effect on my imagination is the one that H.P. Lovecraft conceived in his novella "The Shadow Out of Time," which I first encountered when I was twelve years old and which is a work of such scope and visionary power that it maintains its grip on me to this day. Lovecraft's protagonist, a professor at Miskatonic University in the

New England town of Arkham, experiences dreams in which he is transported into the body of an unimaginably strange creature of the unthinkably distant past. The body he inhabits belongs to a member of the Great Race, creatures of a dying world who, "wise with the ultimate secrets, had looked ahead for a new world and species wherein they might have long life, and had sent their minds en masse into that future race best adapted to house them — the cone-shaped things that peopled our earth a billion years ago."

Lovecraft's Dr. Peaslee, upon entering an archaeological site in Australia that turns out to be the ruins of the city of those billion-year-old cone-shaped inhabitants of our world, is privileged to explore the library of the Great Race, a crypt within a windowless subterranean tower, a titanic repository "whose alien, basalt masonry bespoke a whispered and horrible origin," and there he finds "volumes of texts and pictures holding the whole of Earth's annals — histories and descriptions of every species that had ever been or that ever would be, with full records of their arts, their achievements, their languages, and their psychologies." These records, Lovecraft's narrator tells us, were "written or printed on great sheets of a curiously tenacious fabric, were bound into books that opened from the top, and were kept in individual cases of a strange, extremely light rustless metal of grayish hue. . . . These cases were stored in tiers of rectangular vaults — like closed, locked shelves — wrought of the same rustless metal and fastened by knobs with intricate turnings." Lovecraft's man roams through these books, and then through the world of the Great Race itself, providing readers of the story with one of the richest and most vivid worlds of the imagination ever created.

In my own writing I've done some playing around with library fantasies as well. In more than one story I've sent time-travelers back to the lost library of Alexandria to rescue the treasures that were taken from us when the library and its many thousands of volumes were burned in antiquity: dozens of plays of Sophocles and Aeschylus, dialogues of Plato, much of Livy's history of Rome, Aristotle's study of Homer's poetry, Sextus Julius Africanus's chronicle of the history of the world from 5499 BC on, and much more.

But also I've invented libraries of my own. In the novel *Son of Man*, for instance, which takes place far in the future, my protagonist gets a guided tour of one that probably owes more than a little of its nature to the one in Lovecraft's "Shadow Out of Time":

> "Ti opens a glass-faced cabinet and withdraws a sparkling ruby cube the size of her head. He takes it carefully from her, surprised at its lightness.
>
> "The cube speaks to him in an unintelligible language. Its cadence is strange: a liquid rhythm, rich with anapests. . . . Undoubtedly he is hearing poetry, but not any poetry of his era. A skein of sound unreels. . . . 'What is it?' He asks finally, and Ti says, 'A book.' Clay nods impatiently, having guessed that: 'What book? What are they saying?'

" 'A poem of the old days, before the moon fell. . . .' "

"Now she gives him an accordion-pleated box made, apparently, of rigid plastic membranes. 'A work of history,' she explains. 'The annals of a former age. . . .'

" 'How do I read it?'

" 'Like this,' she says, and her fingers slide between the membranes, lightly tapping them. The box sets up a low humming noise that resolves itself into discrete packets of verbalization. . . . He hears: 'Swallowed crouching metal sweat helmet gigantic blue wheels smaller trees ride eyebrows awed destruction light killed wind and between gently secret in spread growing waiting lived and connected over shining risk sleep rings trunks warm think wet seventeen dissolved world size burn.'

" 'It doesn't make sense,' he complains."

There's more, much more, in this ancient library of the future: "Maps, directories, catalogs, indices, dictionaries, encyclopedias, thesauri, tables of law, annals of dynastic succession, almanacs, almagests, data pools, handbooks, and access codes. . . . His mind floods with a million million questions. He will spend his next three infinities in this hall, mining the past for knowledge." I can't quote it all. If imaginary libraries turn you on, go buy the book.

Nor do I have space here to take you on the full tour of the library I invented for my giant world of Majipoor: "An enormous brick-walled structure that ran like a long coiling serpent back and forth through the core of the Castle from one side to the other and around and around again. Any book that had ever been published on any civilized world was kept here, so they said. Shriveled old librarians who were little more than huge brains with dry sticks of withered limbs attached shuffled around all day long in there, dusting and arranging and pausing now and then to peer appreciatively at some choice obscure item of their own near-infinite collections."

Which, I must confess, reminds me a little of my own library, one floor down from the room in which I sit writing this now: groaning shelves that contain, among much else, just about all the science fiction magazines ever published from the time Hugo Gernsback invented such magazines in 1926 up through last month's *Asimov's Science Fiction Magazine*.

In order to use such a library properly, one needs proper indexes and other sorts of reference materials. A remarkable reference book that unlocks the curious treasures of the Gernsback publishing era came my way a few weeks ago, and I'll talk about it in next month's column.

Asimov's Science Fiction, **March, 2003**

Ancestral Voices

AS I MENTIONED LAST MONTH, DISCUSSING FANTAS-
TIC LIBRARIES, that I have a pretty extensive library myself,
and such a library requires adequate indexing tools in order to be used
properly. One such index tool, a reference book that unlocks the curious
treasures of the earliest decade of science fiction publishing in magazine
form, has recently reached me, to my immense delight and perhaps yours.

Just as jazz came up the river from New Orleans, science fiction in
magazine form emanated from the Manhattan office of a cantankerous gad-
getophile named Hugo Gernsback (1884-1967), who in the early years of
the twentieth century became involved in the new and rapidly evolving
radio and telecommunications industries, but quickly drifted from technical research to technical publishing. He began a couple of magazines called
Modern Electrics and *Electrical Experimenter*, the latter of which became *Science
and Invention* in 1920. In that magazine he regularly ran science fiction stories of a primitive sort, mostly dealing with the wonders of gadgetry, and
they proved so popular that in 1926 he started *Amazing Stories*, the first
magazine devoted entirely to that sort of fiction. Its stories tended to be
heavy on science and technology and generally weak in matters of style,
characterization, and plot, which Gernsback regarded as secondary matters
in "scientifiction" (as he liked to call science fiction.)

Gernsback was a tempestuous businessman, constantly skirting the edge
of bankruptcy. He lost control of *Amazing* in 1929, but almost immediately started a new magazine called *Science Wonder Stories*, which, renamed
Wonder Stories in the 1930s, provided stiff competition for his former magazine *Amazing*. Also in 1930 a publisher of adventure-story magazines began
Astounding Stories (the remote ancestor of today's *Analog*), which differenti-

ated itself from *Amazing* and *Wonder* by running two-fisted tales of fast-paced action in the spaceways.

Fifty years ago, when I was in my teens, I assembled a complete collection of these primordial sf magazines. It wasn't all that hard to do — in 1950, even the earliest Gernsback titles were only 24 years old, and it was still possible to find them in bookstores and even junkshops. They seemed immensely antiquated to me, of course, partly because they went back to a time before I existed, partly because of their archaic 1930s typography, and partly because the fiction in them was, by and large, tremendously creaky stuff by the standards of the 1950s, that golden age of such great sf writers as Theodore Sturgeon, Fritz Leiber, C.M. Kornbluth, James Blish, Alfred Bester, and Jack Vance, among others.

From time to time a great surge of nostalgia for that prehistoric era comes over me, and I take one of those brittle old magazines down from its shelf and fondle it, and shake my head fondly over the stories, and put it back without reading it, telling myself that there's really no point in re-reading such terrible stuff. But there are other times when it occurs to me that the contributors to those magazines are the ancestral voices of our field, the writers who laid the groundwork for such later titans as Asimov, Heinlein, van Vogt, and the other masters I've just mentioned, and I'm filled with the desire to do some literary archaeology in the archives downstairs. But where do I begin? What should I read?

Now I have the key to that archive. It's a huge book called *Science-Fiction: The Gernsback Years*, by Everett F. Bleiler with the assistance of Richard J. Bleiler, published in 1998 by Kent State University Press.

Everett Bleiler, who is now 83 years old, has been performing sturdy service in the field of sf scholarship since the 1940s. Richard Bleiler, who teaches at the University of Connecticut, is his son. Between them they have compiled a monumental work of a grandeur and magnificence verging on lunacy: 730 huge pages that provide biographical entries for all the contributors to all sf magazines of Gernsback and his competitors from 1926 to 1936, *with detailed plot summaries of every single story, nearly 2000 of them (each summary hundreds of words long) and critical analysis as well!* They also offer a long, fascinating historical account of the era, photos of magazine covers and illustrations, and a truly extraordinary index of story themes and motifs, with such entries as, "Glands, effects of manipulation and disorders," "High civilizations of the past, non-human," and "Mad scientist, motivations, purposes." It's a meticulous work of scholarship with an almost medieval intensity about it, the equivalent of what teams of monks might have spent decades producing in the thirteenth century. The degree of passion and commitment that led the Bleilers to devote years of their lives to this project astonishes me. And they have produced a book to treasure and fondle.

If I were a better scholar of science fiction myself these days, I'd have known about it long ago, for it was reviewed by that admirable scholar Gary Wolfe in the July, 1999 issue of *Locus,* science fiction's trade journal. Wolfe called it then "as detailed and unvarnished a picture of modern sf's formative years as we are ever likely to get...a true and relentless picture.... a veritable gold mine of resources for the student of sf." But *Locus* reviews hundreds of books an issue in very small type, and somehow, that summer day in 1999, I skimmed right past the Wolfe review without paying attention. Luckily for me, my eagle-eyed brother-in-law Mark, who does not read sf himself, spotted the book not long ago in a bookstore near the University of California campus and brought it to my attention, and so a copy of it is on my desk right now.

How marvelous it is, too. I roam through it, stirred by the titles of the stories alone: "Mole-Men of Mercury," "Flame-Worms of Yokka," "The Dimensional Segregator." I could quote hundreds more. Bleiler and Bleiler, no romantics they, are unsparing in their evaluations: "Mole-Men" (1933) offers "juvenile writing," "Flame-Worms" is "competent pulp adventure," "Segregator" is "disjointed, boring, very amateurish, but a new idea in dimensional stories." And then there are the biographies of the authors, names out of the misty dawn of our field: Aladra Septama, Ed Earl Repp, Henry J. Kostkos, Captain S.P. Meek, U.S.A, .

We are given both the pluses and the minuses of each story: "The concept of the fighting suits is excellent and is well handled, otherwise the story is confused, overplotted, and unconvincing." ..."The first portion of the story is interesting, but then Miller loses control into a mass of absurdities."..."In the hands of a capable author, this might have been an interesting story." *The Bleilers have actually read all this stuff!* And they do arouse one's interest, at least mine, in taking a look (for the first time in fifty years) at such forgotten tales as Francis Flagg's "The Mentanicals" (1934), Paul Slachta's "The Twenty-First Century Limited" (1929), or Edward L. Rementer's "The Time Deflector" (1929).

In fact I did go downstairs just now and haul out the August-September 1933 issue of *Amazing Stories* in all its pink and purple ancient splendor for a look at Henry J. Kostkos's "Meteor Men of Plaa," famous even in its own day for sheer awfulness and revived in my memory a couple of decades ago by the critic Damon Knight, who had come upon it again and who could not refrain from repeatedly speaking its title aloud with dramatic inflection and unforgettable facial expression. Damon's delight in this story was not unwarranted. Here's its gripping beginning:

> *Gordon Bancroft leaned his gaunt frame forward. "I tell you, George," he said in a voice that trembled with emotion, "this time I will not fail. When the new space flyer is compelted it will hurtle me into the neutrosphere as easily as you can carry a football for a touchdown. And who knows what strange creatures I may discover there?*
>
> *The scientist clasped and unclasped his long, sensitive fingers with an air of nervous preoccupation.....*

The Bleiler evaluation: "Low-grade material, almost juvenile." They *are* unsparing. Of one story we are told, "Possibly parodic; it is difficult to believe that the author could have been serious." Of another, a curt "Of no interest." Of another, "Below routine." And so on, one brutal and no doubt accurate dismissal after another.

Yet out of these magazines came the science fiction we know and love today. And, lest you get the idea that it was all woeful junk, I suggest you try to hunt up two valuable anthologies of the 1970s that should still be fairly easily available: Isaac Asimov's *Before the Golden Age* and Damon Knight's *Science Fiction of the 30s*. I would give priority to the Asimov, not only because it is bigger (986 pages to Knight's 467) but because it includes Isaac's own nostalgic and perceptive essay on each story, and because it gives so much greater emphasis to the first half of the 1930s, when the most characteristic work of this early period was done. But Knight's selection — skewed toward the later part of the decade — is invaluable too.

What these two anthologies show us is just how rich and original and stirring, even in its crudity, much of that early science fiction really was. There is a kind of innocence, of youthful purity, to these stories. Many of them, of course, are amateurish and silly. But not all. The best of them continue to hold rewards for readers, even now. And all of them, even the worst, have the merit of approaching the great themes of sf for the first time, undeflected by knowledge of how Heinlein handled that one in 1941, or Pohl in 1957, or the changes that Brunner or Silverberg rang on it ten or fifteen years after that.

We should preserve and cherish these pioneering stories. The Bleiler and Bleiler magnum opus has served to reawaken my appreciation of that ancestral period, immensely remote to most of you and prehistoric even to an old hand like me, when Gernsbackian science fiction, that rough but fascinating beast, was slouching toward Manhattan to be born. We ought not to despise our literary ancestors, nor even to mock them, for they not only showed us the way but had real virtues of their own. I'm grateful to the Bleilers for providing me with such a comprehensive and masterly guide to an era of our past that is quickly receding toward oblivion.

Asimov's Science Fiction, May 2003

Autographs

———

I DIDN'T WRITE ANY STORIES LAST SUMMER. I SPENT THE TIME signing my name.

Something like 7,000 times, as a matter of fact. That's 14,000 words, which is practically a novella, though not a very interesting one. (Nobody I know would want to read a novella the text of which ran "Robert Silverberg Robert Silverberg Robert Silverberg Robert Silverberg" for forty or fifty pages.) Easton Press wanted me to sign 5500 copies of my novel *Dying Inside* for a leather-bound edition they were putting out, and then there were 250 copies of the limited edition of my fantasy anthology *Legends* to do, and 250 more for its sf companion, *Far Horizons*, and then I went to the Worldcon and signed a lot more books there, and so it went. Nice for the ego, nice for the bank account, very hard on the fingers and wrist.

I suppose I must have done a couple of hundred thousand signatures over the nearly fifty years of my career, maybe more. It's reached the point where I tell people that *unsigned* copies of some of my earlier books must be worth more than autographed ones. And yet the requests keep coming. I sign when asked. It's a small enough thing to do. (The only problem I have is when people ask me to inscribe a book: "Do it 'to Steve,'" they often say. I prefer to write "*for* Steve," not "*to*." It's such a subtle distinction that I don't entirely understand it myself.)

Oddly, although I'm a book collector too, I've never had much interest in owning signed copies myself. Perhaps that indifference stems from the ease with which obtaining such things is available to me. I've frequently entertained other science fiction writers in my home, and vice versa. At the conventions, of course, I have ready access to droves of my colleagues. It would be no problem at all for me to haul out copies of their books and shove them at them. But I very rarely do. I'm not eager to carry lots of books with me to a convention, and in any case it seems somehow out of character, in a way that I can't quite explain, for me to ask a fellow pro for his signature.

I've done it now and then, though, when it's seemed appropriate to do so. It's left me with a nice feeling every time, a pleasant memento of a writer I admire who is also a valued friend. But I once *signed* an autograph that changed my entire life.

That was in Houston, Texas, in April of 1981. I was the featured speaker at a convention taking place at a local university, and did a noontime signing for a long line of students. Midway through the whole proceeding a petite young lady who did not seem at all like a Texan college student asked me to sign a copy of my short story collection, *Capricorn Games*. Something about her caught my interest; we began talking; I asked her if she might happen to be free for dinner that night. She wasn't, but we exchanged addresses anyway and kept in touch. Karen Haber was her name. I married her six years later.

Karen isn't an autograph collector either. When I asked her why she had come across town during her lunch hour to get mine, she explained that her birthday was the same as that of the protagonist of my story "Capricorn Games." The coincidence had amused her, and, seeing in the local paper that I was going to be in town, she had brought the book along to be signed. Little dreaming, etc....

My own autograph-collecting experiences, few and far between, have had less epochal consequences. But I cherish them all the same. As I mentioned a few months ago, when I was a fifteen-year-old fan I timidly asked famed editor John W. Campbell and veteran writer Will F. Jenkins to sign a copy of the March, 1950 issue of *Astounding Science Fiction* at a small convention in New York City. I still own it. Just a few years later I would sit in John Campbell's office, a newly fledged professional writer, while Will Jenkins, at Campbell's request, helped me rewrite a story that hadn't quite hit the mark.

Decades later, at a time of stress and fatigue and general boredom with science fiction, I announced very publicly that I was retiring from writing forever. But I went on buying books, anyway. At a convention in Los Angeles in 1975 — one of the first I attended after my retirement — I picked up an edition of Jack Williamson's *The Humanoids* that wasn't in my library. It's a book I have admired since I was a boy.

Jack Williamson, whom I've come to know very well, happened to be standing quite near me when I bought the book, and the opportunity seemed too good to pass up. So I turned impulsively to him and asked him to sign it, and he did — adding an inscription that made me blush at the time and which probably will enrich my estate by a thousand dollars or so above the $10 purchase price:

"For Bob Silverberg, who used to write great sf — trusting he'll do it again — with a vast admiration — Jack Williamson, LA 1975"

How I treasure that book! And how I sometimes wish I had done the same with other writer-friends of mine! Jack Williamson, who celebrated his 90th birthday last year, seems to intend to live forever. But Phil Dick, who surely would have scrawled something mad and unforgettable in a book had I only taken the trouble to ask him, is no longer available, nor Ted Sturgeon, nor Jim Blish, nor Fritz Leiber, nor Robert Heinlein....

Actually I do have some signed Heinlein books, but I got them on one bounce, so to speak. Near the end of his life, Heinlein turned hundreds of his unwanted foreign editions over to Charles Brown of *Locus* magazine, and Charles got Heinlein to sign every last one of them. I saw them one day at the *Locus* office and came away with a copy of *Die Gruenen Huegel der Erde* and one of the Israeli edition of *Stranger in a Strange Land*, both neatly inscribed, "Robert A. Heinlein." Maybe I *am* an autograph collector after all, at least a collector of the autographs of my favorite writers, and don't fully realize it.

I have just one signed Asimov book, too; and thereby hangs a tale. The book is *The Gods Themselves*. Isaac dedicated it to me, and courteously sent me an inscribed copy. The problem was that there was something I found offensive in his Asimovianly exuberant dedication, and my annoyance led me to ask him to delete it from future editions of the book. Which he did, though somewhat surprised and more than a little miffed. Eventually we patched the matter up, of course; but I feel strange even now as I look at the signature he had so flamboyantly written, not at all foreseeing the ungrateful response the dedication would draw from me.

Another of my favorite writers was Alfred Bester, and at a convention in the mid-1970s where he was guest of honor I picked up Bester's new book, saw him practically at my elbow, and handed it to him to sign. "For Bob from the vice-president of his fan club — Alfie" is what he wrote on the title page. To my surprise, he also *crossed out* the printed line "by Alfred Bester" just above it, explaining that doing that is an old British tradition. Maybe so; but he didn't do it in a signed Bester book from 1957 that I later happened to buy, not even knowing it was signed, from an old-time collector who had decided to disperse his library.

(I once crossed out someone else's autograph, though. This was at some convention around 1980, when I was standing in the hotel lobby talking with Harlan Ellison and someone came up to us with a program booklet for us to sign. Harlan signed first, his big bold jagged signature; and when the booklet was offered to me, the Devil inspired me to draw a line through Harlan's autograph before I signed my own. It's unique and valuable, I suppose: the only Ellison autograph in the world deleted by Robert Silverberg.)

I suspect I would have asked Henry Kuttner, who for half a century has been a personal idol of mine among science fiction writers, to sign a book for me if I had ever met him. But he lived in California and I lived then in New York, and he died very young, in 1958, six months before my first trip west. I mentioned my admiration of Kuttner once to Julius Schwartz, the living legend, who once was Kuttner's literary agent (and H.P. Lovecraft's, and,

I think, Edgar Allan Poe's), and Julie soon after sent me a Kuttner book from his own library that his friend Hank Kuttner had signed long before. (There was a second signature in the book — "Kat Kuttner" — better known to me as the fabulous C.L. Moore, Kuttner's wife and frequent collaborator.)

My collection of books, which is vast, is dotted here and there with dozens of other autographed volumes that I've acquired one way or another over the years. Christopher Priest put a nice couple of words in a book of his that I acquired at the Glasgow Worldcon. I missed out on buying one volume of Joe Haldeman's *Worlds* trilogy, and he sent me a copy with a lovely inscription in his splendid calligraphy. I replaced a copy of a Jack Vance book that I had lost in a fire, and the new copy had an autograph in it, which pleased me, because I admire Vance's work enormously and though he lives five minutes away from me and I see him frequently I have never asked him to sign a book. And I have a number of books that writers have sent to me unsolicited, inscribed, out of recognition of some aspect of my own work that influenced some aspect of theirs: the finest form of flattery for a writer.

I know which one of all my autographed books I prize most highly, though.

About fifteen years ago my dear friend Jerry Mundis, who was staying with me as a house guest, whiled away the late hours of the night reading my copy of Herman Melville's *Moby Dick* — the Modern Library paperback edition that I had owned in college in the 1950s. After Jerry left, I found the book lying on the library table, and before putting it back on the shelf I glanced idly through it. Jerry had playfully added one little touch of improvement on the inside front cover, an inscription that read:

"To Bob with respect and admiration — Herman."

A pity I don't have any grandchildren. I wonder what they'd have made of that one when they found it in my library.

Asimov's Science Fiction, **October–November 1999**

E-mail From Cthulhu

I HAVE NEVER BEEN A PARTICULARLY ADVENTURE-SOME COMPUTER USER. I've been using them for twenty years, but because I was — unlike a lot of you — somewhat past twelve when I got my first computer, I don't have computer skills hard-wired into my reflexes. So when I find a set of specifications and preferences that will make my computer do what I need it to do, I resist making experimental changes in my settings in the hope of "improving" things, for fear that if the improvements turn out to be counter-improvements I won't be able to find my way back to what worked for me before. I just leave well enough alone, at least until circumstances like terminal equipment failure force me to get a new computer, and that doesn't happen often.

Sometimes, though, changes in settings happen anyway, unintended though they may be. That occurred recently on the venerable MS-DOS-based computer that I still use for the bulk of my writing work: I was keying things in more quickly than I should have, inadvertently brought up the settings page that controlled the printer, and changed one of the settings (but which one?) before I could halt my own keystroke. For a while it seemed as though I had permanently interrupted communication between my computer and my equally ancient printer, but eventually I was able to retrace my steps, laboriously figure out what I had done, and undo it.

But then there's the other computer, the relatively modern Windows 98 one that I use for e-mail and Internet surfing. I never change any settings on that one, either. But sometimes, while I sleep, Windows 98 goes to work within the switched-off machine and alters the settings itself, changing them to ones that it thinks I would find more enjoyable. Thus, one morning, I brought up an e-mail from a friend dating from the day before, so that I could check something in my response to her, and discovered that this was how her message now read:

Nun! Gung-f jung V jnf tbvat gryy lbh–fb ibh qba'g unir gb pnyy zr. V gba'g unir "Fpenzoyr" nf n evtug-pyvpx bcgvba, ohg v gb unir "Fbeg" naq bgure cbgragvny gencf sbe gur.

And then came my reply:

Purphxrq mlg gur evhtug-pyvpxre nag glurer'f na "Hafpenzoyr" bcgvboa va guglr zrah. V q'ba'g frr "Fpenzoyr" ohg vg zhfg or hgur-er fbzjurer.

Bemused, baffled, and more than a little alarmed, I checked all the other e-mails stored on my computer. They had all been translated into the same language — a language that I instantly recognized as the one used by H.P. Lovecraft's Elder Gods, a group of which the dread Cthulhu is the pre-eminent deity. This, from Lovecraft's story "The Call of Cthulhu," is a typical example of that language:

Ph'nglui mglw'nafh Cthulhu R'Lyeh wgah'ngagl fhtagn.

The etymological kinship is obvious. But how had it come to pass that my e-mails had been translated overnight into Cthulhuese? Had the Elder Gods taken control of my computer? Were they passing messages back and forth among themselves behind my back like some primordial band of Al Qaeda desperadoes?

I began wandering through the "preferences" section of my e-mail software, looking for the answer, and eventually I discovered a scrambling function that, when checked, obligingly garbles all the e-mail kept on the computer. It has no effect on outgoing e-mail, but transforms all the stored stuff into Cthulhu-language so that the guy in the next cubicle, if he somehow gains access to my computer, won't be able to pore through the secret business information I keep among my old e-mails.

However, I don't work in an office full of corporate spies. The guy in the next cubicle is my wife, Karen, and she's free to read my e-mail any time. There's nothing there that will lead her to steal business contacts from me — or to make her want to run for a divorce lawyer, either. So I clicked on the "scramble" option to get rid of it and all the e-mail on the machine returned to normal. End of story.

Except the idea of e-mail from Cthulhu got me thinking —

Cthulhu's creator, H.P. Lovecraft, was one of the most prolific correspondents of all time. Though he lived only forty-seven years (1890-1937), his published letters fill five or six volumes of very small type — and those are just the ones that survived. Extremely verbose letters they are, too. I open

Volume Two of his Selected Letters at random and find his missive of Oct. 26, 1926, to his fellow fantasy writer, Frank Belknap Long, which starts this way:

"Young Man:

"In replying to your keenly appreciated communication, I must begin in something of my old-time travelogical vein; for the past week has witnessed in a pilgraimage [sic] on my part, more impressive than any I can recall taking in years. This excursion, on which I was accompany'd by my youngest daughter, Mrs. Gamwell, was to these rural reaches of Rhode-Island from whence our stock is immediately sprung; and is design'd to be the first of several antiquarian and genealogical trips covering the Phillips-Place-Tyler-Rathbone-Howard country, and including inspection of as many of the original colonial homesteads as are yet standing. . . ."

And so on in studiedly archaic style for nine printed pages. A lot of the letters are like that. If the irrepressibly communicative Lovecraft had saved the energy expended in all that correspondence to use in his fiction, he would have left us nine Tolkien-sized trilogies. What if he had had e-mail instead? E-mail users tend to be laconic indeed. A paragraph-long query from a friend gets an "I don't think so" response, or, "I sent it last Tuesday," or maybe just "LOL" — but never the kind of flowery and elaborate multi-page exposition that Lovecraft loved to send. We just key in our quick replies, leaving the original queries in place so we don't have to bother explaining what we're responding to, and hit the "send" button. Presto jingo, our reply has crossed the world. A book of Lovecraft's collected e-mails, if there could have been such a thing, would probably be dull stuff indeed, clipped and cryptic little bits of commentary, irrelevant and incomprehensible to any outsider. But we would have those nine trilogies.

Another formidable generator of correspondence was the late, great editor John W. Campbell, Jr. (1910-1971), who was known to answer an author's three-paragraph sketch of a potential story idea with a ten-page essay. His letters have been collected and published, too — only one six-hundred-page volume ever appeared, though many more were intended — and this, a letter of December 6, 1952 to Poul Anderson, is a typical example:

"Dear Poul:

"The trouble with historians is that they'd rather be traditional than be right. It's practically axiomatic; the guy wouldn't be a historian if he weren't all wrapped up and deeply reverent about the traditions of man. There are exceptions, of course — but they're exceptional, and kept well under control by the Traditional Authorities.

"If you think I'm kidding on that, you're wrong. I know whereof I speak.

"Item: Wallace West, scf writer, is also a professional history text writer. But he's a researcher, and not a traditionalist. He dug up some papers which quoted Washington and Jefferson, separately, as saying that our constitution was based largely on the constitution of the Iroquois Nations, as originally drawn up by Hiawatha, the truly great American statesman. . . ."

Campbell's explanation of Wallace West's ideas led him quickly to an analysis of the fall of Rome, the rise of Islamic science, the repression of Galileo by the Church, the development of civilization in the Nile valley, and, six pages later, the position of the electron in the hydrogen molecule. What Poul Anderson made out of all that, we will now never know. But if John only had the use of e-mail, think of the effort he would have been spared! "Story's all wrong, Poul. Go back and read Spengler again. Best, John." And on to the next rejection slip in two clicks of the Campbellian mouse.

Perhaps not, though. Perhaps Lovecraft and Campbell would have been just as assiduous in their e-mail correspondence as they were in their conventional letters. And perhaps they would have fallen into e-correspondence with each other. They were, after all, contemporaries during the late years of Lovecraft's career and the early ones of Campbell's, and the interconnectivity of the wired world brings everyone, sooner or later, into contact with everyone else. So those Collected Letters volumes might include material like this, if only their authors had lived a little longer:

> "Dear John: Do you ever happen to hear the sounds of rats moving in your walls? Beneath the cellar floor?"

> "Dear Howard: Ron Hubbard has developed a fabulous new science-based therapy of the mind that I think you would find of great help in treating your condition. . . ."

Wondrous to contemplate, yes.

And then, the Collected E-mails of Philip K. Dick — what a trail of berserkery there! — and the Collected Rejection Slips of the vitriolic editor H.L. Gold, as terse as haiku and infinitely more crushing —

And there is one Harlan Ellison of Sherman Oaks, California, who actually has lived on into the era of e-mail, but has sworn a mighty oath never to use it. Harlan's correspondence is often, well, rather vigorous in its phraseology. (Our executive editor prefers that I don't quote of it here, alas, to avoid getting embroiled in litigation with Mr. Ellison's correspondents.) Perhaps it's just as well he doesn't use e-mail. He could crash whole strings of servers with a single click.

Asimov's Science Fiction, January, 2003

The Great Whale Hunt

CALL ME ISHMAEL. CALL HER SEASICK.

Intelligent non-humanoid mammals of gigantic size undertake a migration across the face of our planet every year in my part of the world. Nothing more than a couple of miles of ice-cold ocean separates their migration route from the town where I live. The fact that such extraordinary beings do actually share our very own world with us is fascinating to someone like me who has spent most of his life *inventing* non-humanoid life forms, and I've long wanted to get a close look at them, and last week I finally did. As did my wife Karen, though I don't think she enjoyed the experience quite as much as I did.

I'm talking about the gray whale of the California coast. Their scientific name is *Rachianectes glaucus*, which means "gray rocky-shore swimmer," and that is precisely what they are. They spend their summers high up in the North Pacific in the Bering and Chukchi Seas. As the days dwindle down toward winter, they hit the road, one tribe migrating down the east coast of Asia toward Korea, the rest going down the west coast of North America as far as Baja California, a stupendous maritime journey of some 7,000 miles. They bring forth their young down there, in the deepest days of winter, and start up the coast again in January, escorting their cute little fifteen-foot-long newborns back to the icy waters of the far north.

This whole migration takes place, as their Latin name implies, in the shallow waters of the Pacific coast. No other whale comes so close to shore as the gray, which (so I'm told) sometimes will rest in a mere two feet of water along a beach at low tide. Not only do they like to feed on krill and amphipods, tiny shrimp-like creatures that live in the vast beds of the giant seaweed kelp growing just off shore, but they make use of the shoreline rocks to scratch their hides, which are thickly covered with barnacles and other free-loading boarders and are, consequently, extremely itchy.

Because they swim so close to shore, they are reputedly easy to see from the coastal headlands. Gregory Benford, whose home is on a Southern California hillside within easy view of the sea, has told me of watching them with the aid of binoculars through his front windows. I haven't been so lucky. For the past twenty-five years I've been trying to catch a glimpse of gray whales, just one snippety little glimpse, as I drive up and down the California coast in winter, and I've not seen nary a one, matey, nary a one. I've parked on the coastal bluffs and stood staring out to sea for half an hour at a time without any luck at all.

Then, too, I've gone looking for them right in their spawning grounds in Baja California. Baja, as we locals fondly call the long, skinny peninsula that sprouts from the continent just across the Mexican border from San Diego, is (if you like deserts, and I do) a wondrously picturesque place, and about twenty years ago I traversed it from one end to the other, a thousand miles of cactus and other botanical weirdities. Midway down the Pacific side of Baja is Scammon's Lagoon, which is not in any way picturesque — it's a bleak, grim, barren place, cold and windy and raw in winter — but winter is when two thousand gray whales snuggle up in the lagoon to bear their young. Naturally, I went to have a look one February, imagining I would see whales galore, some of them doing the spectacular maneuver known as "breaching" — jumping clear out of the water — and others, at least, "spy-hopping," lifting their heads straight up into view. But something was malfunctioning about the whale migration that year, because the lagoon was empty of cetaceans when I arrived, and after a couple of shivery hours I gave up and went away, utterly unsatisfied.

And brooded about the whole whale thing for years thereafter, until, not long ago, Karen came upon news of a San Francisco outfit called Ocean Society Expeditions, which for a piddling two-figure sum would take us out into the Pacific in a 56-foot motor vessel and, if whales happened to be in the vicinity, bring us right up close to them. So we signed up, despite my glum feeling that I had bad whale karma and that not even this was going to work.

Our boat departed from Pillar Point Harbor, just north of Half Moon Bay on the glorious and still pretty wild-looking Northern California coast. There were perhaps thirty fellow whale-seekers on board. It was a splendid March day, well along in spring in these parts, sunny and clear, the temperature up in the high sixties. But because the Pacific is a very *very* chilly ocean, we had been warned to dress warmly, and there I was, sweltering and miserable in unaccustomed sweatshirt with a windbreaker over it, with Karen beside me in layer upon layer of stuff. Five minutes after we left the harbor, I was glad of it: out there in the actual ocean the air was cold and the breeze was brisk, and I began to wish I had brought a pair of gloves along too.

It's a lovely ocean, the Pacific. It's remarkably large, too, and as the doughty *Salty Lady* went zooming across the billowing waves in search of gray whales I began to think that this was very much like a needle-in-a-haystack kind of operation. All this water; so few whales: how would we ever find one?

Fifteen very chilly minutes went by and I began to feel sure that this would be just one more goddamn wild-whale-chase. Just at that moment our jolly captain announced that he had spotted two whales off the starboard bow. Walk, don't run, he warned, as we all crowded hastily toward starboard, fumbling for our binoculars and cameras and stuff.

Where off starboard, though? We looked this way and that, crying out in erroneous joy at waves and logs and other things. And then we saw the whales. Their vast backs, anyway: ancient, corroded barnacle-covered backs, more mottled-brown than gray, poking briefly up above the surface before they slid from view. We cruised alongside them for perhaps twenty minutes, watching them dive, rise, blow, surface, dive again. One of them obligingly did a headstand, displaying, for a moment, its two huge tail-flukes. Other than that, all we saw was a bit of barnacled back every now and then. But that was plenty.

Gray whales aren't the biggest of their kind, by any means. They generally get no more than forty-five feet in length. (The blue whale, the largest species, averages ninety feet or so.) Nor are they particularly long-lived, however ancient all those barnacles made them seem. Apparently they live thirty to forty years, which I would find a very long lifespan indeed if I had to spend it swimming back and forth in the icy Pacific.

But they *looked* ancient. They looked wise and majestic and wonderful. Even if all I could see of them was a flash of massive back a couple of hundred yards away, it was awesome enough merely to be in the presence of these beings.

And I knew how lucky I was that they were here to be seen at all, if only in glimpses. They used to exist in great numbers in the Pacific, but a fifty-year whale-hunt that began in 1846 saw most of them very efficiently killed for their oil (a large one who had fattened himself up for the southward migration might yield seventy barrels). By 1895 they were thought to be extinct, at least along our coast. But about 100 members of the Korean-wintering segment of the tribe had survived, and gradually they repopulated our end of the Pacific as well. The decline of the San Francisco-based whaling industry, coupled with the coming of modern conservationist legislation (hunting gray whales has been banned since 1937), allowed them to regenerate; there may be as many as 20,000 of them today.

We watched our two until they swam so close to shore, perhaps in need of immediate backscratching, that our boat could not safely follow. For the next hour or so we wandered the offshore waters looking for others. Some of the glow of our triumphant whale-finding began to dwindle during that long and increasingly chilly hour. I am not a patient man at best, and there was nothing much to do aboard the *Salty Lady* except to peer at the Pacific and hope for the thrill of spotting the next whale before our skipper did. And Karen, I discovered, was getting seasick.

I am not susceptible to seasickness, which is more precisely known as "motion sickness." This is not because I am an unusually rugged and virile human being, but merely because the membranous labyrinth of my inner ear, which has charge of my equilibrium, does not react as vociferously to sudden shifts in body position as do the labyrinths of some other people's inner ears. Karen's, for example. So, while I fretted in my restless fashion and wandered the deck looking for ways to keep warm, Karen grew steadily quieter and greener and quieter and greener. "Is something wrong?" I asked, finally, in my sensitive masculine way. "Yes," she said. "I'm seasick." Since I've never had that malady, I had forgotten, in my sensitive, masculine way, that other people sometimes do. I had brought a flask of rum with me to see me through the coldest part of the voyage. "Will this help?" I asked. "No," she said.

But then the captain said, "We're in the middle of a big pod of whales, folks," and color returned to Karen's cheeks and the camera to her hands, and there we all were, again, crowding the bow to stare in wonder at the gigantic non-humanoid life-forms thronging the sea about us, half a dozen this time. One came rushing right toward us, staging a spectacular dive, flukes all aflap, just as I began wondering whether our captain's middle name might be Ahab. We had another twenty minutes of astonishing cetacean diversion.

And then the whales went away and the *Salty Lady* headed for shore and soon we were warm and dry again, and in our car and heading for the nearby city of San Mateo, where we enjoyed spaghetti and red wine in the company of good friends, options that were not readily available to Starbuck and Queequeg and Ishmael and the rest of that crowd.

Our great whale hunt had some dull moments, and some chilly ones, and, for some of us, some icky green-faced ones. But it provided, also, that grand sense of knowing that We Are Not Alone on this world, that we share it with some noble and astonishing warm-blooded creatures of great size and, apparently, high intelligence. I'm glad to have paid a call on them at long last.

Asimov's Science Fiction, **January 1998**

Making Backups

I WAS THE YOUNGEST BOY IN MY ELEMENTARY SCHOOL CLASS, and when I became a professional science fiction writer in 1955 I was for a long time the youngest writer in the business. I am still the youngest writer ever to win a Hugo, for Most Promising New Writer in 1956. All that precocity has left its imprint on me. I continue to tend to think of myself as younger than I am, even though that Hugo, you will note, came to me exactly fifty years ago, and a glance in the mirror is enough to remind me that I am no longer in the first flush of youth. I am, in fact, a man of grandfatherly years, and as a writer I'm a kind of survivor from the Pleistocene, old enough to have been a contributor to the last few shaggy-edged pulp magazines.

There are, of course, still plenty of sf writers around who were already famous when I was just a kid, and who now, in their eighties, are still turning out books and stories. Just last year I was on a panel with three of them — Frederik Pohl, Phil Klass (William Tenn), and Harry Harrison — at the World Science Fiction Convention in Glasgow, and for that one shining hour, sitting among those sprightly codgers, I felt like a boy again.

But I'm *not* a boy. I've had one of the longest careers around, and I'm old enough to remember typewriters, and carbon paper, and manila envelopes, three of the primitive implements that were essential tools of the trade for writers when I was starting out. When, at a more recent sf convention, I found myself explaining to someone what typewriters actually were like, I got a vivid jolting sense of how much the technology of professional writing has been transformed since my earliest days in the business.

The typewriter, for instance: I still keep mine sitting on a side desk in my office as a sort of museum piece. I bought it in 1968, because I needed a new one to replace the one I lost in a fire that wrecked my home that year, but it's essentially identical to the one I was using when I won that first Hugo in 1956. It's a German-made item, an Olympia: a big sturdy box-shaped object with a keyboard that looks something like a computer keyboard, a roller-plus-knobs thingy that allows you to insert a sheet of paper, and a chrome-plated lever on one side that you pull to advance the paper when you've reached the end of the line. A little bell goes "ping" to tell you that it's lever-pulling time. Since each line you typed contained about ten words, and we were usually paid by the word then, each "ping" announced that the writer would earn a dime at the bottom rate of a cent a word, twenty cents if his story was going to a two-cent-a-word market, thirty cents if it sold to *Astounding* or *Galaxy*, the two top-paying magazines.

Some writers of the Fifties used electric typewriters, but mine was the manual kind. The electrics, though they required less muscle-power, made an annoying hum, two or three times as loud as the hum that computers make today, and I found that too distracting. I also was in the habit of resting my fingers on the keys while thinking, and some electrics had such jackrabbit calibration that it was all too easy to type a whole string of unwanted letters during a pause of that sort. Which was a problem, because you didn't just back up your cursor and get rid of such unwanted letters then: they were permanently there, marring the paper you were typing on.

Of course, it was hard work banging away on a manual typewriter, and my refusal to switch to an electric seemed a little quaint to some of my colleagues. But, what the hell, I was young then and had plenty of energy, and in a perverse way I *enjoyed* the physical demands of pounding on the keyboard. (The only writer I know who still uses a manual typewriter is Harlan Ellison. He isn't exactly young any more either, but he's mighty stubborn.)

One big problem we had, back then, was the riskiness of depending on typed copy. Today's computer-using writers can back up each day's work on diskettes, or ZIP drives, or any one of a number of other sophisticated data-storage devices, or they can simply e-mail it to a web site that will store it for them. The closest we could come to making backups back then was to use carbon paper, a messy substance that you slipped between two sheets of conventional typing paper: as you hit the typewriter keys, the impact on the carbon-paper sheet in the middle of the sandwich created a more or less legible duplicate of what you were typing on the sheet below. This gave you an identical copy that you could store in some place other than where you were keeping your primary copy.

That system didn't work so well if you were the sort of writer who typed out a first draft, revised it by hand, and then retyped the whole shebang (or had it retyped professionally) for submission to a publisher. First-draft writing involves a lot of second thoughts as you work; you rephrase stuff, crossing out earlier rejected versions, and sometimes striking out whole paragraphs or even pages. I often wound up with only four or five lines of useful copy on a page. Doing that when you were using two sheets of paper at a time was wasteful and expensive, something to consider in the days when a five-thousand-word story might bring a writer fifty dollars, before taxes. It was also a nuisance when you were zooming along through a first draft in the white heat of creation to pause at the end of every page and assemble a new paper-plus-carbon-paper sandwich. And when you worked over your typed first draft by hand, the changes you made didn't automatically turn up on the carbon copy — you had to inscribe them there too, separately, if you wanted to keep an accurate backup version of your current draft. If you didn't, you risked the loss of all your revisions if something happened to your one and only copy of the manuscript, and I heard plenty of horror stories from my colleagues of just such losses.

Making a photocopy of each day's work would have been a neat solution. Ah, but photocopiers didn't come into general use until the 1960s, and when they did they were the size of SUVs and cost thousands of dollars. Large companies could own them, but not the average science fiction writer. (I bought my first photocopier somewhere around 1980, a huge, expensive thing that was maddening to use. It too is a museum-piece in my office today; I use it as the table on which my nifty pint-sized modern copier sits.)

When I was writing *Lord Valentine's Castle* in 1978, a long, complex novel on which I was essentially gambling the whole economic future of my career, one thing that caused me no little concern was the possibility that a fire or earthquake might destroy my precious copy of my ongoing draft somewhere during the many months of composition. (This was not quite as irrational as it may sound; only ten years before, remember, I had had that fire in my previous house that sent me out into the middle of the night with the half-finished manuscript of my latest book under my arm. And now that I had moved to California, I was living about a thousand yards from one of the most dangerous earthquake faults in the state.) So what I did was store my first-draft copy in a small disused refrigerator in my office, which I hoped might protect it against fire, and every time I finished a hundred pages or so I took them down to the office where my ex-wife was working and had her use the company machine to run off two or three photocopies, which I would store in various places on and off the premises. The process took an hour or so.

It sounds like a ghastly system. It was. But that was how we went about making backups as recently as 1978. Eventually, of course, you finished the first draft. But most first drafts are too messy to show to a publisher, so the whole thing (650 pages in the case of *Lord Valentine's Castle*) had to be re-typed. I could have hired a typist to prepare a submission draft for me, but I liked to revise even while retyping, so I did it all myself, at a pace of some twenty pages a day — more than a month to retype the whole thing.

Then, of course, the manuscript had to go to the agent or book publisher in New York. Today we e-mail them in: instantaneous, inexpensive. But e-mail, in 1978? Don't be silly. We used the U.S. Postal Service to get our copy to New York. You stuffed your paper manuscript into a manila envelope that you hoped was sturdy enough to hold together on its journey across the country, stuck the postage on it (and, if you were submitting a short story to a magazine, usually enclosed another manila envelope with an equal amount of postage on it so you could get your manuscript back in case the story was rejected) and, muttering a prayer or two, sent it off. Five, six, seven days later it reached its destination, if all went well. (We didn't use FedEx. FedEx didn't exist yet either.)

To modern writers it must seem appalling, and I suppose it was. But we had no alternatives in that ancient era. Ray Bradbury and Arthur C. Clarke and Robert A. Heinlein and Isaac Asimov all wrote and submitted their stories and books that way — typewriter, carbon paper, manila envelope, post office — and so did I. Then came computers, and everything changed. By then, I had come to hate the typewriter with a terrible passion, having followed *Valentine* with an even longer novel that required close to three months of retyping to produce a final draft, and in 1982 I bought myself a state-of-the-art computer with a gigantic 10-megabyte hard disk so that future final drafts could be generated just by telling the thing to print one for me. Nearly all the other writers of the typewriter era made the same changeover sooner or later, and those horrible old days seem like nothing more than a bad dream today.

I am, by now, behind the curve once again. After acquiring all the usual gadgets of the era I seem to have contracted gizmo fatigue in this very electronic new century, and I upgrade my computer only when I'm absolutely forced to by the obsolescence of the systems I use. (Isaac Asimov was like that too. He had a modest sort of computer toward the end, but he never even owned a fax machine, and I doubt very much that he'd be an e-mail user if he were alive today.) So I limp along with Windows 98, I have not acquired any of the snazzy new computer accessories of the past five years, and I still use diskettes for my backups. None of that is a problem for me. I'm not all that active as a writer these days, and my current computer setup is good enough for my needs, however laughable it must seem to the likes of today's writers. If I were thirty-five instead of seventy-plus, no doubt I'd install a zorch port and a frammis storage unit just as they have. But I'm content with my equipment. Zorches and frammises will seem ludicrously obsolete ten years from now, so why, say I, bother to learn how to use them? And to anyone who remembers typewriters and carbon paper and sending in typewritten manuscripts by first class mail, the system I use seems downright miraculous as it stands. Yearning to improve on miracles seems to me like tempting the vengeance of the gods.

Asimov's Science Fiction, **October/November, 2006**

Problems Of Time Travel

YESTERDAY I MADE MY HOTEL RESERVATION FOR THIS YEAR'S World Science Fiction Convention in Philadelphia, which is still four months in my future as I write this, but happened a few months ago on the time-line of people reading this issue. And, probably not by coincidence, I dreamed last night that I had traveled back in time to the very first Worldcon I ever attended — also in Philadelphia, in 1953 — and was at it in two identities at once, that of my original 18-year-old self and that of my current 66-year-old self as well.

The idea was so strange that the dream awakened me in a state of bemusement, and I spent the next two hours unwillingly pondering the problems that such an event would create, when I would much rather have finished out my night's sleep.

The first problem I considered was what identity to use for my senior self. I was already registered, under the name of "Bob" Silverberg, as member #148 of the convention. Nothing would prevent me, really, from buying a second membership and walking around the convention with a nametag that proclaimed me to be "Robert" Silverberg. Although I attract plenty of attention at modern conventions when I walk around with my Robert Silverberg nametag on, no one would have paid any attention to the elderly man with the white beard who bore that name at the 1953 convention. The boy who called himself "Bob Silverberg" then was well known in the pages of the amateur science fiction magazines, and a few readers of the professional magazines would recognize the name because of the letters I had had published in their letter columns; but I had yet to sell my first professional story as of September 5, 1953, the Philcon's first day, and in the context of the era I was very far from being any sort of celebrity.

What, though, if some shrewd person noticed the similarity of names? Someone, say, like that smart-aleck kid from Cleveland, Harlan Ellison, who just happened to be my roommate at that convention? I could see him doing a double take at the sight of the old guy who had the same name as his pal from New York. He would study the old guy's eyes, his nose, the way he tended to smile without parting his lips. The resemblance — once you factored out the thinning gray hair and the white beard — would strike him as remarkable.

"What are you, his grandfather?" he would ask.

"No," I would say, truthfully enough. (My Silverberg grandfather was not named Robert, and he was long dead as of 1953, anyway.)

"His father, then?"

"Well, no, not that either." (My father, Michael Silverberg, was at home in New York right then, a youngish man of fifty-two.)

"Well, then, who the hell are you? You've *got* to be some relative of his!"

You see the difficulty.

Another complication I foresaw had to do with my ability to pay for things. Not that the expense of the convention would be beyond my present self — the cost of a hotel room was something like ten or twelve dollars a night, then, and meals were even more laughably inexpensive. But what would I use for money? Credit cards hadn't been invented yet. And the bills in my wallet probably wouldn't do me much good, either. I'm looking at some of the new-style twenty and fifty-dollar bills with me right now, the kind that are full of blank space and seem like fakes even to us twenty-first-century citizens. No hotel desk clerk worth his $50 weekly pay would have accepted one then. And even if I had had some bills of the 1990s with me, not greatly different from those of forty years earlier, there was always the risk that the little line "Series 1995," or whatever, would bring unpleasant remarks if a sharp-eyed 1953 restaurateur happened to notice it.

I would have to borrow money, I decided, from professional writers at the convention, my future friends and colleagues. That would mean confessing my identity as a time traveler to them and swearing them to secrecy.

Frank M. Robinson, for instance. My boyhood self really did meet Frank at that convention, starting a friendship that has lasted close to half a century now. I would go up to him and explain that I came from the year 2001, and whisper a few things to him that no stranger could possibly know about him, even one who was wearing a "Robert Silverberg" nametag. And I'd hit him for ten or twenty bucks, promising to pay him back in a year or two in Cleveland or New York.

"Why those places?" he would ask.

"Because the next two Worldcons we'll attend together will be in Cleveland and New York," I'd say, walking away leaving him dumbfounded.

Then I'd go up to the formidable L. Sprague de Camp — something that my younger self would never have dared to do. I'd let him in on my secret, and prove it by giving him a capsule history of the years 1954-1980, including not only global political events but details of his still unwritten next novel. That would convince him: Sprague, the world traveler, would have loved to believe that time travel was possible. I'd borrow fifty from him. And then I'd give him a more than ample recompense by saying, "By the way, you ought to buy stock in Merck, Pfizer, General Electric, and Standard Oil of New Jersey and hold it for the rest of your life." (I didn't mention Microsoft, because Bill Gates hadn't yet been born in 1953.) "Oh, and you may also like to know that you and Catherine are both going to live to be 92 years old."

I'd borrow ten more from Harry Harrison, who had just bought an article from my other self for his magazine *Science Fiction Adventures,* and another twenty from Lester del Rey. ("Alfie Bester will win the Hugo for best novel on Sunday," I'll tell him. "*Astounding* and *Galaxy* will tie for best magazine. You wait and see.") I think that would have done it, though if necessary I'd have clinched my identity by telling him some inside stuff about his best friends of the era. And that would take care of my financial difficulties.

Then I'd be free to wander around the convention with the other 700 attendees. (Worldcons were a lot smaller in those days. Everything took place under the roof of a single hotel, rather than extending into a gigantic convention center next door.)

One thing I would take care to do would be to keep my distance from that kid Bob Silverberg. He was having the time of his life at his first Worldcon, and I wouldn't want to deflect him from his day-by-day timeline by imposing upon him the weird knowledge that his 66-year-old self was at the con too. I'd watch him out of the corner of my eye, of course, that kid with the crewcut, wearing the Ivy League uniform of khaki slacks and white buck shoes, as he encountered for the first time all the people who would be such a huge part of his life in the decades ahead. But I wouldn't let him see me — not that he'd have been likely to guess who I was, bearded and gray as I am, because he would be accustomed to seeing our face only as the mirror image of the one we actually have. And not even he would have suspected that his self of 48 years to come was at the convention.

The beard might cause some raised eyebrows around the convention hall, though. The writer Fletcher Pratt wore a beard, then, but hardly anyone else did in those days. Sprague de Camp was yet to grow his. The same, I think, with Theodore Sturgeon. Avram Davidson wasn't there. My beard would probably excite some worrisome curiosity. Who *was* this obviously distinguished old guy, anyway? What is he doing here?

My age would have seemed unusual, too. These were still the early years of science fiction in the United States: it was a young guy's game. Isaac Asimov was 33 years old in 1953; John W. Campbell, 43; Sturgeon, 35; Robert Sheckley (the hot new writer of the year), 25; Frederik Pohl, 34; de Camp, 46. The venerable Fletcher Pratt was 56. Willy Ley, the inexhaustible space travel propagandist who was that year's Guest of Honor, was just 47. ("Willy," I would tell him, "we're going to land on the moon in 1969 — I guarantee it." What I wouldn't tell him was that he was destined to die a few weeks too soon to see it happen.) Even Hugo Gernsback, the founder of the whole American sf industry and the man for whom the Hugo awards were named, was only 69 years old then. (He wasn't at the convention.) A man of my present years would have been an oddly conspicuous figure at the 1953 Philcon.

But I'd have managed. I'd have spent an interesting weekend skulking around, attending the program events, oddly skimpy by today's three-ring circus standards. (Willy Ley talking about rockets, Philip José Farmer about sex, Fletcher Pratt about robots, and five or six other things, including what was probably the first appearance of the "Women in Science Fiction" panel soon to become a fixture of these conventions.)

And then, right at the end of it all, I'd go up to my other self, who by then would be pretty well exhausted, since, as I remember only too well, he got something like ten hours of sleep throughout the entire weekend. I would point out our facial resemblance. I would show him the little scar on the back of my left hand. If need be, I would tell him a couple of things about himself that no one but he and I were aware of. And then, as he stood there gaping and goggling, I would say, "Listen to me, kiddo, you're going be famous beyond belief. All your teenage fantasies are going to come true, every single one. You'll sell hundreds of short stories and dozens of novels. You'll win a whole shelf of Hugos and Nebulas."

"Nebulas? What are they?"

"You'll find out in 1965. Oh, and five years after that you're going to be Worldcon Guest of Honor yourself."

"I *will?*"

"As sure as my name is Silverberg," I said. Then I'd give him the most important bit of information of all. "Starting around 1956, kid, you're going to be making a lot of money. Buy blue-chip stocks with it and put them away for your retirement. Write down these names: Merck, Pfizer, Standard Oil of New Jersey, General Electric...."

Asimov's Science Fiction, **June 2002**

Two Worldcons, Worlds Apart

IN A FEW MONTHS THE WORLD SCIENCE FICTION CONVENTION will returns to the British Isles; and, Lord willing, so will I, forty-eight years after my first visit to that green and pleasant land.

I think I know what I can expect from the 2005 Worldcon that is to be held soon in Glasgow — an experience much like the one I had at the first Glasgow Worldcon ten years before, only rather more so. My recollections of Glasgow in 1995 include a pleasant stay on the nineteenth floor of the lofty Hilton Hotel, a bit of whiskey in my breakfast oatmeal and haggis for lunch, a daily jaunt across town to the shimmering, glassy convention center, and having, amid the great throngs of convention-goers, old friends and new, a whirlwind series of encounters not only with British fans and writers but with delegates from former Soviet-bloc countries like Latvia and Poland and the Czech Republic and Ukraine, and visitors from Russia itself, all of them still rarities in the early post-Communist years. At the end of the day there was dinner in one of Glasgow's superb restaurants, and a party at one of the hotels, and perhaps a drop or two of the single malt before bedtime. This time, I suppose, everything will be bigger, shinier, throngier, whirlwindier. I do hope to stay at the Hilton again and to find that the single-malt product is still available, and I will gladly sit down to dine on haggis when the opportunity is presented.

One thing is sure, though: whatever the 2005 Glasgow convention will be like, it won't be remotely similar to the first British Worldcon of all, the one that was held in London in September of 1957. That convention now seems to have taken place in some alternate universe. Those of you whose Worldcon experience is confined to the last ten or fifteen such events would be flabbergasted by the differences between a modern con and that primordial one.

We can start with the attendance figures. I have attended all five of the previous British Worldcons, and I must be one of just ten or twenty people who can make that claim, because there were merely 268 people present at that first one in 1957. (268 attendees, yes: not a typographical error. There will be individual panels at the upcoming Glasgow affair, or autographing lines for the more popular pros, that will have more people than that in attendance.) Attrition of one kind or another must have claimed most of those 268 along the way, and those of us who remember the quaint event out in Leinster Gardens are growing very sparse by now.

Quaint is the right word for it. The venue was the Kings Court Hotel, a very modest affair of Victorian or Edwardian vintage a mile west of Marble Arch. It was my first trip overseas, and London's architecture, primarily of nineteenth-century origin, looked downright medieval to someone like me who had grown up in the high-rise glamor of twentieth-century New York. The Kings Court in particular seemed like something out of the middle ages. Everyone who attended the convention stayed in that tiny squalid hostelry, except for those who commuted from their London homes. All the convention events, such as they were, took place there, too, in one small ballroom. (Certain other convention events, the unscheduled kind, took place in the nearby lounge, where beverages of all kinds flowed freely and uninhibited British fans put on displays of public affection that the staid, puritanical American attendees beheld in bemused astonishment.)

The cost of a room at the Kings Court was one pound a night, including breakfast. Let me repeat that, too: one pound a night, which then was the equivalent of $1.40. You must make allowances, of course, for the carnage that half a century of inflation has wreaked on good old sterling: in those days a reasonable salary for a shopgirl or a young clerk was six or seven hundred pounds a year, a local ride on the Underground was sixpence — 2.5p in modern British money — and newspapers cost a penny except for posh ones like the Times, which might have been tuppence then. Even so, a pound a night for a hotel room was on the low side for the era, so low that when my wife and I hopped over to Paris for a few days during our trip, we simply kept our London room rather than go to the bother of putting our things in storage during our absence.

Of course, the Kings Court was somewhat less than lavish. That pound-a-night fee didn't include heat in one's room, for example. If you wanted that, you fed one-shilling pieces (think 10p. coins) into a meter on the wall. The Americans at the con, perhaps a third of the total attendance, were utterly unfamiliar with that kind of arrangement, but we quickly learned to keep a stockpile of shillings on hand to get us through the night. Another little hotel amenity to which we Americans were accustomed was a private bath and toilet in each room; but no, no, austerity was still the watchword in an England not yet fully recovered from the hardships of the war, and the Kings Court provided just one or two such chambers on each floor, giving us a nice little lesson in old-world privation.

Then there was the matter of breakfast: toast, sausages, eggs, cornflakes. No problem there, except that the toast was prepared the night before and set out on each table in little metal racks, along with bowls of cornflakes. The layout of the hotel was such that the most convenient route from our rooms to the meeting-hall in the evening was through the dining room, but the first time we tried it we were met with anguished cries from the hotel staff: "Please don't walk through here! You'll get dust in the cornflakes!" That became a watchword for the attendees all weekend.

As for the attendees, those brave 268 of the Worldcon Pleistocene who tiptoed past the cornflakes, they included a good many whose names are still familiar today. Among the writers present were Brian Aldiss, Harry Harrison, Arthur C. Clarke, James White, H. Ken Bulmer, E.C. Tubb, John Wyndham, Michael Moorcock, Eric Frank Russell, William F. Temple, H. Beam Piper, and Sam Youd ("John Christopher"). John Brunner — whose death at the 1995 Glasgow convention cast such a tragic pall over that con — was there too, a slender lad of twenty-three. The formidable John W. Campbell, greatest of sf magazine editors, was the Loncon guest of honor. His British counterpart, E.J. ("Ted") Carnell of New Worlds, was the convention chairman. Everyone who was anyone in British fandom was on hand, of course, and a good many American fans, too, most of them passengers aboard a chartered flight organized by David A. Kyle of New York.

You would think that the program would have been a busy one, with that many of the era's best-known professionals there. You would be wrong. The day of the round-the-clock multi-track convention program was still far in the future. The one and only event of Loncon's first day, Friday, September 6, was a brief opening ceremony in the evening, followed by a party. Saturday morning nothing was scheduled except a concert of recorded jazz. In the afternoon came the official convention luncheon, featuring brief speeches by many of the con's celebrities — an event made notorious when the famous American fan Forrest J. Ackerman, who had arrived wearing a string necktie of a type commonly worn in the Western United States but unknown in England, was turned away at the door. "The ceremony is to begin with a toast to Her Majesty," Forrie was told. "Gentlemen must wear neckties." His protests that he was wearing a necktie were unavailing. (I suppose it's still possible to imagine a ceremony at a modern British convention that includes a toast to the Queen, but one for which neckties of any sort are mandatory is unthinkable today.)

The Hugos were handed out on Saturday night — a brief ceremony, because only three were given, one for best American magazine (Campbell's *Astounding Science Fiction*), one for best British magazine (Carnell's *New Worlds*), and one to *Science Fiction Times*, the *Locus* of its day. With that rite out of the way, an official of Madame Tussaud's waxworks spoke for half an hour about Britain's first planetarium, and an auction of old sf magazines and magazine illustrations filled in the time until 10:45, when a costume ball got going in the minuscule main hall, followed by the traditional masquerade and judging of the costumes. Sunday's program was equally light — more jazz in the morning and the showing of amateur films in the afternoon and a hyp-notism demonstration (in which I failed utterly to go into a trance, though some British fans proved hilariously more susceptible). Then, at night, came a film showing (*Mr. Wonderbird*) and another auction for collectors.

Monday, the last day, provided the one and only panel of the entire con-vention — a question-and-answer session featuring half a dozen of the at-tending pros. After that, John Campbell delivered his Guest Of Honor speech (on psionics, of course, the latest of his many pseudo-scientific obsessions), and the rest of the day was devoted to the sort of mild noodling around (more amateur films, another auction) that had filled most of the weekend.

Not much of a program, no. I can't remember much about my own role in it, aside from sitting in on the hypnotism session. I think I was part of that Monday panel, but maybe not. It was all a long time ago and the fifty Worldcons I've attended have begun to blur together beyond repair. My keenest memories of Loncon I have to do with alcohol. Not that I'm a hard-drinking man — which is, in fact, the point. The first episode occurred at a pub called the Globe in Hatton Garden, where on Thursday nights the London sf crowd was wont to gather. Ted Carnell took me to the meeting the night before the con opened, and, when in an injudicious moment I ex-pressed curiosity about British beer, everybody there insisted on buying the young American writer his special favorite. Politely, I tried them all, going way beyond my capacity, and then, at the end of the evening, John Brunner said, grinning diabolically, "But you haven't had barley wine yet, have you?" And coolly foisted a bottle of that high-proof ale on me, a lethal topper that sent me reeling off into the night.

At the convention itself I was inducted into the Order of St. Fantony, a mysterious cult operated by Cheltenham fandom. At the climax of the ceremony the new inductees — I was one of about five — were handed a tall glass of a clear fluid that was described as "water from the sacred well of St. Fantony" and instructed to drain it at a gulp. Which we did; but what the glass contained, I learned a few stunned moments later, was something called Polish white spirits — 140-proof vodka. Ah, yes, a quaint little convention.

Quaint, too, were the bizarre sodium lights that cast an eerie orange-yel-low glow over the nearby streets of the Bayswater Road and over the prosti-tutes who thronged there. Prostitution is not unknown in America, of course, but the streetwalking kind was uncommon back in that distant age, and I had never seen any right out in the open before. The poor girls were not exactly looking their best under those yellow-orange lights, to put it mildly, and for me the sight of them was, well, a nicely alien experience. Long, long ago, that London Worldcon. I do expect that things will be quite different in Glasgow, where the convention will be ten times as big and the streetlamps won't glow orange. Hold the Polish white spirits and pass the haggis, please.

Asimov's Science Fiction, July, 2005

Ghost Stories

I'VE BEEN WRITING A GHOST STORY THIS MONTH. That may surprise some of you, because I haven't written a lot of ghost stories in the past. Possibly this is my first, although I don't pretend to remember every single story I've written over the past fifty-plus years.

I'm writing this one because an old friend asked me to do one for a book of them that he was editing, and while I was considering the invitation a perfectly good story idea popped into my mind. Though nobody who knows my work would ever associate me with ghost stories, I'm been fond of them as a reader ever since I discovered, around 1948, the classic Herbert Wise-Phyllis Fraser anthology *Great Tales of Terror and the Supernatural*. There is something about Victorian England that fascinates me, the fog, the hansom cabs, the Sherlock Holmes atmosphere, and many of the Wise-Fraser stories are set in that era. So I reveled in its vast array of spooky and wonderful Victorian tales by the likes of Arthur Machen, Oliver Onions, J.S. Le Fanu, and Algernon Blackwood, and, ever since, when seeking a change of pace from the robots and spaceships and time machines, I've pulled a collection of ghost stories down from the shelf for a little guilty pleasure.

I call reading the stuff a guilty pleasure because I am, at heart, a rational-minded, logical sort of guy who stopped believing in ghosts around the time I figured out the truth about the Tooth Fairy. The supernatural world has no substance for me. Spooks, haunts, phantoms, revenants — I lose no sleep in dread of them. If it can't be seen, measured, and explained, I figure, it isn't real.

That doesn't stop me, of course, from reading and even (these days) writing ghost stories with pleasure. There's a lot that I read and write about that seems just as devoid of real-world substance as the Great God Pan. I don't believe that we're likely ever to go zipping around the past or future in time machines, but writing tales of time travel has been a specialty of mine for decades. I don't think there's much of a case for telepathy, but that did not keep me from writing *Dying Inside*. I doubt that the Earth is ever going to be invaded by beings from another star, and yet I wrote *The Alien Years*. And so forth: I'm a writer of fiction, not a journalist, and I write about all sorts of things for which I demand (from myself, and my readers) the willing suspension of disbelief.

Having said all that, I need to tell you something that will startle you as much as it does me, because it contradicts my basic view of myself as a rational being. Although I don't believe in ghosts, I think that I live in a haunted house.

Let me try to explain.

The house I've lived in for nearly forty years, in the hills above San Francisco Bay, is quite unusual, architecturally speaking. It was built in 1947 by an unusual architect named Carr Jones, constructed out of recycled brick, slate slabs, and huge beams left over from World War II ship construction. Everything about it is original in concept and very ingenious for its time, which means that doing any sort of maintenance on it is a nightmare. (For example, the heating system was so complex that only one living person, the stepson of the builder, understood how it worked. When he started to show signs of age, and the heating system was doing the same, I had the whole bizarre thing ripped out and replaced with a conventional set of pipes that any capable plumber would be able to work on in the years ahead. But, since I don't want to tear the entire marvelous house down and build a new one, I have to put up with the other strangenesses that the place provides.)

I am the third owner of the house. It was built for a local automobile dealer named Remmer, who after living here for about fifteen years sold it to Rollo Wheeler, an architect. He owned the place for about a decade. In 1971 Wheeler sold it to me, and I have been here ever since.

Both Remmer and Wheeler are long dead. Right after I bought the house, the Wheelers went sailing in the Gulf of California and never were seen again. (They may have been killed by Mexican pirates.) Remmer, the car dealer, died of natural causes somewhere way back. As for the car dealer's wife — well, around 1980 Rollo Wheeler's daughter, who had grown up in the house, came back to visit her childhood home and regaled me with anecdotes of the old days, one of which was the tale of Mrs. Remmer's suicide on the premises here. I hadn't heard about that, and I wasn't particularly eager to know more, so I turned down her offer to tell me where on the grounds Mrs. Remmer's body had been found.

Then in the summer of 1981 I had the house re-roofed. The old roof was the original 1947 one and after thirty-four years it wasn't doing a good job of keeping the winter rains out. I hired someone to strip away the crumbling old shingles and brought in Doug Allinger, Carr Jones' stepson, to do a new roof in keeping with the style of the previous one.

We have two buildings here, the main house and a smaller building that is my office. The workmen dumped the shingles from the main house over the top and down into the driveway, which runs just behind the building. But the office shingles had to be removed in a two-step process: strip them off and pile them up in front of the building, and then haul them the whole length of the property to the driveway. The first step of this job produced a great filthy heap of stripped-off old shingles about three feet high in front of the office door, completely blocking access to the building. Keep that image in mind: a knee-high stack of ancient shingles piled up against the door to the office, and a second such stack in back, where there is a second door. You should also know that I'm a passionate gardener. In Northern California's relatively benign climate I've long been experimenting with subtropical plants that are really a bit too tender even for here (since our winter temperatures do drop below freezing for brief periods every five or six years.) Back then I set up an alarm system programmed to awaken me if the outside temperature ever dropped below 32 degrees. I had some fantasy in mind, I guess, of staggering out of bed in the middle of the night to throw protective covers over the most tender plants if that alarm ever went off.

Two nights after the shingle piles had been dumped in front of my office doors, that bedroom frost alarm went off, about two in the morning. I had no idea at first of what was happening, because the alarm had never gone off since I had installed it. But eventually I figured out that that weird sound was coming from the temperature-reading gizmo on the windowsill; and then I noticed that the gizmo was telling me that the outside temperature was 28 degrees.

It was a mild August night.

Twenty-eight degrees would be unusual in my area at any time of the year. But in August it's simply impossible. The temperature alarm has malfunctioned, I decided, and went back to sleep.

In the morning I realized that I needed to get some reference item from my office that I had forgotten to bring out before the shingles were stripped. I spent a nasty half hour clearing enough of the piled-up old shingles away from the door so that I could squeeze myself inside.

As soon as I entered I smelled smoke.

Sinking feeling in chest. I have already experienced one house fire, in 1968, and I wasn't ready for another. My office was originally the cabana for the adjacent swimming pool. It is equipped with a small refrigerator and a little electric stove. I had never used either one. The refrigerator, disconnected, has served as a storage cabinet for books. I had piled more books on top of the stove.

One of the burners on the stove had been turned on.

The smoke was coming from a slowly charring book sitting on that burner. Probably it would have burst into flames in another hour or two; but I quickly turned off the stove and pulled the book away. Mind you, that burner had never been used in the nine years that this building had served as my office, and access to the office had been blocked for the past couple of days by those shingles, besides. Nor was there any sign that anyone had pushed the shingles aside to enter. Somewhere during the night, though — the same night that the frost alarm had registered a sub-freezing temperature in August — that burner had been turned on.

Had some ice-cold thing walked past the sensor of the temperature alarm in the night, then drifted through the wall of my office to turn the stove burner on?

When the workmen showed up that morning, I asked if anyone had had reason to enter the building the previous day. No, nobody had. (The shingle pile would have shown evidence of entry, anyway.) And when I showed Doug Allinger the book that had been burned he immediately said, "Well, it's Mrs. Remmer's ghost, isn't it?"

The book? Volume Two of *The Encyclopedia of Occultism and Parapsychology*, edited by Leslie A. Shepard.

I don't believe in ghosts, of course. I'm a rational, skeptical man. But there is a useful concept known as Occam's Razor, named for the medieval philosopher William of Occam, which says, "Do not multiply hypotheses unnecessarily" — that is, the simplest explanation for a phenomenon is probably the best one.

What Occam's Razor tells me is that it is simpler to believe that a wandering supernatural being turned that burner on in the night than it is to believe that the burner turned itself on. Maybe the erroneous frost signal had been the result of some electronic malfunction, but the stove did not have electronic controls. Physical force had to be exerted to turn the burner on, and no one had been in my office to exert that force — except, I suppose, the malevolent ghost of Mrs. Remmer.

Would a ghost be able to turn a stove burner knob, though? I don't know. Since I don't believe in ghosts, I have no idea what they can or can't do. One would think that a spirit immaterial enough to pass through the wall of my office would be too ectoplasmic to turn that knob. But no one of this world had entered my office those two days past, and the stove had been turned on, and I can just as readily believe that my house is haunted by the ghost of Mrs. Remmer as I can that a stove can turn itself on.

Since then, all manner of odd things have happened around this house. While we were traveling one winter, the main house's roof sprang a leak during a storm and the narrow stream of water that ran down one wall just happened to descend onto the burglar-alarm keyboard, shorting it out. During another trip, my office sink apparently turned itself on and by the time we got home and noticed that water was running there was a flood in a storage room on the floor below. We have had computer settings mysteriously change themselves, and stored e-mail mysteriously delete itself. *Et cetera.* Our housekeeper of some years back, going into my office to give it one of its rare cleanings, said to my wife, "I feel a presence here."

"Yes," Karen said lightly, indicating my papers strewn all around. "It's Bob." But she knew — and didn't want to say — that what the housekeeper was sensing was the presence of Mrs. Remmer.

As I say, I'm not a person who believes in ghosts. But I do use Occam's Razor as an aid to thinking, and Occam's Razor tells me that all the weird stuff that happens around here can best be explained as the work of some malign invisible spirit, and so be it. A couple of years ago, I told this story to a friend of mine, the anthropologist and artist Winfield Coleman. He is an expert on shamanism, and offered to perform a rite of exorcism for us. I turned him down. I don't believe in ghosts, I said; and in any case, I didn't want to discover that by ejecting Mrs. Remmer I had simply made room here for some even more malevolent apparition.

Asimov's Science Fiction, **October/November, 2010**

Index